MW01254708

DANCING WITH THE MOON

JUNE MARIE SAXTON

authorHOUSE®

AuthorHouse™
1663 Liberty Drive
Bloomington, IN 47403
www.authorhouse.com
Phone: 1-800-839-8640

First published by AuthorHouse 10/28/2009

ISBN: 978-1-4490-1615-9 (e)
ISBN: 978-1-4490-1613-5 (sc)
ISBN: 978-1-4490-1614-2 (hc)

Library of Congress Control Number: 2009911048

Printed in the United States of America
Bloomington, Indiana

This book is printed on acid-free paper.

For my grandpas

Ben E. Weston, the cowboy

and

Francis E. Porter, the athlete

Thanks for your influence!

Long live your legacies.

Special Acknowledgements

I want to thank friends and family members for fueling my fire and expressing an interest in my work. Special thanks to the staff at Bear Necessities of Montpelier LLC. We've had a few laughs! Lots of love and appreciation must be expressed to my parents, Dale and Pam Weston, and my husband, Mike. I appreciate your patience!

Just to make things interesting I included the names of my children and each one of my nieces and nephews into the storyline. Their names represent fictitious characters only, and are not a real life assessment of them as individuals. With the exception of family history names mentioned at the Porterville Cemetery in Chapter Six, all characters in this book are strictly the products of my imagination.

CHAPTER ONE
MORGAN UTAH, MAY 31, 2009

Sabrina brushed the cool wetness from her face. How long had she been there? How absorbed in her own thoughts had she been before the spattering rain finally brought her back to reality? She stood, stretching her aching back, watching raindrops dance in shimmering ripples on the river. Her dark hair clung around her face in dampened tendrils. She pushed the wet tresses away from her chilled skin.

The rain was falling harder now, almost stinging her flesh where it hit. She wanted to escape to the comfort of the house yet she hesitated, intrigued by turbulent patterns on the water. Waves splashed against the bank, spraying mist about her.

The sounds of the storm were powerful! The wind began to howl, bending willows unmercifully along both sides of the Weber River. Angry thunder crashed after a jagged tear of lightning ripped through the blackened sky. The horizon seemed cast in violent hues of bruised purple.

Sabrina turned and quickly stumbled up the slight rocky incline. As she ran across the slippery spring grass of the backyard the wind seemed to steal her breath, making her lungs burn and her chest ache. Heavy torrents of rain beat against her--almost forbidding her to move so she lumbered clumsily until she reached the screen door of the back porch and gratefully flung it open.

Amanda Ashley heard the back door slam shut. "Sabrina?"

"It's raining," Sabrina ventured, kicking off her Nikes and peeling wet socks from her feet. She struggled out of her hoodie and shook her head, sending water droplets spraying in every direction.

"It looks like it's raining in here, too." Amanda teased, eyeing the puddles forming at Sabrina's feet. "Um...it actually looks like you *fell* in the river."

"I know. I should have come in sooner, but..."

"My goodness, your teeth are chattering! I hope you didn't catch pneumonia while you were out splashing around. Get your clothes off and go warm yourself in the shower--but don't dawdle okay? You don't want to miss out on supper--tomato soup and grilled cheese sandwiches!"

"I could use some comfort food. Hot chocolate too, please? Thanks Mom, I'll hurry."

The bathroom door shut between them. Amanda stared at the closed door for a moment, a wry smile turning the corners of her mouth. For one thing, she knew Sabrina couldn't hurry in the shower. It seemed to be a physical impossibility for the seventeen year old girl. Amanda sighed and turned back toward the kitchen. What was it that drew Sabrina to the river? Amanda felt certain the river in their backyard was almost sacred to her daughter. Sabrina called it her *Thinking Place,* but what in the world had she been thinking about today? Sabrina must have been like the rivers own rushing liquid, swept up in the currents of her deepest thoughts and emotions.

Sabrina savored the warmth of the shower, each droplet of water falling like a gentle, soothing massage. Hot humid steam rose around her, encircling her in a soft caress. It was a sweet comfort after the cold, sharp, stinging rain. Sabrina tilted her head back letting the shower spray against her throat. With eyes closed she mentally wandered back to her thoughts at the river. Today she had once again crossed the line that allowed herself to re-live memories: cherished childhood treasures of happiness and forbidden, haunting pains of sorrow.

CHAPTER TWO
RAYMOND, IDAHO JUNE 1, 2000

Golden beams of sunshine tumbled through the window. Ben Ashley studied the beauty of his wife. Amanda's hair fell like spilled honey across her pillow. He mentally traced the delicate lines of her face. A touch of pink played against her cheeks. Amanda's mouth was prettily shaped, soft and kissable. Gentle smile lines teased against her mouth, giving her face a pleasant expression even while sleeping. Dark lashes fringed her eyelids and her brows framed her eyes like honey colored arches. Her nose was small and straight and well proportioned to her face. Ben smiled. His wife was a work of art! He reached out and pulled her to him.

He stroked the glossy satin strands of her hair and nuzzled his mouth against the top of her head, kissing her softly again and again while drinking in her fragrance. Amanda's hair always smelled deliciously of strawberries and sweet clover.

Amanda stirred against him. "Good morning. What are you doing?"

"Sniffing your hair. You smell good."

"Um—it's the shampoo."

"It's not the shampoo. You always smell this way--no matter *what* you use."

"Oh...then...maybe it's the fresh air?"

Ben laughed. "Maybe so."

"Do you think that's why mosquitoes like me so much?"

Ben smiled and kissed the top of her head, harder this time. "Yes. Apparently you seduce the mosquitoes with your scent. They can't help attacking you. Neither can I!"

"Stupid mosquitoes! They think I'm running a delicatessen."

"Amanda, you *are* a delicatessen. I think *I'll* have a bite myself," Ben teased as he nibbled along the side of her neck.

Amanda snuggled against her husband. Her favorite time of the day was breaking dawn, cuddling and talking with Ben before the cares of the day began. He was strong yet gentle; rugged and tender at the same time. Amanda placed her hand against Ben's chest and mused, "I love you Ben. I'm glad I didn't marry a *wimp*."

"Me too, or else I'd have had to kick his butt!"

Amanda chuckled. "No, I mean I'm glad *you're* not a wimp. I like you just the way you are."

"How exactly am I?"

"Strong, sturdy, hard working, kind, dependable, steady—"

"Sounds boring." Ben traced an imaginary square.

"Studly, manly, sexy, hot, *wildly romantic...*"

"Oh, so you noticed?"

"Yes, yes, *yes!*" Ben's mouth covered Amanda's in a lingering kiss. "Well, that's *one* way to shut me up."

"It's time to get up I'm afraid."

"No! Kiss me some more. Shut me up for all day. I'd like to be a mute."

Ben smiled, "Mmm, tempting..." He leaned closer.

A shrill voice ripped through the moment. "Happy Birthday to me! Happy Birthday to *myself!*" "I'm another year older today! I guess I must be about seven...that means lots of presents!"

"Um...I think Sabrina might be awake," Ben ventured.

"How *can* you be certain?"

"Happy Birthday to me for all day long," Sabrina piped in a savagely sing-song tune.

"What a little mood-killer," Ben whispered. Amanda elbowed him playfully and winked, struggling to keep from laughing out loud.

"Can anybody hear that I'm awake and singing to myself at the top of my voice?"

Ben pulled Amanda up. "Let's go pounce on her. I guess that's what she's campaigning for."

The parents playfully crept towards Sabrina's room. Sabrina sucked in her song-singing, suddenly pretending to be asleep. She was so excited that her breaths came out jagged and reckless while she waited for her traditional birthday ambush.

"Surprise!" her parents each took a cheek and started kissing. Sabrina's daddy tickled her tummy while her mom blew raspberries against her neck. "Happy Birthday Bree!" Sabrina opened one eye, groggily pretending to just be waking up. She yawned and stretched and looked almost too rummy to really be conscious. "What an actress!"

Suddenly Sabrina giggled and gasped to life. She sat up in her bed beaming at her parents. "I didn't think you guys were ever going to come in here."

The morning passed quickly. Amanda checked the clock, realizing that while she had barely finished washing breakfast dishes, it was just about time to start preparing lunch. "Where does my time go?" She flipped the oven light on to sneak a peek at the baking cake. "There now, a few more minutes ought to do it."

She pulled a box of candles out of the cupboard, quickly counting them out. *Seven.* She hoisted herself onto a bar stool, loosely rolling the waxy candles between the palms of her hands. *Seven years.*

The house was quiet. Sabrina had gone prattling off to Grandma's. Amanda kept her expression happy and bright for Sabrina's sake, but now as she sat alone at the kitchen counter, tears began to spill from her eyes and stream down her cheeks. Seven years ago today she had given birth to *two* children.

Sabrina was born first, boldly pushing herself into this world. She let out a healthy cry even before the doctor had cleared her airway. "She's not happy with me," Dr. Bainbridge remarked. "Listen to that scolding!" Amanda peered at the tiny creature. A wave of awed emotion washed over her with an intensity which must only be described as mother's love.

Ben leaned down and kissed Amanda's cheek. "You did really good Honey. She is perfect–*so* beautiful. *Look at her*! Look at all that dark hair."

Dr. Bainbridge clamped the umbilical cord and passed the baby to the nurses. "You catch your breath for a second, Amanda. You can cuddle and coo her when you are finished. I don't suppose it will be long now."

Suddenly Amanda was hit with a contraction which made her feel as if she were doubling herself completely in two. "Push!" Dr. Bainbridge urged. "Come on now, harder!"

"You can do it," Ben encouraged, but it all sounded like static in Amanda's ears. She was doing her best. Air hissed through her clenched teeth.

"Breathe again, deeper this time," Doc ordered. "Breathe! Push!"

"Breathe. Push." Ben echoed.

Amanda sucked in a jagged breath wishing she could shut the men up. The encouragements didn't seem to be helping. She wanted silence so she could concentrate but her wishes were impossible to articulate while gritting, straining, and bearing down. She let out one loud yell which was followed by an immense shuddering sensation. *Relief!*

"There he is. There he is." Dr. Bainbridge said, "Easy now, no more pushing." Dr. Bainbridge worked quickly to clear the baby's airway. "This one is a blond." Amanda had been panting, catching her wind. Her head jerked off the pillow to peer at her new little son. *Ten fingers, ten toes. Amazing! So perfect, but so...still. Too still--why doesn't he cry?*

Dr. Bainbridge's nurses hovered near. Amanda couldn't quite see exactly what they were doing. Ben was frozen--holding his breath, not moving. "Is he alright?" Amanda asked shakily. No one replied.

"Come on little guy," Dr. Bainbridge urged. "Breathe. Take a breath."

A fearful sob ripped from the back of Amanda's throat. Ben tightened his grip on her shoulder as they watched helplessly. Amanda was offering up fervent pleas to Heaven for this little son. A minute ticked by or was it two?

The baby boy finally drew in one feeble gulp of air, tasting mortality for the briefest, sweetest moment, and then he exhaled a tiny goodbye.

Overwhelming sorrow pressed upon the room. Sobs racked Amanda's body. The searing burn in her heart was more intense than any labor pain could ever suppose to be. Tears flowed down Ben Ashley's cheeks, but reassuringly he held his wife. "Breathe." he instructed. *"Just breathe."*

Amanda wiped the tears from her cheeks. "The cake," she reminded herself. She pulled herself away from the barstool and started mixing frosting. "This will be a beautiful cake," Amanda said to no one in particular. "A pink pony cake with yellow rosebuds woven in its mane." She studied the instructions mentally reviewing each step.

Amanda smiled as the cake began to spring to life. She enjoyed the challenge of creating masterpiece cakes. "This is even better than the ballerina cake I did last year." She filled the frosting bag again, carefully wiping the tip, and began piping little yellow rosebuds. "Such a cute cake--it will be a pity to poke candles in it."

The kitchen door burst open. "Hi, Mom! I'm just bringing Grandma in to see my cake."

"I'm just putting the finishing touches on it now. Do you like it Bree?"

Sabrina climbed up on a bar stool to get a good look. "I love it! I love it!"

"Well isn't that clever? I never would have the patience to do such a thing." Juliet Ashley said. "Amanda, you are amazing! It's a wonder you didn't make your own wedding cake. Sabrina, your dad never had a fancy birthday cake when he was your age. He only had two choices: round or rectangle."

Sabrina recognized her Grandma's statement as a gentle nudge to remember her manners. "Thank you, Mom."

"You're welcome." Amanda faced her mother-in-law, "We're going to start the picnic tonight about seven. Is that okay?"

"What can I bring besides a potato salad?"

"Fudge," Sabrina said, inserting herself into the conversation. Both women laughed.

Sabrina's cheeks flushed pink.

"You don't need fudge; you have a whole pony to eat."

"I want fudge too."

Amanda closed her eyes for a second. The child could be exasperating at times. "Sabrina!"

Juliet cut her off with a wave of her hand. "Come on then Sabrina. If I'm making fudge for your birthday picnic you're going to help me."

"What do I get to do?"

"Chop the nuts."

"Do I get to stir?"

"Yes, but you'll only stir for a minute and then you tell me your arm is tired."

"But I like to do it anyway. Do I get to lick the pan?"

"If Grandpa doesn't beat you to it."

"Come on Grandma," Sabrina said, pulling her Grandma's arm. "Bye Mom. I'll come home after I'm done licking the pan with Grandpa."

Just as Sabrina was leading Grandma out the door, Juliet paused. "Oh, Amanda–is it okay if Chantry comes to the picnic? He thinks he's one of us."

Amanda thought of the tall, lanky hired boy from across the road. He had worked for the Ashley's for the last couple of summers. "Sure, Chantry can come. He is one of us, isn't he?"

"Good!" Sabrina called out. "I already invited him and told him to bring me a present."

CHAPTER THREE

The Ashley's owned a beautiful plot of land on the Raymond Mountains. A myriad of natural springs gurgled and trickled along the mountainside creating a lush green pasture. Years earlier Joseph Ashley had piped into one of the largest springs, running the water down hill until it formed a small reservoir. Spring water cascaded down rocks and splashed into the pond on the north end. Two big cottonwoods hovered over the miniature waterfall.

Joseph trenched a spillway pipe into the reservoir which carried a constant flow of water several hundred yards further down the hill, where it pooled again, giving drink to livestock and wildlife in lower pastures. Above the reservoir, almost hidden by tangled masses of chokecherry bushes and quaking aspen, was an old cabin. Joseph and Ben worked to preserve the relic. Ben cleared out an overgrowth of brambles and chokecherry wood the fall before, reclaiming the settlers' yard to its former glory while his father gutted the cabin, laying new floor boards, reconstructing the loft, and adding tin to a renovated roof. Ben waged a battle against cockle-burrs and stinging nettle. He chopped, cleared, raked, leveled, mowed, and trimmed. He broadcast tiny grass seeds on the barren patches of black soil. He built an outhouse and picnic tables. Chantry dug a fire pit and rocked it in. Because of school, the hired boy hadn't helped with the project as much as he would have liked.

The men had labored through most of the autumn months, after the harvest was over, to stake this claim on their mountain paradise. Joseph was satisfied with their work. "I've always wanted to clean this up around here. Now we've done it! We've made a mountain oasis where we can get away from it all and only minutes from home. It can't get much better than that."

The cabin was the perfect scene for Sabrina's birthday picnic. June evenings still carried a chill so Sabrina was zipped up inside her new pink windbreaker. She could scarcely wait for the truck to stop so she could interrupt the quiet mountain setting. "Look! Chantry's already up here and has a big bon fire going."

"That was a good idea," Amanda said to Ben.

"I thought the smoke would settle the mosquitoes down so my lady could enjoy herself," Ben answered with a wink.

"Mosquitoes don't bother me," Sabrina chirped. "They can't even catch me, and even if they *could* catch me, I'll bet they can't stick their wicker bills through my new jacket." The truck stopped and Sabrina bolted out the door.

"That girl is a bundle of energy! If only we could harness it..."

"She has been so excited all day long."

Ben looked down at his wife. "And how have you been?"

"Fine."

"Amanda? I know it's kind of a bitter-sweet day. Are you... okay?"

"Yes. I had my moment to reflect and cry when the house was quiet." Amanda bit her lip. "I took Sabrina with me to the cemetery this afternoon. I let her plant a new pinwheel by his headstone. We talked about Brian. It was good."

"What did Sabrina say?"

"She was more inquisitive this year. She wanted to know if her twin would have looked like her. I told her, 'No. You look like Daddy and I think Brian looks like me.' She wondered what his favorite color would have been, and if she would be taller and faster than him."

"It sounds like she was full of questions." Ben jerked the truck door open and lifted Amanda down. "Turn around," he said, spraying her back with repellent. "Turn," he ordered again, misting her side.

"I thought the smoke was supposed to take care of my would-be assassins."

"Turn. With sweet meat like yours? I'm not taking any chances! Nobody's nibbling on my lady but me! Turn."

"Phew! Now I'm going to smell bad. I'll repel people."

"Just the price you've got to pay if you're going to be so irresistible." Ben threw the spray can back inside the truck. He then hoisted a cooler out of the back. "Chantry! Come help me get this other cooler, would you?"

Chantry made long lithe strides toward them. Sabrina was tumbling after him, nipping at his heels like a rambunctious puppy.

"Look Amanda. For every step Chantry takes, Sabrina has to take six." Ben chuckled.

"I can help you carry stuff, Chantry." Sabrina offered.

"I got it."

"Let me help. I'm strong!"

Chantry set the cooler down. "Fine!" He flipped open the cooler's lid and grabbed a package of plastic cups. "You carry this." Sabrina knit her brows together stubbornly. She reached out and snatched the cups. Chantry resumed his load. "Thank you Sabrina. My burden is much lighter now."

Sabrina trailed him to the table and tossed the cups toward her mother. "Now what are you going to do Chantry? Should we hike up the hill? Do you want to hunt for caterpillars?" Chantry looked away, trying to find an escape.

Amanda stepped in, "Sabrina you stay here and help me put the table cloths on, and leave Chantry alone." Chantry flashed a grateful smile at her and made his retreat back toward the fire.

"Why do *I* have to leave *him* alone? I wasn't bothering him."

"Guys don't like getting tagged after, Bree. They also don't like to be hovered over or bossed around."

"I boss Bracken around," Sabrina said, dragging the boy from down the road into the argument. "He likes it."

"But Bracken's only six. When he's fifteen he won't put up with it."

"Humph! Maybe when I'm sixteen he'll just *wish* I'd boss him around! I won't give Bracken the time of day by then." A smile twitched at Amanda's mouth. "Does Chantry think he's *so* big and smart just because he's a high schooler?" Sabrina glared toward the flames licking out of the fire pit. Chantry was poking the coals with a stick, unaware that he was suddenly the target of the small girl's fury.

"Sabrina, don't get huffy! Chantry's done nothing wrong. I just don't want you following after him like a shadow."

"I'm not *huffy*, I'm just *mad!*" Sabrina shot a black look in her mother's direction. She tugged the corner of the table cloth extra hard, yanking it into place. "I wasn't bothering *any*body."

"Grandpa and Grandma's here," Amanda said, distracting Sabrina's wrath. Sabrina hurried down the hill toward their old blue truck.

Joseph and Juliet's doors opened. Sabrina was ready to help them out.

"How's my birthday girl?" Grandpa called. "Have you had your spankings yet?"

"No," Sabrina laughed. "Hi, Grandpa! Here Grandma, let me carry that." Sabrina grabbed a smaller blue cooler. Chantry was crossing the grassy clearing to help them.

"What can I carry for you, Juliet?" he asked politely.

Stubbornly, Sabrina set the blue cooler in the grass. She jerked off the lid and snatched a wooden spoon from inside. She turned, quickly jabbing the spoon toward the unsuspecting teenager. "Here! You can carry *this*." Then she picked up the cooler and marched toward the table. "Thanks Chantry, you are such a help to me," she called over her shoulder.

Chantry's black eyes sprung wide open. His chin dropped with a look of stunned surprise. Amanda caught the whole scene, feeling the energy of Sabrina's sarcasm and Chantry's shock mingle together and sift through the trees. She exchanged glances with Ben. He was struggling to conceal great bursts of laughter. *Oh, Sabrina!*

The fire crackled and popped. Chantry studied the expression of the little girl who sat across the flames from him. She was obviously angry. Twice while he was roasting a marshmallow to golden perfection, she bobbled her roasting stick, nudging his marshmallow into dirty blackened ashes. "Whoops," she commented both times, followed by a surly "I'm *so* sorry." Chantry wasn't completely certain what he had done to offend the child.

Sabrina was a bright, exuberant little thing. She was intelligent and extremely quick-witted. Of course there was a fine line between being precocious and annoyingly obnoxious. Occasionally Sabrina crossed that line. She often followed him around, prattling about some subject or another. Usually her comments amused him. She was a good girl and had been so excited about her birthday. Chantry felt uncomfortable with the knowledge that she was irritated with him now. Her mood was uncommonly somber–especially considering this was her much anticipated birthday picnic.

Chantry searched the other faces around the fire. Ben and Joseph were talking about a fence which needed mending in the meadow. Juliet was humming softly to herself, tapping her foot in cadence to her quiet tune. Chantry's gaze swept over to where Amanda sat. He was startled to see her blue eyes trained on him, studying him. She flashed a smile his way when their eyes met. Chantry felt his cheeks flush and ducked his gaze, pretending to be fixing something on the ground near his boot. Why was he flustered? Amanda was a beautiful woman and sweet as they come. She was gentle and delicate,

15

and *very married* to Ben! He didn't think he was idiotic enough to have a boyish, hopeless crush on Amanda, even though he was sure he'd never tire of looking at her. Surely he couldn't be that much of a sap! No. He blushed and averted her gaze because Amanda was too insightful all of the time. Chantry felt like he was nothing more than an open book and easy to read under her penetrating gaze.

"Sabrina, when are you going to open my present?" Chantry asked the sullen girl across the fire. Sabrina's eyes lit up, excitement dancing to the flames' reflection.

"You really brought a present for me?"

"You told me to."

Sabrina stared at him thoughtfully for a second. "But I didn't *boss* you to bring me one, right?"

Chantry noticed Sabrina pointed the question toward her mother even though she asked it of him. He felt unsure for a second just what his reaction should be.

"Well?" Sabrina demanded impatiently.

"If I say that you didn't *boss* me to bring one, will you stop being mad at me tonight?"

Chantry's question brought grins to the faces of the others. Ben and Joseph leaned closer, careful not to miss a classical *Sabrina Moment*.

Sabrina cast a glare at her mother, biting her lip, and then leveled her stare back toward Chantry. "No deal, Mister! You just answer the question and see what happens." Her hands cut a horizontal slicing motion in the air.

Chantry stifled a laugh. To further enrage Sabrina now would forever cast him into the nethermost pages of her black book. "You didn't boss me," he conceded. "You invited me most kindly, and I appreciated and accepted the invitation with relish." He annunciated each word articulately and carefully so there could be no mistake.

"I thought that's just the way it happened." Sabrina agreed, smiling victoriously at her mother.

Ben and Joseph laughed. "Okay Chantry, Sabrina's just given you a free course in female psychology. Always be agreeable. That's the best policy." Joseph chuckled. "Isn't that right, Mother?" Juliet smiled and clucked something beneath her breath but the others caught the affectionate wink she shot toward her husband.

"And Chantry, always remember the presents." Ben chided. "They score you big time."

"Like you would know," Amanda teased.

Pleasant laughter filled the evening air. Chantry was surprised to see Sabrina had scooted next to him. "Sorry I made you mad at me earlier."

Sabrina turned her hazel eyes toward him, "I just don't like you treating me like a little kid. It ticks me off when I see you go around thinking you're some big high schooler."

A chuckle escaped Chantry's throat. He tried to catch it and recycle it into a twisted cough. He hacked again just to stall. "I'll remember that."

"Now where's my present?"

"Over in my jacket pocket. You can go get it." Sabrina raced over to the picnic table and searched Chantry's coat for the right pocket. She pulled out a small package. She eyed it for a minute and shook it.

"I hope that wasn't breakable," Joseph said.

"Me too!"

Sabrina skipped back toward the fire. She smiled a toothy grin at everyone, happily anticipating the muffled rattling sound which came from inside the package. "Did you specially pick this out for me or did your Mom buy it?"

"*Sabrina*! For Heaven's sakes..." Amanda started to lecture.

"When have I been anywhere to buy anything? But I did pick it out for you, I guess."

Sabrina tore off the wrapping and lifted the lid. She heaved an excited breath as she peered into crinkled folds of tissue paper. She pulled out a black obsidian arrowhead and examined it, running a finger along the ragged, sharp edge. "Wow! Thanks! This is the kind of stuff teachers like for Show and Tell."

Ben looked at Chantry. "Are you sure you wanted to give that away?"

Chantry shrugged and looked away seeming pleased that his gift was acceptable. He stole a quick glance in Amanda's direction. She was staring him down with an amused smile. He feigned a sudden fascination with the ground, casting his eyes around in the dirt as his feet.

"I doubt you'll find another arrowhead right there," Joseph teased.

"I wasn't looking for one," Chantry muttered, obviously uncomfortable with the attention.

"Chantry, did your Mom make this arrowhead?" Sabrina asked.

That inquiry brought surprised chortles from all directions. No one expected such an absurd question. Chantry smiled. "No, I found the arrowhead last fall while I was digging the fire pit." He pointed to the exact spot.

"Oh. I just wondered...because your Mom is an Indian."

"Yes, but she hasn't made any arrowheads that I know of."

"Maybe she could learn some time," Sabrina offered hopefully.

Chantry grinned, peeking in Amanda's direction. He was delighted to see her beet red, with eyes closed, shaking her head as if she were more than slightly embarrassed. Ben was rubbing knots of tension from her shoulders and grinning at his young raven-haired friend.

CHAPTER FOUR

The sun was hot and beads of condensation clung to the icy pop can. Sabrina knew Chantry would gladly accept her fizzy offering. He was in front of the shop working on the swather. "Hi Chantry!" He muttered something but didn't look up. Sabrina waited. She would not be a nuisance to him today. She scowled as she remembered her mother's warning not to bother the hired boy.

Chantry finished sliding the section into place. He stretched upright, wiping his greasy hands on a rag. "Hey."

"Here you go."

"Thanks!" Chantry smiled and popped the tab. Sabrina watched as he took three or four big chugs of the refreshment. His Adam's apple bobbed up and down in his throat as he sucked it down.

"I'd choke to death if I took such a big swallow."

"I'm thirsty. You're a lifesaver, *Breezy-Brina-Thumbelina.*"

Sabrina nodded. She was still mentally pacing herself. *Don't boss. Don't annoy. Don't be a bother. Don't be a shadow.*

Chantry studied the girl. "Why are you so quiet?" he asked.

"I'm just behaving, but it probably won't last very long."

Chantry laughed out loud. "You're a crack-up."

Sabrina felt encouraged by his attention and wanted to capitalize on the moment. "So, you're getting ready to start cutting hay?"

"Yip."

"Do you want to help me build a trading post? Or a fort, maybe?" Chantry didn't say anything so Sabrina tried a different angle of conversation. "Do you like cutting hay?"

"Not as much as I like baseball."

Sabrina considered the statement. It was a well-known fact that Chantry loved baseball.

"You're lucky my Grandpa gives you so many afternoons off so you can play. Dad says you're the best one on the team."

"That's nice of him."

"My Dad is nice to everyone. I'm taking a pop to him, too." Sabrina patted the cold lump inside her back pack.

"He's up in the barn. He's working with the two-year-old colts so you go in nice and quiet. Go in to the tack room and call quietly to your Dad so he knows you're in there. Don't step down into the stall area until he's ready for you. Understand?" Chantry was very deliberate in his instructions.

"Yes."

"I'm serious, Breezy! Sundance is way too skittish for loud noises or sudden moves. Don't let the door bang shut behind you."

Sabrina scowled. "*Okay!* I said *I get it.*" Sabrina whirled toward the barn, glaring over her shoulder. Chantry was watching her retreat. Since she still had an audience with him she hollered, "And Mother thinks *I'm* bossy? Ha!" She swung her head letting dark tangled curls fly around her face.

"So much for good behavior," Chantry called, further infuriating the girl. "But remember what I said about the barn. Be quiet in there!"

Sabrina quickened her march. "Stupid person! There he goes, treating me like a little kid again." Sabrina stomped through the pasture but softened her steps as she approached the barn door. She slowly pulled it open and stepped inside. The pungent aroma of leather and rolled oats greeted her. She adjusted her eyes to the dim barn light. Feed sacks full of grain leaned against the south wall. The fat, plump shapes invited barn cats to curl up there every afternoon. Sabrina took a tiny step toward Jennifer and Slick. She rubbed her hand down Jennifer's well-preened calico. Jennifer stretched and began purring. Slick yawned and rolled closer inviting Sabrina to stroke his sleek black coat. "Hi Babies," Sabrina cooed softly. The cats began to meow. *"Shhh,* Daddy's working with the colts. You have to be quieter." Sabrina heard a boot step up onto the tack room floor. She turned brightly toward her father. "I brought you a pop from my party last night." Sabrina fished the can of root beer out of her pack.

Ben thanked her and sat himself down on a bulging sack of grain. He took off his hat and wiped his forehead with the back of his hand. Unlike Chantry, he sipped his root beer slowly. "Mmm... that's good stuff. Who's my girl?"

"Me!"

"That's right."

Sabrina studied her father. She liked to look at him. Grandma said he had freckles when he was a kid, but now his skin was tanned and brown from being in the sun every day. He was rugged and strong. He wore Wrangler jeans, a blue denim shirt and his boots were Tony Lamas. Strands of dark hair curled against his temples beneath a straw cowboy hat. Smile lines creased the corners of his hazel eyes. His big hands were calloused and rough even though he often protected them with gloves. "You're a real cowboy, aren't you Dad?"

"Darned right."

"And I'm a real cowgirl, huh?"

"I wouldn't have you if you weren't," he answered playfully.

"I know about horses, huh?"

"Pretty much, I guess."

"I know how to act around the colts."

"Let's hope so."

"I need to stay here with you for awhile. I won't wiggle or make any noises."

"Why do you need to be in here? I'll bet Mom is looking for you."

"No she isn't. I told her that I was going out to draw." Sabrina unzipped her backpack and pulled out her sketch pad as proof of her statement.

"I guess you can stay."

Sabrina wanted to squeal but leaned across Jennifer and Slick to give him a hearty hug instead. "Thanks Daddy. I'm going to be an artist when I grow up. I really need to sketch you and the colts. I'm also going to sketch these saddles and stuff in here on another day."

"That's a good plan.'

"I'm going to sketch our whole ranch eventually."

"Have you drawn any pictures yet?"

Sabrina flipped the cover open. "Look," she said, shoving the pad closer for his inspection. Ben was actually pleased with what he saw. Her artwork showed promise, especially for one so young. Ben recognized a depiction of his mother standing in her kitchen stirring something. Behind Grandma loomed a tall, dark haired boy. "That's Grandma. She's making fudge."

"Yes, I can see exactly who that is."

Sabrina pointed to the background character. "That's Chantry. He's waiting for the fudge to get done."

"This is really good. I didn't know you were an artist." He tipped the can to his lips and drained the rest of it. "Well, let's get to it. I'll lift you up on the half-loft. Keep your promises and be extra still up there."

Ben and Sabrina stepped from the tack room into the barn. Sundance and Tessie stirred in their stalls. Ben talked soothingly to the horses. Across from the horse stalls, about seven feet from the floor, hovered a small loft. Ben fluidly hefted Sabrina up on the perch. She scooted back until she leaned against the rough lumber of the wall. She took her drawing pad and pencil pouch from her back pack.

Sabrina was happy with her vantage point. She studied her father and then studied the page. If only her small hands could truly capture what she saw with her eyes. She made a few lines and then grabbed her eraser and scrubbed them out and started over. Being an artist was not as easy as it seemed.

Ben talked gently to the colts while he sidled gingerly up Tessie's stall. "That's a good girl. Take it easy--easy now. I'm walking up here like this. See? Nothing to flinch at." Sabrina listened. His voice was soothing and velvety. "See Sabrina, I keep talking so the horses know that I'm here, so my movements can't startle them so much. They need to get used to me. They must learn that it's okay for me to pet them, curry them, bridle and saddle them. That's what we're working on." Ben talked on while Sabrina's pencil scratched against the paper.

"Now Sabrina, see how Tessie's ears are up? That means she's content. When horses' ears lay back it means they're mad or frightened." Sabrina made a mental note of that. She drew ears on her horse. They were up.

"Good girl, good old Tessie," Ben carefully drew a hand up in front of Tessie. She smelled his hand. His other hand came up holding a hackamore. Tessie's ears flicked back for a second. Ben's hand froze while she sniffed the item. Her ears stood back up. Tessie seemed to be okay with the hackamore. Ben rubbed her nose and continued to talk to her.

Soon the hackamore was on Tessie, and her ears still stood erect. Sabrina was proud of her Dad. He really knew how to work with stock. Sabrina studied her picture. She added a hackamore to her horse. "That's a girl Tessie, that's a girl." Ben's hand dipped into a bucket and came out with a fist full of rolled oats. He let Tessie sniff the treat and then his hand opened.

"You gave her a treat." Sabrina whispered.

"That's her reward for letting me up the stall and getting the hackamore on her." Ben soothed as he worked his way out of Tessie's stall. "I'll let her get used to her hackamore while I introduce myself to Sundance."

Sundance's ears flinched back often. "Don't be skittish. Don't sulk; there now, there now." Ben eased his way up the stall. Sabrina half held her breath as she watched. Sundance was wild! Chantry was right to have been concerned. It seemed like the faintest dust particle dancing in the sunlight would spook him. Sabrina even kept her pencil still a time or two. Her father's voice continued to soothe, velvety and soft. "That's right Sundance. You're an old outlaw. Quick on the trigger, aren't you boy? Come on, let's settle down." Ben's voice droned soothing and monotone.

Suddenly Sundance shied sideways. Ben steadied himself against the stall. "Settle down now, settle down," he huffed firmly. The horse's ears were pinned back and his head kept shying off to one side. A wild gleam danced in the colt's eyes, and one hind leg shot back. Sabrina's breathing froze. *What spooked the horse?*

Sabrina's gaze swept toward the tack room. The silhouette of a woman's body filled the doorway. Ben's eyes must have also seen the intruder. "Please don't move," he said lowly. "I'll be with you in a moment, but please be still." He settled and shushed Sundance. Sabrina dared take a breath only after the horse's ears picked back up. Ben carefully made his way from the stall and closed the gap toward the woman.

Larielle Pritchett's eyes fastened on the cowboy while a sultry smile played against her mouth. "Hello Ben." Her voice oozed a distasteful sugary tone. "Looks like too much horse flesh for one man to handle."

Sabrina winced from her unseen perch on high. *What in the world was Larielle Pritchett doing in their barn?* Sabrina knew her mother hated the woman. The Ashley's didn't have many dealings with the Pritchett's even though they were fellow ranchers in the community. The Pritchett Ranch spread out on the north end of the Thomas Fork Valley. "Ely Pritchett has lots of money but little *sense*." Joseph Ashley had often said. Sabrina wondered what business this spidery woman had with her father.

"What can I do for you Larielle?" Ben asked curtly. Sabrina could tell this visit was unexpected and uninvited. It nearly caused a wreck with the colts. "I'll be happy to help you however I'm able, but please keep your voice low and your movements quiet until we get outside." They stepped into the tack room.

Sabrina watched the woman turn and face her father, barring him from pushing the door open. "Ben, I think you'd better know that once again, I'm making my play for you. You can't put me off forever."

The words sickened Sabrina almost instantly. She saw her father recoil, obviously repulsed by the woman's statement. "I'm married, as are you. Do you need to be reminded of that fact?"

"Amanda is a sniveling, ridiculous girl. I'm not saying she's not *precious*, but you are *way* too much man for her! You deserve someone as wild and unpredictable as those horses, Ben. I always get what I want." The sentences fell off her tongue amid ragged breaths. She grabbed Ben by the upper arm trapping him between the panicky horses in the barn and the freedom of outside. Ben shook his head, backing up a step. Tessie shied, jerking her head into Sundance's stall. Sundance fired with both hind legs. Sabrina watched silent and horrified.

Larielle snatched Ben's hand then, quickly pressing it against the front of her silky blouse. He jerked it away. "Get out of my barn before I throw you through that door!" Ben hissed, prying her hand off his arm. "Get out, *damn it!* Don't you ever come back here! How many times do you have to hear this? The answer is *no*! If you ever come back here again I'll slap a restraining order on you for harassment!"

"You wouldn't *dare*," Larielle seethed between clenched teeth. Her dripping sugar turned to spiteful venom. "I'd smear your name with attempted rape and any other vicious charge I could dream up.

I'd put it all back on you." She shook her dark hair. "No, this is just between you and me," her voice lilted, sweetening the venom, "until you're *mine*."

A sharp slap cracked against her cheek. Larielle's head whipped sideways under the blow. "Damn you, get out." Ben knocked her back a step. The door pushed open behind her and Ben shoved her out into the sunshine. He pulled the door shut in front of him separating himself from her poisonous, gaping, stare. He sat down quickly on a feed sack. Sabrina could see his hands trembling. He clasped them together to quiet the shaking. He ducked his head down toward his knees. He must have felt as sickeningly dizzy as Sabrina did. He examined the hand that slapped the woman. He clenched it instinctively into a fist. He took two or three big breaths then stood and slowly made his way back toward the stalls. His voice kicked into his lullaby tenor as he tried to soothe the horses. "Whoa, whoa, settle down now."

He looked surprised to see Sabrina still sitting statue-still and peering down at him. He appeared shaken and upset. His voice quaked even though he tried to control low even sounds. "I'm sorry either one of us had to see that, Bree. I've never hit a woman in my life, but she is no lady. I don't want your poor mother to know about this. It would just upset her."

Sabrina nodded. "I love you Daddy. I'm glad you slapped her. She said mean things about Mom. She–she–she," Sabrina stammered, "She is a regular mess."

"You are exactly right about that one, Honey. There's a big difference between Larielle Pritchett and your Mother. I just want you to know that I love you and your Mother more than anything in this whole world. I guess that after what you've seen and heard today you ought to know which kind of a woman you want to be when you grow up."

"I want to be a good one like Mom."

"Then you act like her. You make smart choices and you'll be as good as she is."

The horses were settling down. They apparently felt the words shushing from Ben's lips were meant just for them. Tessie's ears picked up. Sundance balked and shied but he was calming down some, too. Sabrina steadied her pencil once more against the tablet.

Ben was inching his way closer to the front of Sundance's stall. Sabrina glanced up just in time to see a flame of light streak in the wild horse's eye. He reared up with powerful front legs pawing the air. Larielle had returned and was again filling the doorway. She was clutching one of Sabrina's cats against her chest. Ben was retreating from the danger in the stall as quickly and as cautiously as he could manage, but the scene was spiraling out of control.

"You *spurn* me?" Larielle shrieked madly. "You *deny* me? You'll be sorry!" Profanity gushed from her ugly lips as she threw herself forward a step or two, and then wildly hurled the cat toward the horses. Larielle then fled the barn, leaving mayhem and chaos raining behind her.

The cat screeched through the air, whirling, landing upright and hissing on Tessie's back. Tessie bolted in a frenzied manner while the cat leapt to the window. Sundance exploded like a cannon, first rearing on his hind legs, then bucking forward with both back legs firing behind him. Ben Ashley dove for safety, ducking his head towards his chest for protection as he rolled. Sabrina saw the right hoof make contact with the back of her father's head. Ben crumpled.

Silent screams exploded in the little girl's throat. Her father lay lifeless and limp on the barn floor. He needed help! She couldn't get down from the edge. Tessie and Sundance were loose from their stalls now, bucking and shying in fits. If her father wasn't already dead Sabrina knew he was in grave danger of being trampled to death.

The little girl was crouched on her knees pleading to God and Heaven for help. Sobs rushed from her throat as she rocked back and forth. "Heavenly Father, help me! Help my Dad. It's bad right now. We need help...*please!*"

The west doors of the barn swung open. Sabrina jerked her head up. "Grandpa?" she called. The horses lunged to freedom removing emanate danger from the trauma scene. "Chantry?" she called louder, staring at the sunlight through the open doors.

Suddenly a boy wearing white clothes was kneeling in front of Sabrina. Sabrina was confused for she hadn't seen this boy come into the barn. How did he get up on the half-loft? "Who are you?"

"Sabrina, I'm your brother."

"Brian?"

"Yes."

"It's bad," Sabrina cried, motioning toward her Daddy's body.

"I'm sorry Sabrina. I've come to take Dad with me. Don't worry about him. I need you to stay here with Mom and take good care of her."

Sabrina listened to the boy. She suddenly realized that she was standing on the barn floor near her father's body. *How did he lift her down?* "Did you let the horses out?"

"Yes."

"Thank you."

"Now you have to go for help. This is going to be the hardest time in your whole life Sabrina. I'm sorry. You'll just have to face it, but I promise that you have the strength to make it. Dad and I will be closer by than you know."

"Promise me Brian!"

"I promise. You'd be surprised. I've always been near. Dad didn't feel any pain Sabrina. One second he was diving out of the way and the next he was meeting his son." Brian was guiding Sabrina to the tack room. Sabrina glanced down. An envelope was lying near the oat bin where her father had tussled with his murderess. She picked it up. "It's from *her*," Brian said. "Don't open it, just keep it."

"I think you look so much like Mom. I always wanted to know you. I miss not having a brother."

"You have one." Brian smiled. His face was brilliant.

Sabrina tucked the envelope into her back pack. When she straightened up the boy was gone. She stood gazing down at her father's body for a sad, sorrowful moment. "I love you Daddy!" Sabrina sobbed then turned and ran screaming for help.

CHAPTER FIVE

Somebody unplugged the sun. Days bled into weeks. Summer work progressed but Joseph Ashley wondered how. Nothing felt real! His family seemed to be surrounded by a thick, dark haze. A dense fog of sorrow and sadness threatened to suffocate any happy thought, any glimmer of promise on the horizon.

Amanda threw herself into the ranch. "I'll do Ben's work for him," she told her father-in-law. She and Chantry operated the swathers. One field after another, the hay fell in windrows. She struggled with sprinkler pipe morning and night. She resembled a robot; mechanically, numbly, going through the motions of work. She didn't eat much, and Sabrina said her mother's sleep was fitful. "Amanda would often cry through the night. The little girl had moved into her mother's room to keep her company but it didn't help much. Amanda wouldn't smile, laughter was void, and joy seemed a thing of the past.

Joseph's jaws worked together as he pondered the perplexing problem at hand. He worried about Sabrina, too. She had been forced to grow up about fourteen years' worth in the last few weeks. She alone had seen one of the barn cats spook the horses. Joseph feared that it was too much trauma for the child.

Sabrina shared her story eagerly with the family, carefully leaving Larielle Pritchett out of the tale. She told a chilling account of Brian's rescue and his sacred words to her. There was definite comfort in her story. Amanda had quizzed Sabrina again and again, prodding for any missed detail. It seemed to be the only thing that she would take comfort in. Sabrina would try to brighten her mother's mood by remembering small details. "Mother, Brian doesn't have one freckle," or, "His eyes are just as blue as yours." Amanda would perk up for a few minutes but never seemed to rally for long.

Sabrina had become the caretaker. She tried to feed Amanda, taking her soup or toast at night. She washed the dishes and kept the house tidy. Games and playing were forsaken. Childhood innocence and pleasures danced into yesterday. Sabrina was the mother now caring for Amanda, the hollow hired hand.

Joseph encouraged Juliet to spend happy time with the girl but Juliet's own heart was broken and bleeding as well. Juliet taught Sabrina how to sort laundry and how to fix easy dishes like scrambled eggs and grilled sandwiches. One day Juliet encouraged Sabrina to play dominos but Sabrina answered soberly, "No thank you, I don't have time for it."

Restless thoughts tumbled around in Joseph's mind. He sucked air into his cheeks and held it there for a second before slowly letting it escape. Something had to change. He climbed out of the tractor and strolled toward the house. Chantry sauntered out the back door, his black brows knit together.

"What's wrong?"

"Amanda and I just came in from cutting at Raymond Creek. She climbed down out of the swather and passed out. I gathered her up and took her in there," Chantry motioned toward the house, "and laid her on your couch. I think maybe she's got heat stroke but who knows? Sabrina confessed she hasn't been eating much. I'm not sure she's been drinking enough water."

Joseph closed his eyes and rubbed his hands across them. "She's okay though?"

Chantry's brows shot up and his head tilted off to one side. "I don't know! She looks terrible! She's got black circles under her eyes and her cheekbones are all hollowed in. Her eyes look dull and she's got sun blisters all across her nose and lips. She's been pushing herself way too hard. She's stubbornly just trying to kill herself off."

Joseph nodded, agreeing with the boy's assessment. "Well, I guess it's time to have a family council. Want to be in on it?" Chantry turned on his heels and followed the graying cowboy back into the house.

Juliet propped Amanda up with pillows. She made her sip a little salt water from a cup. "This will help get some minerals back into you," she said as she placed a cool cloth on her forehead.

"Makes me gag."

"Just get it down. If it comes back up we'll give you some more."

Sabrina entered the front room carrying a few soda crackers on a little plate and a juice glass full of 7-Up. She set them on the coffee table and reached for her mother's hand. "Your skin feels clammy, Mom."

Amanda sipped the salt water and shuddered. "Mmmm." She pointed towards the basin. Sabrina handed it to her quickly then turned her head while her mother threw up.

Juliet took the basin to rinse and Sabrina returned the salt water to her mother's hand. "Again," she ordered.

Tears began to stream down Amanda's cheeks. Sabrina raised her eyebrows toward her grandma. Juliet's hands rested on her hips. "Well it's about time we see some kind of emotion out of you. Madness, sadness, or sickness--it's all better than *nothing!*"

"I cry all night every night," Amanda whimpered. "This is nothing new."

"Yes it is!" Juliet snapped. "You've been a zombie around here just trying to work yourself completely to death to escape the pain. You think two deaths will serve the rest of us better than one?"

Amanda shook her head, tears falling faster. "I haven't meant to do that."

Sabrina nudged the cup back toward her mother's mouth. "Don't cry! You're draining all the salt right back out of you. Here, drink."

A floorboard in the hallway creaked. Sabrina glanced up. Grandpa and Chantry stood in the doorway of the front room. Joseph's eyes surveyed the scene. He ran a hand through thinning hair and eased himself into his recliner. "Have a seat Chantry."

Chantry claimed a spot on the hearth. He stared across the room at Amanda. It hurt him to see her cry. It hurt him to see her so violently ill. He had tried to prevent her from working such long hours but she had been so hopelessly stubborn! Now she lay humbled, exhausted, and spent. Her delicate frame had nothing left.

Joseph cleared his throat. All eyes turned on him. "Things are going to have to change around here. First of all Amanda, I appreciate what you've tried to do for me this summer. You've worked awfully hard. You've done a great job but this can't go on. You weren't meant to labor like a man."

"I'm just trying to earn our keep! Pay rent on our house and earn a living."

"I know, but I told you not to worry about that right now. I told you that you're taken care of. We'll see to things."

"I feel like a leech or something, and–" a sob cut from Amanda's throat. "I don't know what to do! I've got nothing left to give."

"That's what I'm talking about." Joseph said reassuringly. "Brant and Jessie are moving home. Brant will take Ben's place on the ranch."

"When?" Juliet asked, surprised to learn this from Joseph. "I thought Brant was happy in Preston."

"He feels differently about things now. He couldn't come back before without crowding his brother out. Jessie's on board with Brant's decision."

"Where will they live?" Sabrina questioned.

The room fell silent. A frightened look streaked through Amanda's eyes. "They'll have to move into our house."

"But we live *there*," the girl reminded everyone.

34

"Things are changing, Sabrina." Joseph reached his arms out for the child. Sabrina ran to him and he scooped her onto his lap. "You and your mother need a change of scenery. I have a surprise for you."

Amanda took a sip of salt water. "Should I wish this was whiskey? Because I feel like you are about to shatter my world."

"I bought a home for you and Sabrina in Morgan."

"What?" Amanda's chin fell open. "What did you say?"

"I bought a home for you and Sabrina in Morgan," Joseph repeated.

"Morgan, Utah?" Sabrina asked, "That's where my Mom grew up."

"I bought *that very house*." Joseph said quietly. "A Quaint two-story red brick home located on Commercial Street, right along the bank of the Weber River."

Amanda's eyes popped open at this revelation. She had never considered leaving Raymond. "Morgan? I *love* Morgan." A touch of color returned to her pale cheeks.

Joseph laughed. "I know."

"How did you manage it? My parents sold that house to the Pembrooke's ten years ago."

"And I bought it back from them quite recently."

"How recently?"

"Day before yesterday, that's how recently."

Amanda started sobbing uncontrollably.

"Mom? Are you shattered? Because it's hard to tell."

"I think she might be relieved." Juliet offered. "Am I right?"

Amanda nodded her head, "Thank you. Thank you. I love you! This is—too much. How could you buy it for us? It's just too much!" A small laugh tangled with a sob in her throat, creating a strange sound. She shook her head in embarrassment, smiling faintly.

"It's not too much. I figured on Ben getting most of this ranch as his inheritance. Let's just say that your home in Morgan is just Ben's portion. Of course it doesn't add up to the worth of the ranch but I thought we could supplement you from time to time with any necessary income. By the way, that's the first hint of a smile I've seen for the last six weeks."

Amanda sipped the salt water, "Too much excitement. I'm dizzy. This room is spinning." She laid her head against the pillows and closed her eyes.

"What do you think about converting the front portion of the house into a floral shop or something? You are extremely talented with things like that." Joseph suggested. "You could probably eke out a living doing something you enjoyed. You could do weddings if you wanted to. Cakes seem to be your specialty. Just a thought..." That comment sent the room buzzing with ideas.

"That's a good idea. We could use the front room and dining room for it. This is too much to think about with my heavy head."

"I'll order whatever flower coolers or supplies you need to get started."

"How soon will we leave? I don't even know what day it is."

"August second," Juliet said. "You'll need to move soon so that Sabrina can start second grade in Morgan and Brant's boys can get registered here."

Sabrina buried her face against her grandpa's chest and wept. "I don't want to leave you. I don't want to leave Grandma. I don't want to leave Slick and Jennifer. I don't even want to leave *him*!" Sabrina cried, pointing a finger at Chantry.

Chantry ducked his head quickly before anyone could see the liquid swelling in his own eyes. The objects in the room seemed to melt and run together. Ben was his hero and he was gone. Now Ben's special family would soon disappear from his life. Stinging pain clawed against his heart while a dry flame licked in his throat. Of course it was the best thing. It was time to say goodbye.

Chapter Six
Morgan Utah, June 1, 2009

Sabrina studied her reflection in the mirror. Her cheeks looked blotchy, thanks to her slip into melancholy and tears the night before. She leaned closer to the glass. Her eyes were deep hazel rimmed with blue. Grandpa Ashley said the color was bewitching. Her lashes were a thick, dark fringe so she seldom wore mascara. Stubborn freckles dotted her nose and cheeks like sprinkles of cinnamon and nutmeg. Sabrina often wished them away but now wondered how plain she would look without them.

Sabrina smoothed sheer foundation onto her cheeks. *Hopefully that settles the blotchy spots.* She dusted her cheekbones lightly with blush. *Better.* She smiled at herself, studying her dimples. They were just like her dad's. Sabrina was happy to share so many of his features; the dimples, high cheekbones, full mouth, strong jaw line, and dark hair.

She pulled her hair into a pony tail and swept it up with a clip. Springy curls cascaded in every direction. The natural curl made it very easy to achieve a professional up-do look in a matter of minutes. Her junior prom had been proof enough of that. Sabrina's friends had spent lots of time and money at the salon getting done up yet they arrived at the dance looking quite similar.

Sabrina added a hint of eye shadow and covered her lips with spiced mango gloss. She quickly switched earrings, exchanging small rhinestone studs for neon green hoops, hoping the shock of color would coax her mood to brighten up as well. Sabrina slid a matching bangle on her wrist. She loved the look of bracelets but they usually ended up being stuffed into her bag because the constant jangling on her arm became easily irksome to her.

Her white tee shirt was fresh and clean, *If only I could keep it this way*. Her jeans were well-fitting and comfortable. Sabrina threaded her new belt through the loops, careful not to miss one. She liked the belt! It was white leather with neon pink and green hearts and black graffiti hugs and kisses stamped all over it. The Nikes were still wet from last night's storm so Sabrina flung flip-flops on her feet instead. She stepped back for a last minute inspection in the mirror. Grandma Ashley always counseled, "Dress better than you feel and soon you'll feel better than you're dressed." Sabrina supposed there was wisdom in that statement. She always liked to be neat and clean and aimed her fashion meter for the high end of casual. Comfort was paramount!

Sabrina snatched her bag off the closet door handle. She paused in the kitchen to scratch her mother a quick note. She stuck it to the fridge with a magnet and then poked her head around the corner into the flower shop. "Bye Vidalia," she called to the hired woman behind the counter. "I'm going on deliveries then to the library. I'll be gone most of the afternoon. I left a note for Mom."

Sabrina waved to some shoppers as she pulled into Jubilee's parking lot. Ashley Floral kept the grocery store's flower cooler well-supplied with colorful blooms and bright bouquets. Her old blue Chevy lurched to a halt. It had belonged to Grandpa and Grandma Ashley for many years but she bought it from Grandpa for a buck on her sixteenth birthday. It didn't look like much but it was transportation.

Sabrina slung her bag over her shoulder then carefully balanced a basket arrangement on one arm then grabbed a vase full of carnations. She filled her free hand with a trailing ivy plant. She'd have to make two trips. Just as she turned to push the door shut with her shoulder, a voice called, "Hey, can I help you?"

She tossed her head toward the direction of the voice. Her heart sped up a notch and she felt her cheeks flush. She estimated she was looking at five feet and ten inches worth of totally amazing! *Hot* was the only word that shot through her mind.

"Can I help you?" he asked again.

Sabrina stared gaping. The bag slid off Sabrina's shoulder and bumped into the basket. "Um…sure, I'd love some help."

He reached out and took the basket, ivy, and vase. "Do you have more?"

"Just two but I'll have to grab them out of the other side." Sabrina retrieved a dainty bowl of violets and daisies and a green planter. She was surprised to see the boy followed her around to that side of the truck.

"I'll get the door," he said, nudging it shut with his knee.

"Thanks. You'll have to pardon my shock. I'm not used to guys with manners."

"Well, that doesn't speak very well for the hometown variety, does it?"

"Not really," Sabrina laughed.

"I'm Brad."

"Hi, Brad. I'm Sabrina."

"I take it you work for a flower shop? Either that or you're a funeral director."

Sabrina's head bobbed. "No funerals. My mom and I have a floral shop actually."

"I take it we're on some kind of a delivery here?" Brad asked as the automatic doors opened into the store.

"Yeah," Sabrina answered, leading him back toward the floral department. "We stock the flowers for their cooler."

"That's a good arrangement."

"Thanks, I did that one." Sabrina took the basket from him and placed it in the stores cooler.

Brad looked confused. "No, I meant that's a good arrangement between your Mom's shop and this grocery store."

"Oh, I thought you were complimenting my work--my *master-piece*." Sabrina teased with quick wink. *Did you just wink at him?* Color crept into her cheeks. She set the violets and daisies toward the front of the glass shelf so they would be well-showcased. "I did these too, just in case you were curious. I wanted to make sure I got all the credit."

"Breathtaking!"

Sabrina glanced around, looking for another plant to arrange in the cooler, but sadly they were all inside. "Well, thanks for your help."

"So...do you have any more deliveries to make?"

"I do; a couple here in Morgan and a birthday bouquet to deliver in Porterville."

"Birthday bouquets are my passion!" He returned the wink. "Where's Porterville? I'm kind of new here."

"Yeah, I can tell," Sabrina was stalling, not wanting to say goodbye yet. "I could give you a tour if you'd like." She flushed again, hoping her invitation didn't sound too forward or pushy.

"Why do you think I asked?"

"So you want to come?" Sabrina couldn't conceal the surprise in her voice. "You'll have to hold the flowers."

"That's okay. I find myself suddenly fascinated with the whole floral industry. Hey, can I buy you a drink for the road, or are we not allowed to have treats in your truck?"

Sabrina giggled at the thought of restricting food or drink in the old jalopy. "I'll take a root beer."

"Gee, you're hitting the hard stuff pretty early." Brad grabbed a root beer and a Mountain Dew from the pop cooler near the checkout counter. "Do I need to drive?"

Sheila, the friendly woman behind the checkout stand, arched one eyebrow in Sabrina's direction, silently inquiring about the cute guy. "Hey Sabrina, how are you?" she asked, and without waiting for an answer, quizzed, "Who's your handsome friend?"

Sabrina's cheeks flushed again. "This is Brad—"

"She just picked me up in the parking lot," Brad finished.

Sheila's eyebrows shot higher. She motioned thumbs up to Sabrina while Brad's head was down, pulling a couple of bills from his wallet. Sabrina couldn't help but smile.

"Thanks...*Sheila*," Brad said reading her name tag. "If I'm not back by supper time, don't come find me." Sheila's amused laugh escorted them through the doors.

"You sure you want to come?"

"Are you kidding? I wouldn't miss a personalized tour for anything."

The drive up to Porterville was always a favorite of Sabrina's--today especially. The conversation had been surprisingly comfortable. They traded basic information back and forth. Sabrina learned that Brad and his father had only been in Morgan for a couple of days. Brad was seventeen and would begin his senior year in Sabrina's class. He was an only child so they had that in common. The drive was filled with pleasant chatter. Sabrina pointed out various homes which dotted the hills above lush green fields. "My mother is a Porter," Sabrina explained. "Her ancestors actually settled Porterville."

"That's cool. Do you know much about these ancestors?"

"Yeah, I do actually. I'm kind of a history freak and it's very interesting to me."

"You remind me of Mulan."

"Disney's Mulan? Why?"

"She always talked about her ancestors."

"Okay. Um...that's a *first*, being compared to Mulan." A puzzled expression pulled at Sabrina's features momentarily but she pointed to a red brick home on the hill. "See that house right there? That's our delivery."

"Relative of yours? Common ancestors?"

"No," Sabrina shook her head and laughed. "Do you think I'm *weird*?" A touch of defensive tenor sounded in the question. "Because I didn't think that it was so peculiar to tell you about Porterville. You're the one who requested a tour." She scowled sideways at the boy as she pulled into the driveway.

"Don't get nervous--I'm just messing with you. I'll deliver these if you don't mind." He opened the door of the truck and climbed out. "Try replacing that scowl with one of your delicious smiles while I'm gone." He flashed a grin of his own and sauntered up the walk toward the door.

What did he say? The words seeped into Sabrina's understanding causing blood to deepen the blush in her cheeks. *Delicious?* She rolled the word around in her mind. "Speaking of *delicious*," she muttered to herself watching Brad approach the door and knock. He wore Levi's 501 jeans and a white tank top underneath a blue striped, button-down shirt. The sleeves were rolled up to his elbows. His hair was brown with sun-kissed golden streaks that contrasted against deeply tanned skin and his eyes were shocking blue.

"That went well," Brad announced proudly as he climbed back in the truck. "That nice lady was so happy she burst into tears and gave me a hug. Perhaps later I might pass it on to you."

Sabrina let the last comment pass although she decided not to abandon the idea. "We get happy tears a lot. It feels good to people when they are remembered. I think it's the sentiment more than the flowers."

Brad studied Sabrina thoughtfully. "Do you have to get back to work right away? Please say no."

"Okay…no."

"Are you serious?"

"I was going to the library after deliveries, not back to work."

"Do you really have to go to the library?"

"I guess not…why?"

Brad flashed a charming smile at Sabrina. "Because, I'm not done with you yet." He scanned the horizon in front of him. "What's over there for instance?"

"I'm going to go show you but no ancestor jokes, okay?"

"Why would *I* make ancestor jokes?"

"Because I'm taking you to see the Porterville Cemetery."

"Ouch." Brad's lower lip jutted out.

"What?"

"There was this smart remark that I really wanted to say…"

"*Can it,* Brad! Or I'm just going to turn Old Blue around right now."

"Okay, no comment. So what's so cool about the Porterville Cemetery?"

"It's just an old pioneer cemetery on a sagebrush hill. There are all these old headstones. Black wrought iron fences outline some of the family plots. Almost every single person buried there is a Porter. It's pretty cool. Years ago some families planted lilac bushes, others have planted irises. I've seen little purple hyacinths and daffodils there before. They all grow wildly, each year volunteering seeds and blooms. Native grasses, rocks, sagebrush—it's all there together. The grounds aren't groomed, irrigated, or anything. It's just a cool cemetery which takes you back a step or two in time."

Brad listened carefully. This girl was way too serious about liking this place to go joking around about it. "I'd like to see it."

"It's just up this hill." Old Blue chugged up the winding road and lurched to a stop near the cemetery gate. Sabrina started to climb out of the truck. Brad grabbed her wrist.

"Wait a second." He jumped out of the truck and raced around to her side. "Let me," he said, opening the truck door. "You really aren't used to manners, are you?" Sabrina shook her head. "Aren't you going to take your keys?"

Light danced in Sabrina's eyes as she scanned the desolate hillside. "Why? Who's going to take off in my truck?"

Brad followed her sweeping gaze of the empty acres and then shrugged his shoulders. "Too much California in me, huh?"

"California? That's where you're from? I've never been there."

"Never? No Redwood Forrest? No Golden Gate Bridge? Not even Disneyland?"

"Nope." Sabrina unfastened the gate. Brad followed her into the cemetery. Sabrina began showing him different items of interest. "First of all you have to sign this register."

"I've never heard of signing in at a cemetery before."

"Use your California address. It will make it more interesting." Sabrina waited for him to scrawl his information and then began pointing out headstones. "There's a Porter, and there's a Porter. Look over there--those are all Porters. I like reading their names. This guy's name is John President Porter. Isn't that cool? He's a brother to my direct line."

Brad studied the markers as they walked along. "What are those little bronze placards on some of the headstones?"

"That means actually means they crossed the plains with the pioneers."

"Mormons?"

"Yes."

"Are you Mormon?"

"Yes."

"Not me. I'm not really anything. I am a Christian, though."

"Oh." Sabrina nodded then continued pointing things out to Brad. "My Great Grandpa Porter's mother is buried right here. Her name is Susan Lettie Florence Porter. Isn't that pretty?" She waved her left hand marking the spot. With her right hand she motioned off the trail the other way. "These people are my great, great, great, great, great, *great* grandparents." She lifted a finger with each *great* she pronounced, careful to tick off six generations, "Sanford and Nancy Porter."

Brad's eyebrows shot up. "How do you know this stuff?" His question resonated dismay.

Sabrina shrugged casually. "Well you read about them and study them out in family histories and stuff." Brad was staring so intently that she felt uncomfortable. "What's wrong?"

"I'm just trying to figure you out. What makes you *tick*? You're so *multi*-dimensional." Brad's eyebrows knit together thoughtfully. "I've just never met anybody like you."

Sabrina winced inwardly. She felt certain that wasn't good news. She bent down and picked a small weed which was hovering over a tiny grape hyacinth. "Poor little hyacinth, was that mean weed trying to choke you to death?" When she looked up Brad was still staring at her. "We can go if you want to—"

"Why would I want to go?" Brad asked incredulously.

"Well, I don't know...if you think it's too weird up here or something."

"Are you kidding? I like it! It's peaceful." His gaze swept down across the valley they'd driven up. "It's really pretty up here in an isolated, rustic, natural sort of way."

"That's what I think too. I bring my sketch pad up here sometimes and sit for hours just sketching and thinking."

"You draw?"

"Not professionally."

"Is there anything you *don't* do?"

"I don't do drugs."

"Oh my gosh! You are too much!"

Sabrina peeked shyly up at him through her lashes and smiled. She hoped it was one of her delicious varieties. "There are some big rocks down off the trail over there. I wish I'd have worn better shoes and I'd show you."

Brad backed toward the girl, "Here, jump on my back and let me pack you over there."

"No, that's okay."

"Come on, don't be a pansy. I mean, don't be a *hyacinth*," he teased. "I just found out they're delicate. Seriously, climb on." He wrapped her arms around his neck and hoisted her off the ground. "Which way?" Sabrina stifled giggling a fit of embarrassment as she pointed out the general direction.

"Excuse us Ancestors," Brad chimed out as he wove his way between headstones.

Sabrina thumped him playfully against his chest. "You promised."

"Sorry—my bad." He sat her down near one of the big rocks. He draped himself over the other boulder. "Have a seat." He was panting from lugging her through the brush. "Do me a favor, call Sheila and tell her to bring us another drink."

Sabrina smiled and laid back on the rock, soaking in the sunshine. Brad was a pleasant person to be with. He was good at verbal jousting which was Sabrina's term for matching wits. He had a good sense of humor. Sabrina peeked sideways at him. He wasn't bad to look at either!

"Aha! I caught you peeking at me. I know because I was peeking at you first."

"I was just making sure you were still here. I didn't want a giant horny toad to carry you away."

"A *what?*" Brad sat up wide-eyed and in a panic.

"Little lizards? Haven't you ever caught a horny toad before? They like these rocks. I used to catch them all the time when I was little."

"Do they bite?" Sabrina shook her head, laughing lightly. "Then--can I ask another obvious question? Are they really horned or *horny*, or whatever you said?"

Sabrina chortled and choked. "You are so *dumb*," she gasped.

"One more question--are they toads or lizards?"

"Lizards. I don't know why they're called toads. Here, let me find one." Sabrina climbed off her rock and spied the ground carefully. "There's one."

Brad instinctively jerked his feet up on the rock like a woman who'd just spied a mouse. "Where?"

"Right here." Sabrina closed her hands around the tiny creature. Little beady eyes blinked at her as she lifted him up for inspection. "Hi little Guy," Sabrina cooed. The horny toad was only three inches long. She handed the scaly miniature to Brad who looked suspiciously at the harmless grey reptile. He stroked a finger down its back.

"I know who this is! This is Mushu!"

"Who?"

"That little dragon sidekick of Mulan's, he is here to guard your ancestors."

"Brad—"

"By the way, it was very nice to meet your family."

"Brad!"

"Sabrina? I have a confession to make."

"What?"

"I've never brought a girl here before..."

"Correction: I brought *you* here, remember?"

"Please tell me I'm the first guy you've shared this with."

Sabrina giggled. Brad's teasing could rival Grandpa Ashley's. "You're whacked."

"But I'm being serious when I say I'd like to take you out."

"When?" Sabrina held her breath.

"Tonight."

CHAPTER SEVEN

Sabrina hummed happily as she stripped leaves from stems and poked different heights of blooms into place. She kept reflecting on yesterday's unexpected date with Brad Manning.

"You're in good spirits," Vidalia noted suspiciously.

"It's a nice morning don't you think?"

"Oh, I guess it's about the same as it was the other morning when you were brooding."

"Vidalia, what a thing to say. I'm never broody."

"What time did your mom get home yesterday? I felt guilty all day long that I didn't go help her with that wedding."

"I'm not sure. I came home about four and she wasn't home yet. I showered and went out with...a *friend*." Sabrina couldn't help smiling again as she remembered how Brad asked her out even after spending most of the day with her. She liked him quite a bit. Before leaving her at the doorstep last night he asked if he might have permission to relay the birthday lady's hug. Sabrina's cheeks flushed as she remembered the electricity of his touch. It lit her up and she felt as if she still glowed long after she fell asleep. Her dreams had all been pleasant ones.

"For hell's sakes," Vidalia grumbled snapping Sabrina back to their conversation.

"What's wrong?"

Vidalia waved a chubby hand, "Nothing's wrong except you just zoned out and left me talking to myself as if I enjoyed the sound of my gums bumping together," Vidalia murmured crossly and went stomping up the stairs to the work room.

"Sorry Vidalia!" Sabrina called after the faithful employee. Vidalia Davies had worked for the Ashley's for the past eight years. She started off as part-time help but as the business grew so did Amanda's need for Vidalia. She was a dear friend and a loyal worker. She'd often looked after Sabrina, helping Amanda mother-hen the child. She was a skilled florist and willing to assist with Amanda's catering.

Sabrina began wondering what time her mother *had* gotten home. She checked the fridge for messages. In response to her second note her mom wrote: *"Glad you had a good day! I appreciate all you do. I hope you have fun with your friends tonight. The wedding went well. I got lots of compliments and booked three more receptions. (When it rains it pours!) I got home about 6:30, but since you're not here and I'm too tired to cook, I've decided to go out for dinner. In case you get home before I do, don't wait up.*

"*Don't wait up*–is that really what she said?" Sabrina read the note again just to be sure. That sounded so strange. "Where on earth did she go to eat--Salt Lake City?" Sabrina asked herself sarcastically. "Because it doesn't take *that* long to grab something from Subway--it's like three blocks away." But where was Mom this morning? Sabrina mused, her eyes still scanning the fridge. There was another note. *"Good morning, Bree! Sorry I'm already off and gone to Huntsville to meet with a client. Sell lots of flowers today, okay?*

Sabrina furrowed her eyebrows. It was odd to go two whole days without seeing her mother. They were usually on top of each other. The flower shop occupied the original living room and dining room of their home. Amanda had converted the upstairs into a work room. That only left the kitchen, bathroom, two bedrooms, and back porch as living quarters.

Sabrina finished the bouquet she was working on, and checked her work orders for her next project. The door chimed as two female customers stepped into the shop. Sabrina recognized one of them as a regular. "Hi," Sabrina greeted the women warmly. "Let me know if I can help you with anything."

"We're just looking," the more familiar face explained. "I just love this shop! I wanted Claire to see it."

"Isn't this delightful?" Claire exclaimed. "Look at these antique hutches! I love this kind of thing," she gushed.

"I do too. I do too."

Sabrina smiled behind the counter. Her mother did have exquisite taste and tremendous merchandising skills. The tiny shop was filled with antique hutches, shelves and tables. Each surface held gift ware: porcelain pieces, carved wooden collections, stuffed animals, handcrafted jewelry, stationary, cards, bath salts, hand cream, shower gels, specialty soaps, candles, wall plaques, and books. Pre-made gift baskets were scattered here and there. Of course planters, wreathes, swags, and bouquets adorned the room. One hutch boasted specialty chocolates, caramels, cream candies, sugared mints, toffee, hand-pulled taffy, and roasted nuts. Framed art was displayed on easels and available wall space. *What wasn't to love?*

"It's all quality--that's what I like," the familiar face whispered to Claire.

"I'm gaga over the old architecture of this house. Look at that molding; it must be original. The door frames are just like the ones in Grandma's old house."

"Yes they are, yes they are."

"Betty Jo, come look at *this*," Claire gasped, pointing at a candy jar full of old fashioned black licorice whips. "I haven't had a black licorice whip in thirty-five years. I thought they quit making them!" Nostalgia was sweeping the women away.

Sabrina made a mental note: familiar face now had a familiar name, *Betty Jo*. That was valuable information in pleasing returning customers. Now Sabrina could say, "Thanks again, Betty Jo! We just love it when you come in."

"I could just move right in here," Claire cooed. "This place definitely has charm. It just makes you feel better by walking through the door."

"I know, I know," Betty Jo agreed.

Sabrina turned around and smiled at the wall. Betty Jo had a way of saying everything twice. "This is too funny, this is too funny," Sabrina giggled to herself. As soon as composure settled in she turned back to her work.

"Betty Jo! Check out these antique looking perfume bottles! Of course they *have* to be reproductions. Do you remember the dressing tray on Aunt Millicent's bureau? She had three or four little perfume bottles just like this."

"That's right. That's right, I remember. This green glass bottle looks especially familiar."

"How much is that mirrored tray beneath them?"

Betty Jo checked the price and mouthed the amount to Claire, as if she didn't want Sabrina to hear. That action struck Sabrina's funny bone as well, for she was the one who'd marked the price. It was no secret to her.

Sabrina heard Claire whisper, "Well that's not a bad price for quality like this. That tray has genuine crystal roses rimming the whole thing."

"It does, it does."

The door chimed again. Sabrina greeted the new customer warmly. He nodded and quietly and began looking around. Sabrina noticed Claire and Betty Jo elbowing each other and giggling like school girls. Apparently they thought the man was quite a catch. "He smells good," Claire whispered too loudly. The gentleman pretended not to hear. "He looks peachy to me!" Betty Jo hissed. A slight frown tugged at the man's mouth.

"Excuse me," the gentleman said, "but I'd like to order some flowers."

"Sure," Sabrina grabbed her order pad. "What can I do for you?"

"I'd definitely like these to be delivered."

"Okay...what is it you'd like?"

"How many roses do you have in stock?"

Sabrina turned her head back to the coolers. "Well, I think I have plenty to do just about–"

"No. That's not what I asked. I want to know how many roses you can sell me. How many are available for sale? I don't want to short any current orders."

Sabrina's eyes widened. *Surely he doesn't want all the roses!* Claire and Betty Jo clucked and chuckled from the other room. "Hear that? He wants to buy all of their roses! Oh he's a romantic devil, isn't he Betty Jo?"

"He is. He is."

"Let me check. I'll be back in just a second." She dashed upstairs to confer with Vidalia. Sabrina wanted to be sure what they could spare.

Vidalia's eyebrows shot up when Sabrina presented the question. "Who the hell have you got down there--*Don Juan?*"

"I don't know. He is quite good looking," Sabrina said before scurrying back downstairs. "Sir, did you have a preference on the color?"

"No, not if you can arrange them nicely together."

"Then I can sell you five dozen."

"Great. I'll take them. What quality of vases can you put them in?" The question caught Sabrina off guard.

"Whatever you'd like," she stammered. "Is this all one order? I can wrap them prettily in tissue paper if you don't want to stand the expense of vases."

"I want five bouquets arranged in the best vases you have."

"I have some that are cut crystal. They are undoubtedly the best but they are a little pricey, about forty dollars apiece. I also have some nice glazed ceramic ware and I can give those to you for twenty-eight." Sabrina bit her lip, waiting for the man to declare highway robbery and change his mind.

"I'll take the cut crystal vases. They sound just right." Claire and Betty Jo were twittering in fits from the other room.

Sabrina let out a shaky breath. This guy had to be the customer of the year! *He must have money...*"And you want these delivered?"

"Yes."

"Sure, if you'd like to personalize a card and then fill out this address sheet, I'll be glad to take care of that for you."

Sabrina was tallying up the cost. She was half afraid to give him the bill. He'd spent two hundred dollars on the vases alone. She peeked up at the man. His head was down, filling out the information. He seemed to be in his early forties. She wanted to be able to describe this unusual customer to her mother when she came home. Sabrina sorted descriptive words out of her mental thesaurus: *debonair, distinguished, impeccable, polished, articulate...possibly wealthy... now possibly broke...*

"Will there be a surcharge for the delivery?"

"No sir, you've spent enough." A smile twitched at his mouth. "Either you are the world's most romantic man or you have one heck of a guilty conscience," Sabrina said. The man's smile spread. He almost a chuckled but not quite; however, Claire and Betty Jo erupted noisily.

The man pressed six hundred dollars in Sabrina's hand. "There's a little extra for the delivery, please make sure it gets where it's going. Thank you so much." He nodded to Sabrina, and then to Vidalia, who had just pounded down the stairs to catch a glimpse of this gluttonous rose buyer. He also threw a gentlemanly nod to the ladies in the next room. "Good afternoon ladies," he said smoothly before pulling the door shut behind him.

Vidalia reached for the address card and snatched it up. "Well I'll be a one-eyed jack in a stacked deck," she muttered. "I'll be a one-eyed monkey in a box of animal crackers..." she droned louder, shaking her head back and forth.

"Vidalia! You are driving me crazy! Just give me the card! Who are they for?"

"You'll never believe it."

Sabrina gulped at the words. "Well I'll be a one-eyed clown in a three ring circus."

Amanda Ashley

Commercial Street, Morgan Utah

(Please see that these are delivered promptly.)

"It's been a profitable day today." Sabrina punched the buttons on the adding machine. "Betty Jo purchased all of our licorice whips at a dollar ten a piece—complete with the candy jar at eighteen fifty. That comes to a total of fifty-three seventy."

"Those licorice whips aren't penny candy anymore," Vidalia declared soberly.

"Claire finally splurged and bought the mirrored dressing tray at sixty-five, and all five perfume bottles at twenty-five a piece." *Clickety-clickety-click* sounded the adding machine beneath Sabrina's fingers. "That brings Claire's total to two hundred and ten bucks. Add that figure to Betty Jo's purchase, and the six hundred from the rose-buyer...that brings our total to eight hundred sixty-three dollars and seventy cents for only fifteen minutes worth of work! That doesn't even count the rest of our orders for the day."

"That makes a typical work day look right darned anemic," Vidalia said, watching her language "Your mother is going to jump for joy."

"For her flowers or this bonanza sales day?"

"Both. I can't wait to see her face when she walks in her room!"

"I'll bet you she packs all those roses right back out here and puts them in the cooler again."

Vidalia stroked her chin. "No, no, you're wrong. She'll keep every rose in the bunch and those vases too."

Sabrina shook her head. "Bet me. If you lose you have to stop swearing."

Vidalia scowled. "Okay. If I lose I'll watch my mouth but if you lose you must tell me where you were last night."

Color crept up Sabrina's neck and into her face. "Oh, Vidalia..."

Vidalia chuckled. "You've been way too dreamy around here today. Old Vidalia knows what she's talking about, huh kid?"

The back door opened, "Hey," Amanda called. "How's everything?"

Sabrina made a bee-line for the kitchen with Vidalia dogging her heels. "Hi Mom! It's been a good day."

"Did you sell lots?" Amanda asked, setting her purse and keys down on the counter.

"Yeah, we did *okay*," Vidalia confessed casually.

"Great!" Amanda headed into her bedroom. Vidalia and Sabrina followed her in, eager to catch her reaction. It was quiet for a second or two. "Why have you put all the roses in my room? Are the coolers down?"

"No Amanda, they are for you! Sabrina left the card on your pillow. I wish you'd hurry and open it because the suspense has been *killing* us!"

"What?" Amanda gasped and sat down suddenly on her bed. "What do you mean these are all for me?" She cast her eyes around the bedroom. Sabrina had lined up three vases full of roses on top of Amanda's dresser and left another bouquet on the window sill. The last dozen roses were gracing the night stand. Just for dramatic effect Sabrina had scattered a few fresh petals across Amanda's pillows, placing the note card right in the middle. "Somebody actually bought me–roses?" Amanda was dumb-struck.

"They bought every damned one we had," Vidalia triumphed. Sabrina scowled fiercely at the older woman. "I mean every *darned* one," Vidalia corrected.

"For me?" Amanda asked again, a strange quiver in her voice. Tears welled in her eyes.

Sabrina watched her mother. *Is she crying?* Sabrina was surprised by the emotion that five dozen roses could levy. She remembered her conversation with Brad. Her own words now rang in her mind with full import, *"It's the sentiment more than the flowers."*

Amanda's hands trembled as she slid the small card from its envelope. *"Amanda, you are beautiful both inside and out."* That's all. It's not signed."

Vidalia threw her arms in the air with exasperation and pirouetted out of the bedroom. "That's a miserable trick to leave those flowers anonymously! He paid with cash! We have no idea who he was." Amanda's expression seemed far away. She clutched the card to her chest and stared at the flowers.

"You're keeping them?" Sabrina asked, shaking Amanda from her reverie.

"Of course I'm keeping them!" Amanda was shocked at Sabrina's insinuation that she might go stuff them all back inside the flower coolers. "Do you have any idea when I last received flowers?"

"A long time ago, before you were a florist?"

"Exactly."

"Left-over's from Dad's funeral, probably."

"That's right. Those were the last flowers I've had and I was too rotten broken-up to enjoy them." Amanda bent over the roses on her night stand and inhaled their precious perfume. "I love that fragrance." She lifted a finger and softly stroked a velvety red petal.

Sabrina left her mother's room quietly. Vidalia was sternly tidying up the counter area. "I left Mom alone with her roses. She wanted a moment with them. I wish that card would have had a signature."

"Doesn't matter," Vidalia said grumpily. "I've been thinking and she knows exactly who they're from."

The statement stunned Sabrina. "She does--who?"

"Sabrina, a woman doesn't receive five dozen roses from an admirer and not have a faint idea who they're from. No, mark Vidalia's words, your mom knows who they're from, alright. She's just chosen not to tell us."

Sabrina scowled deeply. "You're wrong. My mother isn't interested in men, or dating, or any of that."

"Dream on. You've never seen her as having a life aside from being your mother and the owner of Ashley Floral."

"You're wrong!"

"Ha! I just won the last bet, didn't I? It is a darned good thing, too. If I gave up swearing altogether I'd be giving everyone the silent treatment. You lost the bet though. I'd like to collect on it."

"Not now! I'm not really in the mood to share my life with you at the moment."

"Back to brooding?"

"No! But all your talk about Mother, and admirers, and her knowing who sent those roses to her, has put me in a bad mood! She's never told me about anybody, not in particular."

"She tells you everything, you think?" Sabrina huffed out an angry breath and shrugged her shoulders. Vidalia persisted, "She tells you every single place she goes, and every single person she's talked to--just like you've told her about your date last night, eh?"

"Can it, Vidalia!"

"The truth is sometimes hard to hear, but you'd better be able to take it when it comes. Your mother is a young, vital woman. She just might have a life of her own, aside from you and this place."

"You're crazy," Sabrina snarled. She was feeling stubborn and unreasonable. "My mother isn't young! She's *thirty-seven.*"

Vidalia stroked her chin and laughed at the absurdity of Sabrina's statement. "Just prepare yourself you little hot head," she clucked as Sabrina stomped to her bedroom and slammed the door.

CHAPTER EIGHT

Sabrina was waiting on the porch swing when Brad pulled up. She grabbed her bag and hurried to the car. She remembered to wait while he opened the door for her.

"That's progress."

"So how's Utah treating the California native today?"

"The scenery is great," he replied giving Sabrina an obvious once-over, "But the surfing sucks."

"I'll bet. Seriously, how are you?"

"Alright. We're kind of getting settled in."

"That's good."

"People are really friendly here. I met the *friendliest* girl this morning. She said she was going to be in our class. She offered to show me the ropes which was really kind of her."

"Who?" Sabrina asked soberly. She knew a few overly friendly girls.

"What was her name?" Brad pretended to strain under the pressure of a failing memory. "I've got it! Halsey Redding, do you know her?"

Sabrina's lips pursed into a fine line. She refused to act jealous in any manner; however, frankness was Sabrina's normal policy. "Halsey Redding? Yes, I know her."

"And?"

"I hate her that's all."

Brad's head tipped back and he laughed heartily. "You *hate* her? Why? She seemed very genuine to me."

"Ugh! You know I read once that men were stupid but I never really believed it, until now."

Brad grinned. "She was incredibly kind to me."

"Brad! I don't doubt she's *friendly*. She's also very skilled at *showing boys the ropes*, as you call it."

Brad was grinning at Sabrina's annoyance. "Oh, so you don't much like her then?"

"No I don't."

"That's good. I didn't much care for her myself."

Sabrina brightened, "Really?"

"The Halsey Redding's of the world are a dime a dozen. That's right, they're that *cheap*. I guess I have more expensive taste."

"Seriously?"

"Yes. Besides, I told her Sabrina Ashley was already showing me the ropes."

"I'll bet that killed her dead in her tracks."

"She turned green, alright. It was funny. Her fake smile just froze in place while her small brain processed my intended meaning."

"I also read once that a real friend hates the same people you do. I love you for that!" *Stupid! Why did you say love?* "Um, I just mean... it makes me happy that you didn't fall for her little traps. Most guys around here go stepping right in them."

"Most guys around here don't know enough to open the door for a lady either," Brad reminded her.

"Where are we going anyway?"

"I thought we'd have a cookout."

"Really? I love cookouts!"

"I thought so. Any girl who's happy to sit on rocks at cemeteries, and sketch horny toads and wild daffodils is bound to prefer picnics to restaurants."

"You've got that right."

"So Sabrina, what kind of music do you like?"

"Not rap. Not hard rock. I like pop, soft rock and country, and I know this is square, but I really like vintage music especially from the fifties and eighties."

"Do you have an I-pod?"

"No."

"You're kidding."

"No. Our flower shop supports itself and pays our bills, but things are tight and so I have to be really choosy about my *extras*. I was saving up for one but I spent my money on an online course in herbal medicine instead."

"Why?"

"Why not? Plants fascinate me. I guess it's because of our flower shop that I learned to love plants at such a young age, but it's amazing to me how the Lord created a living pharmacy for us. I started getting interested in edible flowers when I was in sixth grade. I wanted to make sure we could survive in case of an *emergency*," Sabrina chuckled and rolled her eyes at the memory. "Well that spread to an interest in other plants, trees, herbs, roots, and you get the picture."

"Sounds interesting—in a weird way, of course."

"I'd like to add a whole new dimension to our business. I'd like to start carrying fresh herbs, herbal teas, natural balms, oils, and stuff like that. I've already got quite a stock pile of my own remedies. I never get sick and I doctor my mom and Vidalia quite regularly. Grandpa and Grandma Ashley swear by me. It's kind of fun."

"You're the most interesting person I've ever met."

"Does that mean I'm really strange?"

"No but you are very peculiar in your own way. Your interests are so varied and obviously you aren't afraid to explore new horizons. That is an amazing quality. The thing that makes you so attractive is the fact that you're so confident in yourself."

"Conceited?"

"No! Confidence and conceit should never be confused. Most girls our age can't think past the boy next door or what's on sale at the mall. You're different than that. Your interests all build character."

Brad and Sabrina built a bonfire near East Canyon Reservoir. The sun was setting and the evening was balmy. Brad threaded two marshmallows onto his stick. "I'll roast you a perfect marshmallow." He studied his work contentedly, concentrating on transforming the white confection into a melted, golden masterpiece. Just as he was on his last rotation, Sabrina bobbled his stick with hers and Brad's marshmallow dunked into the flames.

Brad's head jerked up in astonishment. Sabrina was wickedly smiling at him and laughing at her stunt. "I did that to our hired boy in Raymond once, a long time ago."

"Oh yeah?" Brad didn't know whether he felt angry, amused, or delighted with the dancing-eyed beauty. "What did the hired boy do?"

"Um...well actually he gave me a present."

"No wonder you never learned a lesson in bon fire etiquette! He rewarded you for delinquent behavior."

"I know I'm naughty, I just can't help it sometimes."

"I'm sure you can't." Brad waited until the flames burnt out on his stick then pulled it from the fire and leaned it against a cooler. "Let's go for a walk, since I see you've got your sensible shoes on and everything."

Sabrina was game. "That sounds good."

"Don't tell me--let me guess, you are an avid hiker, right?"

"Nope, I don't have the time."

"Have you told your mom about me yet?"

"No. She just thinks I'm out with the gang."

"You belong to a gang?"

"You know what I mean."

"So why haven't you told her?"

"I don't know. I'm just enjoying having a secret, I guess. She's been working a lot lately and I actually haven't seen much of her. Does your dad know you have taken me out five times in the last five days?"

"Technically that's not true. The first time you took me out, remember?"

"That wasn't a date. It was a tour."

"Where I come from dates and tours are the same thing." Brad stopped near a large rock and sat down. Sabrina turned to face him, looking for a rock of her own. Brad reached out a hand and laced his fingers through hers. A shock rippled up Sabrina's arm. She couldn't think of anything to say and her heart was beating rapidly.

Brad scooted further back on the rock and then pulled Sabrina down to sit in front of him. One of his arms was around her, still holding her hand. His chin and mouth rested against the back of her head. "Your hair smells good."

"It does? My mom's hair always smells good so maybe it's hereditary."

"Well I'll be sure to thank her later on." Brad murmured against her hair, "When I'm allowed to know who she is."

The moon cast a silvery path across the water. "It's pretty tonight." Sabrina noticed her voice was shaky. She had never felt this jittery about anybody before. Involuntary shivers were shooting down the back of her head where Brad's breathing moved her hair. Goose bumps rose against her arms.

"Are you cold?"

"No, I'm fine," Sabrina answered then wondered what she should have said, because she shivered again.

"You must be cold."

"Well I guess I am then."

"Here, let me give you my sweat shirt." Sabrina leaned off the rock so Brad could pull it over his head. He handed it to her and she struggled into it. "Whatever your many talents might be, getting dressed doesn't appear to be one of them," he teased, helping her find an armhole.

"I know--I struggle." Sabrina chuckled at her awkwardness. "There, how's that?"

"My sweatshirt's never looked better," Brad said thickly, reaching out and pulling Sabrina toward him. His hands closed around her back. "You are more beautiful than the night."

Sabrina realized she wasn't breathing. Even her subconscious movements seemed haywire in this close proximity. She felt woozy almost. "You're quite beautiful your own self," she blurted honestly. Brad smiled, studying her face intently. Sabrina's heart was pounding louder than her ragged breathing. *He's going to kiss me.* "Your hoodie smells good, like *you do*, and I think it's making me drunk."

Brad pursed his lips together to keep from laughing. "You're so cute," he said before covering her mouth with his. "Mmm…delicious. They don't make lips as sweet as yours in California."

Sabrina's knees felt weak as new sensations coursed through her body and so both of her arms reached instinctively around Brad's neck, clinging for support. That action initiated another kiss, infused with tender passion. The moonlight shimmered approval on the budding romance while stars danced and twinkled over two young people falling in love.

CHAPTER NINE

"What day is it?" Amanda asked.

"July first, believe it or not."

"Oh my word, summer is dancing away in a blur. I can't believe it! Where did June go?"

"You've been too busy around here to enjoy any of it and that's a pity." Vidalia clucked.

"Ever since you got the talented women of Ashley Floral featured in that bridal magazine, things have been manic. It's amazing we don't all kill over dead."

"Now Vidalia," Sabrina interjected, "you always told me that hard work makes you healthy."

"I'm so darned healthy now I'll probably never die." Vidalia said, reaching for another batch of Russian tea cakes. The woman was rapidly rolling the hot cookies in powdered sugar then placing them to cool on the counter behind her. "How many of these did you tell me we're doing?"

"Nine hundred, I need a commercial baker's kitchen, huh?"

"Dream on," Sabrina and Vidalia answered at the same time.

"Jinx!" Sabrina cried enthusiastically.

"Oh jinx, *my foot*," Vidalia muttered.

The women were all working around the kitchen table together, keeping an ear open for the shop door to chime. Amanda was busy slinging batches of cookies in and out of the oven. Vidalia powdered hot cookies on one end of the table while Sabrina hand dipped strawberries on the other. "It's these weddings that are making life so frantic," Vidalia complained.

"I know. I've opened a whole can of worms haven't I? But I just love what I'm doing! I couldn't do it without you two though." The oven's buzzer sounded and Amanda dumped another sheet full of hot tea cakes onto the table for Vidalia to roll.

"Vidalia's hands can fly at lightning speed," Sabrina observed. "She makes me look pathetic."

"Hogwash!" Vidalia blustered. "There's not another seventeen year old in this town that can handle an order for nine hundred chocolate dipped strawberries. You are doing just fine. I would dare match your skills against anybody's."

Sabrina smiled. Vidalia's praise wasn't easily earned but it was sincere when given. "It's because I was apprenticed out at an early age," Sabrina said, flashing a playful smile at her mother.

"What I wonder is what we'll do without you here next fall?" Vidalia's brows furrowed. She turned her head in Amanda's direction and said, "I guess I'll just pack my bag and go off to college with Sabrina."

"Don't you *dare*," Amanda said shaking a wooden spoon in Vidalia's direction.

"I'm not planning on going anywhere. I'll pick up some botany and business classes at Weber State, but I don't need to move thirty minutes away to do that."

"Heaven forbid we pry you away from the plants!" Vidalia snorted.

The oven buzzer sounded again. "There, that's the last of the tea cakes," Amanda chirped pleasantly. "I think this is the prettiest batch I've done yet."

"Practice makes perfect," Sabrina and Vidalia said again, simultaneously.

Vidalia looked wide eyed at the girl and shook her head.

"Jinx!"

"I'll *jinx* you! We've been around each other too much. We're starting to think alike and talk alike."

"We don't talk *exactly* alike.

"And it's a damn good thing! Or else Vidalia would have to wash your mouth out with a bar of soap."

"I need to hire some more help." Amanda interrupted their banter. "The problem is I'm picky. I need to clone the two of you. I just don't know if I have time to train a new person. If training is more work than we're doing now then it's not worth it. Can you think of anybody who could help us out, Vidalia?"

"My sister Vandaline just moved here from Boise. Her damn, dumb, alcoholic husband died last year and she's moved in with Mother."

"Would she be interested? Could she do the job?"

"Vandaline's worked for the Owyhee Hotel for the last twenty-six years. She was supervisor in charge of special events. That means she was in charge of catering all banquets, conventions, receptions, and stuff like that. She can fold a mean napkin, if that means anything to you. She can fold those things into lilies, roses, ladybugs and only Heaven knows what else."

Amanda blinked her eyes, processing the information. Sabrina's mind was still playing on Vidalia's stinging words regarding her dearly departed brother-in-law. Vidalia was brutally honest! "Is Vandaline anything like you?"

"She's a mouse," Vidalia answered with a disgusted tone to her voice, "but she's a quiet mouse and shouldn't cause too much trouble."

"So she's nothing like you then?" Sabrina prodded.

Vidalia ignored the comment. "She could use the job and I think she's very well qualified."

"Okay, well...I'll consider this. I need to think about it for a couple of days." Amanda sprayed off the baking sheets and stuck them in the dish rack then turned and quickly helped Vidalia roll the last batch of cookies. "I've got some deliveries to make in Mountain Green today, and then I think I'd like to slip on down to Ogden and do some shopping. Is that okay with you?"

"Sure," Sabrina said.

"Vidalia, would you mind making the other deliveries? There's a planter to go to North Morgan, one to Echo, and two bouquets ready for Henefer. Then you can call it a day."

"Sounds good, I'll stop and see Mother while I'm there."

"Thought you'd like that." Amanda smiled before hurrying to her room to change.

"Guess I'll stay here and dip seven hundred more strawberries," Sabrina said out loud to the empty chairs in the kitchen. Her phone buzzed. She wiped her hands and fished it out of her pocket. There was a text from Brad.

"Wanna do something?"

Sabrina's thumbs flew over the miniature key pad. *"Come help me dip strawberries. I will be alone in ten minutes."*

"I love strawberries. See you in ten."

Sabrina heard Brad's tires crunch against the gravel in the driveway. She hurried to the porch and flung the screen door open. "Hey you," Sabrina greeted cheerfully. "I'm excited to show you the place! Welcome to the back porch."

"Hi," he smiled pulling her to him in an embrace. "The last three weeks have been the best ones in my whole life. I can't believe I gave my old man static about moving to Utah."

"I'm glad you're here."Sabrina grabbed Brad's hand and led him into the house. She showed him around the kitchen first. Brad's jaw dropped when he spied stacked trays of cookies and strawberries.

"You weren't lying about the strawberries, were you?"

"I'm afraid not." She guided him through a doorway. "This is my mother's room."

"It looks like a shrine for aging roses," Brad mumbled, noticing several wilting vases full.

Sabrina opened a door into the bathroom. "This is where you go if you need to."

Brad laughed. "Well, thanks for the information. It could be vital. You are just the most proficient tour guide I've ever known." Another door led from the bathroom into Sabrina's adjoining room. Brad looked around curiously. A cat was curled up on Sabrina's bed. "I thought you said we'd be alone."

"This is my Mia." Sabrina stroked her hand down the back of the sleeping feline. Mia yawned and stretched and lazily began purring. "She's my baby."

Brad noticed several books about herbs and plants leaning against her night stand. Jewelry was scattered across the top of her dresser along with sunglasses and nail polish. A rumpled hoodie was tossed carelessly across a chair in the corner. Several belts and a bag were draped over the closet door handle. "I like this room. It smells like you in here."

"It just smells good because we live in a flower shop," Sabrina said, pulling him from her room into a small hallway. She motioned at the stairs with her left hand. "Our work room is up there." A floor to ceiling bookcase stood across from the stairway. Brad studied the items on the shelf.

"Is this a picture of your dad?"

"Yes."

"You look like him."

"I know." Sabrina pointed at another photograph. "This is my mom." A beautiful blonde face smiled pleasantly from the frame.

"She's pretty! She's very young in this picture?"

"That was only taken two years ago. She just looks like a kid. Really, she is only five foot two. I'm five inches taller than she is. Everybody always thinks we're sisters."

"Wow! She's really *hot.*"

"Shut up," Sabrina muttered taking the picture frame from his hands and placing it back on the shelf. She tugged his hand, leading him away from the bookcase and into the floral shop.

"Well, this is it!" she announced proudly. "Ashley Floral!"

Brad walked around the shop looking closely at everything. He appreciated the fact that Sabrina took so much responsibility in her mother's business. Sabrina happily pointed out various projects that she had done. She led him to a card rack. "Do you like these cards?"

Brad studied the assortment. There were different pictures of blooms and bouquets; some had pictures of old barns and buildings. One of the cards featured a lazy cat curled up in a rocking chair. "That cat looks like Mia."

"It *is* Mia."

"What?" Brad picked up the card and studied the picture. *Sabrina Ashley* was scrawled on the bottom corner of the card's image. "You did this? This is your artwork?"

"Yes."

Brad grabbed several cards examining them closely. "*Sabrina!* You are incredible."

Sabrina pointed out a card with a cowboy. "Recognize this person?"

"It's your dad. These cards are unbelievable."

"I'm glad you like them."

Brad stared at the girl intently, emotion building in his expression. "Sabrina, I wonder if you know how special you are. Can you possibly know how important you are to me?" Brad reached out and smoothed a wayward strand of Sabrina's hair. She returned Brad's gaze, startled by the intensity playing in his features. She was becoming accustomed to the electrical current which pulsed between the two of them but was now caught off guard by his reaction to her artwork. It seemed to be causing an extra zing.

"You are important to me too."

"I love you, Sabrina." Brad's voice sounded raspy.

He said it! Sabrina couldn't breathe again. Emotion pressed against her body's ability to function properly. She finally drew in a ragged breath. "I love you too. Please don't break my heart."

His mouth sought hers to silence any insecurity. A few teddy bears from a nearby shelf stared unblinking at their affection while tiny buds in vases nodded approval. Sabrina finally drew back. "I can't breathe right." Her heart was pounding audibly.

"Need mouth to mouth?"

"That's what caused my condition in the first place, you idiot!" Sabrina smiled at the good looking face. "So you really love me?"

"Yes."

"Then I want to show you something." Brad looked astonished, as if Sabrina just leveled a very juicy proposition. "You're so *dumb*," Sabrina laughed, tugging him toward her bedroom.

"Well, I don't know—look where you're leading me!" Brad feigned a frightened yet delighted expression.

Sabrina knelt down and slid a box out from under her bed. It was plainly labeled in child's handwriting, *"You spy you die! Keep Out. Personal Property of Sabrina Lyn Ashley"*

"What's this?"

"My special treasures." Sabrina rummaged a hand down through the box.

Brad grabbed an empty root beer can. "This is a treasure?"

"My dad drank that root beer right before he was killed. I found it in the barn a few days later and put it in with my keepsakes."

"Oh," Brad said, laying the can tenderly back into the box. He didn't want to trespass any further into this complex girl's cherished items.

Sabrina pulled out a sketch pad and flipped it open. "Look at this."

An image smiled from the page. "What? Oh my gosh Sabrina!" Brad stared at a portrait of himself. He was sprawled on the rock near the Porterville Cemetery. "You haven't sketched this from memory have you?"

"No, I snapped a picture of you with my phone when you weren't looking."

"I thought I was always looking."

"My hand is faster than your eye."

"Can I have it?"

"No. Always and forever I want to remember you just the way you were that day. It was the beginning of the best summer of my life--besides, I'll use this one to help me sketch other pictures of you."

"Thank you for showing me." Brad handed the sketch book back to the artist.

Sabrina rearranged it in the box and shoved it under her bed. "Well let's go dip some strawberries, shall we?"

An hour later Brad complained, "I hate strawberries."

"You said you loved strawberries and just think; there are only another hundred to go. Luckily the shop has been slow today."

Brad crinkled his forehead at the girl in a pained expression. "When do you have to have these done?"

"The reception is tomorrow evening but we have to have the food done because tomorrow we'll be working on the bridal bouquet and corsages. We want everything to be as fresh as possible."

"I couldn't work with such deadlines. It would drive me crazy worrying."

"We employ Vidalia for that. She worries enough for all of us."

"She sounds like a real character."

The shop door chimed. Sabrina left Brad in the kitchen with the strawberries and went to greet the customer. "Hi," Sabrina called out cheerfully before she noticed who was there. Halsey Redding and her friend Tiki Gordon were hovering near the jewelry. Halsey cast a long look down her nose in Sabrina's direction while Tiki gave the Sabrina an impatient eye roll, swinging her head back to the case. "Let me know if I can help you."

"I seriously doubt it," Tiki whispered harshly to her friend. Both girls giggled cattily.

"I was hoping to buy some *cute* jewelry," Halsey complained, "but you just don't have anything that shouts *me* to me."

"I'm sorry. Perhaps you could try a second-hand store. They may have what you're looking for. They have a lot of cheap and worn out things just lying around."

Tiki began profaning. "I'm going to slap you down!"

Halsey's eyes narrowed and she stomped toward Sabrina with a haughty strut. No doubt she learned the moves from watching *America's Next Top Model*. "Listen Peach," Halsey said shrilly, "I heard you are chasing after Brad Manning. I just came in to tell you to forget it since I've practically been out with him every night."

Sabrina listened to the lies, feeling amused. "Then you have nothing to worry about. I wouldn't *dare* run competition with you, Halsey." Sabrina hoped the strawberry dipper in the next room was listening. Apparently he was, for Brad donned a grand entrance from the kitchen.

"Hey, where did you go?" he asked Sabrina, wrapping his arms around her waist and nuzzling her hair for good measure. He feigned shock at seeing customers in the shop. "Oh hi, Halsey," he stammered, kissing Sabrina's neck. "Have you met my girlfriend? This is Sabrina Ashley. She's keeping me away from home quite a bit lately."

Sabrina smiled at the girls' reactions--jaws gaped, eyes bugged, and cheeks flushed. The two turned and stomped from the shop. Sabrina followed them to the door then turned the lock and flipped the *closed* sign in the window.

"The nerve of that little vamp," Brad exclaimed. "She totally lies!"

"See why I hate her? Oh, Brad...the look on her face when you came in the room! It was priceless." Sabrina laughed until tears streamed down her cheeks. Brad was too unnerved by the nasty girl's untruthful tales to fully appreciate the humor in the situation.

"They treated you *awful*. I was getting so ticked off out here I accidentally strangled a strawberry. I made jam out of it. Do you think anybody will notice if there's only eight hundred and ninety-nine?"

"Correction: only eight hundred and ninety-six. I ate three of them while I was waiting for you to get here," Sabrina confessed. "I was so excited I just started mindlessly popping them in my mouth."

"Good, that means we'll get done faster," he murmured, reaching for another berry. The two worked steadily and without talking for a few minutes until Brad swirled the last one in chocolate and raised it high in the air with a triumphal flourish. "Hooray! We're done. Well let me help you do the dishes. I'll wash and you can dry."

"You don't have to help me wash."

"I didn't see a dishwasher."

"No, you're looking at the dishwasher. It's me but I don't expect you to do them."

"I can't believe you guys don't have a dishwasher with as much catering and cooking as you're doing." Brad said, ignoring Sabrina's request not to wash dishes. He started hot water in the sink and squirted detergent under the stream. "I like lots of suds."

"A dishwasher's next on our wish list."

Brad clanked dishes around noisily albeit cheerfully. "I'm good at dishes. We didn't always have a dishwasher either. It was always my job to clean up if Dad cooked."

"How long has it just been the two of you?"

"Ever since I can remember, my mom ran off when I was a year old."

"I'm sorry--I can't imagine *any* mother doing that."

Brad shrugged his shoulders. "Oh well, I guess you don't miss what you never had."

"Your mother missed out on one great kid! She'll suffer the consequences of her rotten choices someday." Sabrina scowled and bit her lip. *Who could be so uncaring?*

"Maybe...It's kind of weird. She walked out and never looked back, I mean *never*. Dad got served with divorce papers about a week after she packed up, but that's it--never a birthday card, phone call, or anything."

"Does your dad know why she left?"

"No. He came home from work one night and there I was, sobbing my eyes out from my crib. I guess I was starving and my diaper hadn't been changed for a long while. He assumed she left early that morning and I was alone all day long."

Sabrina winced at the mental picture. A shiver of melancholy ran down her spine. "Brad, that's so sad. I'm sorry that you ever went through any of that." A disturbed knot tied itself in her stomach.

"Doesn't matter now. Dad struggled for awhile though. He was trying to get through school, work, and take care of a kid. I'm telling you, he had it rough."

"Well he did a great job in raising you. I know that because I'm looking at the proof."

"Well thanks."

"I'll share my mom with you, okay?"

"That's a hoot--you wouldn't even let me hold her picture for more than ten seconds. You won't even let me meet her!" Brad playfully flipped suds in Sabrina's direction.

"Thanks for your help. Come on now, rinse out that wash rag. I want to show you my Thinking Place.

"Your what?" Brad asked, wiping the last suds from the sink.

"My Thinking Place. You know—where I go to think."

"You mean when you're not at the cemetery?"

Sabrina laughed. "Maybe I think too much, huh? This is my regular spot for thinking." The porch door slammed shut as Sabrina led Brad from the house and across the yard toward the river.

The Weber flowed languidly that evening. Crickets and frogs generated a summer night's symphony from unseen places. Water bugs skated recklessly on the lazy reflective surface. "The river's always changing. Only a month ago it roiled and boiled violently with muddy spring runoff. The water is so brown and frothy then and it rages down the banks looking like a flood of chocolate milk."

"Tonight it's calm," Brad observed. "The sound of it is powerful, though. Listen to the rushing depths. Maybe there's a stronger under-current than meets the eye."

Sabrina yawned and lay back in the grass. "This time of year the sound of the river is like a lullaby—very soothing." She propped herself up on one elbow and peered at Brad. "It's wicked in a storm, I tell you. I was here doing some thinking the night before I met you. Suddenly this awful thunder bumper hit like Mother Nature was throwing a temper tantrum. The river seemed anything but soothing to me that night." An involuntary shiver shuddered down Sabrina's arms.

"I remember that storm! We'd just finished hauling stuff into the garage and *crack!* Lightning struck a big pine tree just down the road from where we were standing. A jagged streak of blue lightning singed down the tree, buzzing and popping. We could see balls of electricity dancing out of the pine boughs. It was eerie as heck!

Suddenly there was this loud bang and the whole top of the tree flew off and landed in flaming toothpicks about twenty yards closer to us."

A fish jumped sending ripples cascading outward. "One less water bug to worry about--I should run grab my pole."

"Let's fish tomorrow night; I have something else on my mind right now." Brad smiled and reached for Sabrina. "Come over here," he said, wrapping his arms around her tightly. "See what I caught?"

A night breeze rattled through the canopy of leaves above them. Starlight streaked through a network of branches, illuminating rippling patterns on the river. "I'll never be able to sit and think here normally again—not without thinking of you."

"Good," Brad muttered against her hair.

"I feel a little bit drunk again. Do you think it's the starlight, the moonlight, the sound of water, or just *you*? My heart hammers every time you kiss me."

"Mine does too."

"It does?"

"Here," Brad said, placing Sabrina's hand against his chest. "See?" She smiled at the racing rhythm beating against her palm. "I guess I'm not so different from your river," Brad whispered softly.

"What do you mean?"

"Listen to the rushing depths," he repeated, but this time his words fell like poetry. *"Maybe there's a stronger under-current than meets the eye."*

The words seeped into Sabrina's consciousness, entering her blood flow like intoxicating wine. She reached out, curling her fingers in his hair. She pulled his head down to meet hers anxiously. He kissed her again and again, each time reinforcing his earlier declaration, "I love you, Sabrina...I love you...I love you..." It was a beautiful echo which danced like magic on the breeze.

CHAPTER TEN

"Happy Independence Day!" Vidalia hollered as she unlocked the front door and stepped into the shop. "I've brought Vandaline to show her around while we're closed for the holiday."

"Welcome," Amanda greeted warmly, "I'm happy to meet you."

"This is Amanda, the sweetest and kindest gal in the world," Vidalia's introduction was gracious. "Here is the real ramrod of this outfit!" Vidalia waved a finger at Sabrina. "She runs a tight ship around here. Keep in mind that she's a fiery little hot head and be sure to toe the line or you'll walk the plank."

Sabrina reached out and shook the bony hand. Vandaline bobbed her head nervously toward Amanda and Sabrina but didn't say a word. Her hands twittered nervously at her throat and then fussed incessantly against the rings on her fingers, running them around and around as if fastening nuts on bolts. The sisters didn't look a thing alike. Vidalia was hearty and plump with gentle character lines etching her round face. She always complained about packing fifty extra pounds but her cheeks were pink and she looked robust and healthy. Her eyes were brown and shiny. She wore her hair in a tidy bob, keeping stubborn streaks of grey neatly concealed under frequent trips to the salon.

Sabrina studied Vandaline. "Vidalia was right, she is a mouse," Sabrina thought. She was well coifed, with her hair cropped into an uncommonly short pixie cut. *Too short.* The poky spikes of hair reminded Sabrina somewhat of a hedgehog. Her face was thin and long. Deep lines carved furrows between her eyebrows, giving her an unnecessary worried expression. Vandaline's black eyes were small and deeply set in their sockets. She blinked often and seemed to stare down her sharp, shrew-like nose. Her lips were thin and pinched. Hard lines tugged around her mouth, making the corners droop downward. She was however, impeccably dressed.

Long spangly earrings dangled from her ears. Her hands often fidgeted from her throat to her earrings as if constantly checking to make sure they were still there. Vandaline wore a black elbow-length blazer over a caramel camisole. A silk scarf of deep indigo and purple paisley was tied smartly around her neck, making it look less thin and bony. Her wrists were layered with multiple bangles but she pulled the look together neatly without looking gaudy. She definitely had a flair for fashion. Sabrina felt confident that she would also have a special touch with the needs of Ashley Floral.

"There you go," Vidalia said, producing a set of linen napkins and thumping them down on the table. "Show us some of your napkin tricks. I was bragging about them the other day."

Vandaline looked embarrassed and shook her head rapidly. "No, no," she twittered. "I mustn't bore them." She fussed with the table-cloth as her eyes darted wildly around the room.

Vidalia pounded the stack of napkins. "Do it!"

Vandaline's small eyes screwed shut. "I'd certainly like to see your talents," Amanda encouraged soothingly. Vandaline exhaled slowly, charging the room with released ripples of tension and then quickly folded the napkin like an origami specialist.

"A sailboat!" Vidalia triumphed. "Do another one." Amanda and Sabrina exchanged impressed glances. Vandaline grabbed another napkin. Her nose twitched while her nervous fingers fussed at the fabric. Suddenly the linen transformed into an oyster holding a pearl. "Well I'll be damned." Vidalia muttered. Again the fidgety fingers flew, folding and pleating until a dove was born. "Look at that!" Vidalia crowed proudly. Vandaline sculpted a linen rose; it budded and blossomed in less than a minute.

"Why Vandaline, that's marvelous!" Amanda announced. "I'd love to have you join our team if you're willing."

The thin lips twitched a quick smile. "She'd be happy to," Vidalia volunteered, apparently assuming the role of body language interpreter on behalf of her high-strung, mystic sister.

Sabrina reached for a folded napkin. She wanted to try her hand at this strange new art form. The others watched. Sabrina made a couple of folds and pleats, trying to replicate the sailboat. The fabric didn't respond as magically to her touch as it had Vandaline's. With a roar of sheer frustration Sabrina pounded the napkin flat then grabbed it and wadded it into a crumpled ball.

"What the *H-E-double toothpicks* is that supposed to be?" Vidalia asked.

"A shipwreck," Sabrina said, shaking her head.

A shivery laugh trilled from Vandaline. It poured from her mouth like liquid crystal, shattering somewhere overhead with each trill. Sabrina and Amanda looked startled at the tinkling sound so merrily ringing from the fidgety little woman. "You have a cool laugh," Sabrina commented.

"You should hear her sing," Vidalia said. "Like a bell peeling from a church tower...well, come on Sis, I'll show you around." Vidalia led the way upstairs. Her familiar pounding steps sounded in the kitchen. A nervous echo of scurried footsteps scrambled after.

Amanda listened, shaking her head slightly. "What do you think?"

"Vandaline's the jitteriest person I've ever met, that's for sure. I think she'll do a good job though."

"I hope so. I really need her right now. So how have you been lately?"

"Fine."

"I'm sorry I've been gone so much. I feel quite guilty about it."

"That's okay." *I haven't been here much myself.*

"You're alright then...and happy?"

83

What's she heard? Sabrina knew her mother was going to learn about Brad sometime. They'd been all over town together. "Sure, I'm great."

"Want some breakfast?"

"I'd love some!" Sabrina smiled, thinking that cooking should take her mother's mind off the inquisition. "I'll help."

"Oh, let me." Amanda pulled an apron from a drawer.

Strange. Sabrina's eyes swept her mother. She'd been too occupied with Vidalia's sister to take notice of her mother earlier. Sabrina scowled. "Is that a new outfit?"

"Oh, do you like it?" Amanda brightened. "It's not too *blue* is it?"

Sabrina gazed thoughtfully. "What do you mean by too blue? I mean—it *is* blue."

"I know, but the shade—is it alright? I just wondered if it was too much." Amanda whisked eggs in a dish.

"It looks fine." Sabrina's voice was sharp. The suit was a striking robin-egg blue and was smartly tailored, fitting Amanda's petite build perfectly. Dainty pearl buttons trailed down the front of the short sleeved jacket. The v-shaped collar revealed a sparkling necklace. A delicate silver chain wove intricately through a myriad of shimmering diamonds and glossy pearls. *Of course they couldn't be genuine.* "New necklace too?"

"You like it?" Amanda's hand instinctively flew to her throat, caressing the soft jangles which danced beneath her touch. "I have earrings, too." She pulled back her hair so Sabrina could see.

"Nice." Sabrina knew she should have made a bigger fuss. Amanda seldom indulged herself with anything. She was self-sacrificing to a fault. Sabrina forced herself to elaborate, "That color is flattering on you, Mom. It really brings out your eyes and makes your cheeks look pretty and pink."

"Thank you, Bree!" She slid a light fluffy omelet from the pan and onto a plate. The toaster popped and Amanda spread creamy butter over warm golden toast. She sliced it diagonally, just the way Sabrina liked it.

"Thanks Mom. Aren't you eating anything?"

"Not this morning."

Sabrina gave her mother a scrutinizing look. "Breakfast is the most important meal of the day! Somebody I know often tells me that." Sabrina grabbed a fork and dug into the omelet. A string of melted cheese clung to her fork, stretching toward Sabrina's mouth. "This is really good."

Amanda didn't answer. Sabrina looked up. Her mother was staring at nothing in particular. Sabrina sat her fork down and studied her mother. What else was different? *Her hair!* Amanda usually pulled her honey blond wisps into a neat French braid. This morning her hair was loose with gentle curls cascading around her neck and shoulders. *She looks like Carrie Underwood in a recent music video.* "What's up with your hair?" Sabrina demanded impatiently, jarring Amanda from her thoughts.

"I just needed a change...Sabrina, have you made plans today?"

"I thought I'd wear a Revolutionary War costume and sell tea in the town square...why? Do *you* have plans?" Sabrina didn't want to offer any more information than necessary.

"I just wondered." Amanda bit her lip. "I needed to meet someone this morning, would you like to come?"

"Clients on the Fourth of July? Ugh. No thanks."

"Not a client, *exactly*..."

"I'm busy," Sabrina pronounced defiantly.

"Sabrina—I've been seeing someone."

Ding, Ding, Ding, Ding, Ding! An alarm sounded in Sabrina's mind. *The roses! Vidalia was right.* "What? The roses? Were they from this anonymous person?"

"Yes."

"And that outfit and jewelry you are modeling—did *he* give them to you?"

"Yes."

"Why didn't you say something sooner?"

"Because I was afraid you'd scream at me like you are doing right now."

Sabrina pursed her lips together tightly and closed her eyes for a few seconds to collect herself. "Mom, you can't be serious about this guy--I don't even know who he is!"

"Sabrina," Amanda said intently, "he is wonderful."

Wonderful? "What about my *Dad?*" Sabrina drew his name like a knife and hurled it at her mother.

"Your Dad was the best. I'll always love him. Sabrina, you know that! The feelings that I have now don't detract from the love I feel for your father but I don't want to face the next fifty years alone."

"You have me," Sabrina pointed out stubbornly.

"For how much longer? Sabrina, you're seventeen! You're graduating next spring, and your life is just beginning. Are you going to pack me up and tote me along with you wherever you journey in life? No! You're not and I wouldn't want you to. You'll go off to school, become a world-class botanist, or perhaps host your own show on the history channel. You could get married or start a revolution somewhere. Who knows what you'll do? What about me then?"

"How long have you known this–this–this *guy?* I don't even know his name."

"His name is Dorian. I've known him since March."

"March? Are you serious? You've known this guy for months and you're just telling me now?"

"Four months ago I didn't know it would grow into something so special. You and Vidalia would have ganged up on me, making me the target of every joke, now admit it! I didn't know quite what to expect so I thought it would be best to just keep it to myself for a while. This secret has been deliriously wonderful, though."

I'll bet! Well, I've got a few secrets of my own and maybe I'll never share them with you! I'm in love my own self, now how about that! I've met someone wonderful, too. Sabrina's thoughts fired like arrows from a well-stocked quiver. *How dare you, my mother, become all breathless and worked up over some guy? I know what that's like now and it irritates me that it's happening to you! So there!* "Does he take your breath away in the moonlight?"

The question startled Amanda. "Yes. As a matter of fact he takes my breath away everywhere."

Sabrina rolled her eyes. *Disgusting!* "Do you like the way he smells?"

"Yes."

Sick! He's an old man, how good could he smell! "Do you kiss him very often?"

Amanda's eyebrows arched. "Yes."

Scandalous! "Does it make your heart beat faster than a race horse with his tail on fire?" Amanda choked and blinked her eyes but didn't say anything. *Aha! You should be ashamed of yourself, Mother!* "You didn't answer my question."

"Yes."

Unbelievable! The nerve of these people—carrying on like a couple of seventeen year olds! "Do you feel this is a healthy choice?" Sabrina grilled. "You could be taxing your cardio-pulmonary system, you know!"

"Oh for Heaven's sakes, Sabrina! My cardio-pulmonary system is fine."

Ha! "You could make that old guy have a stroke."

Amanda rolled her eyes toward the unreasonable girl. "Sabrina, he's not old. He's only forty-one. I'm sure his heart and circulatory system can handle whatever I throw at him. He's very physically fit."

"You're both old enough to know better." Amanda's hands clenched together tightly. Blue vessels bulged in her wrists. Sabrina had pushed her arguments and sauciness just about as far as she dared. *Careful.* "It's just that I don't want things to change. We're a team, right Mom?" Sabrina's chin trembled.

"We're still a team, Honey. Nothing needs to change between you and me unless you let it."

Don't use the sound of reason on me! "So how serious are you about this guy?"

"This serious," Amanda said laying her left hand on the table. A large diamond ring glinted from her finger.

Holy crap! "That looks pretty serious," Sabrina gulped. Her hands were sweating and her lungs began to burn.

"Do you like it?"

"No." Sabrina's heart was pounding in her ears. Her body was ambushed by a full-blown anxiety attack. Her lungs were yearning for air. She needed oxygen but her chest felt too heavy to suck it in correctly. *Whoosh, whoosh, whoosh,* sounded in her ears now with every beat of her heart. Sabrina's face felt prickly and her tongue was thick. Tears stung her eyes like hot darts.

Amanda grabbed a wet cloth and quickly held it against Sabrina's forehead. "Breathe. Slower...deeper. It's okay, it's alright," she soothed.

"I can't breathe!"

Sabrina's first anxiety attack took place after Grandpa Ashley announced that he'd bought the property in Morgan. It had frightened Amanda to death at the time, not knowing what was wrong with the child. A doctor suggested counseling but the counselor assured Amanda that anxiety was normal after experiencing trauma. "I've tried to unlock her pain center," the counselor said, "but her emotions are buried too deeply. It's like she's carrying a heavy burden inside of her; a desperate secret of sorts. She won't let me in. She's locked it up and thrown away the key. Someday she'll have to face it. The anxiety will dissipate when she finally does." Sabrina had struggled with bouts of anxiety intermittently ever since.

"What can I get you?" Amanda asked, as Sabrina's breathing became less labored.

"Valerian. It's in the cupboard above the fridge. I need some minerals and B vitamins."

Amanda quickly grabbed the remedies and handed them to her daughter with a cold drink. She often wondered if Sabrina was interested in natural healing just to help herself find relief.

Several minutes ticked by. Sabrina wiped beads of sweat from her upper lip. She was breathing easier but now felt a pounding headache stretch over the back of her neck. "The valerian will help in a little while," she told herself, feeling that her nerves would relax if they understood relief was on the way. "Mom, will you grab me a couple of Tylenol too? Thanks."

Amanda stared at her daughter, resolved not to let Sabrina's anxiety deter her plans. "I'm sorry that you're upset. I didn't want to invite an attack. Perhaps that's why I've kept this all under wraps."

"How long have you been engaged?"

"Dorian proposed to me last night and *yes*, there was moonlight involved."

The fire had all burned out of Sabrina. The sass and arguments were exhausted. "Oh."

"Sabrina, do you know how many times I've been to the temple praying about this lately?"

"I just thought you were religiously doing your duty."

"And I've been fasting."

"That's why you didn't have breakfast this morning?"

"Yes. I needed strength to survive telling you."

"Why did you bother telling me at all? Since your big secret romance was so much fun, I'm surprised you didn't just elope and save yourself all this misery." A fiery ember was rekindling.

"Because I want you there--I want you to be my maid of honor. Sabrina, I really feel that I'm doing the right thing. I'm meeting Dorian for lunch and I'd like you to come."

"I feel like crap."

"I know. I'm sorry."

"I look worse than I feel."

"This isn't about you. Now go get in the shower and get cleaned up."

Sabrina scowled. "Who are you and what have you done with that nice lady who used to be my mother?" Sabrina grumbled to herself as she walked into her bedroom and slammed the door.

Amanda heard the second door slam so she knew Sabrina was really going to shower. She felt a little bit victorious since battling wills with Sabrina was like trying to stop Teddy Roosevelt from charging up San Juan Hill. A little thrill of exhilaration shivered down her arms. "Congratulations self and happy Independence Day."

CHAPTER ELEVEN

Sabrina followed her mother into the restaurant with as much enthusiasm as Joan of Arc displayed on her way to the fire. She was determined to be miserable. Sheer disgust washed over her like a tidal wave when she once again locked eyes with the infamous rose buyer. She looked away when her mother greeted him with a kiss. She noticed several local residents' eyes bulge at the scene as well. A newspaper write-up highlighting the upcoming nuptials would certainly be unnecessary, as word would spread like wild fire all over town.

"Dorian, this is Sabrina," Amanda said, praying the girl would mind her manners.

"Hi Sabrina." Dorian extended a hand to the girl.

Sabrina didn't want to shake it but years of good upbringing took effect and she found herself behaving congenially. "Bought any roses lately?"

Amanda twittered nervously, reminding Sabrina somewhat of Vandaline. Dorian just smiled.

He keeps his emotions very tucked in–Mr. Calm, Cool and Collected. My Dad was open and didn't hide anything. Brad is like my Dad. I prefer warm to cool. Sabrina's thoughts tumbled haphazardly.

A sweaty waitress galloped up. "Hi folks!" she called. "Happy Fourth of July! It's a beautiful day aint it? My name's Connie. What can I get you all to drink?" Sabrina glared at the woman. She was too down-home and perky for Sabrina's mood. "I'll take a whiskey," Sabrina said sarcastically. She felt he mother's foot jam her shin bone from under the table. "I mean a root beer," she amended. She didn't notice what the others ordered. She focused all of her attention on the menu.

"Dad?"

Sabrina's head jerked up. Brad was standing by the table looking confused. His eyes flew to Sabrina momentarily and then swept back to Dorian. "Dad?"

Dad? Panic welled inside Sabrina as realization swept through her consciousness. A flood of emotion rippled through her body like molten lava. Her heart was racing again but she steeled herself against a full-fledged attack in the public setting. *Whoosh, whoosh, whoosh!*

"Have a seat Son," Dorian motioned. Brad pulled out a chair next to Sabrina. He shot her a deer-caught-in-the-headlights expression.

"What's up?"

"Son," Dorian began, "I'd like you to meet Amanda. This is the amazing woman I've been telling you about."

Amanda leaned across the table and hugged the shocked young man. "I'm so happy to meet you! Your dad has told me so much about you." Amanda beamed sincerely at the boy.

"We're getting married, Son."

Sabrina felt Brad's body stiffen into granite. He wasn't breathing. Under the privacy of the table she reached one hand out and patted his leg soothingly. She felt him unfreeze as one hand squeezed hers firmly for a moment. She could feel his mind laboring to process the meaning of his father's words. Brad swallowed. His Adam's apple bobbed uncomfortably as if his throat was very dry. Amanda quickly poured a glass of water from the slushy pitcher in the center of the table and handed it to him. He accepted the water gratefully. He took a sip. "Congratulations," he muttered softly. "When is this all taking place?" Sabrina listened for the answer with a keen interest. The table was silent. In fact, many nearby tables also seemed hushed.

Sabrina imagined curious locals were straining to catch each juicy scrap of information.

"I rode shank's ponies at top speed getting these drinks back to you all," the obnoxious waitress interrupted. "Here you go," she said to Sabrina, "one double whisky root beer on the rocks."

Sabrina closed her eyes. This day was a nightmare. "Howdy young feller! I didn't see you here before," Connie drawled at Brad. "Did you just ride into town?"

Dorian looked annoyed at the waitress. "He just got here."

"Well in that case, what can I fetch ya from the old watering hole?"

"Do you have Mountain Dew?" Brad asked. Sabrina noticed his voice was uncommonly quiet.

"*Dew* we ever!" she snorted. "Get it? *Dew* we ever!" she disappeared laughing raucously at her pun.

Brad cast a sideways glance at Sabrina. Her head was down not daring to meet his gaze. "Oh for Heaven's sake!" Amanda said. "I'm sorry--Brad, this is my daughter Sabrina. She'll be in your class at school this year. She just turned seventeen a few weeks ago."

This is so awkward! Lame! Stupid! Unbelievable! Almost hilarious! Totally tragic! Sabrina's thoughts screamed inside of her. Brad's head turned. "Hi, Sabrina. It's nice to meet you."

I want to laugh! I want to cry! "Hi Brad, where are you from?"

"California," he said, a smile twitching slightly at his mouth.

"I've never been there."

"Never? No Redwood Forrest? No Golden Gate Bridge? Not even Disneyland?" He sounded incredulous.

"No." Sabrina felt Brad's hand reach for hers under the table. His finger traced letters on her palm. *I l-o-v-e-y-o-u,* he spelled. She squeezed his hand tightly in return.

"When is that idiot waitress going to come take our order?" Dorian grumbled.

Sabrina cast her eyes toward the counter. Connie was stuffing French fries into her mouth at a rapid pace. "Looks like she had to stop and feed shank's ponies."

Dorian smiled at his future step-daughter. "The service here isn't nearly as prompt as it is at Ashley Floral, nor as charming."

Perhaps he's warming up. "Thanks." She then turned her attention toward Brad. "So how do you like Utah?"

"The scenery is great but the surfing sucks," he recited.

"I'll bet." Dorian and Amanda looked slightly puzzled by the teenagers' reaction to each other. Amanda was especially surprised by the improvement in Sabrina's mood.

"Here's your Dew," Connie bellowed, setting the long-anticipated soda in front of Brad. "I'll be back in one switch of the cow's tail to take your orders."

"No," Dorian interjected before she could saddle up and ride away. "We're ready to order *now*." Connie's eyes bulged and blinked but she complied, grabbing her tablet from her pocket and producing a pen from behind her ear.

After the dining quartet finally ordered, Dorian cleared his throat. "In answer to your earlier question Son, we are planning on getting married on the tenth."

"Of this month?" Sabrina asked.

"Yes. I'm not waiting another day," Dorian said, rubbing an affectionate hand down Amanda's back.

Idiot. "That's kind of sudden."

"It's none too soon for me."

"Me neither," Amanda agreed gazing at him adoringly.

Give me a break! "The *tenth*...it's still kind of sudden," Sabrina repeated.

Brad leaned forward and dryly quipped, "Especially when you realize Connie won't be back with our lunch until the *ninth*." Everyone laughed heartily, even Dorian. Brad sneakily laced his fingers through Sabrina's under the table. "So Sabrina, are you going to share your mother with me?"

Amanda's face brightened at the boy's question. "Of course she will! I can't wait to have a son."

"Sure, I'll share. Hey, guess what? The Weber River runs right in my back yard. Want me to show it to you later?"

"Absolutely! Do you ever catch any fish?"

"Sometimes."

"Great, I'll grab my pole."

Dorian smiled at Amanda. "See Amanda? I told you they would get along."

Brad offered to drive Sabrina home after lunch. Dorian and Amanda thought it would be a good idea so the two kids could become better acquainted. The day's events had left Sabrina feeling hung-over. Brad's mood was also subdued but he tried to brighten Sabrina's spirits. "I'll be the luckiest kid at Morgan High School. My old man just told me that he's letting my girlfriend move in. It's right nice of our parents to let us live together."

"Brad, this is a disaster! You know what this means? If our parents really go through with this then it's the end of *us*."

"It doesn't have to be," he said, turning into the Ashley's driveway. "Come on, let's walk. We need to talk." He took her hand and led her to the river. He sat on the grass and pulled her down to sit next to him. "Oh man, I nearly flipped when I saw you and your mother sitting at the table today--*surreal*!"

"I was just as stunned to see you! In fact I felt sick to my stomach."

"That's complimentary."

"Just because I didn't want *this* to end!" Sabrina mourned.

"Lunch was horrifying and hilarious at the same time. When you asked me where I was from and that whole conversation played out, I just wanted to grab you and kiss you."

"Ha! Actually that would have served our dumb parents right."

"I knew my dad was getting seriously addicted to some *incredible woman*, as he commonly refers to her, but I was too dense to put it all together. I never realized it was your mother."

"I'm confused. The first day we met you told me you and your dad had only been in Morgan a couple of days. My mom claims she's been seeing your dad since March."

"Dad's been working on some Utah projects. He's been flying back and forth quite a bit. He met Amanda on his second trip out here. He fell for her hard. I'm telling you, he's had it *bad;* so I guess I wasn't dumbstruck at the marriage announcement. The realization of who my new sister was going to be however, now *that* slapped me sideways."

Sabrina noticed Mia's eyes staring from a tall thatch of grass. She stealthily crouched into a lioness position, ready to pounce. "Prepare yourself, you are about to get ambushed." Just then Mia sprang, boxing Brad's arm with her paws.

"Hi, Mia." Brad stroked a hand down her fur. "Did you hear the news? We're all getting married."

Sabrina laughed miserably. "I'll probably just have to leave Mia here at the shop. I'm sure she'd never stay in a new location."

"That's just because she hasn't seen her new room," Brad quipped.

"You're funny."

"Why aren't you laughing more then?"

"Because I'm too devastated! I was so excited to flit through the rest of the summer completely punch-drunk in love. I wanted to strut into my senior year sporting my summer's conquest, which would have been you."

"I rather like the sound of that." Brad plucked an over-grown dandelion and wiggled it in the grass, baiting Mia playfully. "Sabrina, we're moving in together, literally. I fail to see the earth-stopping devastation in all of this."

"How freaky would that be? Picture this: I go lugging myself into school with my arms draped all over you, saying to my friends, *'Hey this is my brother–isn't he dreamy?'* It's just stupid."

"We could keep things on the sly."

"Brad, I can't keep feeling as strongly for you as I do now and live with you!"

"Why not? Our parents are giving it a try."

"Be serious! Brad, I need to keep myself morally clean. It's a big part of my faith. I can't fling temptation into my own path purposefully and not trip over it." Her chin quivered and tears again began to jet down her cheeks.

"I don't want to make you break promises to yourself. Where do we go from here?"

"I don't know. I love you!"

"Whatever else happens, I love you too." Brad hugged his knees to his chest. "Hey, I have something for you. I was actually going to give it to you tonight at our cookout, but I have a feeling that our date's been canceled." He shoved his hand into his pocket and drew out a small package.

"You brought me a surprise?"

"Yes."

"Why?"

"Because I knew that you would dunk my marshmallow into the flames again--at least I hoped you would and then I was going to give you a present just like that hired boy did a long time ago."

Sabrina ripped through the delicate folds of tissue paper. A gold bracelet dropped into the palm of her hand. "I love bracelets."

"It's an identification bracelet." *Sabrina* was engraved on the front of the bracelet in a delicate cursive font. "Turn it over," Brad instructed. Sabrina's breath caught. *Summer Love* was etched in dainty print. It was so simple yet packed with so much meaning.

"Thank you." Sabrina traced her finger over the words.

"It doesn't matter what happens to us Sabrina. The truth is plain. Neither one of us will ever forget the magic of this summer."

"Do you think my mom and your dad are as much in love as we are?"

"Yes and probably more. They've both hurt too much and been alone too long. You can't believe the change in my dad. I've never seen him so giddy. I guess I've probably never seen him happy. Your mom has morals too, by the way."

"How do you know?"

"You know how in the movies, people have to take cold showers a lot to help them cool down?"

"Yeah?"

"Well, Dad's been running us out of cold water."

"That's kind of funny."

"Then laugh. I need you to be happier!"

Sabrina wiped tears away with the back of her hand. "I don't trust myself at this point. I might end up taking a lot of cold showers my own self...that's why we can't just frolic away in some secret affair."

"I like that word, *frolic*. We don't all end up married to each other for six more days. Wouldn't it be legal to frolic a little bit until then?" Brad lifted the dandelion stem and softly batted it in Sabrina's face.

"Legal? Yes, but wise? No."

"What's your verdict then?"

"We need to put the skids on this thing."

Brad was quiet for a few minutes but the melancholy was too painful. He tried to change the subject. "Guess what? I think you're going to like your new bedroom."

"Really? Where do we live anyway?"

"Dad's been frantically finishing a brand new home ever since he met your mom. He's paid crews double over-time to finish it. He's got an artist in there today decorating your bedroom so it will be ready for you."

"But it's a holiday!"

"Don't worry--I'm sure she's being compensated for her work. What Dad should have done was let you paint your own room--you're such an artist."

"I don't understand...why is anyone special painting my room? Doesn't that just entail a roller and a brush?"

"You've got a mural."

"You're kidding! Are you serious?"

Brad laughed. "Do you want to know if I'm kidding or I'm serious?"

"Both!"

"Okay then...yes, I am serious. No, I'm not kidding."

"I want to see our new house. Can you take me?"

"Let's give the artist a chance to work her magic first. By the way, I feel better seeing you brighten up a little bit."

"Does my mom know we are getting a new house?"

"I'm sure she does. Dad's had her over there a lot."

"Then why didn't you know she was my mother?"

"Every time she was over there with him I was over here with you." Brad chuckled at the bizarre tangle of fate. "I made myself scarce because I didn't want to hover around and get in their way."

"She didn't know it was going to be her house though. He only proposed to her last night."

"Sabrina, I'm sure she had a pretty good idea where things were headed. She's been instrumental in the whole decor of the place. The proposal last night was only a formality, I think. Amanda's the one who commissioned the artist to do the work in your room. She designed your suite."

"I have a *suite*? Are you serious?"

"No I'm kidding." Brad said playfully. "Of course I'm serious, you silly little nut! But if you ask me one more time if I'm serious or kidding, I'm going to throw you in the river!"

"My mom's always dreamt of decorating a new home. She's really great at that kind of thing. I'm happy for her I guess, in a very weird way."

"I learned something interesting about women and men from all of this." Brad said as he chucked his dandelion stem into a swirling eddy near the bank.

"What?"

"I found out it doesn't take very long for a man to decide on a wedding when a woman doesn't offer an early honeymoon." Brad ran a hand through his hair leaving his bangs spiked in an unruly manner. "It sure as heck didn't take my Dad very long! I heard Mormons were kind of...different, you know? But I think you and your mom's values make a lot of sense actually."

"Most guys would ridicule our standards and call us old-fashioned."

"Whatever..." Brad tossed another stem into the river. "Sabrina, can I tell you something?"

"Anything."

Brad turned to look at her, grabbing her hand. "I've never seen goodness like you before, but I felt the same energy from your mom today. Dad kept telling me that she was beautiful inside and out, but now I understand where he was coming from."

"He sent her roses; a *lot* of roses. That's what he wrote on her card."

"All those roses in your Mom's room--those were a tribute from my old man?"

"Yes."

"That's too much! See what I mean? Your mom's totally transformed him into some romantic, unrecognizable guy. He's willing to give up whatever, including beer in the fridge."

"Did you know your dad's girlfriend had a daughter?"

"Yeah, he mentioned something about it. He said he met her, I mean he'd met *you*."

"Weren't you worried about inheriting a sister if things got serious?"

"I didn't think about it too much at first but after I knew he had gone ring shopping I broke into a sweat. I started picturing every face in this town, *except yours*, and wondering if they'd be moving in soon. The night after we dipped all of those stinking strawberries, I got worrying about it really bad. I got down on my knees and pled to God in Heaven that it wasn't Halsey Redding."

Sabrina snorted out a sudden freakish laugh. It sounded like a horn blasting. It startled Brad and made him jump. Sabrina's cheeks flushed and she laughed harder, embarrassed by the grotesque outburst. "Sorry, I wasn't prepared to laugh just then. You caught me by surprise."

"Blast away, it's a free country."

"Thanks for being you." Brad reached out an arm and pulled her close, kissing the top of her head. "And thanks for my bracelet," Sabrina continued, "and for letting me cry and be a mess." Brad rubbed her back and kissed her head some more, breathing deeply the fragrance of her hair. "And thanks for being the best brother in the whole world…" Sabrina rambled sarcastically.

Brad tilted her chin up to meet his face. He kissed her with a flame of intense longing. "Thanks for one last *frolic*." He stroked her hair and held her close then kissed her tenderly one final time, "I guess this is goodbye."

Chapter Twelve

"I've got a million things to do before Friday," Amanda said, busily sorting items from her drawers and closet. "Thank you for being such a good sport at lunch." Amanda paused for a word from her daughter. Both bathroom doors were open, making communication easy. They had chatted this way thousands of times since moving to the little house.

Sabrina was lying on her bed facing the wall. She didn't answer her mother although she could hear Amanda's comments.

"Guess where we're getting married?" Amanda asked brightly, ignoring the silence.

Nothing–

"We're getting married on a pier at Dana Point Harbor, in California. Dana Point is located between Los Angeles and San Diego. Dorian says it's beautiful–absolutely the best kept secret in the state! Dorian's friend is a sea captain and that's who will be performing the ceremony. How does that sound?"

Silence–

"Of course you and Brad will be coming with us. You're my maid of honor and Brad will be Dorian's best man. You'll also be acting as witnesses, I think. I guess you can be a witness before you're eighteen? I'd better check on that..."

Blank–

"Then Dorian and I will take off for our honeymoon. Brad will show you around California. Doesn't that sound fun? I know you've always wanted to see the ocean. This will be great holiday! I called and talked to Vidalia just after lunch today. She cried happy tears for me, although she scolded me for not telling her sooner. Anyway, Vidalia and her sister will see to things here while we are gone. It's nice to not have to worry about the shop. Do you realize this will be our first real vacation since your Dad died? I wouldn't have dared leave it all for Vidalia alone and I think Vandaline was heaven-sent."

Dead zone–

"So you need to pack your bags. We're planning on being gone about nine days. We're flying. I know you've always wanted to go on a plane. We couldn't prolong the wedding. When I looked at my planner, I realized I had a three-week window of opportunity without any catered events scheduled. Dorian and I thought we'd better take advantage of it."

Void–

"I'm sorry you're still upset. I would like you to talk to me though," Amanda invited Sabrina to participate in the conversation but the stubborn girl was acting the part of a mute. "I can't wait for you to see the house! The thing that's wonderful is, it's *our* house. It's new to both parties; not *his* house, or *her* house, but *our* house. I planned something extra special for your bedroom. Tomorrow we will start moving some of our stuff over, okay? We'll leave all of our furniture here though. Then if we're here and we need to stay for some reason we're already set."

Bam! Sabrina's bathroom door slammed shut so Amanda stopped talking. Five minutes later the back porch door slammed as well. Amanda pulled her bedroom curtains back and watched as Old Blue backed out of the driveway. She quickly dialed Vidalia's number.

"Hello?"

"Vidalia–watch out for a teenage runaway, will you? Sabrina's pretty upset and I think I have a fair idea where she's going. Let me know if she shows up...thank you. Bye." Amanda hung up the phone. A knot was tightening in her stomach.

Vidalia was watching a documentary about the Revolutionary War on the television. The town fireworks display had been a good one and she'd come home feeling very patriotic. After Amanda's rattled phone call Vidalia stepped into the kitchen and put on a kettle of hot water. A little cocoa always soothed Sabrina.

Vidalia sat back waiting for the kettle to whistle. She remembered the first time Sabrina had run away. She was about eleven. Sabrina had quarreled with her mother about something and stormed out of the house, riding away on her bicycle with her pillow strapped to her back. She arrived at Vidalia's about ten minutes later. On another occasion, when Sabrina was fourteen, Vidalia had once again found her sobbing on her doorstep. Vidalia smiled, feeling needed, like a surrogate grandmother.

It wasn't long, the kettle hadn't yet whistled, before Vidalia saw headlights pull into the driveway. "Poor little wretch," she muttered before opening the door.

Sabrina stood in the porch light. Tears were streaming down her cheeks. Her eyes were just puffy slits. She had her pillow tucked under one arm and a bag slung over her shoulder. "Hi, Vidalia," she cried, trying to smile.

Vidalia's arm reached out to the girl, pulling her into the house. "What's the matter, honey? Come in and tell old Vidalia all about it. Come on, now. I've got some cocoa all ready and I'm ever so happy to have someone to help me drink it." Sabrina followed her to the kitchen table.

"I've just got to phone my mother," Vidalia lied, grabbing the phone and dialing Amanda's number. Vidalia waited until Amanda answered and then said, "I can't seem to get anyone. I guess Mother's already gone to bed."

"Thanks Vidalia," Amanda said into the receiver, understanding the signal that Sabrina was there and safe.

Vidalia set a soothing mug of chocolate in front of the pathetic girl. "Look there, I put marshmallows in it just the way you like it."

"Thanks Vidalia." Tears continued to stream down the puffy cheeks so Vidalia passed a box of Kleenex across the table.

"What's the matter with my girl? Has it been a nightmare, has it?"

Sobs racked the girl's chest. Vidalia let her cry. "Go ahead and let it out, you can tell me when you're ready."

Minutes ticked on the clock. Butterscotch jumped onto Vidalia's lap and settled in for a snooze. Vidalia lazily stroked the dog's ears. The hour was getting late but she could wait.

"Thanks for letting me come," Sabrina sniffled. "I didn't know where else to go."

Vidalia nodded, listening. "I need to tell you what's been going on with me." Sabrina blew her nose and sucked in a ragged breath. "About a month ago I met this boy."

Vidalia's eyebrows furrowed slightly. This wasn't exactly the conversation she was prepared for. She thought Sabrina's woes were concerning her mother's engagement, not boys.

"His name is Brad and he's the best person I've ever met. Anyway, I was supposed to tell you about him after I lost the bet with you over Mom's dumb roses but I didn't because I'm awful."

"That's okay, dear. I wasn't going to stop swearing if you'd have won the bet. Go on."

"Well, I've been running around with him a lot. I'm in love with him, Vidalia! I love him so much that it's making me crazy! I haven't even told Mom that I've been dating anybody and she hasn't noticed because she's in love her own self. I kind of kept him a secret at first, because he's not a member of the church and I didn't want a big lecture about dating do's and don'ts. I'm also not supposed to go steady with anybody until I'm eighteen but I broke that rule, too. It's not like we officially said, "Wow, we're going steady," or anything. It just happened! It felt steady though."

"How steady?"

"I saw him every single day." Sabrina admitted, taking a sip of the cocoa. "Well, before I knew it, we were saying we loved each other and we do. Vidalia, when he kisses me I can't breathe right and my heartbeat gets all messed up..."

"Sounds great..."

Sabrina smiled a wary smile at her friend. *Dear Vidalia! She never judges me. I love Vidalia!* "I was going to tell Mom about it pretty soon, honest I was. But then she dropped the bomb on me this morning that she's engaged, so I go to the stupid lunch to meet this guy, Dorian, and guess who shows up?"

"Who?"

"Brad! He's Dorian's son...." Sabrina puffed air in her cheeks and then slowly exhaled like a deflating balloon. Her words bounced across the table and smacked Vidalia.

"Oh my hell! Not really?" Vidalia's eyes were the size of quarters. "No wonder you're a blubbering mess."

Sabrina's elbows propped on the table and she rested her chin on her hands. "Mom and Dorian don't know. We were both so surprised at lunch we didn't say anything. We just acted like strangers, accept for under the table we were holding hands."

"*Damnation.* This doesn't bode well, Sabrina."

"I know. After lunch Brad drove me home. We walked back to my Thinking Place and talked. I told him that we couldn't see each other romantically anymore. He said we could see each other on the sly but I can't move in the same house with him—not with a breathing disorder and a messed up heart beat!"

Vidalia was rubbing her chin thoughtfully. "No!"

"We kissed goodbye at the river then he walked me back to the porch and it was so hard watching him leave! Oh Vidalia, I just wanted to die! I was crying and he was too. That really wrenched my heart, seeing him tear-up. Then he drove away. I know it's a different kind of heart ache but I really haven't felt this torn up since my Dad got killed."

Vidalia nodded, "It's a loss," she consoled. "Of course it rips you up."

Vidalia and Sabrina sat in silence for a while. Butterscotch was snoring from Vidalia's lap. The kitchen clock ticked obnoxiously. It seemed to say, "What now? What now? What now? What now?"

Sabrina cleared her throat, "Vidalia, I don't think I can bear this. What if I'm not strong enough? I could tell Mom, and maybe I should, but then you know what she'll do?"

"Yes, I know just what she'd do—call off the wedding. She'd never put you in this position. Never!"

"So am I being selfish by considering telling her and having her call a halt to the whole thing? That would ensure my happiness but destroy hers. Or am I being dishonest by not saying anything and letting her go through with it?"

"That's a good question and this problem needs some sorting."

"I'm so angry at her I could just spit! Part of me wants to hurt her and deny her the happiness she's feeling now, just as she's denying me if this wedding takes place. What on earth is she thinking anyway? Dorian is not a member of the church! I was all guilty about Brad, and she goes off and does the same dumb trick! She's getting married on a *pier*! She's always lectured me about the virtues of temple marriage and she's getting married on a pier! What kind of an example is she setting for me anyway?" Sabrina was ranting unreasonably now but the release felt healthier than silently grieving.

"She's an idiot!"

That comment stopped Sabrina short. The girl's eyes blinked a couple of times. A furrow creased her brow and she bit her lip. "Well, she *was* married to Dad in the temple, so she's already sealed to him forever. I guess it doesn't matter as much then—if she marries Dorian by the ocean...they are really good people, these Manning's. I know because Brad's character seems nearly faultless. I've decided not to ever like Dorian but he should be given *some* credit for the way he's raised his son." A smile twitched at Vidalia's mouth as her reverse psychology methods were working. "And she's set a good example for Dorian. She's got him to take the beer out of his fridge and everything...anyway Brad said something about that. She's kept her values, too. Brad says his dad's been running them out of cold water at their house because he's taken so many cold showers." The smile tugged harder. Vidalia covered her mouth with a hand in a yawning gesture. "Brad needs a mother. Oh Vidalia! If you only knew how awful he's had it. His mom left him when he was only a year old. He doesn't know what it's like to have a mother. Wouldn't he love mine? Mom is awesome, and I could share her with Brad. I mean, I don't think I could share her with just *anybody*, but I love Brad! I want him to know what it's like to have a mother. I think he needs one, even if he is seventeen."

Vidalia nodded, listening to Sabrina's rambling justifications. "So you think your mom should go through with this then?"

"Yes," Sabrina lamented miserably, tears streaming again.

"Then I don't want you to say anything to her about you and Brad just yet."

"She'll cream me when she finds out."

"You let old Vidalia take care of it."

"You'll help smooth things over with her?"

"Yes." Vidalia said then raised a finger at Sabrina and began wagging it. "I think you *should* be horsewhipped! But if anybody's going to do that it'll be me. You high-headed little firecracker! You knew better than to go cavorting around *every* day with that boy; I don't care how perfect he is! You've done this all to yourself and then you convicted your mother of wrong-doings by your own guilty conscience."

"I know." Sabrina gazed unflinchingly at Vidalia. She knew Vidalia would get around to scolding her at some point. It actually felt good to hear it. "I knew I shouldn't but I did. It was such a rush."

"It was. It was a fairy tale–possibly too good to be true."

"And now my heart is wrenched sideways forever."

"Not forever."

"For how long then?"

"A while."

Sabrina reached for a fresh Kleenex. "Have you ever had a broken heart, Vidalia?"

"Oh hell yes I have."

"Really?"

"Three of them."

"Three of them?" Sabrina sounded mortified. "But how did you survive it?"

"One day at a time, just breathing in and out...oh, and chocolate helps a *little*..."

Sabrina stared wide-eyed at her seasoned friend. "Want to talk about it?"

"I don't make a habit out of prattling on and on about myself--but maybe you should hear it." Sabrina settled back in her chair, this time *she* waited. "I was crazy in love with a kid named Phillip Masters. He got drafted in '67 and sent to Vietnam. He gave me a promise ring before he shipped out. I wrote him faithfully and he answered whenever he could. It was tough finding stationary and envelopes in a foxhole, of course. He was in the marines so he had a thirteen month tour of duty. I prayed like a saint for Phillip! He caught some shrapnel in his hip not long before his tour was up, so he spent a few extra months in a military hospital there. His mother notified me that he was finally coming home; he would be arriving by bus at Evanston. I was so happy! I splurged on a new dress and shoes so I'd look my best. I drove to the bus stop in Wyoming and then stood waiting, practically drunk with anticipation. The bus pulled in and I made my way through the crowd. When Phillip stepped off the bus, I took off in dead run, high heels and all." Vidalia paused, swallowing hard.

"And?" Sabrina prodded, "Go on."

"He saw me. His face never lit up. His expression looked pained and pinched. I then saw a Vietnamese girl climb off the bus behind him. She was out to here," Vidalia said, moving her hands in a swollen motion, "with child. Phillip placed his hand on her back and guided her off the curb and into the crowd. I froze in my tracks. At that moment I wished that he had been killed in that God-forsaken foreign country. At least I could have cried the merciful tears of honorable, unfulfilled, expectations, and the sorrow for what could have been. Phillip would have been enshrined in my heart as the dearest of patriots and martyrs. But...instead of him dying, I did. I died right there on that sidewalk in Evanston, Wyoming. I couldn't breathe, I couldn't think, I couldn't move. I just watched him walk away. The love in my heart turned to ashes and soot."

Sabrina was now crying for Vidalia's heartache. "Oh Vidalia, it's awful! It's so awful. I'm sorry."

"Of course the Masters' were torn up over it. Phillip's mother sent me the kindest letter, trying her best to apologize for him. It didn't help one damn bit, but it was kind of her just the same."

Raucously the kitchen clock ticked, "That hurt, that hurt, that hurt, that hurt."

Vidalia stood and cleared the mugs from the table. "Let Butterscotch out will you?" Sabrina led the whining dog to the door and then listened for the dog to scratch, signaling she wanted to come back inside.

"Let's go into the front room where it's more comfortable," Vidalia suggested. She grabbed sheets and a blanket and made a bed for Sabrina on the couch. "Here you go, my girl. Climb in and get comfortable. Vidalia doesn't host slumber parties very often."

It was midnight. Sabrina felt guilty for keeping Vidalia up so late, but Vidalia wasn't protesting. She settled into her recliner, throwing an afghan over herself. Butterscotch once again nestled comfortably on Vidalia's lap. The woman stared thoughtfully at the dog, petting it lovingly, and then continued talking. "I went ricocheting around in a daze. I swear to you my senses were dead. Some guy named Stan came along. I can't tell you much about our courtship. I was just on the rebound from Phillip and willed myself not to truly feel anything. Anyway, he offered marriage and I accepted. We ran off to Reno in '71. That was stupid! What did that do, except break my mother's heart? I wish I could have done that one over again. Live and learn!"

"You should have been horsewhipped you high-headed little firecracker!" Sabrina couldn't imagine Vidalia doing such an impetuous thing. "What happened then?"

"Stan and I had been married for a couple of years. I was working at Walgreen's in Salt Lake, trying to put his lazy butt through school. I came home to our apartment one afternoon and Stan met me at the door. "I've fallen out of love with you, Vidalia," he said smugly. "I've fallen for someone else." I told him to just get the hell out. The divorce didn't take very long but you can imagine my surprise when just a week after it was finalized, he ran off with my sister, Vandaline."

"No!"

"The very sister you met this morning. That would be Stan's heartthrob."

"Vidalia, that's horrible." Sabrina's eyes closed tightly, fighting sympathetic emotions for her friend. "You were betrayed by two people who should have loved you."

"Stan was no good. He just played on Vandaline's youthful vanities. She was a proud little cuss and had quite worried our folks to death. Stan flattered her along and she swallowed his bait like a dumb sucker. Of course I was angry. I felt a terrible, tumultuous dislike for both of them! Mother tried to reconstruct a happy family for a long time. After a decade of declining invitations to dinners and family functions, I softened and joined the folks for Thanksgiving. Stan and Vandaline were there. Boy was I ever shocked to see the two of them. Vandaline's conscience had eaten her alive. She was a shriveled, mousy, nervous wreck. Stan, the dumb lally-bump, was a bigger nothing than I'd remembered. He was just a mean booze-hound. I looked at him and laughed out loud. I wrapped my arms around that waify, frail little sister of mine, and thanked her for taking him off my hands."

"You did? That's kind of funny, Vidalia."

"Well, that broke the ice. I started writing to Vandaline. Stan had moved her off to Boise, and she was kind of separated from the rest of us. I figured she'd suffered in solitude long enough and getting stuck with Stan was punishment enough for whatever her past crimes may have been. I forgave her. She's had the saddest life out of all us sisters."

"How many are there?"

"Five of us. Vondessa, she's the oldest. Then me, followed by Valyncia, Vandaline, and Velveteen."

"Did your mother have a special soft spot for *V* names or what?"

"Yes," Vidalia laughed. "Father's name was Von and mother's was Vivian, so naturally they just lined us up. Father used to say our family created a V formation just like a flock of geese."

Sabrina chuckled and settled further down into her make-shift bed on the sofa. "I'm sorry for keeping you up so late, Vidalia."

"Nonsense. Girls have to talk sometimes. You needed me and I need you to need me."

"Thanks Vidalia. You've always been my shoulder to cry on... what was your third broken heart, anyway?"

"Well, after the train-wreck I made of things with Stan, I woke up. I decided I'd better take charge of my life a little better. I started going back to church. I met an insurance salesman named Keith Davies. He was a good man. My feelings weren't as intense as they'd been for Phillip, but I was older and more sensible I guess. Aint that something? I went from sense, to no sense, to *sensible*! We took it kind of slow. Anyway, Keith took me to the temple on my thirtieth birthday and we were married. We were happy and getting along fine but he died of cancer fourteen months later." Tears sprang again from Sabrina's eyes. *It's not fair!* "Luckily he'd taken out an insurance policy on himself. I've budgeted carefully and I've just gone forward, one day at a time. What else can a person do?"

"You've had a hard life, Vidalia. I feel guilty for bawling so much. I'm just selfish and awful!"

"Hogwash! You're just a young girl in love. You're experiencing your first romantic heartbreak and it's painful. It's not easy. Hell, if it was easy what would we learn? How would we be smart enough to recognize true love, if ever it fell again into our paths?"

"I just wish it didn't hurt so badly."

"Good night, Honey. Things will be brighter in the morning. Don't worry about a thing. Old Vidalia will help you get through it all. You can be strong enough if you have to be. Just remember my sad tale of Phillip. His immorality crushed our hopes and plans. It left his parents' hearts broken, and worst of all, he shattered his own dreams and ideals. He gathered the broken shards of his honor and tried to repair the damage where he could. Did he leave that girl pregnant and in disgrace? No, he did the right thing by her. But if he could have dug deep enough, fighting temptation as hard as he fought for our country, then things would have been different."

"You'd be Mrs. Vidalia Masters."

"That's right. I probably would be."

"Have you ever been able to forgive Phillip?"

"Kind of I guess. Those boys went through hell in Vietnam. I can't be anyone's judge because luckily I wasn't there. I don't know what he went through. I've softened my opinions about him over the years. I hope he's happy. I haven't spoken to him in forty-one years."

"How old are you?"

"Sixty-one."

"Thanks for everything Vidalia."

"You're welcome, Kid." Vidalia disappeared into her bedroom with Butterscotch.

Sabrina's phone buzzed in her pocket. She retrieved it quickly. There was a text from Brad. "Are you awake?" he asked.

"Yes."

"Miserable?"

"Yes," Sabrina answered back.

"Me too. Good night. I love you."

"Goodnight," Sabrina typed. She hesitated momentarily and then flipped the phone shut.

Chapter Thirteen

Sabrina pulled into the driveway and turned off the ignition. The sun was extraordinarily hot for nine o'clock in the morning, even in July. A jacked-up Dodge truck was backed up to the porch door. The candy-apple red paint job glinted with metallic flakes shining beneath the morning rays. *Nice truck!* Sabrina peered in through tinted windows to admire grey leather upholstery and a clean, sleek interior. *Dorian has good taste.*

"Hello Sabrina."

Sabrina startled--her hands and face jerking away from the glass where they were pressed. Her head shot up. Chantry Cantrell leaned against the truck, a bronze hand casually running across the glossy surface of the truck bed. He was taller than Sabrina remembered, at least six foot five. *Has he grown even taller since his mission?* He was well proportioned; the muscled contours of his body balanced out his height. His dark hair was groomed short and neat. Chantry's dark eyes burned like chips of obsidian. His face seemed perfectly chiseled, from high forehead and cheekbones to his angular jaw. He wore a brown plaid western shirt with sleeves rolled to his elbows, tan Wranglers, and snake skin boots. Sabrina's eyes absorbed it all in just a spit second. *He reminds me of home--of Raymond.* A pang of homesickness jolted through her center. Chantry's eyebrows shot up, waiting for a reply.

"What are you doing here?"

"I was in Morgan and thought I'd better say hi to old friends," he explained. "Looks like I barely got here in time as I see you're moving. I thought since I had time this morning I'd help if I could."

"That's nice of you."

"I helped move you into this house, remember? I guess I'd better help you move out," Chantry smiled and kicked a lanky leg up on the running board, casually resting it there.

Sabrina stared at his boot. "Tony Lamas?"

"What else is there?"

"My Dad always wore Tony Lamas."

"Yes he did. He was my fashion icon."

"So how are you, anyway?"

"Good. We haven't seen you around Raymond much this summer. Your Grandpa and Grandma are kind of sad about that."

"Well...I've been kind of busy. I was planning on going up there in a couple of weeks, but I guess my mom's getting married. I'm not sure what to expect for the rest of the summer. I'd like to get up there though."

"How do you feel about her remarrying?" Sabrina shrugged her shoulders. "That pretty much says it all," Chantry said quietly.

"How long have you had this truck?"

"Couple of months. You like it?"

"What's not to like? It's *hot*."

"The guy who sold it to me said it was a chick magnet. That was the selling point right there."

Sabrina laughed. "Yeah, you look like you need help with the chicks alright," she said sarcastically. "So...are you still at Oregon State?"

"I'm done thank goodness–except I'll miss playing ball."

"Not going to the majors anytime soon?"

"I've had some minor league teams squabbling in my ear but I think it's time to grow up and settle down."

"So your ball playing career has wound down, huh? Grandpa Ashley will be sorry to hear it."

"He's a good man. Did you know your grandpa and grandma came to watch me play every time I was within five hours of home? I could look around and count on seeing Mom, Dad, Juliet and Joseph in the stands."

"Your very own traveling fan club."

"Exactly. I remember you and your mom coming to a few games over the last four years. That was pretty nice of you."

"I just tagged along for the snow cones," Sabrina teased.

"I'll still be playing league ball every chance I get."

"I'll bet you bleed little baseballs don't you?"

"Baseballs and horses," Chantry agreed.

"You haven't forgotten your country roots then?"

Chantry shook his head, gazing intently at Sabrina, black eyes searching. "You've been crying?"

"Bees! I was attacked by a whole swarm of them. It happens sometimes when you work with flowers..."

Chantry looked unimpressed by the lie. "That's the lamest story I've ever heard."

"Um...would you wait ten minutes while I grab a quick shower?"

"I'm timing you. Your mother says you can't hurry in the shower."

"Bet me!" Sabrina challenged running into the house.

"The clock's ticking."

Forty-one minutes later Sabrina reemerged.

"You lost the bet," Chantry said flatly.

"I was out of the shower in ten minutes! Hair and makeup took a little longer..."

"Whatever," Chantry said, grabbing a box full of Sabrina's books. He had already packed up most of the room. "I didn't touch anything *too* personal," he teased. "I thought I'd leave that for you, although the first ninety pages of your journal were pretty good."

Sabrina wrinkled up her nose and smiled. "Ha, ha! I doubt I've written *nine* pages in my journal. I'd rather illustrate my life's story than write it."

"I appreciated the cards you sent me every once in a while. Your artwork is really improving!"

"Thanks. I thought you'd like the ones of my dad and Raymond."

"You just tried to make me homesick."

"Did it work?"

"Yes, a couple of times. Once I drove out to some farmer's field just to stare at his horses and smell his hay. That helped a little."

Sabrina dumped drawers of clothes into boxes. She packed her belongings into boxes and Chantry carried them out to the truck. Soon the room was empty. "I just need to leave enough stuff here to get me through this week." The empty closet made her feel melancholy. "I guess this is one way to help me clean my room."

"Where to?" Chantry asked, sliding the last of Sabrina's things into the back of his truck.

Sabrina shrugged, "Maybe you should go ask my mom."

"Why don't you ask?"

"I've taken up a vow of silence."

"Sabrina–don't be a brat, okay?"

"Shut up! I don't want to talk to her yet." A deep furrow set in Sabrina's brow.

"*Stubborn!* My gosh, aren't you ever going to grow out of that stubborn streak?" Chantry huffed at the girl before pivoting toward the house. Sabrina smiled. "Amanda!" Chantry called from the kitchen door. "Where the heck am I supposed to take this to?"

"I forgot Sabrina's never been there," Amanda called. "Okay, you go down the Milton road. It's a brand new home off to the left hand side–kind of on the hill. It's a two-story white house. You can't miss it. I'll be there in a minute! Tell Sabrina not to go inside until I get there. I want to show her around and see her face!"

Chantry turned and sauntered back through the porch. "Did you catch all that?"

"Uh-huh."

"I shouldn't reward you for bad behavior, but would you like to drive my truck?"

"Absolutely!" Sabrina climbed in. Chantry's seat was cranked so far back she couldn't even reach the pedals. "How tall are you anyway?" She asked, hefting the seat forward and adjusting the mirrors.

"Six foot seven. I grew two inches on my mission and another inch the year I came home."

"Put your seatbelt on," Sabrina instructed.

"My gosh you're bossy. This is my truck, remember? Put your seatbelt on Sabrina."

"Thanks for letting me drive." Sabrina maneuvered the truck off the yard and into the driveway. "I love this truck!"

"It's not Old Blue but it tries hard."

Sabrina eased the truck onto the road. "I hope everyone I know drives by and sees me today."

Chantry leaned his head against the back of his seat and laughed. "As if you ever cared what people think! You just live to defy everybody."

"I don't know what you're talking about, Chantry Cantrell!"

"You do too. No other girl would drive around in that old beat up Chevy. You're happy to go chugging around in it because you are independently different. Today you want people to see you in this outfit just so you can prove that you're versatile."

"Versatility is important! Besides, maybe I look good in this truck."

"Oh, I imagine it suits you alright." Chantry cast a look sideways at the driver.

Sabrina was tiptoeing Chantry's truck up Commercial Street, waving animatedly at everyone she saw.

"I don't have all day. Are you going to wave and smile at everybody between here and Milton?"

"I'm a very friendly person."

"With everyone but your mother."

"Let's listen to the radio," Sabrina said, snapping it on and cranking up the volume.

Chantry shook his head. "You're rotten!"

"Sorry, I can't hear you."

"Be nice to your mother." Chantry turned the radio off.

"I *am* nice! We got along just fine until yesterday morning. She dropped the news on me like an A-bomb! I didn't even know she was dating anybody. Pardon me if I'm not thrilled about packing up and moving out of my house the very next morning."

"*Feisty!* I'm sorry it's tough on you but your mom is so excited about you seeing this new house. Just play along, okay? *Pretend.*"

"I'm going aren't I?" Sabrina grumbled. "Now help me watch for a new house."

Chantry pointed ahead. "Is that it?"

Sabrina eyed a large home on the hillside. "Too much house for the four of us, I doubt that's the one." The Dodge crept by the property slowly, but Sabrina caught a glimpse of Brad's car in the driveway. "Oh my heck, this *is* the house," she said, making a loose turn in the road and backtracking to the lane. Chantry's truck rumbled up the grade and parked in front of the home.

Chantry whistled between his teeth. "Nice digs, Sabrina."

"I'll bet Mom's twittering a fit about this place. I hope she's not marrying this guy just for his house."

"Amanda's too level-headed for that. I'm sure this is a rush for her though."

Buzz. Sabrina pulled the phone from her pocket and flipped it open. Brad's text read, "What are you doing just sitting out there?"

Sabrina's thumbs flew. "Mom's making me wait until she gets here to show me the house."

"I was hoping to be your tour guide," printed across the screen.

"You can help."

"Nice truck. Who is that guy?"

"Where are you spying at me from?"

"Upstairs window."

Sabrina craned her head over the dash, looking up. She saw Brad staring at her from up above. She smiled and waved.

"Who are you waving at?" Chantry asked.

"My new step brother." The words burned like gall in Sabrina's throat.

"Who are you texting?"

"A really good friend," Sabrina answered nonchalantly. Her phone buzzed again.

"Who is that guy?" Brad demanded again from the tiny screen.

"He used to work for us in Raymond." Sabrina typed.

"Teenagers!" Chantry shook his head. "You know Sabrina; it really bothers me when you go around acting like a big high-schooler." He smiled at the girl, wondering if she remembered accusing him of that on Raymond Mountain so long ago.

Sabrina cracked up. "Oh Chantry! You weren't supposed to remember that! I was *so* dumb. That's embarrassing."

"You were such a spunky little thing," Chantry laughed. He studied Sabrina thoughtfully. "I see nothing's changed. You're still a spitfire! You're Dad was right."

Sabrina smiled at the childhood memories. "We had good times."

"I miss your Dad. He was my hero."

"Mine, too." *Buzz, buzz, buzz.* Sabrina ignored the phone. "How's Grandpa Ashley getting along this summer?"

"Good. He's making Brant's boys all play summer baseball. Bear Lake has such a good program you know, so all of his best help is still gallivanting off most afternoons. Joe and B.J. are playing on the American Legion team this summer. Little Ben made the little league all-star team. He's quite a pitcher."

"Really?" Sabrina was happy to hear about her cousins' activities. "I'll bet they like it when you come home."

"Yeah, we had a Raymond baseball game the other night. It was fun! Brant's kids all look up to me like some kind of a star or something. They're all eager to learn and it was fun giving them some pointers. They're coachable and that's important."

"What positions do Joe and B.J. play on the Legion team?"

"Joe plays catch. He's got about the best gunning arm I've seen for a junior. Well--he'll be a senior this year. There aren't very many guys who are going to steal bases on him. If the basemen play their positions well, Joe should be able to pick them all off. B.J.'s a fielder. He's learning how to gage heights and distances pretty well."

"That's good."

Knock. The sound startled both Chantry and Sabrina. Amanda was standing at the window, smiling. "Come see the house," she called through the glass.

"Be nice," Chantry hissed before opening the door and easing his long legs out onto the pavement.

"Killjoy!" Sabrina fired back before facing her mother with a painted-on smile.

"I love you," Amanda said, catching Sabrina's wrist. "I'm sorry," her voice quivered fragilely.

"Love you too, Mom." Sabrina reached out and hugged her tiny mother. "I'm sorry I've been a brat."

Amanda patted Sabrina's back soothingly. "Nonsense! It was wrong of me to spring it on you so suddenly. Please forgive me."

"I will sometime."

"I'll accept that offer," Amanda smiled. "Well, follow me," she called cheerily, blazing the way to the front door.

A strong hand clapped Sabrina's shoulder, giving it a squeeze. She looked up. Chantry was smiling down at her, nodding approval. "Good job," he whispered. "Now keep it up."

CHAPTER FOURTEEN

Sabrina's eyes swept the foyer and front room. A large stone fireplace dominated her first glance. It stretched up the wall and beyond the soaring ceiling height. Dark hard-wood walnut framed a square of plush carpet in the center of the room. Two sturdy armchairs flanked the fireplace on either side, angling toward a large tufted leather sofa. Caramels, chocolates, and burnished reds created a mouth-watering potpourri of color in the room. Shards of light glimmered from a stately bronze chandelier. It was grand but not pretentious. Amanda's collection of five crystal vases graced the mantel.

"Oh my gosh," Sabrina uttered, her eyes still sweeping the room. "Mom, we could fit our house into this one five times over."

"Isn't it wonderful? Do you like the colors?"

"Did you do all of this?"

"Yes!" Amanda answered enthusiastically. "Oh, Sabrina! Shopping for this house has been a total blast."

"I'll bet."

"Come in here," Amanda urged. Chantry and Sabrina followed her into the kitchen.

Sabrina felt a quick touch on her arm. She knew Brad had entered the room. She glanced sideways at him. He was smiling, eager for Sabrina's reaction to their new home.

The kitchen was a sprawling mass of stainless steel appliances, dark granite counter tops and antiqued cream cabinets. "It's gorgeous!" Sabrina triumphed. "I love the contrast of the dark granite against these lighter cabinets," she said, opening a cupboard door for inspection.

"Look at all this counter space! We can cater up a storm in this kitchen," Amanda said brightly, "and look at *this*, Sabrina!" Amanda motioned toward the range.

"A commercial sized oven!"

"It should come in handy."

"Oh Mom, it's awesome!" Sabrina opened the oven and peeked in. She wandered into the pantry and squealed again. "This pantry's as big as our whole kitchen! Awe, look at this! Two more refrigerators! We can store *everything* in here. Oh my gosh!" Sabrina whirled around the pantry, studying brand new appliances which lined the shelves. "Get a load of this Bosch mixer," she uttered in dismay. It was all too much to take in at one time.

Sabrina heard the others laughing at her excitement from the kitchen. "I think she likes it," Chantry suggested.

"Oh my heavens—my manners!" Amanda cried. "Chantry, this is Dorian's son, Brad. He's Sabrina's age. I'm looking forward to knowing him better. Brad, this is Chantry Cantrell. He's a dear friend from Raymond. He used to work for my husband and father-in-law on our ranch."

The two shook hands. Sabrina was busy pulling drawers out and examining brand new cooking and baking utensils. She wasn't paying too much attention to the others. She faintly heard Dorian come in the house. The introductions started all over again.

"Chantry has played baseball for Oregon State for the last four years on a full-ride athletic scholarship," Sabrina heard her mother boast. Dorian was impressed and the two men exchanged information back and forth about the formidable Oregon State Beavers, batting averages, and the Pac-Ten Conference in general.

Sabrina wandered back into the pantry. Brad followed her in. "You like it?"

"Brad, it's wonderful!"

"So my old man's not too bad after all huh? He enlarged everything in this kitchen for your mom's business."

"It's great," she repeated, feeling a little bit defensive. "I love it and I'm sure Mom appreciates it too."

"She's cool," Brad nodded. "So that guy out there, is he the little hired boy you told me about?"

"Chantry? Yeah, but I never said he was *little*."

Brad's brows furrowed. "You sort of implied it though."

"No I didn't! I was *little*, he was a teenager. I never implied anything." Sabrina gave Brad a suspicious look. *Is he jealous?* "He's like eight years older than me, so wipe that scowl off your face."

"I'm not scowling. I was simply trying to figure out who was keeping you so darned enthralled in that truck outside."

"I wasn't *so darned enthralled!* We were simply talking about my dad, my grandpa, and my cousins. I haven't even seen Chantry since Christmas."

"Don't get nervous," Brad said, flashing charm to smooth things over. "You didn't answer my text and I panicked."

Sabrina jerked her phone from her hip pocket to study the message. "Did you tell your mom or are we playing it cool?" the message read.

She looked up at Brad. "I'm not going to say anything until after they're married. Otherwise, I'm afraid my mom will bolt."

"Okay, suits me. I'll just keep pretending I don't *really* know who you are. By the way," he grinned mouthing the words, "I love you!" Sabrina smiled and emerged from the pantry.

"What were you doing in there?" Amanda quizzed.

"I had to stop her from baking something," Brad teased. "She wanted to whip up a double batch of cream puffs or something. Don't worry though; I made her put all of the ingredients back neatly."

Amanda chuckled, easily persuaded by the boy's charm. "Come on everybody! I want to show you the rest of the house."

Sabrina sauntered into the dining room. A china cabinet gleamed against one wall. A collection of scarlet sandwich glassware glimmered behind the panes. The extraordinary dishes had been Great Grandma Porter's. Little cups and saucers twinkled and winked beneath the cabinet's light. "The dishes are happy to show off."

"I think so too. Do you like the chandelier in here?"

An oblong chandelier hung from a tray ceiling. It was in perfect scale with the table, anchoring it to the room. It was a Tiffany-style cut glass fixture. Brilliant shades of red and amber glass sparkled between black seams. "What's not to like?" A large bouquet of fresh pinks and carnations livened up an elegantly carved table. Sabrina counted eight sturdy dining chairs. "Are we planning on taking in boarders?" Sabrina asked, "foreign exchange students or something?"

Amanda dismissed Sabrina's sarcasm with a wave. "No, I want to be able to host plenty of company. Isn't this set exquisite?"

"Sure is," Brad agreed leading Amanda by the hand, coaxing her to speed up the tour. "I have a feeling this next room will be a hit with Sabrina. I can't wait to show her!"

A pair of chaise lounges rested beneath sunny beams streaming through a paneled glass wall.

Plants clung to a small table between them. Ivy and rhododendron trailed from hanging baskets and a giant fern spilled from a plant stand with its feathery foliage draping the floor. Book cases lined the opposite wall from floor to ceiling. "I don't have these all stocked yet," Amanda said, "but I'm looking forward to it."

A menagerie of bird cages inhabited a corner. Greenery trailed up the birdcages, weaving in and out; clinging for support. Three colorful canaries chirped from one cage. A pair of lovely white cockatiels cooed from the tallest one, while two golden finches trilled softly from the third.

Water cascaded in trickles down rocked panels near the room's entry. Sabrina turned and walked closer, noticing a shallow pool cut right into the floor and running the length of wall. Several golden coi swam lazily blowing bubbles to the surface. A few water lilies floated on the little canal.

"This room is where I plan on spending most of my time!"

Brad was fairly bouncing with enthusiasm at Sabrina's declaration. "Do you like my pet birds?"

"Yeah, I do. How long have you had them?"

"Four or five days." The group laughed.

"Your mom told me you always wanted a bird," Dorian said. "I thought I'd surprise you, but when I went to the pet store, the sales lady confused me about which birds made the best pets. I wasn't sure what you wanted so I just bought a whole collection."

"An aviary!" Brad piped.

Chantry was casually leaning against the door frame. He raised one eyebrow in Sabrina's direction. He remained silent but Sabrina felt his thoughts tumbling across the room toward her. *"See? This Dorian--he's a pretty good guy. He's gone to big lengths to indulge you and your mother. Be kind to this new family, Sabrina. Ben would have wanted it this way."*

Sabrina plopped herself down on a chaise. "I don't need to go any further. I love this room! Whose idea was the fountain and fish?"

Amanda pointed to Dorian. "Well," he explained, "I wanted this to be a nature solarium. I know you two are crazy about flowers! I was afraid you'd miss the shop too much. The glass wall opens out to the hillside. I've got big plans for the back yard. It will be an extension of this room, really. I thought the birds and fish would feel right at home with all the sunshine and plants. Sabrina, if you decide you want one or all of the birds in your room then you're welcome to take them up there."

Buzz. Sabrina checked her phone. "I'm happy you like it in here. After I found out you were the one that was moving in, this whole room made sense to me." Brad's message said. She glanced across the room and saw the phone in his hands. She smiled and shoved her phone back into her pocket.

Amanda led the group through a utility room and Dorian's den before they tromped upstairs. "I can't wait for you to see this, Sabrina," Amanda said, opening the door with a sense of drama. "Voila!"

Sabrina entered another realm. The color of the walls was pale honey and filmy, gauzy green fabric draped from French doors which opened to a private balcony. Potted plants and hanging baskets enclosed the balcony in a colorful jungle of leaves and blossoms. A small outdoor sofa nestled against the house. Sabrina had a beautiful view of the hillside and a shady glen which cut a seam into the mountainous slope.

"Trust Sabrina to head straight outside," Chantry said.

Amanda guided her daughter back into the bedroom. A queen size bed sat on top of a raised platform, three staggered steps up. A built-in desk, complete with a whole computer set-up, balanced the room on the opposite wall. Floor to ceiling bookcases flanked the desk.

"My own computer," she gasped. "No more library? What kind of wood is this? It's beautiful." Sabrina stroked an appreciative hand along a shelf.

"Pear wood. I got the idea from touring your church's Conference Center. I was taken with the color and grain," Dorian explained, delighted by Sabrina's interest.

A mural of the Raymond Mountains emerged from plush shag carpet and spread upward, drenching the wall in nature's majesty. A portion of the mural splashed onto the ceiling. A hawk circled near Sabrina's light fixture. Tears sprang to Sabrina's eyes. Emotions choked her throat while she gazed, drinking in every delicious detail.

Amanda gently nudged Sabrina toward her bathroom. A vanity of matching pear wood housed a copper basin. A sunken tub beckoned her in for a closer look. Above the tub was another mural of Sabrina's Thinking Place. Swirling eddies and willows' reflections danced on the languid surface of the Weber River. Sabrina could identify each branch, each stone, and each tree. A walk-in steam shower was situated beside the tub. *How well Mother knows me!* A spacious closet boasted room for a dressing table and built in drawers.

"It's too much," she cried. Tears were streaming down her cheeks and she didn't even care. "It's too much," she said again.

Buzz. When Sabrina's tears cleared, she checked her message. "It's your river in the summertime! That's what the artist was working on yesterday only she wouldn't let me in to see it."

"I'm speechless."

Chantry's eyes were twinkling at her. He was propped against her new desk. "This is pretty much a dream home if you ask me. Well, I guess I'd better be going. I have a twelve-thirty appointment. I'll put your stuff in the garage, Sabrina. Nice room--see you around."

"Thanks for coming!" Amanda said, crossing the room to give Chantry a quick hug. "We love you and hope you'll come back often. I'll keep a place set for you at the table."

"Thanks, I might take you up on that sometime."

Dorian and Amanda followed Chantry from the room and down the stairs. Sabrina stared at them from her window watching them unload boxes.

Brad slid up behind her wrapping his arms around her waist. "What are you thinking?"

"Brad, I don't know what to think! It's all too much. I can't believe my mom's been in on this these past few months. No wonder she's been gone so often!" She stepped away from his hold.

"You think you'll be happy here?"

"Absolutely–how could I not be?"

"I was excited for you to get here this morning. I knew you would appreciate it."

"Brad, can I ask you a dumb question?"

"Shoot."

"Are we rich?"

"Not by California standards, just upper middle class."

"If this is upper middle class then my whole life has been spent in the ghetto."

"You're funny you little nut!"

"Was your house in California this fancy?"

"No. We'd have had to have the *Beverly Hillbillies'* oil money for that. Our house in California cost twice as much as this one but it's only one-third of the size. It's a nineteen-fifties style rambler. Ironic huh?"

"You've lived here since I met you?"

"Yes but it wasn't done. The decor just started getting pulled together the last couple of weeks. Every night when I got home from being with you another room would be decorated. I was having a great time exploring."

"But you never once looked down your nose at our house. We must have seemed terribly inferior to you."

"How superficial do you think I am? Don't be ridiculous! Your house has character. *You have character!* Dad was impressed by your mom's ability to make due and be creative with limited space and re-sources. He knew she would be a great manager and appreciate every single thing he could provide for her. 'She's not high-maintenance, Son. She's a keeper,' Dad said more than once."

"Brad, if we're not rich, are we drowning in debt? I don't mean to be nosy but if I need to chip in on the cost of my computer, or my bed, or something, then I will. I have a bit of money tucked away in my college fund."

Brad's head tipped back in a hearty chuckle. He reached out to lightly pinch the freckles dancing on Sabrina's nose. "Save your money, Honey! There's a principle which my Dad has picked up from your church. He won't start projects unless he has money to finish them. We're not in debt."

"Then we *are* rich, I don't care what you say!"

"Okay, whatever," Brad said shaking his head.

"What does Dorian do, anyway?"

"He's an architect. He's landed some big projects the past few years. He always invests in his work. He says it keeps him striving for excellence on any project. Some of the investments have paid off pretty well. I'm not bragging but Dad's made some smart moves, financially speaking.

"Even with the economy as shaky as it is? Did he lose a lot?"

"He gained more than he lost."

"That's lucky." Sabrina once again peered from her window, studying the progress in the driveway. Sabrina opened her window and called out a farewell to Chantry, "Don't let that hot truck go to your head! And wear your seat belt!"

Chantry waved a hand at Sabrina. "Don't be so bossy!" he hollered up at her before climbing in his truck and driving away.

CHAPTER FIFTEEN

The ocean breeze was cooler than Sabrina expected for the tenth of July. A tiny shiver crawled down her back spilling to her arms. *Or am I just nervous?* She checked her reflection in a shop window along the harbor. Dorian had bought Sabrina a simple white dress. It was shorter than Sabrina was used to with the hemline five inches above the knee, but compared to California standards she felt as trussed up as a pioneer. It was casual, yet elegant. Dainty rhinestone flip flops made walking comfortable. Sabrina wove daisies into her upswept hair. She felt dressy but not over-done.

Amanda was stunning! Sabrina had swept her hair up also. Tiny white roses and pearls peeked between blond cascades of curls. She wore a white suit, delicately tailored to compliment her petite body. White satin pumps clicked along the cement as she walked. She wore the diamond and pearl jewelry Dorian had given her and Sabrina learned that they were, indeed, genuine. Sabrina fashioned a bridal bouquet for her mother to carry. It was an elegant cluster of white roses, bridal wreath, and baby's breath. The monochromatic white on white color scheme was sophisticated.

Dorian led his bride by the hand, weaving her between the shops along the harbor and toward the pier. He had planned the wedding to take place at sunset. The fiery rays lit the horizon in a brilliant burst of tangerine and crimson. The reflection seared the ocean's surface making it blaze passionately.

The paintbrush in Sabrina's mind dabbed and mixed colors to indelibly capture the moment forever.

Captain Sparling waited at the end of the pier, along with the photographer, Jaques. The Manning's and Ashley's had spent much of the afternoon with him posing for family pictures along the coast. Flashes zapped at the family as they took their places before the captain. Jaques must have snapped a thousand photos.

The ceremony was simple, not taking more than ten minutes. Sabrina's heart flip-flopped as she realized this was the real thing. Her mother was now Amanda Manning. Captain Sparling said, "You may kiss the bride." Dorian's happiness was evident as he pulled Amanda to him in a gentle embrace, kissing her softly. Eyebrows shot up when Amanda grabbed Dorian around the neck, pulling him down for a real smacker. Brad laughed but Sabrina's cheeks burned with the sunset. *Mother!*

Captain Sparling interrupted the newlyweds. "Congratulations Dorian. You've found yourself a jewel among women." The men clapped each other on their backs. "Mrs. Manning, may I also congratulate the bride?" Captain Sparling requested cordially. He bent down; giving Amanda a hug then kissed her graciously on both cheeks.

Brad stepped forward. Dorian reached for his hand and began pumping it up and down then tugged Brad closer, crushing him with a father's embrace. "Good job Dad."

"Thank you, Son."

Dorian addressed Sabrina in the same manner Captain Sparling had done with Amanda, with a polite hug and cordial kisses on each cheek. "Welcome to my family."

Sabrina returned the affection but didn't know what to say so she just smiled and nodded. Amanda then grabbed Sabrina by the wrists. "I love you, Bree!"

"I love you too, Mom. I hope you'll be happy." She leaned down to plant a kiss on her mother's petal-soft cheek. "You're not setting a very good example for me," she whispered playfully in Amanda's ear.

"Forgive me, but I'm *not* sorry!"

Sabrina smiled at her mother. "Have a fun honeymoon."

Amanda's cheeks colored. "You behave yourself and be careful. Call me if you need to okay?"

"I'm not calling you! I'm sure I'll be fine. I'll see you in a few days."

"Brad's promised to take good care of you."

The group wandered down the pier toward the shore. A yacht, *the Pacific Rose*, was docked close by. "Mrs. Manning, it will be my pleasure to carry you over the threshold," Dorian said gallantly.

"What? We're honeymooning on a *yacht*?"

"Won't it be wonderful?" Amanda squealed and laughed excitedly as Dorian lifted her into his arms. "Bye kids," Dorian called. "Don't wait up."

Sabrina suddenly felt like a trespasser on the unfolding scene. "Bye," she called, hurrying her pace toward the lights of the harbor. Brad quickened his step to match her stride.

"So...that was...fun."

"I can't believe your Dad's taking her honeymooning on a yacht! Could anything be more romantic?"

Brad shrugged. "Come on, Sabrina. I'm taking you to my favorite restaurant." Brad's hand clasped Sabrina's. Her mood was too strange to disengage the handhold. The ocean was breathtaking and now as the sun and moon changed places in the sky, the water deepened to black. Dark waves washed against the boats in the marina and rippled beneath a network of docks and walkways. Harbor lanterns shimmered on the surface creating a magical, mystical atmosphere. The air seemed charged with some unexplainable energy. Of all the bodies of water which seemed to affect Sabrina, the ocean was definitely the most intoxicating of them all.

Brad and Sabrina glided past several buildings then skimmed the steps to El Torito.

An attractive hostess in a black mini skirt greeted the pair warm-ly. Brad slipped a twenty dollar bill into her hand. "Window seat," he requested. She smiled and led the two to a cozy table with an incredible vista.

The windowed wall overlooked the dark water below and lamp-light jittered in dizzying patterns. "It's gorgeous! What a view! Brad, I'm afraid this trip is going to ruin everyday life for me from now on."

The blue eyes smiled at her. "I'm glad you like it. Everything on the menu is good, and I mean *everything*, but you've got to try the fresh guacamole."

"I'm not sure I like guacamole."

"You'll like this," he promised. "I also recommend the tortilla soup."

"I'm not sure I like tortilla soup."

"Trust me," he said, one hand reaching out to hers. Sabrina met his gaze and felt zinging tingles tangle up and down her spine.

A waiter appeared. "My name is Mauricio. Can I get you started with drinks and an appetizer?"

"Yes," Sabrina said. "I'd like your soup with guacamole." Mauricio's eyes blinked a couple of times.

Brad stifled a laugh. "We'd like two virgin pina coladas, torti-lla soup, and an order of chips and guacamole. That should get us started."

"I'm an idiot! From now on you order everything, because re-questing anything more sophisticated than a six inch sandwich at Subway taxes my mind."

Brad reached out for her other hand. "You're beautiful--taxed mind and all. That dress is perfect on you. I think Jaques took a mil-lion pictures of us today just because he had a thing for your legs."

"Oh stop!" Sabrina giggled at the fun-loving boy sitting across the table.

Mauricio reappeared, wheeling a small cart. He sat two beautiful icy drinks, complete with mini umbrellas in front of them. He then took avocados, peeled and pitted them in one sleek movement. He mashed them in a dish then added fresh salsa and seasoned it with salt and pepper. His fingers could fly as fast as Vandaline's when making napkin art. He presented the guacamole to them, waiting for Brad's nod of approval. He then delivered a basket full of warm chips. "I'll be back with the soup," he said courteously.

"He's not quite as efficient as Connie, but he'll do," Brad announced.

Sabrina's head bobbed as she chuckled. She loaded a chip conservatively, staring suspiciously at the green stuff. She popped it in her mouth. *Delicious!* "That's good," she said hungrily, grabbing another chip and super-dunking it. "I don't even care much for avocados."

"These are fresh. It makes a huge difference!"

Sabrina took a sip of her pina colada. "This is good too–very refreshing! Why would anybody spoil it with rum?"

Brad shrugged. "Pirates like it."

Mauricio placed colorful mugs of soup on the table. "Would you care for grated cheese, Senorita?"

Sabrina nodded, watching him rapidly grate yellow slivers of mellow cheese into the steaming soup. *This is service!* Sabrina tried a bite and again her eyes lit up. "Brad, I don't think I've ever enjoyed a meal so much." She sat back against the booth, crunching on a chip, and staring at the water sloshing against the harbor. "I love you," she said without thinking.

Brad swept Sabrina from the restaurant with one arm around her waist. Instead of leading her to the car, the couple strolled along the harbor. Their eyes scanned the waves, looking for any twinkle of light from *the Pacific Rose*. A few visible glimmers shone from boats here and there, but of course it was impossible to identify the honeymooners.

Sabrina's artistic sensibilities were keenly soaking up the sights and sounds of the ocean at night. A cool breeze stirred goose bumps on her arms. Brad draped his jacket across Sabrina's shoulders. The smells of the harbor were varied. Tantalizing aromas drifted from the restaurants dotting the marina but they were dull in comparison to the briny odor of the sea. The water was black and the sky was black. Small stars winked from the heavens while pale lights flickered and blinked from bobbing ships, sailing it seemed, on the edge of the earth. The pattern from below was reflected above--or was it vice-versa?

"It's hard to tell where the ocean ends and the sky begins," Sabrina said.

"I feel dizzy when I study it too hard."

"This is the stuff good poetry is made of."

"It's intense isn't it?"

"Yes," Sabrina said, feeling heady and a little dizzy herself.

Brad pulled Sabrina beyond the harbor lights and onto the sandy coastline of Doheny State Park. The beach was deserted, yet Sabrina wondered why the whole city wasn't out sitting in the sand, watching the tide ebb its way up on the shore. Brad pulled Sabrina to him. She had resisted his touch and not returned his declarations of love since the couple had kissed goodbye at the river six days before, but the ocean's magic seemed to be casting a sorcerer's spell over her firm resolve, numbing it.

She had surprised herself at dinner, blurting "I love you" to the boy. Sabrina had hoped she was getting a better grip on herself than that, but now realized she didn't have a grip on anything—not with the surf roaring in her ears; not with the moonlight dripping like anesthetic in her veins. She shook her head slightly, trying to clear her thoughts but the intensity of Brad's blue eyes seemed to cloud her vision even more. "I'm messed up."

"Me too," Brad whispered, his mouth searching for hers in the darkness. The kiss was an explosion of pent-up emotions bursting with fiery sparks of raw sensation. It was neither tender, nor gentle, but fiercely wild. Sabrina felt her lips bruising beneath the passion yet she strained hungrily for more. Brad pulled back. "Sabrina—"his voice wavered.

Sabrina took a step backward. Her heart was pounding in her ears, drowning out the surf. She stared at Brad. He was breathless and appeared somewhat shaky. His eyes looked black and as wild as the sea. *Or are they just a reflection of my eyes--like the ocean mirrors the sky tonight?* The idea was sobering. She took another step away from the boy; still their eyes locked, neither one speaking. A gull circled the two, gliding gracefully to the sand. Little eyes blinked at the gasping statues, intrigued.

A wave lapped around Sabrina's feet, startling her. The tide had crept up on her unaware. She dodged a second wave, springing herself further onto dry sand. "That snuck up on me," she said.

The statement was fitting given the scenario. "Uh-huh. I guess we'd better go before we're both carried away."

Sabrina understood the meaning of his words. She took another step and the gull skittered sideways, flapping awkwardly. *"Go home! Go home! Go home,"* it shrieked, disappearing into the night. Brad took Sabrina's hand leading her along the moonlit shore, not saying anything more.

Brad's car wound through the streets of Dana Point, finding the way to the old driveway.

Lights were streaming from the windows. Brad scowled. "Who's here?"

Fear prickled down Sabrina's neck. "Why are all the lights on? Mom checked them before we left the house this afternoon."

"Stay here while I go check it out," Brad commanded, climbing out of car and sauntering warily toward the house. Sabrina grabbed her cell phone from her bag, ready to call for help if necessary. Suddenly the front door burst open and a woman stepped from the house.

"Where the hell have you two been?" Vidalia Davies thundered.

Brad stopped dead in his tracks but Sabrina leapt from the car, relief washing over her like a tidal wave. "Vidalia!" she squealed, "What are you doing here?"

Brad scooped his chin from the pavement pulling himself together. "Hello Vidalia," he greeted courteously. "I was afraid we had an intruder."

"Nope, just me. Get inside you two, it's late. Don't you little idiots know what time it is?" Sabrina and Brad followed Vidalia into the house. "How was the wedding anyhow?"

"It was good," the kids said in unison.

"Well it's the best thing. I'm so happy for Amanda," Vidalia blustered. "She's a young, vibrant, beautiful woman. She deserves some happiness."

Sabrina stared at her friend. "Why aren't you home tending the shop?"

"Hmph!" Vidalia scoffed. "That's a welcome if ever I heard one."

"I'm happy to see you, I'm just surprised--that's all."

"You should have just come to the wedding," Brad added pensively.

"Awe, that was just for the four of you. It needed to be that way. Well, yesterday I had a little visit with your folks," Vidalia said. Brad looked stricken, his eyebrows arching high with un-asked questions. Sabrina's brows furrowed.

"What do you mean, Vidalia? A talk about *what*?"

"Oh, wipe those expressions off your innocent little faces. Your secret is safe with me but I leveled a proposition at Amanda and she took it."

"What proposition?"

"Old Vidalia's rather crafty. You see, Amanda was fluttering all kinds of orders and advice about the shop and just how to run things for the next several days. I spoke right up and said, 'Now don't you worry about a thing. Vandaline's learned the business really good the last few days.' Your mother looked confused and so I illuminated, 'I know that you want me to take care of things while you're gone, but who's taking care of Sabrina?' Dorian gets all puffed up and crows, 'Brad, that's who! He can show Sabrina around California. They'll have a great time.' I nodded my head, listening, and then I said, 'Sure, they'll have a super time. I just hope all the neighbors don't get the wrong idea, or anything. I wouldn't want a shadow cast over Sabrina's reputation.' You should have seen their faces! The realization that you two *could* be more than brother and sister, casually thrown together by the tangles of fate, settled in on them. Amanda seemed a trifle-bit pale, so I said, 'Nothing to worry about of course, it's just that I don't want the neighbors to talk of scandals where there are none.' I told Amanda that my sister Valyncia was coming to stay with mother for a couple of weeks, and she could help Vandaline manage the shop. I generously offered my services as chaperone. Dorian gave me a house key and a healthy expense account. I flew in on the eight-thirty."

Brad studied Vidalia. He didn't yet know her well enough to love her. "So, basically you're baby-sitting?" His charm was tucked away, eyes firing daggers.

"Do you need baby-sitting?" Vidalia asked directly.

"No, I *don't*."

"I do," Sabrina volunteered quietly.

Brad rolled his eyes and shrugged. "Okay, well...goodnight."

"What's on the docket for tomorrow?" Vidalia called to the retreating boy, undeterred by his mood.

Brad whirled around, a mix of emotions played across his face. It wasn't in his nature to be surly or disrespectful. He truly understood the wisdom in Vidalia's mission yet his honor felt questioned and his masculine ego was bruised. He bit his lip, eyes casting from Sabrina to Vidalia. He let out a controlled breath. "We're going to Catalina Island." He coaxed a gallant smile.

"Oh," Vidalia clucked. "Catalina Island? I always wanted to go there! It's the island of romance, you know." She winked at the boy in the hall. "I'll be sure and bring my sunbonnet."

"You do that. I'm sure it will be very romantic; just the *three* of us," Brad said, retreating behind his bedroom door.

Vidalia turned to Sabrina. "Are you okay?"

"Yes," Sabrina nodded. "I'm glad to see you Vidalia. I don't trust myself. I'm not as indestructible as I thought I was."

"None of us are." Vidalia cocked her head off to the side. "Your lips are puffy so I know you've been kissing that boy."

"If Brad hadn't come up for air, I would have still been kissing him," Sabrina admitted, crimson rising in her cheeks by her own admission. "Tonight I didn't even care."

"Well, Sabrina, if that's the case, then I'm mighty damn glad I showed up."

Chapter Sixteen

The *Catalina Express* sliced the surface of the ocean. Vidalia rode comfortably inside the ferry boat but Sabrina was hungry for an adventure on the water so she stood on the front deck, facing the wind and salty spray. A ponytail streamed from a pink ball cap. She kept a tight hold on the brim preventing the wind from whipping it away. Brad stood behind her, scanning the waves for any sign of ocean life. "There," he said to Sabrina, pointing out a couple of dolphins.

Sabrina spied the frolicking pair. They dove and splashed alongside the boat for a while. Sabrina clapped her hands at their antics. "I love them! They want to race us I think."

Brad pointed again, "Look, there's more over there." Sabrina's eyes focused in on the spot. Ripples splashed, dorsal fins crested, and silvered bodies arched and flipped from the water. Other passengers were calling to each other. The captain's voice called, "We seem to have driven into a pod of dolphins. We'll cut the engine and watch them for a minute." Tourists applauded heartily.

Sabrina tried to count the dolphins, but they seemed to be multiplying rapidly, and it was impossible to track them in the waves. *One hundred? Two hundred?* Brilliant silver arches danced from the water as nine dolphins simultaneously surfaced, jolting into the air in a dynamic un-choreographed flip. The crowd cheered. "That's what you call water ballet," the captain commented over the loud speaker. "I present to you the synchronized swimmers of Orange County."

A dolphin glided right beneath the deck, turning on her side, showing off her baby. The miniature dolphin swam against his mother. He rolled over and over in the water, waving a tiny flipper, entertaining the masses. "They're friendly!" Sabrina squealed. "They look right at you and smile." Sabrina watched the pair dart beneath the bow.

Brad squeezed her arm, "Oh man! *Look!*"

It seemed that another pod of dolphins had surfaced from deeper playgrounds, now connecting, chattering, and splashing all around the craft. "Ladies and Gentlemen, we seem to have engaged what is called a *super-pod* of dolphins," the captain announced. "My spotter estimates there are about twelve hundred dolphins currently encircling the *Catalina Express*."

Sabrina watched the dolphin follies with wonder. "Amazing," she breathed. Silvered arches twirled and flipped, soared, and dove, again and again. The water was their stage. Bubbles frothed and foam surfed on ripples.

Brad was snapping pictures as furiously as he could. "I'm afraid I'm missing more action than I'm capturing," he said with a tenor of frustration.

"Glad we didn't go to Sea World today. Imagine all of those people hoping to see a show like this one." She held her phone up, recording a video of the unplanned spectacle.

"I was going to take you on a dolphin safari tomorrow but now I don't need to. It would be anti-climactic anyway. I've never been in a super-pod before. This is unbelievable."

Vidalia elbowed her way to the ship's bow. Sabrina could hear her coming. She envisioned her dear friend shoving fat men in Bermuda shorts and stepping on small children to catch a better glimpse of the grand dolphin finale. She bustled between Brad and Sabrina. Her plump hands gripped the deck railing to steady herself. "It's thrilling!" Vidalia triumphed. "It's gosh-all-heck-a-mighty-shoot-dinging, darn-tooting, for hell's sakes, sure a sight!"

A crowd of people within earshot of the comment laughed and snorted at the enthusiastic dolphin-watcher. Vidalia didn't notice.

She was leaning over the railing, pointing at every one she could see. "See them jumping, there! Look, now, over there! Heck-a-heck-a, hit the deck-a," she chanted, "What a stunt! Did you see *that*? Just imagine what these dolphins could do if they *practiced*!" The merry sight-seekers laughed again at Vidalia.

Sabrina snuck a look back at Brad. He was beet red and falling back a person or two in the crowd, careful not to fully own knowing Vidalia. *Chicken!* Sabrina flashed a smile at the good looking boy. He met her gaze and winked.

The water was a crescendo of activity. It was alive with dancing dolphins, gliding to their own rhythm, creating a joyous symphony of movement. Skimming, swimming, rolling, splashing, diving, flipping, arching, teasing, dolphins flirted boldly with the audience. Quickly and quietly the ripples began to dissipate. The dance was over and the water cleared. *The Catalina Express* rumbled to life once again.

"Can I help you back inside?" Brad asked Vidalia.

"Hell no. A person might miss something in there."

"It's still about forty-five minutes to Avalon," he persuaded.

"That's alright," Vidalia chirped. "I brought my sea legs with me today."

The trio faced the wind, watching for anything, as the boat conquered the waves and closed the distance toward the tiny island. Catalina donned from an ocean mist. It was smaller than Sabrina expected. As the boat drew closer to the dock she could pick out familiar landscapes from books and old movies. Palm trees draped lazily along the coastline of Avalon, but it was easy to see they weren't indigenous to the whole island. "It reminds me of the Poconos," one lady said, lounging against the rail. She spoke condescendingly, checking her lipstick in a small mirror.

"Well aint that grand?" Vidalia asked the high-brow traveler.

The woman scowled down her nose at Vidalia. "You've never been there, I presume," she whiffed.

149

"Naw!" Vidalia blasted. "I make it a point to avoid all those *hoity-toity* places, if you please." The woman shoved her sunglasses down on her nose and moved further away from Vidalia. "I'd like to throw her overboard," Vidalia muttered to the kids. "She thinks she's the queen of the travel channel, I see."

"Don't let her bother you," Sabrina soothed, rubbing Vidalia's back.

"*You've never been there, I presume,*" Vidalia mimicked the woman, throwing her head haughtily to one side.

"Let's go have some fun, shall we?" Brad asked. "Come on, Vidalia; escort me ashore, will you?"

Vidalia smiled warmly at Brad. "Don't mind if I do! Thank you," she draped her arm through Brad's and fluttered a snooty wave in the woman's direction. Brad tugged her along, patiently guiding her from the ramp.

"What now?" Vidalia asked.

"I want to look around in the shops," Sabrina said.

"I'm going to load up on souvenirs my own self," Vidalia chirped.

"I'm taking the two of you to a really great restaurant for lunch, the El Galleon. It's my favorite one on Catalina."

"How do you know so much about where to eat?" Sabrina asked.

"Not having a mother, that's how! I used to bring myself out here a lot when I was a kid."

"You're kidding?"

"No. Dad would be working, so I'd be all alone. I'd ride my bike to the harbor and buy myself a ticket, and come here."

"All by yourself?" Vidalia asked, eyebrows working together. "That's lonesome."

"Expensive too." Sabrina added a quick tally in her head.

"Not too bad. Dad used to keep a jar of money in his bedroom. It was where he always put loose change and any stray dollar bills. That was my money cache. I was supposed to use it for lunches, or whatever I needed. I'd let the money accumulate for a few weeks and then I'd come and spend the day. I probably came four or five times every summer since I was nine. I pretended I was the captain, sometimes I pretended to be a pirate. I made a friend on the Island. His name's Tony Raduccio. We used to explore the coves together. We even made ourselves a hideout."

The little group crossed the street. "I'll slow you two down. What time do you want me to meet you for lunch?"

"One o'clock?"

"Sure. Behave yourselves," Vidalia muttered, entering a gift shop.

"Come with me," Brad urged, tugging Sabrina's arm up the street. I want to introduce you to Tony." Brad led her to a small sport shop.

A bell chimed. A dark haired kid was leaning over a counter, fixing a fishing reel. "Hey," he said, not looking up. "Welcome. Just chill out and I'll be with you in a second."

"Hey man," Brad said.

Tony's head jerked up. "Hey hey! It's Brad, my buddy from the mainland. How you doin'? I haven't seen you all year." He came around the counter, firing a series of motions at Brad in a secret handshake. The moves were too complicated for Sabrina to master. "Who's the babe?" Tony asked, appraising Sabrina from head to toe."

"This is Sabrina, isn't she cute?"

"*Cute* is not the word, Man! This chick's smoking' hot. No wonder you haven't been hanging out with me lately. Sizzle, sizzle, fry, fry! This girl's enough to make me cry," Tony chanted. He jutted a dirty hand out to Sabrina. "I'm Tony. I'm flamboyant."

Sabrina's eyebrows rose at the random scrap of information. "Thanks, I'll remember that," she said, shaking his hand warily.

"That means he's *full of it*," Brad interpreted.

"So Manning, are you spending all your time at Disneyland or what?"

"Actually," Brad said, examining a new pole from a nearby rack, "I live in Utah, now."

"*Jump back!* No freaking way--Utah?"

"That's where I picked her up at," Brad explained, pointing to Sabrina.

"You two shacked up?"

"Sort of," Brad stalled. He was enjoying the expression on Tony's surprised face. "Our parents just got married."

"We're on our honeymoon," Sabrina blurted. She blushed instantly. "I mean–um...our parents are on *their* honeymoon. We are just, uh...never mind." Her head tossed from side to side, wishing she had kept her mouth shut. *Idiot! Stupid!* The boys laughed at her discomfort. Brad winked affectionately at her.

"Utah," Tony shook his head. "That sucks, dude. Are you a Mormon?"

"I'm not but Sabrina is."

"Far out! I thought Mormon girls wore gray bonnets and aprons. They like to churn butter, right? That's how I pictured them–I must have been tripping out, huh?"

"I haven't met anybody dressed that way. You must be thinking of the Pilgrims," Brad teased.

"I've never made butter," Sabrina said defensively.

Tony's eyes glinted toward Sabrina. "I'm suddenly eager to be baptized, Honey. What do I need to do to join your church?"

"You'll have to give up beer," Brad said.

152

"No way? Dude, that's harsh. I work in a bait and tackle shop. I drive a golf cart to work every day and you want me to give up beer?"

"If you ever get to Utah, come look me up!"

"I'll do it, I sure will."

"Tell your Mom hi for me."

"She's working the town tour today; better tell her yourself. Nice meeting you Sabrina. Hey, did Manning ever tell you about the time we tried smoking seaweed?"

Sabrina bit her lip. "No, he didn't. I guess he must have missed that one."

"It was freaking hilarious," Tony laughed. "Remember, Manning? You turned green and started to cry. You were afraid you'd turn into a donkey because that happened to Lampwick and Pinnochio on Pleasure Island."

"You're the bright mind that rolled the smoke, you fiend!"

"How old were you?" Sabrina asked.

"Ten."

"That was dumb," Sabrina said, shaking her head.

"It was great!" Tony bellowed, still chuckling at the memory. "Are Mormons allowed to smoke genuine seaweed cigars in Utah?"

"I doubt it," Sabrina answered. "It tends to stain our aprons."

Tony and Brad laughed raucously, giving each other the razzle-dazzle handshake one last time. Sabrina waved goodbye to Tony and waited outside of the shop.

When one o'clock rolled around Vidalia was waiting on a bench outside of the *El Galleon* fanning herself. She had a couple of sacks on her arm. "Hi, Vidalia," Sabrina called. "Have you finished shopping?"

"These trinket shops all have the same stuff in them; different shops, but all of the same merchandise. If I'd have known that in the beginning I'd have saved myself walking in every one. I got a great shirt for Vandaline. Want to see it?" Vidalia pulled a red t-shirt from the sack and held it up for Sabrina's inspection.

"Pirates just want me for my booty" was printed across the front. Sabrina laughed. "Vandaline will never wear it."

"I know and it will distress her because she will think I'll expect her to," Vidalia confessed wickedly. She pulled a second shirt from her bag. "I also bought another one. It says, *"Be a fruit and avoid the scurvy."* Look at the picture!"A drunken banana with an eye patch was wearing a pirate scarf and an earring. It was just plain stupid yet annoyingly humorous at the same time.

"It's hard to beat good taste like that," Brad mused.

Lunch was pleasant and it was cool inside the El Galleon. "So everybody on Catalina Island drives golf carts, huh?"

"Yeah, there's only two hundred permits for regular cars even allowed on the island," Brad explained. "But where is there to drive to anyway? The roads are narrow and steep, and there's really limited parking."

"What are you kids doing after lunch?"

"Taking you on a semi-submersible submarine," Brad said.

Sabrina's eyes lit up. "You really are showing us a good time. Vidalia and I will be so spoiled we won't be able to stand around poking flowers in vases anymore."

"Turnabout is fair play," Brad recited. "You showed me around the Porterville Cemetery. I'm showing you around Catalina Island."

"Oh yeah–that's really even!"

"What in the hell did you take him to a cemetery for?" Vidalia quizzed. "That's odd, even in my book."

Brad dismissed Vidalia's comment with the wave of his hand. "It was great," he said, shaking his head. His foot reached out and tapped Sabrina's playfully. "Ladies, we've got to scoot. We have an Avalon bus tour in five minutes."

"We do?" Vidalia and Sabrina asked.

"Well, there's only so much you can do in Catalina, besides drink beer and drive golf carts, so I think we should pack our day with activities. We catch the *Express* back to Dana Point at six. We can watch the sunset from the deck, but I'm warning you, it gets really cold."

Sabrina's eyes shot up when the bus rolled in. It was a topless tour bus that had once seen better days. A blue cloud of smoke belched behind the monstrosity as it lurched to a halt before the ten or twelve waiting passengers. The driver quickly sucked a few last puffs from a cigarette then ground it under her boot as she dismounted the beast.

"My name is Regina," she said warmly. Her voice was full if gravel and grit but it fit her weathered, raw-boned face. "I'll be your guide and driver. Step up now and give me your tickets. No tickets no tour."

Brad reached a hand out with the tickets. "Hi, Mom!"

Regina jerked sunglasses from her nose to study him. A large smile cut through the leathered lines of her face. "Brad! You made it back to us! How are you?" She threw her arms around his waist. "Does Tony know you're here? Oh it's so good to see my boy. You're a handsome devil you are! Regina looked at Vidalia and Sabrina. "Who are they?"

Brad put his arm around Vidalia. "Regina, I'd like you to meet my girlfriend, Vidalia."

Vidalia perked right up at the boy's comment. Regina shook Vidalia's hand eagerly. "It's about time I met you, take good care of my boy. I'm pretty partial to him."

"And this is my new sister Sabrina."

"New sister? Your father got married? Wonderful! Brad, you have a mother now!" Regina hugged the boy again, patting his back.

"This is Tony's mom, Regina Raduccio," Brad explained.

"I figured," Sabrina said. "Nice to meet you." Vidalia and Sabrina climbed onto the rickety tour wagon. Regina held Brad out at arm's length to look him over again.

A fidgety tourist, who had been waiting behind Brad, stirred impatiently. Regina scowled at the man. "Take a Prozac! You don't like my line? Find another line!" The man's eyes bugged and his face turned red, but he quickly straightened up and waited for the tour guide to finish talking to her young friend.

"Utah?" Sabrina heard Regina say to Brad. "You be sure and write to Mama Raduccio, won't you? Now look me in the eye and tell me what I've always told you."

Brad laughed. "Seriously? Okay...never play poker with a man named Ace."

"That's right! Now you remember that and life will be easy. Give me one more hug."

Brad climbed onto the bus and took a seat with Vidalia. "Hey Darling," he said, sliding his arm around her shoulders. Vidalia erupted into giggles. Brad was making the most of his so-called babysitter. He knew how to turn on the charm and soon he'd have Vidalia eating out of the palm of his hand. Sabrina's gaze trailed to Regina. She felt that Brad's pull towards Catalina had more to do with her than Tony. She pictured Brad as a young boy, so hungry for a mother's affection. Regina was genuine and kind. What else mattered?

"She makes good ravioli," Brad was explaining to Vidalia. "Every time I'd come to the island, she'd fix it for lunch. Once she sent some home a plastic container for me and Dad's supper. Tony always lugged me home with him. It was better than eating at the restaurant alone, although I did that too, if Regina was working. I used to pretend she was really my mom. In school, whenever I had to make something for Mother's Day, I made it for her. In seventh grade I had to write an essay about my mother. I didn't have a clue about her so I just wrote about Regina and got an *A*."

The tour was interesting. Sabrina held her breath a time or two when the bus rolled down the hill, waiting for Regina to catch a gear. She wasn't keen on the idea of a four hundred foot plunge into the ocean! Regina's knowledge of the quirky town was top-notch. She drove the bus by Zane Grey's home, Wrigley Gardens, and other worthy sights. The tour even included a drive by of Avalon's famous nine-hole golf course. Regina pointed out the exact site where the Chicago Cubs used to hold held spring training. *Chantry should see this!* All in all it made Sabrina smile.

The submarine tour in the *SS Nautilus* was a funny experience with Vidalia. She kept fidgeting about getting claustrophobia inside the vessel. "I'll feel closed in," she said. "How deep will they take us?"

"It's only a *semi*-submersible," Brad encouraged. "It won't be bad at all."

"I could get sea-sick."

"You won't," Brad said.

The others in the vessel scattered away from Vidalia, just in case. Sabrina noticed a sly smile creep onto her face. *You old rogue! You just did that for more space!* Vidalia spread out comfortably, setting her souvenir sacks on the vacant seats next to her. She settled in and hummed softy while the sub motored to a select place in Lover's Cove. The vessel bubbled downward. The riders could turn in their seats and fire torpedoes of fish food into the water. Vidalia made sound effects from World War II as she launched a feeding frenzy outside her window. Fish of all sizes, shapes, and colors clamored against the glass. The colorful menagerie of ocean life sent little shivers down Sabrina's arms.

When feeding time was over the *SS Nautilus* rose to the surface. "No," Vidalia complained. I wanted to go deeper. I wanted to see an octopus!" She was clearly disappointed.

"I'd better sign you up for deep-sea diving," Brad quipped.

"I'm too claustrophobic for that."

157

The three travelers disembarked from the submarine and walked back toward the *Catalina Express* loading dock. The day was nearly spent. "What time is it?"

"Five twenty," Brad said. "We'll just sit on the pier and enjoy the sights until it's time to load."

Sabrina noticed a ripple in the water. At first she just thought a big fish jumped but then a pair of black eyes blinked at her. "A sea lion! Come here, Vidalia!" The sea lion disappeared into the emerald depths then reemerged a little bit closer. His head poked out of the water. "He's smiling at us! I love dolphins *and* sea lions." Sabrina held her phone out to record another video clip.

Buzz. Sabrina pulled her phone closer to examine her message. "And I love you. Every time I think about that kiss you laid on me last night my knees go weak."

"I love you too and I'm not sure what to do about that right now," Sabrina typed, thumbs flying fast. "I'm a big, fat, hypocrite."

"Hypocrites are special. Hypocrites are my favorite."

Sabrina laughed at Brad's absurdity. "Not really!"

"The politically correct term for hypocrite is Self-excluding Pious American. Please use that term for it sounds much nicer."

"I'll be damned, look at that!" Vidalia called. Another sea lion appeared, dragging a lunch box in his mouth. The two creatures passed the lunch box back and forth, bunting it with their heads. "This is better than the circus!"

One sea lion barked, "Awrv, awrv, awrv," and slapped the lunch box through the air. It zinged between Vidalia and Sabrina's heads. The lion clapped his flippers enthusiastically.

"Let's see what's for supper," Brad teased, unzipping the soggy vinyl box. His expression froze.

"What's in there, a *tuna* sandwich?" Vidalia goofed.

"Drugs," Brad said, biting his lip.

"No way!" Sabrina crossed the cement to look. Sure enough, tiny plastic zip-locked packets full of white powder were crammed inside. Brad pulled his phone from his pocket and dialed the Sport Shop.

"Hey Tony–could you call the authorities and tell them to come to the pier? I've just found a bunch of drugs…I *know* April Fools is over…no I'm not kidding. A sea lion just dredged up a lunch box and flung it at Sabrina's head. I opened it and it's full of cocaine… yeah? Tell them to hurry…because I've got a boat to catch, that's why."

It wasn't long before the area was bustling with excitement. Several officers milled around the pier, asking questions and taking statements. A couple of reporters materialized out of thin air, snapping photos and rolling tape. The snooty woman, who Vidalia had crossed swords with earlier, came snooping over to the scene. "What's going on? What's going on?"

"Curiosity killed the cat," Vidalia intoned.

"I wasn't talking to you!"

"Drugs! Stuff that in your Poconos pipe and smoke it."

CHAPTER SEVENTEEN

The ride from Catalina was choppy and rough. Evening winds were stinging and bitter. Vidalia claimed a seat inside the cabin, along with the majority of worn-out travelers. Sabrina could see her through the window. She was sleeping and her head lolled off to one side uncomfortably.

A few diehards remained on deck. Brad and Sabrina hunkered down, snuggled in a dolphin throw which Sabrina had purchased with her Catalina souvenirs. Brad's arms wrapped securely around her, adding extra warmth and comfort. "Where do you think our parents are?" Sabrina asked, eyes sweeping the vast horizons of the Pacific.

"They were docked on the other end of Catalina, actually. Two Harbors is a famous docking spot for yachts. They were exploring Isthmus Cove."

"How do you know?"

"The old man sent me a text. He was checking up on us." Brad scrolled through his messages. "See?" He handed the phone to Sabrina. *"We are having a great time. We docked at Two Harbors last night and are taking in Isthmus Cove this morning. Amanda is amazing. I am one happy man!! How is Sabrina? She is beautiful also, so please watch yourself. No funny business!!! Sorry about Vidalia. I didn't mention her to you because I didn't want a hassle."*

Sabrina read the message again then handed the phone back to Brad. "No funny business," she teased, kissing him under the privacy of the blanket. "I'm so bad," she confessed guiltily.

"Bad is good!"

"I just want you to know that as soon as we go back to Morgan, I'm your step-sister and that's *all*. That's the end! I thought I already made that resolve but last night un-did it. I stayed up half the night worrying about it, and finally decided I'd be happier and less stressed, if I didn't fight my feelings on this trip. Apparently the ocean drugs my senses and disables my conscience. You totally sweep me off my feet and I'm at your mercy because I'm in *your* territory, and it's terribly exciting."

"Is that a fact?"

"Yes!" Sabrina lamented. "I wish there were dolphins in my river, but there's not."

Brad laughed. "You funny little nut." He arranged the blanket around them so only their eyes were exposed to the biting wind. "We have to be able to see the sunset."

The western sky was beginning to pink up with mottled clouds of lavender and purple. "It doesn't look real," Sabrina observed. Within moments a tangerine glow splintered the horizon behind the distant, tiny black mass of Catalina Island. The rays streamed upward, engaging the clouds, igniting the purple hues until they burst into flaming crimson. The white wake churning from the boat now gleamed golden in the fiery twilight.

"It's so beautiful. I could never get tired of seeing it. Do you think my mom and Dorian are watching the sunset?"

"Yeah, unless they're busy doing something else," Brad replied. Sabrina threw an elbow into his ribs.

The splendid majesty of the sky's fire began to fade, subtly morphing into shades of worn-out orange. The clouds dimmed to periwinkle then grey. The inky stain of black settled across the water.

"It changes so quickly! It dims from brilliancy and passion to the grays of nothing in such a short time."

"Kind of like us," Brad said soberly. "We're supposed to dim into the *grays of nothing*, too."

"But not tonight...not yet."

An hour later Sabrina was shivering as the wind had eventually crept through the blanket and sept into her bones. "I'm a frozen, wind-blown mess," she moaned, climbing out of the car at the Manning residence.

"A hot shower will fix you right up," Vidalia said.

"Don't you two want to go to dinner?"

Vidalia shook her head. "I'm bushed."

"I'll cook for you but I've got to run to the store first," Brad volunteered. His keys jangled as he unlocked the door.

"Don't bother."

"I am starving!" Brad thundered. "What is it with you women? Let me annunciate it more clearly: I AM STARVING!" Sabrina and Vidalia snickered at Brad's hungry outburst.

"I'll go eat with you but I need a shower first."

"Can you hurry? Your Mom said you needed a steam shower for your suite in our new house because you love showers but she claims you can't hurry."

"How much time do we have before you're dead of starvation?"

"Twenty minutes, tops."

"I'll hurry."

Vidalia switched on the television. "Brad, what channel does the news come on? I wondered if they'd mention the drug thing we got involved in this afternoon."

Brad grabbed the remote and started flipping through stations. "This channel, probably..."

A caveman commercial was on. "I love this one!"

"I know, right?" An *Outback* commercial aired next. "That's cruel," Brad stated, staring lustily at the jumbo *Bloomin' Onion* on the screen. "I'm so hungry."

"That does look tasty."

Brad walked to the kitchen and grabbed a jar of peanut butter and a spoon. He took his place by Vidalia on the couch. "Want some?"

"No thanks. I'm not too hip on peanut butter."

"Survival food."

An anchor woman's face plastered the screen. "We have an interesting story from Catalina Island. Here's Ronald Salisbury with the story."

"Thank you, Giselle. Some tourists at Catalina Island today alerted authorities after finding a lunch box, containing approximately three pounds of cocaine. Sixty-one year old, Vidalia Davies, of Morgan Utah, and two seventeen year olds, also from Utah, had this to say..."

Vidalia's face covered the giant screen. "Well we were just watching a couple of sea lions swimming right here," Vidalia pointed. "One of the sea lions dove down in the water and came up carrying this lunch box. They passed it back and forth like a couple of kids playing catch. Suddenly, one of the sea lions barked and flung it through the air. It nearly hit me in the head! I jerked to one side and it sailed between the two of us..." The camera panned to include Sabrina in the shot then zoomed to Brad, who was talking to the police. Vidalia's voice continued, "He opened the lunch box and saw what was in there. He immediately called to report it."

"Did you know what the powder was?" the reporter asked.

"Hell, I didn't think it was baking soda!"

"Do you think the sea lions knew what they'd found?"

"I didn't ask them," Vidalia said disgustedly. "If you'd like to bark a couple of times and clap your hands together, maybe they'll surface for an interview."

Brad was laughing, slapping his leg. "Vidalia! You are priceless. I didn't know they interviewed you for the news!"

"You were busy answering the officer's questions. That was an idiot reporter! No wonder the media can't seem to cover a political event correctly. They ask stupid questions."

"Did they get your age right?"

"Yes, but why did they go splashing *that* all over Tarnation?"

The reporter continued, "Police ordered the *Catalina Express* not to leave the island until they were finished interviewing the three eyewitnesses. That put the ferry's departure time at six thirty, halting the return trip by thirty minutes. One traveler had this to say..."

The snooty woman's face hogged the screen. Vidalia groaned. "It's such an inconvenience," the woman said. "I've traveled all over and this is a first! I wouldn't have *dreamed* we'd be delayed over something as insignificant as a lunch box. I may have to cancel my dinner reservations."

"Did you realize the lunch box contained illegal drugs?"

"Yes, a rude person pointed that out to me."

Ronald Salisbury's eyebrows shot up. "Well, there you have it. Reporting from Avalon, I'm Ronald Salisbury, now back to you, Giselle."

Vidalia turned off the set. "That high-faluting busybody! I knew I should have shoved her overboard this morning."

"Vidalia, we made the news and Sabrina missed it! How long has she been in the shower?"

"Thirty-five minutes."

"Oh man…"

"Take old Vidalia's advice, get used to it."

Sabrina breezed into the room, seemingly revitalized. She smiled brightly at Brad, "I'm glad to see you're still alive." She had straightened her hair and it hung down her back, glossy and smooth. She was wearing a black skirt, actual heels, and a red blouse. She had taken more pains with her makeup than usual, giving her bewitching eyes a dramatic evening look. "Sorry to make you wait."

Brad looked a little bit stunned. "No problem—it was worth it. You'd better give me minute though, because now *I* have to change."

Ten minutes later Brad strolled down the hall. He wore black dress pants, red shirt and black tie. His hair was washed and freshly gelled. The scent from his cologne faintly wafted into the room. *Oh my gosh!* It was Sabrina's turn to stare.

"I take it you two aren't eating at *Burger King!* It looks more like you're jetting off to the prom together. My feet hurt and I don't want to go anywhere, but I'm worried about the two of you keeping your hands off each other. For one thing," she droned, pointing a finger at Brad, "You smell *good!*" Brad smiled at the baby-sitter. "And you, little Missy," she pointed at Sabrina, "are not helping your cause any. I haven't seen you that *dolled up*, not even for Easter Sunday. I can't blame you for wanting to go out on the town with this kid over here," her thumb jutted back in Brad's direction. "He's adorable and quite the smoothest little charmer I've come across. *But*...what the hell are you thinking? Don't answer that, because I already know--you're *not* thinking! That's the trouble with teenagers—they don't know how to think."

Brad looked pensively at Vidalia. "We were planning on you coming with us, Vidalia...I didn't realize your feet hurt. We'll be glad to bring some food back to you and I'll go to the store tonight and get groceries for breakfast."

Vidalia put a hand up. "Don't try sweet-talking; don't even try to rationalize any of this to me. I understand that you're punch-drunk in love. Look at the two of you! I've never seen a better matched pair. Hell, I can feel your sparks fly clear over here. I have a feeling that even if you had only met each other last night at the wedding, you'd have fallen for each other by today. The chemistry is just there."

Sabrina considered Vidalia's words. She felt they were true. She looked at Brad. He was nodding in agreement. "Fate's been a little bit cruel, and old Vidalia's not completely unsympathetic to your plight. I'm going to let you go out tonight. Live it up! Have a good time! You *need* to get it out of your systems! Just remember that every spell you cast on each other must be broken, and the stronger the spell, the harder the break. If you can walk out of this house, on those terms, knowing full-well that it's going to sting like hell in about a week, then all the more power to you. I want you home by twelve-thirty. I'm not waiting up, I'm not calling, and I'm *not* going to come find you. You both know what I expect. If you break my trust then the rest of this trip will feel like a sentence in Baby Hitler's boot camp. Understand?"

Brad's brows rose. His mouth opened and shut. Sabrina answered, "Yes, Vidalia."

"Now, I'm not as anciently unaware of tripped-out hormones as you think I am. I remember the wild excitement of being young and in love! But I want to give you one piece of advice."

"Okay," Brad gulped. "I'm listening."

"Don't let the heat in your pants melt the sense in your head." Sabrina's cheeks burned crimson, her gaze fixed to the floor. Brad's shock rippled like a seismographic shift reverberating around the room. "Understand?" Vidalia asked.

"Yes." Brad said timidly.

"Sabrina?"

"Yes, Vidalia...but...I can't believe you just *said* that!"

"My grandmother said that to me a long time ago. I know it's shocking, but I doubt you'll forget it. Good night and have a nice time." Vidalia walked to the door and opened it into the balmy night air. Brad and Sabrina filed past her in silence.

The door closed with a quiet thud behind them. Brad guided Sabrina gently down the stairs and to the car. He opened her door, then walked around to his side and climbed in. "Holy crap!"

Sabrina was still blushing at Vidalia's lecture. "I know."

"Holy crap...I've never imagined even God's judgment to feel *that* scathing."

Sabrina giggled. "Well, I guarantee we'll be home by twelve-thirty."

"No wonder you have good morals--growing up with *her* around."

Sabrina bit her lip, careful not to smear the dark raspberry-raisin gloss. "You really look nice, Brad."

"A departure from the casual wind-blown looks of the tourist, huh? You do too."

"I didn't mean to get so *dolled up*, as Vidalia put it. I just looked so awful from the boat trip. My hair was frizzled, my lips chappy, and my nose sun burnt. I just wanted to fix up a little bit better. I knew I was taking too long, but...a girl does have a little pride."

"You look great–in fact I nearly choked to death when you came out of your room."

"Really?"

"I've never seen you in heels before. I kind of have a thing for heels..."

"Most guys do. That's because they don't have to walk around on them."

"They make your legs look amazing. You really are stunning, but...modest at the same time. There's something very alluring about modesty, you know."

"It leaves something to the imagination. *The modest are the hottest*, that's what they say."

"I've never heard that before."

"That's because you haven't lived in Utah long enough. There's a lot of stuff I've got to teach you so you don't start school and go, *Huh? What did I miss?*"

"I've already noticed Mormons speak a different language. Remember three weeks ago; when you said you had a fireside at the steak center? Well, I drove all over Morgan County looking for a steakhouse! The closest thing I could find was Larry's Spring

Chicken Inn. There was nobody in there sitting by the fire side. They don't even have a fire."

Sabrina was laughing at Brad's tale. "Memo to self: take Brad to the *stake* center."

"I thought *Especially for Youth* was a teen clothing store. I can't find it anywhere in the yellow pages, so I'm assuming *that* is something else as well."

"*Especially for Youth* is definitely not a store."

"The other day I heard Amanda telling Dad about the temple. She was talking about doing work for the dead. I immediately thought of someone planting lilac bushes at the Porterville Cemetery."

"You're silly!"

"Dad took me to Morgan High School to see what I needed to do to register. The secretary, um...what's her name?"

"Mrs. MacL'main."

"That's her. Anyway, she said I could be released from school to join the seminary. Dad looked puzzled and I was confused. I said, you mean you want me to become a minister? Then *she* looked confused and said, 'or you can just take auto shop'...I wasn't very excited about either prospect. Mrs. MacL'main wasn't really all that much help."

Sabrina was giggling. "Seminary is an optional religious course that you can take if you'd like to but it's not mandatory. I know there are other options besides auto shop but that's *so* funny! In seminary last year we studied *The New Testament*, so this year we'll be learning about *The Book of Mormon*. If you want to really understand what makes me tick then you might consider taking it. You don't have to be a member of the church."

"You mean something can actually explain what makes you tick? Incredible! Sign me up."

Brad pulled into the harbor parking lot and walked to Sabrina's side to let her out. She was beginning to get the hang of being treated like a lady. Brad took her hand and led her toward The Wind and

Sea. Sabrina laughed at the name. "It's a perfect ending to our whole day!"

Sabrina kept silent during ordering. Brad ordered steak and lobster for two with a side order of crab legs. "I don't know if I like lobster," the girl confessed.

"You'll love it."

"I've never had crab..."

"Sabrina! Trust me. Last night you didn't think you liked guacamole, remember?"

"You think I could forget last night?" she asked coyly, gazing at the blue of his eyes, the strange, heady sensation washing over her again.

Brad grasped her hands. "Baby, I have a question for you."

"Yes," Sabrina breathed, wondering was he could possibly ask with such intensity.

"What's a *Mia Maid*?"

Snort! Sabrina had been sipping her drink through a straw but Brad's question caught her off guard. Strawberry lemonade shot into her sinuses and seemed to spray from every orifice of her face. Lemonade spewed from mouth and nose, and the tangy, misplaced, citrus burned her sinuses causing tears to shoot from her eyes. She coughed, choked, chortled, gasped, and spit, drawing unwanted attention from three tables away. Brad laughed until tears brimmed in his own eyes at the spectacle.

"You *idiot!*" Sabrina hissed, when she could get her bodily functions back under control and muster enough of a breath to speak.

"Me the idiot? You're the one who just showered our whole table with recycled lemonade..."

"I was expecting you to say something really romantic by the look in your eyes. Your face was all intense and then you said," she laughed an irreverent outburst again, 'What's a Mia Maid?' I don't know why I bothered putting mascara on...it's probably all flooded away, along with my blush and lip gloss." She grabbed her bag and disappeared to the restroom to reconstruct her face.

"Welcome back," Brad said when she returned. He was still grinning at her discomfort.

"I have another question for you. I'm giving you plenty of warning on this one."

"Yes?" Sabrina asked, steeling herself for anything.

"Can the *Book of Mormon* really explain all my questions about you?"

"No! I thought it could help but now I see I'm beyond all human understanding. I'm sorry I sprayed you."

"It's okay. It was refreshing."

"I'm sorry I called you an idiot."

"That's okay too, I'm used to it."

The waiter delivered massive trays of food to the table. Sabrina's eyes were huge as she calculated the square mass of food before her. "How can I ever eat all of this?"

"Don't worry I'm hungry enough for both of us." Brad gave Sabrina a course in crab cracking.

"This is tedious," she complained, digging out her first succulent morsel. She swirled it in butter just as Brad instructed then popped it in her mouth. *Mmmm....*"Brad, you were right! Crab is undoubtedly, unmistakably delicious." She zealously attacked the plate, cracking, hunting, digging, prying, poking, butter-swirling, then tasting. "You actually work up more of an appetite while you eat this stuff."

"I've never had so much fun watching anybody indulge themselves in my life! You should star in commercials for the entire shellfish industry."

Sabrina felt as full as a tick as Brad led her from the restaurant. He walked her directly to the car, but instead of going home he drove the car up a winding hill which overlooked the harbor. The couple walked along the bluff, hand-in-hand, studying the splendid scenery below. The tide pounded against the rocky crags creating a low, roaring lullaby.

Brad took his *IPod* from his pocket, and fumbled for the right song. He stuck one earphone in his ear and the other one in Sabrina's. As the song began to play, soft and mellow, he wrapped his arms around her and began to dance. "Vidalia was right," he murmured against her hair, "our own private prom."

Sabrina rested her head against his chest, moving when he moved, swaying when he swayed. The moonlight's golden pathway skipped across the water and shimmered in time with their steps. One song after another they danced with the moon. Brad reluctantly checked his watch. "Well Cinderella, it's time to leave the ball. Unfortunately the clock's just struck midnight."

Sabrina's lips brushed against his mouth softly. "Thank you for my fairy-tale."

Chapter Eighteen

"I can't believe I'm actually here," Sabrina squealed as she followed Brad and Vidalia through the gates of Disneyland. "Brad, why didn't you ever tell me you worked here?"

Brad shrugged. "It just never came up. I worked here four days a week until we moved to Morgan. I was lucky enough to get bumped to occasional help and not dropped completely. That allows me to keep my employee status but still live in another state. I'll be flying out here every so often to work."

Sabrina wondered why she was even surprised. This certainly explained Brad's common references to all things Disney—Cinderella, Mulan, Mushu, Pinnochio, and on and on. He was always quoting the Disney characters and drawing comparisons from fairy tales to real life.

"You'll spend more than you can make," Vidalia pointed out

"I don't want to give it up. It's pretty difficult to get on here."

"What exactly do you do?" Vidalia quizzed.

"I can't tell you," Brad said. "I'm not allowed to discuss it but you'll find out later."

"You're some kind of secret service man for Mickey Mouse?" Vidalia guessed.

"Not quite." Brad was wearing an identification lanyard around his neck. He gave the gals their tickets. "Keep them around your necks so you don't lose them."

"I can't believe I have a season pass!" Sabrina said, full of wonder. "I wanted to come to Disneyland when I was a little girl. Dad promised to bring us the summer he was killed." A Percheron work horse was pulling a street car. Sabrina studied the animal. *Dad would have already liked this place.*

"Look," Vidalia pointed. Honest John Foulfellow the crafty fox, and Gideon, his bungling feline sidekick, leaned against a lamp post. A group of small children looked warily at them.

"They're from *Pinnochio*!" Sabrina cried. "Now Brad, if they give you a ticket to Pleasure Island, don't take it! No more smoking seaweed cigars and making a jackass out of yourself."

"Yes, Mother."

"What a happy place!" Vidalia exclaimed, sweeping her gaze up and down *Main Street USA*. "The music makes me feel like dancing."

"Allow me, if you please," Burt offered, tipping his hat to Vidalia. Mary Poppins smiled sweetly from few steps away. Vidalia's eyes were huge when Burt whirled her around and around in a jolly dance. "That's the way to step in time," he called, tipping his hat once again. He and Mary Poppins linked arms and merrily skipped up the street.

"Thank you, Burt!" Vidalia turned back toward a stunned Sabrina and a delighted Brad. "Hell, I did not see that coming."

"Pinch me! I can't believe I'm really here." Sabrina immersed herself in the gaiety of the magical place. She wanted to search every shop and stomp her foot to every tune. Music was everywhere! "Look at all the hats going by! People really do wear mouse ears here."

"I own about fifty different Disney hats," Brad said. "I collect them."

Brad led the ladies to *The Mad Hatter*. Mickey ears, Minnie ears, Goofy ears, Pluto ears, and Dumbo ears lined the shelves. There were Donald hats, Daisy hats, Robin Hood hats, and Grumpy hats.

Vidalia proudly purchased a red and white polka-dot Minnie cap to help keep the sun from her eyes.

"I'm glad you're a good sport, Vidalia. You look good with mouse ears."

"Which one are you getting?" Vidalia asked.

"I'm not sure I'm ready for ears just yet."

"What's one more freckle on your face anyway?"

"We'll look in all of these shops later," Brad said, pulling Sabrina away from the nostalgic buildings. "I'm too excited to show you the Disneyland that I love. Follow me and don't get lost!" He took Vidalia by the hand, leading her through crowds of people. Sabrina happily tagged after. "We're going to Adventure Land first because I want to get fast passes for Indiana Jones, that will help us avoid a terrible line, then we'll slip up to New Orleans Square and ride Pirates of the Caribbean. I have a little tradition. Pirates of the Caribbean is always my first and last ride at Disneyland."

"Must be your favorite," Vidalia said.

Swarms of people jostled through the park. Sabrina was glad to follow Brad through the maze. "I'm glad you know what you're doing," she called to Brad. "I would be overwhelmed if I was here alone."

"I'm better than Tour-Guide Barbie."

The atmosphere was super-charged! Walt Disney and his skilled associates had spared no expense in creating the magical kingdom. It was truly a fantasy world--an escape from real life. Sabrina was enchanted with the detail and imagination in everything. *Amazing!*

The sun was stifling. Little beads of perspiration dotted Vidalia's forehead as the line snaked toward the entrance of Pirates of the Caribbean. A cool breeze greeted them at the door of the ride. Sabrina was struck with amazement. "Okay Brad, I know that we just entered a building, right? We were outside and we just walked inside, but it feels reversed. It feels like we just walked outside on a summer's night."

"Welcome to the bayou," Brad said.

Employees wearing buccaneer costumes loaded passengers onto to boats. Brad, Sabrina, and Vidalia climbed onto the front seat. The journey was pleasant and Sabrina was swept into another world entirely. The boat sailed past an indoor restaurant—which, again, actually seemed out of doors. Wisteria climbed up white lattice panels resting against a grand, southern mansion. The vines trailed through second-story balcony railings. Japanese lanterns hung from the branches of a sprawling tree, giving illumination to dinner guests seated at tables beneath the leafy canopy. Drab gray and brown moss clung to the network of sturdy limbs which lazily extended over the murky waters of the swampy bayou.

"That's the Blue Bayou," Brad said. "We have reservations there for lunch today."

"You mean we get to eat *there?*" Anticipation dripped heavily from Sabrina's question like moss from the swamp.

The boat floated past an old man rocking on a rickety porch. *Creak. Creak. Creak.* Fireflies danced in the night. An eerie chill of excitement splashed down Sabrina's backbone. The boat skimmed along in the darkness. A voice warned the passengers, "Dead men tell no tales..." Suddenly the craft fell down a small waterfall and then another. It wasn't a scary thrill-ride kind of a fall for it was even better.

Sabrina found herself immersed in a strange entertaining underworld of catacombs, skeletons, haunted curses, pirates, wenches, and treasure. The animatronics and special effects were unreal! Pirates sang, and fought, and battled. They drank, and danced, and chased each other around. *Comical!* Cannons blasted and embers smoldered. The smoke and haze were acrid in Sabrina's nostrils. Vidalia clucked delightedly at every turn and every scene.

"I love this," Sabrina whispered.

"I knew you would. You're such a little pirate your own self."

"I'm not a pirate!"

"You stole my heart away."

"You stole mine first!"

"You're both scurvy pirates, you little bilge rats," Vidalia cackled. "I'm afraid it's going to sting like hell when you walk the plank." She illustrated her point with a sound effect of a body slapping against water.

"Memories are golden," Brad called pleasantly. "I plan on burying mine like a treasure and no one can ever steal them from me. So there, Matey!"

"Don't *Matey* me," Vidalia grumbled good-heartedly. Sabrina was sorry when the boat chugged up the hill to unload its passengers. "Yo-ho! Yo-ho!" Vidalia sang.

The next three days began and ended the same way.

On the third day, just after two in the afternoon, Brad spoke privately with Vidalia. She nodded and cooed excitedly. Sabrina couldn't make out the gist of their conversation. Vidalia glided away. Brad breezed across the street and grabbed Sabrina's arm. "This way, Princess," he said, pulling her toward Tomorrow Land. Sabrina was still confused, not quite sure of her bearings in the park. She thought he was leading her toward Star Tours, but then there was a maze of doorways and stairways, and suddenly Sabrina found herself in a room, far removed from boisterous crowds and bustling activities. She wasn't exactly certain where she was.

"Brad," a woman's voice called.

"Hey Jetta, this is Sabrina."

Jetta stepped forward, invading Sabrina's bubble, inspecting the girl from every angle.

What's going on? Sabrina didn't say a word but she felt claustrophobic with Jetta in her face.

"She'll do just fine, Brad. You sure can pick them! Come into my office." She led the teens through a doorway and into a small space.

"What's up? Why are we here?" Sabrina whispered to Brad.

Jetta arched one brow quizzically. "She doesn't know anything about this?"

"No," Brad answered.

Jetta's other brow raised to meet the height of its twin. Sabrina had never seen anyone's face do that before. "Sabrina, you don't know what's going on?"

"No Mam." Sabrina swallowed. She felt as if she'd been summoned to a principal's office for no good reason.

"Management called..."

"I thought you *were* management," Brad said to the woman.

"Excuse me; *upper* management called," Jetta said, articulating the words carefully. "They said Brad Manning would be bringing someone special in for a cameo crash course. This is highly uncommon."

"What is?" Sabrina's throat was dry.

"Young lady, we have strict standards here at Disney. We go through extensive, and I do mean *extensive*, interviewing and auditioning processes here. Only a very select, very talented few are ever cast as our beloved characters. The most highly sought-after positions are of course, our face characters..." Jetta paused, looking intently at Sabrina. "Jane Porter, I would like you to meet Tarzan."

Sabrina blinked a couple of times, scowling slightly. "I'm sorry, I don't understand."

"*Upper* management says you are to be Jane Porter in the parade tonight. When they speak, who am I to argue? Brad has obviously never clued you in that he is one of our characters, currently cast to play Tarzan. This pleases me because he is under contract not to disclose his particular job here at Disney. He is allowed to say, "I am a *friend* of Tarzan's," but not make actual claims. It is important to maintain the integrity of the Disney magic and all it stands for. Each character lives for itself, not for the actor or actress giving it life. Understand? If someone were to recognize you on the street tomorrow and ask if you were Jane, you would say only, *I am a friend of Jane's.* Jane will continue to live; completely independent of whomever is cast to portray her. You see?"

"Barely," Sabrina said timidly.

"Say it," Jetta demanded.

"I am a friend of Jane's."

"I need you to fill out a contract which says you will not disclose any information about portraying this role. You will conduct yourself within the Disney code of conduct...yada, yada, yada. I'll give you a minute to examine the papers before signing. This is a cameo cast appearance only and you will not be paid for your performance."

Sabrina chanced a look at Brad. He was grinning at her. "We're going to be in the parade? The same one we saw last night?"

"Yes."

"You're a friend of Tarzan's?" Jetta ducked her head to keep from laughing.

"Yes," Brad answered directly.

Sabrina drew in a jagged breath. "You're really good at keeping the rules. You never told me about your *friend.* I'm kind of shocked."

"Tarzan's great guy," Brad confessed. This time Jetta chuckled. "I thought you'd make an awesome Jane Porter. She has a familiar last name...maybe her ancestors hail from Porterville."

"I can't believe I'm going to do this," Sabrina said, signing the contract.

"Great." Jetta retrieved the paper. "You'll spend the next couple of hours with a character coach and then Simi will get you into makeup.

"What have you done to me?" Sabrina asked Brad.

"Trust me," he said winking.

Jetta strolled from the room "I'll send Nickole in."

"How could you give all this up just to move to Morgan?"

179

"My dad needed your mom."

"Were you ripped up?"

"I felt *ripped off* for a couple of days, and then I met you." Brad's words lilted across the room.

Sabrina took deep breath and then closed her eyes tightly for a second. She exhaled slowly. "Let me get this straight. You are used to practically living at Disneyland, yet you enjoyed the tour of Porterville? East Canyon Dam? My Thinking Place? *Unbelievable!* You've probably met world-class artists and animators but you liked my stupid little note cards? You sincerely made a fuss over my art-work? Forget all of the reasons why *I'm* strange—what the heck makes *you* tick?"

"You." He kissed her once, twice, three times before the sound of Nickole's high heels clicked in the hallway.

CHAPTER NINETEEN

"Hi, I'm Nickole," the striking, strawberry blonde said. *She's even smaller than my mother!*

Sabrina reached out to shake her hand. "It's my challenge to help you become an animated character. Welcome to the world of make-believe where fairy-tales spring to life. Come with me." Sabrina followed the pretty girl into the unknown, feeling gargantuan and awkward while walking behind her.

"Nickole, you're very nicely put together...um, are you a cast member here, too?"

"I used to know Tinker Bell," she said without hesitating.

Nickole was a grueling task-master. Sabrina soaked in as much information as she could about Jane Porter; how she moved, talked, looked, and held her head. She wasn't going to have to say anything, but she needed to think like the character. "You *are* Jane," Nickole encouraged. "*Be* Jane. *Feel* Jane!" Again and again Nickole put Sabrina through her paces.

At last Nickole put an arm around Sabrina's waist and gave her a quick squeeze. "Good job Jane. Break a leg! Remember to react to the baboons the same way along the route. Remember how we've choreographed your movements. Each person watching the parade deserves the same energy coming from you. You basically have six expressions, run through them like a continuous film reel. That keeps you fresh and interesting all along the parade route. Little children will be so excited to see the real Jane Porter!"

Her instructions circled in her mind. *What if I forget?* Her heart-beat accelerated. *This is no time for an anxiety attack!* She uttered a silent prayer. Her hands were sweaty and her joints felt stiff and contracted, but she managed to hold it together.

Simi was a work of art! She was an eclectic collection of extreme fashion. Her hair was styled after an exotic bird. Shaggy, staggered lengths of chartreuse and fuchsia hair jutted away from a cropped tangle of jet black. Her makeup was a colorful palette of creativity and self-expression. Graduating sizes of safety pins climbed their way up one earlobe. A florescent orange question mark dangled from the other. She wore a neon yellow mini dress, black fishnet tights, and white go-go boots. Sabrina counted seventeen bracelets in all. A tiny butterfly was tattooed across her throat. "Did that hurt?" Sabrina asked.

"Not really," Simi said casually. "Let's get you into makeup." Sabrina did not want the creature to touch her! *How can an expert in make-up look like that?* She followed Simi with fear and trembling through another doorway.

An explosion of activity was bustling inside the sprawling room. Princesses were evolving before a long, mirrored wall. Sabrina couldn't help but notice the beautiful girls. They were rare and ex-quisite. Plush characters were stuffing themselves inside of hot bulky costumes. There were gallant princes, villains, heroes, and animals. Captain Jack Sparrow stood in one corner, receiving facial hair and heavy kohl eyeliner.

Brad winked at Sabrina. Her mouth opened when she saw him. He was wearing only a loin cloth, standing near the middle of the room. He was receiving a spray tan and airbrushing. His chest, arms, and abs were astonishingly toned and well-defined. *Does he work out every day?* The airbrushing really made his muscles ripple. He got bulkier and more ripped by the second! A Tarzan wig was being woven into his hair. Brad was Brad no longer. He was becoming Tarzan the ape-man.

Quickly Simi worked, applying thick, theatrical foundation on Sabrina's face. Gone were the freckles! Sabrina stared wide-eyed at her reflection. "I've always wondered and now I know," she gasped.

"What?" Simi asked impatiently.

"What I would look like without my freckles. Ordinary foundation doesn't erase them like this."

Simi shrugged. "I'm not using anything *ordinary*. You'll be *okay* as Jane I guess. Your bone structure would have been even better suited for Belle." Simi bobbed her head decidedly. "I would like to have made you into Belle."

Even better! "Seriously?" Sabrina blushed beneath the foundation.

"Well, duh!" Simi snatched Belle's wig for a quick try-on. She fit it over Sabrina's head then turned her to the mirror.

Unbelievable! Now that the freckles were gone, Sabrina's own eyes stared from the princess Belle! "My eyes are the wrong color, though."

"We'd take care of that with colored contacts," Simi countered.

A gorgeous girl glared at Sabrina in the glass. "Can I get my hair back now?"

Simi grumbled something at the princess then returned the wig. "She's just jealous," she whispered in Sabrina's ear before pinning up strand after strand of Sabrina's curly tresses. Soon Jane's hair was secured onto Sabrina's head. By skillfully applying contours of shadows and highlights, Simi gently coaxed Jane's features from Sabrina's face. The process was amazing and the results were stunning. "Simi, you're a magician with your powders and brushes! You've created me." Sabrina turned her head from side to side.

"Thanks." Simi seemed pleased with the attention. "Let's finish. Scoot back here and let's get you dressed."

Soon Jane Porter twirled in the mirror, complete with her sunny yellow dress, high-necked white collar, purple tie, grey hat, and matching, old-fashioned button-hook boots. She swung her lacy yellow parasol gleefully at the reflection. Tarzan smiled behind her.

The airbrushing and make-up techniques had transformed Brad into a wild, ferocious, jungle man. His jaw and chin looked long and angular, just like the animated version. Only his blue, penetrating eyes seemed the same. "No living person will ever believe this," Sabrina thought ruefully.

She cleared away from the mirror so others could morph into their respective characters.

Sabrina noticed a delicate-boned blonde girl. She seemed younger than Sabrina by a couple of years. She was exquisite even without make-up. "What's your name?"

"Whitlee," the girl said shyly.

"Who are you going to be?"

"Can't you tell by my blue nightgown? I'm Wendy."

Of course--Wendy! "Wendy's almost as pretty as you are."

Whitlee smiled. Simi carefully fit a weave of brown ringlets over Whitlee's blonde curls. She then whisked soft pink powder across her cheekbones and forehead. She tinted the girl's lips and darkened her lashes. Wendy smiled at Jane in the mirror. Sabrina was fascinated by the whole process.

"You're obviously not the regular Jane," Whitlee commented. "You're nicer."

Sabrina noticed Jane Porter smile in the glass. "Thank you, *Wendy*...you know, when I first saw you standing there I thought you might be Alice in Wonderland–it was your blonde hair, I suppose."

"I've done Alice before," the girl said, "but our Peter Pan is short, like a *boy* of course, so they needed an even shorter girl to match up. That's me!" Perfect teeth gleamed behind her smile.

Two of Peter Pan's lost boys tumbled past Wendy's feet. "Knock it off!" she scolded.

The lost boy dressed in a bear cub suit climbed off of a smaller skunk-clad kid. "I pinned you," the bear cub grinned.

"Save it for the parade, P.B.!"

P.B. didn't pay an ounce of attention to the lecture. Once the skunk kid stood up, P.B. rolled him over again. "I got you times two," he said pleasantly.

Whitlee looked annoyed at the boy, and huffed an exasperated breath at him. "He's my little brother," she explained to Sabrina. "The lost boys scuffle all along the parade route but he takes wrestling to an extreme!"

"The Neverland float is wonderful! I saw the parade last night." Whitlee nodded, grinning. "I liked the interaction between you and the mermaids."

"Want to meet them?"

"Sure!"

Whitlee led Jane across the room to meet the vixens of *Mermaid Lagoon*. "This is Morgann, she likes to make a splash," Whitlee teased.

"I'm Sabrina. I actually live in a town called *Morgan*."

Morgann was tall and willowy–built like a model. Dark eyes fired mischievously beneath sequined lashes. Her flowing wig was black and mermaid tail shimmered turquoise. She gauged Jane suspiciously, not saying anything.

Her stare made Sabrina feel uncomfortable. "You could pass for a real mermaid. You looked like you were having fun in the parade last night," Sabrina continued.

The mermaid's head leaned slightly toward Whitlee. "What did I miss? Usually the princesses and main characters strut around here like golden prima donnas."

"I'm only here for tonight. I don't know how I'm supposed to act. I'm shell-shocked."

"You're supposed to behave like the queen of the jungle," Morgann explained, flipping her nose toward the ceiling. The movement was synchronized with a haughty shoulder roll. "Like this."

A shorter, younger, mermaid peered from the mirror. She was applying amber sparkles to her eyebrows. Her hair was vibrant orange and her tail was reminiscent of the golden coi swimming at the new house in Morgan. "I'm Lindsey," she said, "But all my friends call me *Zee*. My Aunt Bobbi started calling me that and it stuck. Some day I'm going to be a major princess and treat everyone like poo." She giggled at her idea. Her smile was engaging and her friendliness quite bold.

"I doubt that," Sabrina said.

"*Brad!*" Morgann's voice peeled, "You're back! It's been like six weeks since I've seen you."

"Miss me?" The Neverland cast buzzed around Tarzan. *Obviously he's a favorite.*

Another model-like mermaid appeared from her dressing stall. Her wig was a fun fantasy of brilliant yellow. Her mermaid's tail dazzled like dripping rubies. She hopped up to Brad. "Are you here to stay?"

"Naya! How are you? I've missed all you guys--"

The ruby-adorned mermaid smiled, seeming pleased with his acknowledgment. Naya's eyes scrutinized Sabrina. "Who are you?"

"This is Sabrina," Brad said. "Isn't she great?" Naya's eyebrows rose with casual nonchalance. Her flippant expression remained unfazed. The Neverlanders laughed. "Naya's famous for her stoic, unconcerned, *unimpressed* expressions," Brad teased. "We all think she got her job here from staring at management that way."

Morgann's head bobbed. "Yeah! Like, she glared and Jetta jumped. *Presto!* She got the job."

Naya shrugged. "Treat people like they don't matter and suddenly they want to."

"She's intimidating," Whitlee agreed. "She stares at me all throughout the parade like she wants to drown me in *Mermaid Lagoon*. Whenever certain people get huffy around here we send Naya to wither them with a cold stare."

A smile suddenly broke through Naya's exterior shell. It was a beautiful smile and Sabrina was taken with her pretty features.

"If that doesn't work," Brad piped playfully, "we unleash Morgann's mouth on them."

The raven-haired mermaid doubled up a fist. "How about a knuckle sandwich Monkey Boy?" Brad playfully guarded his face. Morgann grinned. She seemed a little bit too smitten with Brad to actually enact violence. *How old is she?*

"You're all friends then?" Sabrina asked, sorting names, characters, and faces. She was trying her best to catalog the experience.

"The Neverlanders are younger than most of the characters so I guess I relate to them better. We usually grab that last ride in the park together, huh gang?"

"Brad!" A red-headed Peter Pan broke away from Simi's grasp and stepped toward the group. "Wanna go paint-balling or something tomorrow?"

"Hey Scottie! How's it going man? I can't tomorrow. I've got plans with Jane, here."

"She could come too--we could all go fishing."

"He's busy with *her*," Naya said, flipping her head impatiently. "What part of that don't you understand?"

Scottie's shoulders drooped with disappointment. "You're not really supposed to date a co-worker," he muttered.

"This particular Jane is just here for tonight," the mermaids said. *Do they sound happy about that?* Sabrina felt suddenly inferior to the close-knit group of beautiful, make-believe people.

"I wish she could stay on," Whitlee said sincerely. "She's nice."

Chapter Twenty

Over and over Sabrina ran through Jane's reel of antics and expressions while Brad performed a choreographed series of athletic vine swinging and acrobatics. About every two minutes Brad's stunts would lead him, wildly hanging upside down, to discover Jane in his jungle. Every two minutes chemistry popped between them as they would gaze at each other again...for the first time. Tarzan's hand would extend and Jane would take it. The crowd cheered and cameras flashed. It was a rush, a thrill, a moment suspended in memory's making.

Sabrina was vaguely aware of Vidalia as the float scooted by. Vidalia had claimed squatter's rights on a bench near Sleeping Beauty Castle. Jane cast one quick smile at her friend then engaged in her role acting again. *Was Vidalia crying?* Sabrina longed to look back at her friend but Jane Porter forbade it. Instead she struggled with baboons for the possession of her boot, followed by amazement at the fiercely handsome jungle man's piercing blue eyes.

The parade wove a serpentine pattern through the park. The Neverland float loomed just ahead. Sabrina could see the mermaids, Morgann, Naya, and Zee, flirting shamelessly with the red-haired Pan. Whitlee--*Wendy*--teetered pensively on a rock, overlooking an emerald pool and the dazzling water vixens. Once she telegraphed a tiny smile and little wave in Jane's direction. Sabrina caught it gratefully.

The parade ended too quickly! Sabrina peeled Jane's clothes from her body with a sense of melancholy. This was a once-in-a-lifetime evening. *I'll never forget it!* Sabrina was envious of her new friends.

This experience would play out for them again tomorrow night. *How could Brad ever have given all this up?* Sabrina's phone jangled her from mournful thoughts. "Hello?"

Vidalia's voice sounded in her ear, "Oh, Honey! You did so well! How 'bout that? That was some terrific surprise that boy cooked up for you huh? My hell, Sabrina, I'm falling in love with him myself! Did you see him swinging through the trees and doing all of those tricks? He's really something, that's all I know."

"Yes he is."

"You were wonderful, too! I'm so proud of my girl. You just made old Vidalia cry. You looked so pretty and you really acted like Jane. I'm marching right to the *Emporium* this very minute and buy me a copy of *Tarzan*."

"Thanks, Vidalia."

"What's the matter, Honey?"

"I'm just sad it's over that's all." A tear streaked the makeup on Sabrina's cheek.

"It was a great fairy tale wasn't it?"

"Uh huh," Sabrina sniffled into the phone.

"Kind of like your whole summer but don't cry! Have fun tonight. Brad's made arrangements with some other kids from the parade. You're all going to do something together. I'm meeting you kids by the front gate at eleven. Have fun! Dry those tears."

"Okay. What did you do all afternoon? I feel guilty because I just jilted you."

"Nonsense! It was a relief not to have to drag you along with me everywhere I went! I walked through all of the shops and I saw a couple of shows at the *Golden Horseshoe*. I bought Vandaline a coon-skin cap! I rode Mark Twain's big river boat and pretended I was sassier than Tom Sawyer. I listened to a barbershop quartet for awhile and then I lapped up a pineapple whip near the *Tiki Room*. I caught a glimpse of Woody and Buzz, and saw a talking, moving garbage can play tricks on people. If all of that were not enough,

I saved myself a front row seat for the parade and watched people go by. There are a few weirdoes in every crowd, I'm telling you that right now. I spied myself a few cowboys though, so the view wasn't all bad."

Sabrina smiled. "That's good." She wiped more tears from her cheek, sniffling away from the phone so Vidalia couldn't hear she was still crying.

"Speaking of handsome cowboys...that luscious Chantry Cantrell called for you three times this afternoon."

"Chantry? Why did he call? Is everything alright at home?"

"Yes, everything's fine. He said he just wanted to see how you were getting along. He was thinking of you and hoping you handled the wedding okay. He seemed kind of worried about you."

"Why didn't he call my phone?"

"He couldn't get you. It's been off all afternoon, hasn't it?"

That's right. It's been shoved in this locker. "Yes. What did you tell him?"

"I said, 'Hell, she's just fine! She's been kissing on that kid a lot. She staggers into the house punch-drunk in love every night then wakes up flushed from the hangover and eager for another fix in the morning.'"

"Vidalia! You didn't!" Sabrina felt herself flush with panic. "Please tell me you did not say that!"

"Relax. I'm just kidding you." Sabrina let out a pent-up breath. Relief trembled from head to toe.

"But he knows, anyway," Vidalia said.

"*What!* How? Did you say something to him?"

"No, he had it all figured out in Morgan the other day."

"How do you know?"

"Hell, Kid! The whole world aint as oblivious as your folks are. What does it matter?"

"I don't know. I just don't want Chantry thinking about...*I don't know!* I just don't want Chantry thinking, *period.*"

"I'll wager he's thinking something though. I told him I'd have you call him later."

Well maybe I will and maybe I won't! "I'm irritated that he thought he needed to check up on me."

"Settle down. He was just proving his friendship. He's been your loyal friend forever."

"He's never *called* me before."

"I fail to see that as bad news."

"What do you mean, Vidalia?"

"Sabrina...a tall, dark, and handsome, baseball playing cowboy *might* just be the anecdote for your soon-to-be broken heart."

Sabrina scowled into the phone. It was a fact, and not disputable, that she'd *secretly* loved Chantry ever since she could remember. It was a hopeless, childish, infatuation! She remembered when Chantry reported his mission; little butterflies had done triple flip-flops inside of her thirteen year old stomach. "Chantry Cantrell doesn't even know I'm alive," Sabrina stated gloomily.

"Oh, I see..." Vidalia said, sounding like a wise old sage. "That's why he's called my phone all day wondering where you are, huh? Just think about this, Kid; while you're here romping around in a storybook, he's home fixing fence and saddling up a horse in the real world. Reality isn't all bad you know."

Rap! Rap! "Are you okay?" Whitlee asked.

"Yeah," Sabrina called. "I'll be out in a second."

"Goodbye," Vidalia's voice sounded in her ear. "I'll see you later. Think about things."

"I've got makeup remover and a brush and stuff, if you need it," Whitlee offered.

"I do! Thank you." Sabrina opened her dressing space.

Whitlee handed Sabrina her makeup bag and waited patiently while Sabrina washed Jane Porter away. Traces of the fairy-tale swirled around in the sink before gurgling down the drain. "I'm sad to have it be over."

Whitlee just nodded her understanding. She was a good listener. "I'm sorry too. I know you're a little older than I am but I think we could be good friends."

"I know we could! Let's trade cell numbers and E-mails, okay?"

"Can I ask you something?"

"Shoot."

"Are you a Mormon?"

"Yeah!"

"Me, too." Whitlee smiled. "Brad is too, isn't he?"

"No, he's not."

Whitlee's brows rose. "I thought he was...he acts like it. His language is clean and he seems like a good kid. I don't think he parties or anything."

"I know."

Whitlee pursed her lips together thoughtfully. "He *is* a member," she decreed. "He just doesn't know it yet!" A broad smile lit her pretty features. "Sabrina, I'm putting you in charge of his conversion."

Sabrina laughed. "Okay, I'll work on that."

Whitlee started giggling. "It's kind of funny."

"What?"

"Brad asked me out earlier this spring. I thought he was a member and so I said, "I can't--I'm only a *Mia Maid!* I'll bet he thought I was whacked."

So that's where the Mia Maid question came from! "That is funny," Sabrina agreed. The girls giggled and shared information back and forth while Sabrina quickly found her own features again. She brushed her hair into a neat pony tail, and applied a touch of gloss to her lips. Her cheeks were already rosy from too much excitement. "Let's scoot," she said to her new friend.

Morgann, Naya, Zee, Scottie, and Brad were congregated in a hallway.

"Has anyone seen P.B.?" Whitlee asked with a flash of concern.

Down the hall a garbage can suddenly skidded sideways. Two lost boys tumbled from behind it, rolling each other. Their costumes were gone but their actions were still going. "Pinned you again," P.B. said smugly.

"Knock it off!" Whitlee barked. "Come on P.B.! We're all going to Pirates of the Caribbean together."

"Come on, Buddy," Brad called to the boy. "We're gonna dine on turkey legs and churros while we watch the fireworks."

The group enthusiastically merged into the jostling, merry throng of the park. They were no longer in the limelight. They were suddenly just a group of kids who happened to be friends with: Tarzan, Jane, Peter Pan, Wendy, a Lost Boy, and the dazzling beauties of Mermaid Lagoon. They walked anonymously among the crowd. Whitlee shepherded P.B. along the congested walk-ways for she was a responsible sister. Morgann flirted innocently with Brad, Naya meandered nonchalantly, firing a few withering stares to old people and small children alike. Zee smiled and chattered a mile a minute. Scottie trailed behind Brad, hanging on his every word and making random statements about sport fishing and motorcycles. Sabrina brought up the rear. She listened, watched, smiled, and wondered. *How did Brad pull strings for me today? Does he possibly know someone in upper management? Does he cast a magic spell over everybody? And what the heck does Chantry Cantrell want?* Brad held an arm out for Sabrina to catch up. "

TWENTY-ONE

It was midnight before the car's headlights illuminated the Manning's California residence. Vidalia was asleep in the back seat. "Vidalia, wake up Sleeping Beauty," Brad said tenderly, patting her shoulder.

Vidalia's head jerked. She shook the sleep from herself and then swung her legs onto the driveway. Brad grabbed an arm and helped pull her from the car. "My dogs are dead," she said, motioning to her aching feet. "Don't wake me in the morning when you kids leave. I think I'll stay here and relax."

"We can stay with you if you'd like," Brad offered, always the gentleman.

"Nonsense! You kids go have fun."

"I'll show you where the keys are in case you want to take the other car some place tomorrow."

"Okay, sounds good." Vidalia followed Brad into the kitchen.

Sabrina wandered out onto the patio. She was too lit up to sleep. The lights of Dana point twinkled and an ocean breeze gently washed the night air with a briny fragrance. "Good night Honey," Vidalia said from the patio door. "In bed by one, okay? Sleep well. You've had a big day."

"Good night Vidalia. Thanks for everything."

Sabrina turned back toward the patio gate. A splintered view of the harbor could be seen from the house. *I don't want to leave the ocean.* A pair of strong arms wrapped around her from behind. "Hey," Brad said. "You did really well tonight! That was the most fun I've ever had being Tarzan. The crowd could feel our chemistry too. You could feel it in their energy. It was a *trip*."

"I didn't want it to end."

"I know...me neither. It was good though, huh?"

Sabrina nodded. "How did you manage it?"

"I've got a couple of connections."

"Such as?"

"Do you remember going into the clock shop on the Main Street U.S.A. this morning?

"Yes,"

"That old man who looked like Geppetto, remember him?"

"How could I forget? He was sitting there drawing. His artwork was amazing! I'm supposing he's an actual animator for Disney."

"Not just any animator. He was a close personal friend of Walt's, actually. Walt took him on as a young apprentice in nineteen forty-nine. He even helped Walt sketch some of his early visions for Disneyland. Anyway, Walt showed him the ropes–literally trained him in every aspect, you know? He's worked on masterpiece greats like: *Alice in Wonderland, Sleeping Beauty, One Hundred and One Dalmatians, Sword in the Stone, Winnie the Pooh, Jungle Book, the Aristrocats,* and *Robin Hood,* just to name a few!"

"That's an impressive list."

"Walt was about thirty years older than he was but they really became close friends."

"Like me and Vidalia."

"Exactly. Well, Haskel is in his eighties now. He's still going strong for Disney and his close-knit history with Walt and the company places him in an honored, revered, position. He's commanded a lot of respect over the years. There's not many of the good old boys left who can say 'Let me tell you what Walt said about that,' or 'this is what Walt wanted.' His mind and abilities are still sharp. He's invested in Disney since Walt took him under his wing, and is one of the oldest stock-holders."

"That's interesting."

"Haskel thought so much of Walt Disney that he named his oldest son *Elias*, which was Walt's middle name."

"Really?"

"Elias was killed in Viet Nam. Dad grew up without a father around, just like you. Haskel Manning is my great-grandpa and the only one I've ever known."

A shiver splashed down Sabrina's arms. "He's your grandpa?"

"Uh-huh. He threw his leverage around and landed my dad his first big break. Dad's done some work as an Imagineer. He actually had a lot to do with the architecture of Disney's California Adventure Park. Without knowing it you've marveled many times in the last three days, about his work. You've also complimented Haskel's ideas and art again and again. His work is prominently displayed in Storybook Land."

"So...the man who designed our new house also designed elements of California Adventure Park? No way..."

"And Downtown Disney..."

"Unbelievable!"

"He's still doing some work for the company but he's not exclusively there anymore. He's branched out on his own. He was the architect for Tenselley's Technology. Have you heard of them? You know? Their slogan is the five *T*'s. It goes, *Testing Tomorrow Through Technology Today.*"

Sabrina shrugged, "That's not ringing a bell."

"It's okay. The Tenselley's contract was huge and Dad bought stock in the company with the bonus he was paid for finishing before deadline. The current frenzy over alternative energy, bio-fuels and stuff, has made his investment kind of golden."

Sabrina drank the information in, hungry to know about her new family. "Sounds like you can be really proud of your dad."

"I am. None of it came easy, he's earned every bit. His work is genius, I think. I also like his principal of investing in his own projects. It keeps him striving for perfection and builds confidence in his own worth as an architect. That's Grandpa Haskel's tradition. A long time ago Walt Disney paid him a bonus for his work in his first animation experience. He turned around and reinvested the money in Disney's next feature. That move impressed Walt. It kind of proved his loyalty."

"I'll bet. I'm finding out all kinds of things tonight. I can't figure out why you and your dad can leave all this behind just to come to Utah."

"We haven't really left anything. Dad's work is here, my work is here, *occasionally*, and our home is here. We're keeping all of it. Actually Dad can do the majority of his projects from his home office in Morgan."

"Why the move, though?"

"Dad was studying the architecture of Temple Square. He's been fascinated by the San Diego Temple, and then when the Newport Beach Temple was being built he'd run up the coast every week, just to watch the progress. He decided to check out more of the Mormon churches' buildings. He flew to Salt Lake City and began touring, sketching, and studying. The tour of the Conference Center just about blew his mind. He was thrilled by the utter perfection that the L.D.S. people put into their projects. On his next trip to Utah, Dad visited with a man from the churches' building department."

"That's cool."

"That man recommended a place where Dad could get a good lunch. He went to the Joseph Smith Memorial Building. He was en-thralled with it—just totally overwhelmed. He sat down in one of the chairs, studying the grand molding and marbled pillars. Suddenly this little blond chick goes strolling by, trying to wheel a large wedding cake into one of the reception rooms. Dad jumped up to help her."

"That's how our parents met?"

"Yes. He helped her lift the heavy layers of cake onto supports. "What are they called? Mini cake-pillars?"

"That works." Sabrina smiled in the darkness.

"Amanda put the finishing touches on the cake while Dad watched. He was stunned by her precision and attention to detail. She's just as fussy over her cakes as Dad is his blue prints and plans. Amanda knocked his socks off! She must have been more exquisite than the building they were standing in because Dad forgot all about the stunning architecture, he said. He asked her to ride to the top floor with him for lunch at the Garden Restaurant."

Sabrina was laughing at the scene in her head. "How come I didn't know about any of this?"

"They hit it off. He walked Amanda to her car just to be near her longer. As he was boarding the plane to come home he said he realized that it was time to invest in something that really mattered. He was hooked! He flew back to Utah only three days later."

"I was ignorantly blind to all of it."

"You haven't been as privy to the information as I was. Dad started spending so much time in Utah; he actually bought a car to keep at the airport in Salt Lake. I felt like an orphan around here. It's a good thing I was working a lot. I spent a few nights at Grandpa's house playing Disney Monopoly."

Sabrina smiled at the thoughts of Tarzan and Geppetto going after premium real estate in the board game. "I'll bet it was hard to fall into the status of only *occasional* help."

"Yes, but I think I can come back after graduation. I'm on kind of tight terms with Jetta. She likes me."

"And you've got Haskel in your corner. That helps too."

"I try not to play him like a trump card though. I want to earn my own stripes. He pulled strings for you today but only after he sized you up in the clock shop. It was totally his call."

"I'm glad he approved. It was such a fun experience! If I could do it every night it would probably go to my head. I would become one of those golden prima donnas that Morgann the Mermaid was telling me about."

Brad laughed and turned Sabrina around to face him. He studied her eyes intently. "No it wouldn't. It wouldn't change you one bit."

"It obviously hasn't gone to your head. I'm glad."

"How could it go to my head? When I'm in costume I'm Tarzan, but out of costume nobody knows who I am!"

"Your friends know you. You have some kind of a magnetic pull on people. They just gather around you, thrilled to be within your scope of recognition. You ought to set Morgan High on its ear when school starts. You'll have students, teachers, and administration all eating out of your hand!"

"I doubt it. I'm really nervous. I'm petrified."

"You are not!"

"I know but it sounded like the right thing to say."

Sabrina grinned at the handsome boy. "I felt special tonight while we were all walking toward Adventure Land, that I was the one who your arm was around."

Brad leaned closer. "You did huh?" The question was mellow and velvety.

Sabrina nodded her head. "I was feeling really lucky."

"Maybe I was feeling lucky, too," Brad said softly, the velvet tones of his voice sounded even plusher in Sabrina's ears. It stroked her sense of hearing with pleasure. A tiny shiver trickled down her neck.

"I like your voice," Sabrina confessed.

A smile curled Brad's mouth. His brows rose quickly. "I like your face so we're even."

"I *love* your face so you're still ahead."

"So it's a contest, huh? Okay...there are other features of yours which I'm plenty crazy about..."

"Like what?"

"Your freckles, for one." Brad's face loomed closer. He lightly kissed her nose and both cheeks. "I missed them when they were gone." He suddenly knelt down.

"What are you doing?"

"I'm still pointing out your good features. Your legs," he said, kissing Sabrina squarely on both knee caps.

She couldn't help laughing at the boy! "You're so dumb," she reminded him playfully.

Brad stood back up. "Your hair," he continued, as one hand lifted a wayward wisp of dark curl to his lips. That movement sent a jolt of adrenalin coursing through Sabrina's body.

"Well...you're not really *so* dumb," she muttered weakly.

Brad's hand closed around Sabrina's throat, gently tilting her head. "Your neck, "he whispered trailing tantalizing kisses along her hair line.

Sabrina's heart rate accelerated violently. "My heart is pounding." Brad lifted Sabrina's hand to once again feel his own heart's racing rhythm. It was beating as wildly as hers. She raised her face toward his.

"Your mouth," he murmured, tracing a finger along her lower lip.

Sabrina curled her fingers in the soft waves of his hair where it fell over his collar. "Kiss me." Brad did.

Dong! Sabrina drew away. "The clock chimed, it must be one o'clock"

"We don't have a chiming clock," Brad said wryly.

"Vidalia?"

"Yes, Vidalia's dong has dinged."

Sabrina giggled recklessly under her breath. The kids headed through the open patio door and into the house. "Goodnight," she whispered to the boy as he snuck sheepishly past Vidalia's room and on down the hall.

CHAPTER TWENTY-TWO

Sabrina woke early. *Chantry!* It had been too late to call him last night. She peered at the clock in her strange California bedroom. It was seven. She knew he'd probably be out of the house, moving sprinkler pipe already. Just then her phone jangled. "Hello?"

"Hi, Sabrina. Don't you ever return your calls?"

The girl smiled. "Hi Chantry! It was pretty late last night," she explained.

"But Vidalia did tell you I called didn't she?"

"Yes...it was just really late when I had a chance. I couldn't call you at the park. It was too noisy. I was just thinking about calling you now, but I thought you'd be out moving pipe."

"I've already finished moving pipe. It's eight o'clock here. Did you forget?"

"Yes; so that means it would have been extra, *extra* late for me to call you last night."

"Maybe you shouldn't be out so late," Chantry said.

Sabrina rolled her eyes. "You're stubborn."

"Whatever..."

"So...is everything okay? How's your truck?"

"Things are okay. The truck's good."

"Was the dealer right? Is it the very chick magnet you'd hoped for?"

"Not exactly," Chantry grumbled.

Sabrina beamed. "How delightful…"

Chantry let her little comment pass. "How was the wedding?"

"It was good! It really was. Dorian has whisked Mom away on a yacht! Can you believe it?"

"Wow that *is* something. Were you well-behaved?"

"Of course! I played the part of an angelic child."

"Ha! That's a stretch and I don't believe it. That would have required acting lessons."

Sabrina's head bobbed back in her pillow. "Chantry! Your statement cuts me deeply."

"I'll mail you a band-aid."

Sabrina laughed. "Did you wake up on the wrong side of the bed this morning?"

"Not really."

Sabrina's eyebrows knit together. *Why did he call?* "Then what's your beef with me?"

"I don't have a beef with you," he sounded exasperated.

"You're just jealous because I've been on a delicious vacation out here, and you're home working!" She intentionally baited him.

He stepped in the trap. "How *delicious* of a time are you having, exactly?"

"*Tasty*…positively *mouth-watering*, that's how delicious."

"Maybe you'd better try dieting a little."

"Killjoy!"

"Glutton!" he fired back.

"Chantry, seriously…are you mad at me?"

"No! Why would I be *mad* at you? Frustrated? Yes! Irritated? Yes! Mad? No."

What a strange answer! "Why are you frustrated and irritated with me? I *said* I liked your truck!" Sabrina deliberately tagged the last sentence on just to add another dimension of exasperation.

"You're so innocent, aren't you? You know you've always loved to irritate and frustrate me! It can't possibly be news to you now."

"Why did you even call me then, if I'm so bothersome to you?"

"Because, *Breezy-Brina-Thumbelina*, I wanted to make sure you're okay."

The childhood nickname sizzled and popped through the phone's receiver. *He remembers!* It had been many years since Chantry had greeted her that way but she loved hearing it now, just as she'd adored it as a girl "You remember my nickname!"

"Of course I remember." Chantry seemed surprised by her reaction.

"That's good."

"It is?"

"Yes." The conversation was quiet for a second. Sabrina felt uncomfortable but her mind was blank. She was willing to provoke him for a conversation but she felt too rattled to come up with anything.

"Are you still there?"

"Yes, I....um, guess what?" Sabrina stalled while her mind flew for something to say.

"What?"

"We went to Catalina Island and found some drugs in a lunch box. Vidalia got interviewed for the news and everything--except I missed seeing it because I was in the shower."

"I can't imagine that," Chantry said sarcastically.

"And Brad's taken us to all of the *greatest* places. I've had the best food! Guess what Brad did for me yesterday?"

"Put you in a parade at Disneyland?"

"How did you know?"

"Vidalia told me when I called."

"Oh," Sabrina stammered. "Well, it was really fun."

"I'll bet. That Brad is really something, huh?" The statement had a bite to it.

"Yes..." Sabrina realized that Chantry now seemed *amply* provoked. *Now what?*

"He's a good brother," she added quickly.

"Mm-hmm."

"So, what did you do yesterday?"

"I saddled up old Rio and went riding," Chantry paused for dramatic effect. "I let the wind whip through my hair and smelled our fresh mountain air. I picked a bouquet of wild flowers and took them in to Julia."

Sabrina smiled at Chantry's melodramatic description. "That was nice of you."

"They miss you."

"I'll be up there soon. Will you go riding with me? You made it sound so tempting a moment ago."

"I did?"

"Yes. I'm sure I can outride you." Sabrina knew Chantry was always game when a challenge was levied.

"I doubt it. You've probably gotten too fat on your delicious vacation."

"Bet me!"

"You're on!"

"Guess what else happened on Catalina?"

"I can't imagine, exactly."

"I thought about you."

"You did?"

"Yes...our tour guide drove us by the place where the Chicago Cubs used to hold spring training."

"That's cool. I don't know anything about Catalina Island."

"I'm an expert now, you know."

"Yes, I figured you would be. You usually know a lot."

"Jerk," Sabrina said playfully.

"So, I actually have a little bit of news."

"What? You're not getting married are you?"

"That was random." Chantry sounded puzzled.

"What's your big news then?"

"I didn't say it was *big* news...I just said I had a *bit* of news."

"What is it? For heaven's sakes, Chantry! I feel like your dentist trying to pry a tooth out!"

"Shut up!" Chantry laughed. "You are maddening! Will you let me talk for one minute please?"

Silence.

"Sabrina?"

"I'M LISTENING!"

"Remember the appointment I had the other day in Morgan?"

"Yeah?"

"It was an interview for a teaching and coaching position in Morgan. I am the new varsity baseball coach and I'll be teaching history at the high school."

Shocked silence.

"Sabrina? Are you still there?"

"Yes. You're moving to Morgan?"

"Can you handle that?"

Sabrina thought of seeing Chantry every day just like old times. "Yes!"

"Promise?"

"Of course! You'll have all of the girls in school passing out in the aisles just like they used to at Elvis concerts. They'll be positively swooning."

Chantry's laughter peeled through the phone. "I doubt that."

"You'll be awesome for our baseball program! Morgan loves baseball just as much as Bear Lake does."

"I know. I'm really excited to be a part of the program; it's been going strong for several generations. Your Great Grandpa Porter helped to begin a very lasting tradition in Morgan County."

Sabrina was pleased with the acknowledgment of her grandfather. "He was legendary, at least to me."

"I know..."

"Congratulations about the job!"

"So now it's your turn to help me move into my apartment."

"Okay!"

"You can give the old bachelor pad a feminine touch."

"I'll bring you a little violet for your window sill."

"Sounds good. Well...talk me up to your friends and any of the team. I'm a little nervous about this. It's my first teaching job you know."

"I will. I hope I get you for history."

"Sabrina, don't think you'll get any special treatment just because you're an *old friend.*"

"Don't think I'll show the teacher respect just because it's you, then."

Chantry laughed. "Okay you little firecracker! Well, I guess I'd better let you go. Thanks for penciling me into your morning."

"Not a problem. It was good talking to you--even if you were kind a grumpy with me a time or two."

"Bye, Sabrina. I'm expecting a horse race sometime in the near future."

"Okay, but don't get your hopes up. I'm sure to win. Um... Chantry? Thanks for calling."

"I'll talk to you later Sabrina."

Sabrina held the phone against her chest for long minutes after they'd said goodbye. An excited, heady sensation was sweeping through her. She knew her romance with Brad was hovering near the brink of ashes and ruin. The thought of a broken heart loomed like a black, unavoidable cloud. *Is there possibly a flicker of hope dancing on the horizon? Can life ever be as magical without Brad's romantic enticements? Will Chantry ever see me as anything other than an old friend?* "Friendship's not all it is cracked up to be," Sabrina said to herself. *Will the teacher and student relationship crush any budding chances anyway?* "I'm going to hunt up a gypsy and buy myself a crystal ball!"

A slight knock rapped against the door. "Sabrina?" Brad's voice called out.

"Yeah?"

Brad pushed the door open and stuck his head in the room. "Who are you talking to in here?"

"Myself...I was hungry for an intelligent conversation."

"How was that going, exactly?"

"Not very well."

"Can you get ready sometime in the next hour?"

"Yes."

"I have something special planned today."

"Oh, good...it was time we finally got around to doing something *special*."

Brad smiled. "I'm glad you've enjoyed your week."

"Mom and Dorian can't possibly be having more fun that we are."

Brad's expression locked into place. "Oh...we might be surprised."

Sabrina flushed. *Why do I open myself up to blunders all of the time?* "Is Vidalia awake?"

"She's still snoring. I think we wore her out."

The morning drive was brilliant. Brad's car motored along the Pacific Coast Highway. Sabrina enjoyed the ride. The ocean was deep blue beneath the sky. The air was clear, fog and mist had seemed to roll away on the sea. Sabrina was amazed with the swanky streets of Laguna Beach. Porsche and Ferrari dealerships dotted the highway. "You don't see those in Morgan," Sabrina mentioned.

Surfers were crashing on waves at Newport Beach. Brad pointed out the new Mormon temple.

Sabrina's eyes surveyed rows and rows of identical houses, spreading along the hills, morphing into subdivisions and developments. "They all look the same. Where are we going, anyway?"

"Huntington Beach. It's not too much farther. Look," he pointed out. "That's the Boeing Corporation." Sabrina appraised the impressive property from her window.

Brad's car maneuvered through the pretty streets of Huntington Beach. The cookie cutter houses were gone. Here each home radiated its own personality. Burgundy bougainvillea clung along fences and trellises of a beautifully landscaped street. Palm Trees and lush tropical foliage lined walkways. A brilliant burst of daylilies, crimson vine, and phlox poked from well-manicured flowerbeds. A colorful potpourri of daisies, dahlias, pansies, roses, and snap dragons exploded against dense green lawns. Marigolds bobbed cheerily from pots. Lemon trees, orange trees, and date trees perfumed the air, adding variety to the green thatch of orchards and yards. Brad's car stopped in front of magnificently cared-for home. It was pale yellow, with green shutters. Two small dormer windows peered from an upper level like happy eyes. Sheer white curtains fluttered against their panes. The front door was welcoming and quaint, with a large oval window. Geraniums lined the walk way to the front steps and splashed from window boxes against the house. Hanging baskets of trailing ivy swung from the porch. Deep purple clematis blossoms climbed large lattice panels near the garage door. The house and yard donned a profusion of color and set the little home apart from all of the rest along the pretty street. A green garden hose was neatly coiled against the house. A pair of garden gloves and a spade was lying nearby.

The door opened. Geppetto stood smiling. "Hello Kids! I've been waiting for you."

"Hi Grandpa Haskel," Brad said, hugging the white haired man. Sabrina had wondered if he was in costume to resemble the wood-carver from *Pinocchio* or if that's just the way he looked. *He wouldn't be wearing a costume in his own house!* It made it even better that he actually looked like the kind, snow-topped Geppetto. "This is Sabrina."

"My Dear," Haskel bowed gallantly. "You were beyond compare last night."

"You saw the parade?"

"Of course! I wouldn't unleash you on the park without staying to enjoy the show! You were the belle of the ball; a splendor; and a vision."

"Thank you."

"And welcome to Haskel's family! I always wanted a grand-daughter. I didn't believe I would ever get my wish but here you are. That's proof that wishes do come true isn't it Dear?"

"Yes," Sabrina agreed.

"I can't wait to meet Amanda. Can she possibly be as exquisite as this bright girl here?" he asked Brad doubtfully.

"Oh yes, she's even better," Sabrina said.

Haskel disappeared into the kitchen and came back carrying a tray full of chocolate chip cookies and tiny blue glasses of milk. A stack of miniature blue plates were stacked on the tray. Sabrina wondered if the dishes were part of a child's tea set. She'd never seen anything so fun. Brad shot a wink at Sabrina, hoping she would accept the eccentricities of the little man. "How fun!"

Haskel set the tray down on a small ornately carved table. He was very fastidious in arranging everything just so. He then strolled to the kitchen and carried in matching baby bowls full of buttery popcorn. "Just enough for a taste," he winked. "I always like a little salt to balance out the sugar. When your bowl gets empty we'll just dash to the kitchen and get some more." Sabrina pictured Haskel scooping the popcorn from a teeny tiny pan.

Sabrina reached for a cookie. Haskel shook his head. "First, let us offer our thanks to the Lord in Heaven." Sabrina wasn't used to blessing snack-time. She quickly set her cookie on her plate and bowed her head, realizing she had many lessons to learn. Haskel cleared his throat "Dear Lord, we are so thankful for thy bounty. We are thankful for the beauty and imagination in our lives. We are so thankful for friends, and family, and every magical moment of promise. We are most thankful that thou hast sent Amanda and Sabrina to adorn our lives with beauty and grace. Please bless us to always keep our hearts and hands clean and pure, and our lives ever in tune with thy will. Bless these bites of food that they might gladden our hearts and strengthen our bodies. We ask thee for health and strength and the wisdom we need to appreciate such glorious blessings. Amen."

"Amen," Brad and Sabrina echoed.

"That was a beautiful prayer, Haskel," Sabrina said sincerely. "I had a distinct impression you were speaking with a friend."

"The dearest friend," Haskel agreed.

Brad comes from good stock! Sabrina wondered if she'd met a more faithful, or sincere fellow in all of the church. Her eyes scanned the cozy room. A collection of cuckoo clocks ticked noisily from one wall. *Just like Geppetto!* A menagerie of animated prints lined another. Sabrina studied them. "Did you do these, Haskel?"

"Yes." Recognizable scenes from Disney movies pranced across the wall.

"Original sketches from the film cells?"

"Yes."

"Haskel, these must be worth millions!"

Haskel and Brad laughed outright at Sabrina's exaggeration. "Not millions, surely," Haskel corrected.

"Lots of thousands then."

"Perhaps someday, after I'm pushing up daisies of course. I'm glad you like them, my dear."

"You're amazing Haskel. I feel kind of star struck standing here, talking to you."

"If that's the case then I feel as dim as a candle when compared to the polar star in *your* presence, for your beauty and potential shine like a bursting gleam of celestial glory." Brad grinned at the words spewing from his grandfather's mouth. He was obviously used to it, but still intrigued.

"That was *poetic*! Could you say it again, one more time?"

"My Dear, I could not if I tried, although my feelings remain the same as they were only a brief moment ago."

The girl chewed on his words. They were lovely but still sincere. "Are you a poet as well as an artist?"

"I don't make any claims. I just like to use pretty words on pretty girls."

"Brad's not so different! He's just more casual about it."

"You mean *hip*." Haskel smiled at his grandson.

"I learned from the master," Brad declared.

"Would you like more popcorn?"

"Yes please." Haskel scooped up the tiny bowls and swept into the kitchen for refills.

"He could use his regular dishes but what fun would that be?" Brad whispered.

"He's an amazing little man! His attitude is keeping him young. He gets around very well!"

"Here you go," Haskel placed the trial-sized portions of popcorn on the table.

He looked kindly at Sabrina. His merry blue eyes twinkled at the girl. "These are quite good," he said, drawing a bundle of cards from his pocket and arranging them before his guests.

Sabrina gasped as she recognized her own artwork. "Oh no! Where did you get those?" She cast a violent look in Brad's direction. "I'm embarrassed for you to see them."

"Child!" Haskel chided sternly. "You've just erred against the gift which God has given to you. Never be embarrassed of your talents! Don't hide them under a bushel! Always find joy and happiness in your endeavors. Celebrate the things which you've done, for you are very young, and I see so much promise in your work."

"Really? Haskel, you can't be serious!"

"These are wonderful! They are very good. Tell me, my dear, have you ever received training or special lessons in art?"

"No."

"Nothing but raw talent, eh? That's the best kind! Never be afraid to learn, but never become over-coached. I would like to share some tricks and skills with you today if you are a willing party to my plan."

Tears brimmed Sabrina's hazel eyes, making the unique objects and people in the room swirl into unidentifiable liquid blobs. "I would love it Haskel! I really would."

"Let's finish our tea party, and then I will lead you upstairs to my studio."

The hours of the day flew, orchestrated by a cacophony of cheery cuckoos every sixty minutes.

The chorusing cuckoos would call upstairs. "This day is going too fast," Sabrina lamented. "Of all of the brilliant things that I've gotten to do this week, today has been my favorite."

Haskel's hand clamped her shoulder affectionately. "I'm very pleased to hear that and look how much you've progressed since arriving! My dear, your work has blossomed like a rose, right before our very eyes."

Brad was working quietly on a car model while Sabrina labored through Haskel's exercises. Brad told Sabrina that, as a boy, he always looked forward to visiting his grandpa because Haskel kept a well-stocked supply of models for him to make. "After I got them put together Grandpa would help me paint them. We created some real dandies, huh Grandpa?"

"I should say we did, my boy! If only the car companies had our skill and ingenuity, they would surely not be in a fix." Haskel whistled, hummed, and drummed his fingers quietly as he supervised Sabrina's progress.

"Haskel, can I ask you a question?"

"As long as I am able to answer it. I don't care for questions which make me feel foolish."

Sabrina smiled. She felt she could listen to the little man's strange prattle forever without tiring of it. "Do you believe in angels?"

"I do."

Sabrina sucked in a wary breath and continued. "When I was a little girl I saw my father be killed. He was kicked in the head by a horse. I was all alone with him in the barn. The horses were going crazy and I was so afraid! I prayed for help—I mean I *really* prayed. Suddenly this...person was with me. He let the colts out of the barn and then carried me from the loft safely. He was Brian, my twin brother, who died when we were born. I had always wondered what he would have looked like. Haskel, he was *beautiful!* Brian's face is still locked in my mind—etched in every fiber of my heart, I think."

Liquid brimmed in the kind, merry eyes as Sabrina told her tale. Brad was staring intently at the girl, obviously dumbstruck. She had never confided the story in him before.

"My question is," Sabrina continued, "how can I draw my memory? I've always used a photograph or an object as a pattern, but I feel very strongly that I'd like to capture Brian's image on paper. Mom would love to see the son she bore but could not raise."

"You will come back tomorrow," Haskel said resolutely. "I will not accept any excuses. Did Brian resemble any living family members?"

"Yes. He looked like Mom."

"Then bring a photo of her, if you have one. We can use her as a missing link, you understand, to help us fill in any missing details. Sabrina, with your memory and our combined skill, we shall pull it off! Such a delectable challenge, my dear." Haskel rubbed his hands together thoughtfully, knitting his white, bushy brows. "Capturing angels is my new, favorite pastime. Yes, I believe we can do it!" Haskel thumped his hand down on Sabrina's paper. "Continue practicing. I'm going downstairs to whip up a light supper. We shall dine in grand fashion on cucumber sandwiches and sliced tomatoes." Haskel paused. "Do you quite care for tomatoes, Sabrina?"

"I find them a delicacy of bursting red—a sumptuous gift from the garden of goodness,"

Sabrina spouted, copying a page from Geppetto's eloquent speeches.

A large smile spread across Haskel's features, lighting his face like a harbor lantern. "My dear," he said quite grandly, "you shall blossom most beautifully on Haskel Manning's family tree!"

CHAPTER TWENTY-THREE

"Hi, kids!" Vidalia called when they breezed through the door. "You're home extra early. Did you have a nice day?"

"Super! Oh Vidalia, this was the best day yet! I'm in such a good mood."

Brad set bags of groceries on the counter. "I hope you're hungry Vidalia! I stopped and bought everything we need for a steak fry. Grandpa Haskel fed us cucumber sandwiches, but that only whet my appetite."

Sabrina started rinsing and chopping veggies and making fresh dill dip while Brad headed out to the patio to fire up the grill.

"This is a nice change; having you two come home at a decent hour. It's only six o'clock!" Vidalia rubbed her eyes, "Or am I only hallucinating?"

"Suppertime," Brad said. "Did you starve today?"

"No, I drove myself down to the Ocean Institute to look around then I grabbed myself a burger at the harbor. I came back here and flipped on the air conditioner and read a good book all afternoon. It's been very restful."

"You look good."

"I soaked in the tub a long while, maybe that softened me up." Sabrina giggled at Vidalia's comment. She carried a tray of shish-kabobs out to Brad.

"Your hair looks extra nice. You look younger," Brad persisted.

"What the hell do you want?"

Brad's hands flew up in a defensive motion. "Absolutely nothing, Vidalia! I just thought you looked extra nice this evening." Vidalia studied Brad suspiciously.

"It smells good already," Sabrina called.

"What do you kids want me to do? I *can* cook you know."

"Nothing! I'm king of the grill." Brad waved a pair of tongs like a royal scepter.

Ding-Dong.

"Somebody get the door," Brad commanded.

"Bossy!" Sabrina said.

"I'm the king, remember?"

Sabrina opened the door. A tall man stood on the front steps. Sabrina judged him to be about six foot two. He was wiry built. He wore Wranglers, boots, and a red shirt. His face was charactered-- raw, yet ruggedly good-looking. His eyes were like steel, grey-blue, with crow's feet creasing the corners. A mustache of sandy red hugged his lip beneath a perfectly straight nose. His brows were furrowed, giving him an urgent look of serious intensity. His mouth was pulled into a hard line, as if the man's jaws were clenched very tightly. Grey-streaked sandy red hair teased against his temples. A cap covered the rest of his hair. Sabrina's gaze swept to a Harley parked in the driveway. *Nice ride.*

The man studied Sabrina, reciprocating the once-over.

"Can I help you?"

"I'm looking for somebody."

The voice fit the face like a hand in a glove. It reminded Sabrina of Sam Elliot's voice while narrating a beef commercial. "Who?"

"Is there anyone here named Vidalia..." The man's voice trailed into nothing. He was staring past Sabrina as if he had just seen an apparition. Sabrina's head followed his gaze. Vidalia stood just behind her in the doorway, eyes wide, vision locked on the stranger, unblinking. Sabrina heard Vidalia gasp shakily. She ducked out of the way, scurrying past Vidalia into the front room.

"Daisy," the man said, taking an uninvited step into the room.

Daisy? Who the heck is Daisy? Sabrina noticed Vidalia's hands. They were trembling uncontrollably at the greeting. She worked them furiously together, trying to calm them. The cords in her neck also seemed to spasm uncomfortably. Brad stood in the open patio door, watching Sabrina watch Vidalia watch the stranger. Sabrina was having a hard time deciphering Vidalia's body language. The woman was uncommonly silent and every nerve seemed pent with tension. Her complexion washed ashen.

"Daisy?"

Brad's eyebrows arched. "Daisy?" he mouthed silently at Sabrina, his face full of questions.

"Phillip." Vidalia answered as calmly as her shuddering body would allow.

Phillip? Phillip Masters! Of course! No wonder Vidalia seemed to be shaken to the core and coming apart at the seams. The two former flames stood facing each other in confrontation's fire. The emotion was scorching. A dry fire licked in Sabrina's own throat as she felt for the sudden shocked discomfort of her friend.

"How are you?" Phillip asked meekly. Tears brimmed against the steel grey, penetrating gaze.

Vidalia's jaw worked manically. She couldn't seem to control her jerky movements well enough to speak. *She needs help!*

"Won't you come in and sit down?" Sabrina said to the man. She motioned toward a chair. She grabbed Vidalia by the arm and quickly pulled her to the sofa to sit. "I'll be right back," Sabrina said in her ear. Sabrina dashed to her bedroom, retrieving a couple of anxiety supplements. She pressed them in Vidalia's hand, along with a drink of cold water. Neither Phillip nor Vidalia had said another word.

"Can I get you anything, Sir?" Sabrina asked as congenially as possible.

The man's vision shifted momentarily to Sabrina. "Could I also have a glass of water?"

"Certainly." Sabrina crossed the room to the kitchen. She fumbled with ice cubes from the refrigerator.

"Thank you," he said. Sabrina took a step back, wringing her hands against the discomfort in the room. Vidalia's cheeks burned scarlet which a vast improvement from the ghostly pallor of a few moments before.

Brad had fled outside to the grill. Sabrina could see him making the most of his steak flipping and shish kabob seasoning.

"Is this your granddaughter?"

Vidalia did not say a word. Sabrina smiled brightly, coaxing false ease and sunshine into her demeanor. "Hi, I am Sabrina Ashley. Vidalia is my dear friend. We work together. Vidalia doesn't have any grandchildren." Sabrina paused. She felt like an idiot in the situation. She didn't want to be there but it seemed Vidalia needed her so she conjured up another pleasant expression and dredged forward. "How on earth are we so lucky as to receive visitors today?" *Haskel would have been proud of that sentence!*

"That's the graceful and polite way of asking you what the hell you're doing here." Vidalia was awaking from her catatonic spell. *Cue! Exit Sabrina.* Sabrina backed quietly toward the patio door then slipped outside. She stole quickly over to Brad.

"Who's that guy in our house with Daisy?"

Sabrina couldn't help but smile at Brad's question. "That's Phillip Masters. They were in love forty years ago but he broke Vidalia's heart by bringing a souvenir home from the war."

"What kind of souvenir?"

"A pregnant Vietnamese woman."

"Oh." Brad poured his attention back to cooking. His Adam's apple bobbed nervously. Sabrina eased a little closer to the door, straining for any scraps of conversation.

"I was watching the news the other night," she heard Phillip say, "And boom! There you were, all over my screen. At first I just couldn't believe it but then they said your name was Vidalia *Somebody*, and I knew I had to trust what I was seeing."

"Davies. My name is Vidalia Davies."

"You're married then?"

"*Was*...I've been a widow for the past thirty years."

Silence.

"Psst, Sabrina! Sneak into the kitchen and bring us some plates and stuff. We'll eat out here. Grab the sodas."

Sabrina scowled at the Grill King. "Yes your Highness." She snuck through the front room, feeling like a fool. "Excuse me," she mumbled quietly. It didn't matter. Phillip and Vidalia were oblivious to the earth in its orbit. Sabrina loaded her arms with items from the kitchen, including napkins, utensils, pop, plates, steak sauce, veggies and dip. "Excuse me again," she said traipsing past.

Brad loaded plates of food. "Should we take them some?"

"I don't know. Go ahead. Feel free. Be my guest."

"I'll give you fifty bucks if you'll do it."

"It's not like you to be so uninvolved," Sabrina accused.

"Oh yes it is! I'm not touching this scenario with a ten foot shish kabob."

"Coward! Let me guess--your favorite color is yellow?"

"Absolutely." Brad grinned, plating up food for the fate-torn, yesterday-faded lovers.

Sabrina sauntered back into the house. Phillip's face was buried in his hands. *Is he crying?* Sabrina felt her eyes grow large. She quickly set the plates down on the coffee table. "Here's some dinner if you two would like some." She hurried back outside.

Brad motioned Sabrina to join him at the patio table. The picnic hadn't turned out quite the way they'd planned. Sabrina had pictured the three of them laughing and lounging in good humor and fun instead of Vidalia being held hostage to discomfort in the house, with Brad and her in exile outside.

"I called information," Phillip's voice said from the house, "and got Vandaline. She gave me this address."

Brad popped the tab on his soda. "Shhh..." Sabrina scowled. "I can't hear." Brad gave Sabrina a dirty look. He picked up his knife and began sawing his meat. "Shhh..." she said again. "I think Phillip's saying something." He threw his fork down on the table and huffed impatiently at the eaves-dropper. Sabrina couldn't help but laugh at him.

"Shhh!" he scolded, to even the score. Sabrina took a bite of shish-kabob. "Chew softer!" Brad commanded. "We're just getting to the good part...Phillip was about to learn that Daisy's name is really *Vidalia*." Giggles trilled from Sabrina. Brad snorted irreverently as well. "I feel like I've been sucked into a worn-out episode of *How the World Turns*."

"I've got a better one," Sabrina announced proudly, "*How Their Love Still Burns*."

"Tony could come up with a soap opera for you Sabrina, *How Your Butter Churns*."

"Now we're getting punchy. By the way...this is good steak."

"Thanks. Hey Sabrina, sneak over to the door and see what they're talking about in there."

Naughtily Sabrina did. "Vidalia's crying," she relayed softly to Brad. "Ah-oh...Phillip is moving closer towards her."

Brad's curiosity moved him next to Sabrina, just to see for himself the goings on.

"It's been a long time," Vidalia cried.

"Too long," Phillip said fervently. "I've wasted too damn much precious time."

"They might be a good fit for each other," Brad observed wryly in his new sister's ear.

"I'm sorry!" The man's voice was laden with pain. His eyes seared with sorrow.

"There's an awful lot of pent up emotion in there," Sabrina said. "If the dam breaks there could be a flood."

Brad silently retreated back toward the table to finish his meal. Sabrina followed. The two sat stationary, banned to the patio long after they'd finished eating. "I don't dare go in there. They are really having a heart-to-heart."

Vidalia's voice raised shrilly a time or two. Sabrina's chest burned for her friend. "She's finally facing forty years of grief, pain, and loneliness."

"And he's facing the holy tribunal of Vidalia's wrath, as well as his own guilty conscience. I feel sorry for him."

"He's either courageous or an idiot."

"He's both. He's an idiot for not explaining himself before now but he's courageous to come crawling here today."

Brad pushed himself from the table and ambled toward the grass. He swung himself onto his hands and began walking around upside down."

"Show off! I always wanted to do that."

"Try it."

"I have tried it!"

Brad sprang back onto his feet. He then launched himself into an acrobatic tumbling routine, finishing with a grand bow.

"Why didn't you tell me you were such a gymnast?"

"Never came up. I took tumbling classes twice a week since I was about eleven. It helped occupy my time after school. That's how I got the Tarzan gig. I could maneuver the stunts pretty well."

"Have you ever competed?"

"No, I haven't been that serious about it but I thought I was a real stud on the playground in sixth grade."

The mental picture of Brad performing for his classmates made Sabrina smile. "I'll bet."

"I practically took state in monkey bars. What did *you* do at recess?"

"I just stood around waiting for somebody to blow my mind on the monkey bars. No one ever did."

"Seriously--what?"

"I liked to hula hoop. I liked to jump rope. Mostly I used to catch insects with Danforth Wycliffe MacL'main."

"*Who?*"

"Danforth Wycliffe MacL'main," Sabrina stated again.

"Sounds like a one-person law firm."

"I *know*. You met his mother, Mrs. MacL'main. She's the secretary at the school. Well, she used to work at the elementary. One day in fifth grade Danforth was in big trouble. He chucked an ice ball at Halsey Redding during noon recess. Halsey ducked and the ice ball smacked into a school window and shattered it. The bell rang and we all scuttled into the school leaving the playground monitors to unravel the mystery of *who done it*. When the guilty finger was found pointing toward Dan his mother pitched a fit! She huffed and puffed into the intercom microphone, "Danforth Wycliff MacL'main! Report to the front office at once...and you'd *better* be afraid!" The announcement peeled all over the school. It was so funny! Even the teachers and faculty got a kick out of it. Danforth turned red and slunk from the classroom completely mortified. From that day until now he's referred to as *Danforth Wycliffe MacL'main*. Everyone uses all three handles."

"It's a strange name anyway, poor kid. It wouldn't have been so funny had his name been John Robert Jones or something."

"He's a really good baseball player. When coach calls him from the bench he yells his three names, followed by, *"You'd better be afraid"* It's kind of a hoot. Danforth's really good natured about it. You'll like him. I'll introduce you to him as soon as we get back to Morgan. He'd make a good friend. He has a younger sister. Her name is Robina Josephine MacL'main, but we all call her Binny Jo, much to her mother's chagrin."

"Those are quite the names alright." Brad checked his watch.

"What time is it?"

"Almost nine. They've been venting in there for three hours. I've got to use the bathroom; do you think I dare interrupt?"

"I'll come in the house with you. I've got to go too...then maybe we should just call it a night."

Sabrina followed Brad quietly into the house, catching the action as she went.

"You're beautiful Daisy," the man said, reaching a hand out and covering one of hers.

"Nonsense. I've made it a goal to gain two pounds annually for the last twenty-five years."

"I think you're beautiful. What's fifty pounds? Look," he said, sweeping his cap from his head. "My hair's starting to thin. Big deal!"

"I would rather have thin hair than thick hips," Vidalia said pleasantly, furiously wiping tears away with the backs of her hands.

The kids slipped down the hall without Phillip or Vidalia even noticing. An hour later Sabrina crept to her bedroom door and pushed it open a smidgeon. She lay down, putting her pillow in the doorway and rested her head, listening to the sorting process coming from the front room. She was startled to see Brad's pillow in his doorway too; his head poked from his room like a curious ground

225

hog. He wrinkled up his nose at the girl. Sabrina stifled giggles in her pillow. Brad glared placing his finger to his mouth to shush her.

Phillip's voice was sounding, low and raw.

"He could certainly sell me beef for dinner," Sabrina thought, being reminded once again of Sam Elliot's narrated commercials.

"Her name was Tuyen. That means *angel* in Vietnamese. She was a refugee, helping alleviate some of the nurses' duties. I wasn't as bad off as most of the guys in there. I was just laid up, depressed, and out of my mind with boredom. Tuyen would load me in a wheelchair and take me for walks. Sometimes I think she was my salvation for getting me out of that terrible hospital. Other times I feel she was my damnation for ripping me from you." Phillip let out a ragged breath. "I found solace in her black eyes, all the while dreaming about your brown ones. I was loyal to you until the end Vidalia, but then..."

Sabrina wasn't even breathing, her lungs seared with shared pain. Brad's face looked solemn as well.

"Did you marry her when you found out?"

"No. I nearly just bolted. I wanted so badly to walk away and leave her there. I willed the whole war experience to just go away and stop haunting me. I wanted to come home to you! We had big plans together, didn't we Daisy? I was boarding the damn plane to come home with some other troops when...I couldn't do it. I couldn't walk away and leave that little dark haired angel to face hell alone."

Vidalia was crying again. Sabrina wanted to cradle her head in a comforting hug.

"I went back to the hospital. Tuyen burst into tears when she saw me limping through the door to get her. It took a few months longer to get clearance to bring her home with me. I salved my conscience toward Tuyen, all the while knowing I would destroy you. Vidalia, I swear to the heavens above I never meant to unplug your world. I never meant to crush our dreams." A twisted sob choked from the hickory-smoked voice. Sabrina felt like a rat for listening, yet she couldn't pry herself away.

"I know you can't ever forgive me. I don't expect that you could, but after forty years of oppressive guilt I've come to tell you that I *did* love you. I've always loved you. I've condemned myself to a life of hell and misery. I've been tormented by the left-over battlefield fiends who sometimes blaze in my mind from the war. I've been hounded by nightmares and buried beneath shrouds of unpleasant memories, but the one that causes me the most pain, is the recollection of your face in Evanston that day. It took you less than one second to comprehend. Your beautiful face shattered, Vidalia. I'm sorry I did that to you."

"Are you still married to Tuyen?"

"No. My drinking got out of control. I was a coward hiding in a bottle. Tuyen tried to make me happy but she finally took the boy and skedaddled back across the sea to her mother in '78. I sent money regularly. I missed them after they'd gone. I've never remarried."

"Have you seen your son since?"

"No. He's bitter. The last time I talked to him, he was spewing a lot of anti-American crap in my ear. Hell, I'm not going to listen to that. He was born here, he's legally an American citizen, but he feels entitled to trash the stars and stripes and everything I battled for. I don't have room in my life for that kind of blatant disrespect. He can call me what he wants to--hate me, despise me, but when he starts in on my country, by G-- I won't tolerate it."

"So where have you been all of this time?"

"I'm a career military man. I've been around. I just retired last fall."

"Are you still hitting the bottle?" Vidalia didn't pull any punches.

Brad grinned at Sabrina, not surprised by the woman's direct question.

"I dried out about twenty years ago. I finally kicked the smokes too."

"When was the last time you stepped a foot inside of church?"

"Forty-one years ago, Daisy. The last time I went to Sunday school I sat by you."

"Maybe you ought to give it a try."

"Don't start polishing my shoes and pressing my suit just yet. I'm not interested. Any sparks of testimony I had have burned out. You can't rekindle a dead fire."

"No, but any Boy Scout is smart enough to know you can always light another one! You *are* a coward," Vidalia said coldly. "You think you can come crawling in here confessing your sins before me and begging for *my* mercy? Who am I to grant such pardons? You'd better make good with the Lord first...and then who could I be, to deny or doubt His sweet forgiveness? Think about that."

"If I did...come back to church...would you consider...would you risk becoming reacquainted with a wretch like me?" Phillip asked tentatively.

"I thought we just *were* reacquainting ourselves. I don't want you doing anything for me that you aren't willing to do for yourself. If you came to the conclusion that for your own peace of mind, you should make things right with your Maker, then the answer is *yes*."

The room was silent. Brad waved at Sabrina then gathered his pillow and quietly shut his door. Sabrina followed his lead. She said her prayers and climbed under the covers. Sabrina tried to settle down and sleep. This was the first night she'd even hit the sack before midnight but she couldn't relax. She felt fitful and restless. She needed a drink. She quietly opened the door and padded down the hall to the bathroom.

On her way back to her room she beheld a sight. Her dear friend Vidalia was dancing slowly with the tall, roughly handsome man. His arms were wrapped around her tightly, his head tilted down with one cheek resting against Vidalia's hair. Soft music tripped from the Manning's stereo. Sabrina's eyes and ears were frozen on the scene. Suddenly Phillip stopped dancing. Vidalia looked up at him, studying his face. Phillip bent closer. His hand gently touched her cheek as he kissed her. Sabrina's body flushed with the thrill of energy radiating from the two fate-thrown lovers. Sabrina quickly ducked into her room and closed the door. She felt as if she'd trespassed where she didn't belong. Her own heart was trilling. "Please don't let Vidalia be hurt ever again," she silently pleaded, climbing back into bed.

Buzz. Sabrina reached for her phone on the night stand. Brad's text read, "Do you think Daisy knows what time it is? If this were last night her one o'clock dong would just have dinged."

"This has been an exhausting evening but I can't sleep."

"Do you realize we never even kissed one time today?"

Brad's message forced the realization to settle in on Sabrina. "Maybe last night was our last," she typed hesitantly.

"Maybe so." *No argument?*

Sabrina considered the text. It felt right. Something was changing. Perhaps last night's parade and all of the wild fanfare and excitement was the crescendoing height of their romantic performance. She remembered the dolphin's leaping frenzy at the peak of their activity, and then how very quickly, how very quietly, the ripples had dissipated and the waters smoothed. She cross-examined her feelings for several long minutes. She loved Brad! She would always love Brad, but the waters were definitely settling. The realization didn't sting as badly as Sabrina had feared. "It feels right," she typed in the darkness.

"I know. I will always love you Sabrina, but now you are my sister. We are both blossoming together on Haskel Manning's family tree, remember?"

"Sleep good...by the way...Whitlee turns sixteen in November." Tears of melancholy trickled from Sabrina's eyes, pooling against her hair. She wasn't destroyed, just blue, and as strange as it seemed, worn out with relief. She drifted off to sleep, dreaming first of dancing dolphins then of the flaming fire of a setting sun. As she sank deeper into the enfolding comfort of blissful rest the sunset dawned--for it wasn't a sunset at all, but a sunrise. Brilliant rays burst over the tops of the Raymond Mountains, bathing the valley with golden light. She walked along the road, holding her Daddy's hand. A handsome raven-haired cowboy loped toward them on a horse. "Hello Chantry," Ben's voice called out. "I have a little something for you."

Chantry paused, shifting in his saddle. "What's that?"

"This," Ben said, hefting Sabrina onto the horse with the rider. "Take good care of her, Son. Don't ride too fast, she's pretty young. She's fearless though, and she trusts you. She's ready to ride."

Suddenly Sabrina wasn't seven anymore. The wind whipped her hair and the sun felt warm against her neck. She was keenly aware of every detail. She tossed her head over her shoulder to look once again at her father. He was smiling and waving. "I love you Dad," she called.

CHAPTER TWENTY-FOUR

Brad quickly hit his blinker easing the car into Bolsa Chica State Beach. He jerked the Mustang to a stop in the parking lot then took off running down the beach. Sabrina watched him go, hurting for the boy she loved. His anguish was genuine. She shared his agony but the confirmation of peace in her soul the night before had felt so reassuring. Hot tears burned her eyes as she waged against conflicting emotions.

She climbed out of the hot car. Her mouth was dry and she felt queasy. She leaned against the door. Brian's portrait stared at her from the backseat. She and Haskel had indeed been successful in *capturing angels,* as he phrased it. She studied his brilliant face peering from behind the glass. She remembered his soothing words to her so long ago.

"...This is going to be the hardest time in your whole life Sabrina. I'm sorry. You'll just have to face it, but I promise that you have the strength to make it. Dad and I will be closer by than you know."

"Promise!"

"I promise. You'd be surprised. I've always been near." The words danced in yesterday's script, fresh and alive, and with a renewed urgency.

She could see Brad's distant form, growing smaller and smaller as he pounded down the beach.

Sabrina wandered on the sand, making her way near the water. She shuffled along in her flip-flops, letting the waves wash her feet. She gathered pretty shells and interesting bits as she walked.

Occasionally tears would fall from her cheeks but the hungry, swirling ocean waters quickly lapped them up.

Sabrina's phone jangled. "Hello?"

"Sabrina?"

"Hi Vidalia. How are you? I didn't want to wake you up this morning...you had kind of a late night."

"Can you believe it, Kid? Can you really believe this has happened? I never dreamed in a million that my trip to California would bring me face to face with Phillip. You and Brad's frolicking romance led me towards my future I think."

"Maybe that was the purpose of it all then."

"What's wrong, Honey?"

"Last night we kind of ended things. It felt like our *zing* transferred to you and Phillip. I felt so peaceful that I settled in and slept, *really* slept. I've had another amazing day. Haskel helped me draw Brian, Vidalia! Can you believe it? I'm going to give it to Mom as a delayed bridal gift. But this afternoon all of our steeled-up resolves seem to be waning some. Brad's really having a hard time right now. He was even babbling about us running away together. I told him not to be ridiculous because there's no way I'm getting married while I'm still in high school! That's just plain *dumb*! He just jerked the car off the highway and took off running down the beach. I'm not chasing him because I figured he needed to think, yell, be alone, or whatever."

"I've been fasting for you two kids. I broke my fast yesterday with that hamburger down at the harbor. It sends shivers down my spine to know that you felt peaceful about things last night. Let that boy have some space. He's grieving. It probably feels to him like every important female in his life just gets ripped away."

"It was nice of you to fast for us."

"Oh Kid! I've prayed, pleaded, pondered, and poured over the two of you. You'll never know. I hope you won't be too angry, but I invited Joseph and Juliet to join me in my fast. Valyncia and Vandaline did too."

Sabrina sat down in the sand. She rested her elbows on her knees. She felt a little panicky knowing everyone knew about her business. *No secrets?* "Valyncia and Vandaline scarcely know me," Sabrina complained. "What did Grandpa and Grandma Ashley have to say when you told them?"

"They were concerned. They love you Sabrina! Don't you know they worry about you? They said they'd scarcely heard from you this summer. The news cleared things up a little bit, I think."

"I don't want to go see them now! I wish you wouldn't have called them. That's going to be awkward."

"What in the hell did you want me to do? You kids were respectful enough of my rules but your feelings for each other were soaring pretty high. Your folks were due home in a couple of days. Forgive me, but I needed some help!"

Sabrina closed her eyes, gathering her loose wits about her. "Don't get me wrong, Vidalia. I appreciate it, and I know something helped. I guess your prayers are potent ones."

"Prayer is especially powerful when it's united with others. That's why I called in the recruits to help me. Today I've been fasting for Phillip."

"You're bound to lose twenty pounds on this trip."

"I'm down ten, if you can believe it," Vidalia purred proudly.

"I *can* believe it. We've walked you to death, for one thing." Sabrina mindlessly drew pictures in the sand. "Vidalia, Phillip is very handsome."

"He is."

"Why does he call you *Daisy*?"

"My father used to call me his little *Vidalia-Vidaisy*. Phillip adopted it from Dad then shortened it down."

"That's kind of cute."

"He called me just a little while ago. He wants me to go home with him--on the back of his Harley. Phillip says we'll go north along the coast. That's the scenic route. We'll drive through the Redwoods; travel past Tahoe, then over the Sierra Nevada Mountains. It should be a beautiful ride."

Sabrina choked at the mental picture of Vidalia all trussed up in bikers' gear. "What?"

"Phillip still owns the old family place in Henefer. I didn't know that. It's sat around empty for so long. He wants to go home and have a good look around. He's invited me to go with him."

"Surely you're not considering it."

"As a matter-of-fact I *am*."

"Vidalia, you don't want to ride a motorcycle clear to Utah," Sabrina reasoned.

"Who the hell says I don't? I *do*."

Sabrina's finger drew a Harley in the sand. "Okay then…"

"Phillip sort of challenged me. He said if I would go home with him, he would try praying and read *The Book of Mormon*. He just called me a while ago and told me. He's sincere and I know he spent the whole night soul-searching."

"Not the *whole* night, a big majority of it was spent out in the front room with you. How did you get him to soften up about the church?"

"Last night I walked him out to his bike. I said, 'I'm an imperfect person, too. I'm rough around the edges. I've got a lot of faults; I swear too much, I judge other people, and I'm too damn proud. But every night I kneel down and say my prayers. I acknowledge my weaknesses, my failures and shortcomings before the Lord. He knows all of them anyhow and do you know what, Phillip? In the morning He sends the sun to shine on me anyway.' Phillip motored out of the driveway with a pretty thoughtful expression on his face."

Sabrina's finger traced a sun. "When are you leaving?"

"Just as soon as your Mom gets back but I'm in San Diego right now, so I won't be at the house when you get home tonight."

"Okay. Bye, Vidalia." The phone went dead in her ear.

Too much to think about, too much! Sabrina absentmindedly traced the Raymond Mountains in the sand, with a large sun cresting between their peaks. She was vaguely aware of a small pair of sandaled feet standing next to her. "That's good," a young voice said timidly.

Sabrina looked up. A dark haired girl stood peering at Sabrina's sand picture. Her brown eyes twinkled brightly. She smiled shyly at the artist. Sabrina then noticed the girl's tiny tongue poked a little mound in her cheek.

"What's your name?"

"Mady. I'm five."

"Five? That's my favorite age."

"We're on a picnic. We've been to Disneyland all week."

"That's fun! I've been there too."

"Why were you crying?"

How long has the little girl been watching? Sabrina's hands flew to her cheeks, rubbing any evidence of tears away. "I don't know. I didn't realize I was."

"That's funny. You've been crying for awhile. I always know when I'm crying."

"That's because girls are always more sensible when they are five."

"Can you draw a fish?"

Sabrina did. "Here, like this." She took Mady's hand in her own, helping the girl draw a fish in the sand. Mady clapped joyfully. The pink tip of her tongue slid excitedly back and forth along her lower lip.

"A bird?" The liquid brown eyes fairly danced with anticipation.

Again Sabrina guided the girl's finger, swirling in the sand until a bird flew beneath their fingers.

Mady bounced with increased enthusiasm. "I'm going to go show my Daddy what I can do," she called, skipping gleefully along the beach.

"Little darling," Sabrina mused.

"Should we go?" Brad asked.

Sabrina startled, she hadn't noticed him ever come back. "How long have you been there?"

He was sitting on a large boulder studying her thoughtfully. "Long enough to know you're still hurting, too."

"Of course I am, you idiot!"

Brad smiled. "Be patient with me Sabrina. Gearing down is going to be a little tedious for me." He gently took her arm and guided her up the shoreline.

The last two days in California were a mix of happy and sad. Sabrina was thrilled to see her mother! Amanda was tanned with a radiant, sun-kissed glow in her cheeks. The house was abuzz with conversation as the new family traded travel-log experiences. Dorian and Amanda lavished souvenirs and gifts on the kids.

"Thanks Pops," Brad said, examining a new hammock. "I'm hanging this in my room."

Sabrina was eager to see her mother's reaction to her special gift. She retrieved the portrait from her bedroom. "I have something for you Mom. Haskel helped me. It's Brian, just the way I remember him."

Amanda gasped at the likeness of her angel son. Tears trickled down her cheeks as she stared at the portrait. She hugged it to her chest then stared again. "It's wonderful!" Amanda threw her arms around Sabrina's neck and wept against her hair. "I love it, Bree, and I love you. I love Brian! Thank you for such a gift."

"Haskel's awesome. He helped me so much. I would have been too overwhelmed on my own to know quite how to begin. Haskel has referred to this undertaking as *capturing angels*."

Dorian's expression seemed odd as he gazed upon the portrait of Sabrina's twin brother. Furrows etched his forehead and he studied the artwork thoughtfully. Sabrina felt a little bit uneasy by his reaction, hoping he believed her account of actually seeing the boy. "Sabrina, ride with me to the market, will you? I'd like to talk to you."

Strange! Sabrina felt awkward fastening her seatbelt in a car which was only occupied by herself and her new stepfather. She didn't know him that well. Perhaps this was his attempt to make friends but Sabrina thought the whole experience was a little bit weird. The car ride was quiet for a few minutes. Sabrina's mind flew for something to say, "Haskel really is amazing. I figure he taught me about twenty years' worth of art lessons in a couple of days. It was thrilling for me to learn from him."

Dorian nodded thoughtfully. "Yes he is. Sabrina, has Brad told you how I met your mother?"

"Yes. He said you met her in Salt Lake City, and you took her to lunch."

"That's right. I had meetings that morning with a guy from the church building department. He answered many of my questions. He told me where I could get a good lunch. A young man approached me in the hallway and offered to show me just where to go. He led me into the Joseph Smith Memorial Building and said, "Wait here. You will shortly find what you have been looking for." I was puzzled to say the least, but I took a seat, thinking the young man was referring to the architecture of the grand structure. Suddenly your mother wheeled a cake past me. She was taking it into a reception hall."

"Yes, that's what Brad told me."

"Sabrina, the young man who led me to the building and told me to wait—he looked just like your portrait of Brian." Tears welled in Dorian's eyes and his voice was shaky.

Goosebumps raced against the flesh on Sabrina's neck and arms as the realization of Dorian's suspicions of divine guidance settled in on her. "You think Brian guided you to Mom?"

"Yes. I've never experienced anything like this before—it's a little bit unsettling to me. I knew your mother was Heaven-sent, but I didn't realize the power of those feelings until just a few minutes ago. Thank you for capturing an angel today." His expression bespoke sincerity. He seemed a trifle bit rattled by it all and quite chagrined at the emotions which tugged at his spirit.

Sabrina smiled at her new stepfather. They both wiped tears from their cheeks. Dorian slid sunglasses over his eyes to camouflage all traces of emotion while they hurried into the grocery store. Sabrina walked with him, up and down the aisles, feeling a sudden kinship to this man. Perhaps he was good enough for her mother, after all. They bought ice cream, and ribs, and lots of good things for a barbeque, and their conversation was easier on the way home. Sabrina and Dorian both felt a certain reverence for the revealing twist in the afternoon.

Dinner that night was enjoyable. The new family exchanged stories and conversation while they ate on the patio. A cool breeze swept in as the sun went down, carrying the briny odor of the sea and a slight chill on the air. The family moved inside the house where Brad set up Disney Monopoly.

Brad's phone jangled and he stepped into the kitchen to take his call. "Hey Pops," he said, covering the phone with his hand. "This is Jetta. One of the other Tarzans cracked his wrist. She needs me to work for the next two or three weeks. Is that okay with you?"

Dorian considered the request thoughtfully, finally nodding approval. Sabrina felt gutted. She was returning to Utah without Brad and once again an only child.

CHAPTER TWENTY-FIVE

Sabrina's head bobbed excitedly from the backseat as Dorian turned onto the Raymond Road. The car ride with her new step-father had actually been very pleasant. Sabrina had been determined to visit at least once this summer then an invitation had arrived from Grandma and Grandpa Ashley. They wanted to meet Dorian.

"Look! See that big rock sign right there? My cousin Joe just completed that for his Eagle Scout project. You're going to like Joe. He's just like me, huh Mom?"

Amanda nodded. "That's right. Whenever Aunt Jessie and I would take you kids out, people always asked if you were twins.

"We're the same age," Sabrina babbled to Dorian."We have the same dark curly hair and freckles."

Dorian grinned at Amanda. "Do girls always talk this much?"

"She does."

"That first house right there, that's Uncle Brant's house. We used to live there. The house right next to it is Grandpa and Grandma's. Remember Chantry Cantrell? They live across the road, over there."

Dorian nodded thoughtfully, trying to take it all in. The car pulled into the driveway. "Wish me luck," Dorian said pensively, obviously apprehensive about meeting Amanda's former in-laws.

"Nonsense," Sabrina said, sounding eerily similar to Vidalia. "You'll be fine."

Juliet burst out the back door to welcome her guests. Sabrina nearly knocked her down with an exuberant hug. "Where's Grandpa?"

"Out in the shop," Grandma said.

Sabrina left the introductions up to the others, running in search of her Grandpa.

He was standing near the shop talking to Joe and B.J. "Hi guys," Sabrina sang out. Joe grinned, wrinkling his freckled nose at the girl. Both cousins were sitting on four-wheelers, each with a cute girl peering from behind. Sabrina hugged her grandpa. "You remember these cousins of yours, don't you?"

"Don't be silly, Grandpa! Of course I do."

"Well I hardly recognize them anymore. They don't stay around here much—too busy running off and playing ball. Here they sit tonight with a couple of girls. What good are they to me?"

B.J.'s face flushed, and he rolled his eyes. "This is Brittney," he introduced. A mischievous smile peeked from behind B.J.'s shoulder. She had light brown hair and a hint of a dimple in one cheek. Her nose wrinkled in a playful manner.

"I'm Sabrina." Brittney didn't say anything; she just grinned shyly and bobbed her head.

"This is her older sister Kaylee," Joe motioned, jutting a thumb toward the girl sitting behind him. A pair of large, chocolate, doe-eyes twinkled brightly. Her smile was warm and friendly, lighting her features. The girls were cute in an attractive, down-to-earth fashion.

"Sisters?"

"Where's that kid who's your new brother?" Joe asked bluntly.

"Oh, Brad? He's in California. He works at Disneyland." Both girls raised one brow. *Must be a family trait...*"He got called into work for two or three weeks so he stayed in Dana Point.

"Well, we were just gonna play four-wheeler tag, but uh...we need another couple," Joe explained.

"There's Chantry, I'll go get him to play," B.J. said anxiously.

"Oh, don't bother him," Sabrina implored.

B.J. paid no attention to her. The four-wheeler rumbled to life, roaring past the gaping girl. Brittney turned her head back toward Sabrina, shrugging.

"He won't want to be bothered," Sabrina said quickly to Joe.

Grandpa Ashley laughed at her discomfort. "What makes you so sure? You think he's too old for a little fun, do you?"

"Yes. I don't think he wants to be bothered with a bunch of teenagers. He's going to be a school teacher you know."

"Is that a fact? Well...there won't be any teenagers *there...*" Grandpa teased.

Joe grinned at the man he was named after. "Sabrina's acting shy. What's wrong with her?"

"I'm not *shy*. I just don't want to bother Chantry. Let's call Bracken instead."

"I'd rather just play with two teams than drag him along,"

Sabrina chanced a look across the road. B.J. and Brittney seemed to be holding a conference with the painfully good looking neighbor. Chantry caught her looking and waved. Sabrina turned quickly. Her cheeks were flaming hot and she stared at the dirt, feeling ridiculous.

Joe gauged her reaction. "What's the matter with you? It's just Chantry...he's easy about stuff."

Grandpa Ashley winked at the pink-faced girl. "I guess I'd better go to the house and be sociable. Good to have you back here where you belong." Grandpa hugged Sabrina. He nodded to Kaylee. "Nice to meet you Kaylee. Make sure these knot-headed boys don't wreck every outfit on the place. They're apt to be showing off." It was Joe's turn to feel awkward. He ducked his head and groaned. Kaylee just smiled and giggled nervously.

B.J. and Brittney sputtered back across the road. "He's coming," B.J. triumphed. He's going to bring his wheeler but first he says he has to *change*." B.J. shot an accusatory look at Sabrina. "I said, 'Don't waste time changing, she didn't even want you to play.'"

Brittney thumped B.J.'s arm. "You did not."

"While we're waiting for Chantry to come, these are the rules," Joe said. "You have to hide as a couple *with* the four-wheeler. It's against the rules to stash the wheeler and sneak off somewhere. Each couple has to stay together. One couple will hide first. The first team to find them gets to hide next. The hiding team gets a ten minute head-start."

"Sabrina and I hide first," Chantry called. Sabrina startled for she hadn't heard him cross the road.

Joe scowled at his idol. "Okay."

"Let's play ball," Chantry said decidedly.

"We're not playing ball," Sabrina muttered, following him across the road to his four-wheeler.

Chantry glanced down at the girl, as noticing for the first time who his teammate was. "Oh hello, Sabrina. Are you home from your *delicious* vacation?"

"Yes I am!" Her heart was hammering as she saddled up behind him. "You smell good," she noted without thinking.

Chantry turned toward the girl, grinning. "Isn't that lucky? Hold on." The four-wheeler rumbled to life and peeled out of the Cantrell's driveway. Sabrina's arms instinctively threw around his waist for support. Chantry lapped the block a couple of times, trying to give the other teams the slip, then he urged the four-wheeler into the south end of a long, dark, calving shed on the Cantrell property. Sabrina helped him close the double doors. They were parked near the dark end of the barn, partially hidden behind splintery slab panels, a pyramid of salt blocks and a few spools of wire fencing. "If they come in down there," Chantry said, pointing to the far end of the shed, "They'll have a hard time seeing us because of the sun. It's really shadowy down here."

"But if they come through these doors we're caught dead to rights."

"Uh-huh." Chantry swung his long legs off the four-wheeler and eased himself down on the ground to wait.

Sabrina followed his lead. "I can't hear them coming yet."

"Awe, we gave them the slip. Dollars to doughnuts Joe's driving west and B.J.'s heading south to Raymond Creek."

"How do you know?"

"Because those are the places they like to hide."

"You've played this game with them before?"

Chantry nodded, "But never with girls. I think Joe's got a case on Kaylee. This is the second or third time I've seen him with her."

"Oh." Sabrina strained to hear the rumble of a *Polaris* motor but couldn't.

Chantry squinted across the dim light at the girl. "You'd better over here and sit by me. I'm afraid they can see your head silhouetted against that window right there."

"Okay," she whispered, scooting towards the tall, perfect outline. "So much for my clean jeans." Sabrina slapped dust from her knees when she sat.

"Glad to see you're not so citified you can't have some good old country fun."

"I'm not citified at all!"

"You're not all puffed up with yourself over Disneyland?" Sabrina threw a playful elbow into his ribs. "Ooof," Chantry's wind hissed out. "Don't get violent."

A motor rumbled in the distance, purring closer. Sabrina tried to shush her breathing as a four-wheeler sputtered to a stop. Footsteps sounded outside of the shed. She heard Joe's voice. Suddenly Kaylee's silhouette filled the double doors at the end of the barn.

"Are they in here?" Joe asked, stepping beside the dark-eyed beauty.

Kaylee's eyes scanned the darkness. It was hazy and dim. "I don't think so. Hey! Are you in here?" she demanded to the dark shadows on the far end.

Chantry's voice caught in his throat, stifling a laugh. He reached out and squeezed Sabrina's hand under the adrenaline surge of being hunted. Her fingers tingled beneath his grasp.

Joe took two or three steps closer, his eyes working the haze and din. "I don't think they're in here."

Kaylee turned, giving up too easily, and headed back towards the sunlight. Joe reached for her hand, pulling her to a stop. She giggled something but Sabrina couldn't quite make out her words. Joe chuckled too, reaching for her other hand. *Oh, Joe! If only you knew you had an audience!* Kaylee giggled again. Joe tugged her hands so she had to take a step nearer. Their heads leaned closer, closer, until...*bump!* Noses collided. Kaylee tittered but Joe was not deterred. *Bump*, once more. Joe reached a hand up to steady the girl's chin and finally nailed the kiss.

"After two strikes he slides into second." Chantry whispered softly in Sabrina's ear.

Sabrina stifled a laugh by biting on her lip. *Poor Joe!* She chanced a look at Chantry. He was smiling down at her. His eyes were purely black in the dim shadows. Her heart picked up a stray beat.

Suddenly a second four-wheeler screeched to a stop. Joe and Kaylee leapt away from each other, posing an innocent distance. The south door flung open and sunlight instantly lit the shadows. Chantry and Sabrina were exposed.

"There you are," B.J. called triumphantly. "We win!"

Sabrina noticed Joe's chin drop to his knees. Kaylee's eyes widened comically and she peeled out of the double doors, trying to

244

escape as quickly as possible. Sabrina could hear the girl's mortified, uncomfortable hysterics from outside.

"You *jerks!*" Joe thundered. "Why didn't you say something when we hollered?"

"Because we were *hiding*," Chantry explained, grinning at his young friend. "We'd be pretty poor sports if we just called out our positions. We did appreciate the half-time entertainment though."

"If you say one word of this *Sabrina*," the boy threatened. Joe was shaking his head, blushing, flushing, and gawking foolishly. "I can't believe it! You two suck," he muttered, staggering out of the doors and rumbling away with a red-cheeked, tongue-tied, embarrassed girl.

B.J. and Brittney had roared off in a cloud of dust, innocent of Joe and Kaylee's romantic folly.

Chantry was still laughing at the spectacle. He pulled Sabrina to her feet. "That was great," he said, dusting the seat of his pants. Sabrina noticed his faded blue Wranglers looked good even dusty.

"I feel sorry for them! I thought poor Kaylee was just going to cry when the doors opened and here we sat, witnesses to a tender moment."

"Love spies," Chantry agreed.

"It's not funny!" Chantry questioned her statement by arching his black brows. "Well...it's kind of funny," Sabrina conceded, climbing on the back of the four-wheeler.

"It will give them something to talk about later," Chantry said wickedly.

The game was exhilarating! Chantry and Sabrina found B.J. and Brittney right off the bat. Chantry was correct; B.J. had driven to Raymond Creek, concealing the four-wheeler in a thatch of willows.

"No fair," Brittney whined when Chantry called them out. "We barely got to hide at all."

"You're so predictable," Chantry said to the younger Ashley.

B.J.'s eyes rolled. "Where's Joe?"

"I couldn't be certain. Maybe he and Kaylee are sandwiched between two haystacks trading kisses."

B.J. rolled his eyes. "Joe doesn't know anything about *that*."

Chantry grinned and shrugged his shoulders. "I don't know then. If you see them, tell them they're looking for us again."

B.J. and Brittney ambled back onto Center Lane, putting north to wait at the shop. Chantry steered the four-wheeler south toward Grandpa Ashley's big meadow. The sun was creeping toward the western hills, dampening the heat of the day.

Chantry eased the four-wheeler down into a dried-up slough, following it into large culvert.

"They'll never find us in here," Sabrina said.

"Not if they don't hurry...but I doubt Joe could see anything tonight if he actually saw it. He's too love-struck."

Chantry had to walk hunched over to avoid whacking his head on the curved culvert's top but Sabrina followed him uprightly. "Hey Slimy, get out of here," Chantry said to a tiny, coiled up water snake. "This is my hiding place." He flipped the scaly reptile from the culvert's opening with a stick then sat himself down to wait. Sabrina slid down across from him. Chantry was fiddling with his watch; Sabrina took advantage of his down-swept gaze to study him.

"So where's that *delectable* new brother of yours?" Chantry asked without looking up.

"What an odd question! Has Brad done something to offend you?"

"No...I was just wondering."

"He's probably getting his muscles airbrushed as we speak."

"Attractive! Painted on Pecs."

"He happens to be quite nicely built all by himself! He just has to undergo the *Tarzan* touch, that's all." Sabrina scowled at Chantry. "He's very athletic. You of all people should appreciate that. You should see Brad's acrobatic stunts. He's a real gymnast!"

"In a make-believe place, maybe."

"You big jerk!" Sabrina clawed a dried piece of mud from the bottom of the culvert and flung it at Chantry.

He shied sideways, easily avoiding contact. A smile twitched at his mouth. "You throw like a girl."

Sabrina's hot glare fired missiles at the man. "You make me *crazy!*" She hurled another mud clod but Chantry extended a long leg, blocking it in mid air. It crumbled and bits of dirt sailed back in Sabrina's direction. Tiny fragments invaded her eyes, nose, and mouth. "Ooh!" She shrieked, climbing to her feet and stomping furiously to Chantry's side. She swiped at his head but he caught her by the wrist.

"Feisty," he appraised smoothly. He applied gentle pressure to Sabrina's wrist, forcing her to sit down. "Why do you let me get you so riled up? I'm just playing with you and you know it. What a little hothead."

Sabrina was mesmerized by the finely chiseled features of his face. She forgot all about assaulting him. She was only aware of the electric sensation pulsing up her arm from Chantry's grasp. His brows rose, expecting a response from her. Sabrina gulped once. "Oh."

"Now if you can behave like a lady I'll let go of your wrist."

"Then act like a gentleman," Sabrina countered.

Chantry released his grip. "You're too maddening Sabrina. You positively bring out the worst in everybody." His voice was rich and pleasant, and Sabrina knew he wasn't being cruel, but she quickly jutted an elbow into his ribs because he expected a reaction.

"*Ooof!* Stop doing that! I'm going to turn you in for *friend* abuse."

"I'll turn you in for child abuse!"

Chantry winced slightly. "Actually I really should have more sense than to be caught sitting in a culvert with a *minor...*"

"Whatever...We're just playing a game. There's no law against culvert-sitting!"

"Still...I'll have to watch myself when school starts..."

What does that mean exactly? Sabrina felt confused. She began picking at a hang-nail, drilling her mental reserves for something to say. "Brad's probably swinging from jungle vines right now. He'll have the crowd eating out of the palm of his hand. He's very good at it."

"Delightful."

Sabrina peeked sideways. Chantry's mouth was pulled into an annoyed grimace. *Good.* "Guess what? I got to meet his Great Grandpa. He's the most darling little man! He fed us cookies and popcorn on little blue dishes."

"Little blue dishes?"

"This teensy," Sabrina said, illustrating the miniature size with her hands.

One black brow arched suspiciously.

"And tiny glasses of milk..."

Chantry blinked a couple of times then cleared his throat and said, "My great-grandfather once slaughtered a grizzly bear with his bare hands to save his tribe. Did I ever tell you about that? Later they ate the bear and didn't use any dishes at all."

His larger-than-life Indian story tickled Sabrina's funny bone. She sputtered and choked, laughing obnoxiously. Chantry's chuckles mingled with hers and the happy echoes reverberated around inside of the culvert. "You're dumb," Sabrina gasped.

"I know I am! I'm a perfect fool sitting in here with you." There was an edge to his voice.

Concern knotted Sabrina's stomach. "Why?"

"Because--those idiotic cousins of yours are never going to find us." Chantry's answer pleased Sabrina and she bellowed heartily yet again. "Oh, listen..." Chantry said, stifling Sabrina's gaiety. "Hear that?" A four-wheeler purred in the distance, growing closer. "Bet you ten bucks it isn't Joe."

Sabrina smiled. "My heart always beats fast when I'm trying to be quiet."

"Mine, too."

Sabrina shivered. "It's getting cold in here."

"You should have brought a jacket."

"It was hot when we left."

Chantry nodded. Sabrina shivered again, giggling softly, trying to reign in her ragged breathing. The four-wheeler chugged closer and the engine stopped.

"They've got to be around here someplace," B.J. said.

"Over in those cattails?" Brittney offered.

"Maybe. Let's walk over there. We'll surprise them." Footsteps sounded overhead.

Sabrina sucked in her breath. Involuntary shivers danced along her arms, raising tiny goose bumps. Chantry quietly slid an arm around her, rubbing her chilly arm. The warmth of his touch popped and sizzled against her flesh like a droplet of water falling in a hot frying pan. Her heart thumped sideways. The footsteps softened, crunching through meadow grass a little further away.

Sabrina exhaled shakily.

"Are you okay?" Chantry whispered against her hair.

"Um...I'm not *sure*," she stammered blankly. She missed seeing a large smile spread across Chantry's features in the darkening shadows of twilight.

Chapter Twenty-six

Grandpa Ashley enjoyed cooking and eating breakfast outside. "Nothing," he often decreed, "tastes better than pancakes and bacon in the crisp morning air." He was chief commander in charge of hash brown operations, while assigning Uncle Brant to bacon and sausage detail. Chantry and Dorian were busy flipping golden pancakes. The backyard was filled with delicious aromas and happy voices.

"Make some juice will you Sabrina?" Grandma asked. "Amanda, let's you and I go out and cover the tables." The back door slammed behind them.

Sabrina was happy to stand at the sink, watching the men cook in the yard. She deliberately fiddled longer than necessary with the cans of frozen concentrate. Her mind replayed seasoned memories of so many breakfasts, shared together before her dad was killed. He always cooked the pancakes to what he termed to be, *"Aunt Jemimah's standards."* Sabrina smiled subconsciously while yesterday's fragments skipped across the stages of her mind.

"That smile suits you."

Sabrina startled. "I didn't hear you come in."

Chantry's expression was pleasant. "I don't suppose you did. Your thoughts were a million miles away. I just need to get some paper towels."

Sabrina reached beneath the sink and handed some to the ruggedly handsome neighbor. "I was just remembering my dad and how much he loved morning cookouts. He was just as fanatical about them as Grandpa."

Chantry nodded, sharing the recollection. "A person has to swear a secret oath just to help your Grandpa cook," he raised his hand in scout's honor, "I promise, in the name of all that is golden, light, fluffy, and known as *Pancake*, that I shall do my best."

Sabrina chuckled at the exaggeration. "Where are Joe, B.J., and little Ben?"

"B.J. and Ben are out moving sprinklers. Joe and Kaylee are probably still looking for us."

Sabrina laughed, "Poor Joe!"

"What? That will teach him for getting big ideas about little girls. He needs to keep his mind on baseball."

"Ugh. You really are a coach aren't you?"

"I'm trying to get my mind geared for it anyway. You still need to help me move, remember?"

"Yes! I know I owe you."

"So...I was wondering...how about you stay in Raymond for a couple more days and then I'll take you back to Morgan with a load of my stuff. Would that be okay?"

"Yes! I wasn't ready to go home yet."

"You're sure now? You're not just telling me that?" Chantry baited the girl even though her feelings were blatantly obvious.

"I want to stay! Now we can go riding together." Sabrina felt as if she'd possibly suggested too much. "I mean...if you wanted to." She looked down feeling embarrassed.

A large hand tipped her chin up. Chantry's gaze was penetrating. A myriad of emotions flooded the girl as she focused in on his dark, searching eyes. "I do," he said before strolling from the kitchen.

Slam! The back door banged shut. Sabrina was frozen in the same place he'd left her, her chin and jaw searing from his touch. She took a deep breath then turned back toward the frozen clump of juice and began to stir. Her eyes trailed to the pancake grill, sweeping over the top of Dorian's head, and settled in on Chantry from a safe distance. His eyes looked up and locked with hers once again. A soft smile teased against his mouth. He reached up and touched a spatula to his forehead in a small salute. "Here's to Aunt Jemimah," he called, loud enough for her to hear.

A few neighbors began to trickle in. Chantry's family sauntered across the road, followed by the Brehman's and Spicer's. Joseph and Juliet welcomed each neighbor warmly, introducing Dorian to each one. Bracken Spicer followed Sabrina like a puppy. She'd forgotten how irksome the boy could be.

"I heard your Mom got married."

"Duh--that's why Grandpa's invited everyone to breakfast."

"Oh. So where do you guys live now?"

"We are still in Morgan."

"Oh. I thought you were moving to California."

Sabrina rolled her eyes, finding it hard to be courteous. "No."

"Remember I took you to prom last spring?"

How could I possibly forget? Sabrina scurried over to the grill, retrieving a Dutch oven full of hash browns from Grandpa's hands. Bracken tripped behind her a few paces. She suddenly understood why Joe and B.J. didn't want him playing four-wheeler tag! He was *too* annoying.

"Well, do you?"

Chantry breezed by with a loaded plate of *Aunt Jemimah* pancakes. "Do you Sabrina?" he asked with a quick wink.

"Of course. It only happened in April. I couldn't possibly forget that quickly."

"Did you like my tuxedo? I've studied our prom photo and I think it was pretty good."

"Fantastic," Sabrina said flatly. "The cummerbund looked like a piano keyboard. How could I forget?"

"A brilliant Sonata in D flat," Chantry called pleasantly as he glided back to the grill.

Sabrina bit her lip to keep from laughing out loud. She unwrapped squares of butter and placed them, here and there, on the picnic tables.

"Did you like our prom picture?"

"Sure," Sabrina said without giving it much thought. She was pouring syrup from a gallon jug into small pitchers.

"When is your Homecoming dance? Maybe I should come to Morgan and take you to it."

Aunt Jessie shot Sabrina an *"I'm so sorry"* look, while Amanda also appeared similarly pained.

Sabrina stalled by dashing in the house for napkins. "Bracken's a perfect idiot!" she muttered as she went. When she came out of house Grandpa Ashley was gathering everyone together for a blessing on the food.

"After the prayer you can get your plate and come through the line. Enjoy! There's plenty and if there isn't the boys and I will gladly cook you some more!"

After *amen* was said, Sabrina grabbed a plate and dodged into line between Joe and Ben. "Save me," she mouthed to Joe.

Joe flushed at the very sight of Sabrina but knowing she had a secret on him, he felt obliged. He put a quick hand up, blocking Bracken from squeezing in. "No cutting Spicer! You know the rules; it's the back of the line for you."

"Awe Joey," Bracken mumbled. "No fair. You let Sabrina in."

"She just slipped me twenty bucks. If you've got twenty dollars to burn I'll let you in right behind her."

Bracken's head drooped and he shuffled to the end of the line.

"*Moron,*" Joe whispered against Sabrina's ear. "Aren't you glad Chantry played last night, instead of him?"

"You'll never know! He just asked me to Morgan's Homecoming."

"No way? Wasn't Bear Lake's prom enough punishment for one girl to bear? *Even if it is you.*"

"I didn't commit to anything."

"His sister is just as bad. She stares at me on the bus," Young Ben added. "One time she doodled balloons all over my math assignment."

Sabrina walked to a table and set her food down, doubling back to get some juice. As she approached her selected seat for the second time, she noticed Bracken had arranged himself across from her plate. He was smiling eagerly at her. Sabrina's pace slowed, inwardly scheming how to get away from the boy without being completely rude. Just then Chantry's form strode past, scooping up Sabrina's plate. "Over here Breezy, I saved you a seat."

"Thank you," she sang under her breath. "Chantry Cantrell you saved my life," she trilled softly, following him to a different location. At that very moment she would have followed him anywhere.

The next two days were great! On the second day Chantry took Sabrina riding up Raymond Canyon. It had been years since she'd ridden so far. "Dad used to bring me up here."

Chantry nodded. "Your dad loved to ride. One night, not too long before he was killed, I couldn't sleep. I got up and got a glass of milk and went out on the front steps to drink it. It was a starlit night with a full moon and all."

"Was it one of those glowing nights that you can drive without headlights?"

"Yes, exactly. Anyway, I saw your Dad gallop up to the front of your house. He whistled and your mom came running outside in her nightgown. He scooped her up onto the horse, and they started riding toward Raymond Creek on a dead run. The wind was whipping Amanda's nightgown and hair. It was quite a sight and it left me wishing for a girlfriend."

The story was appealing to Sabrina. She never contemplated her parents doing romantic things like taking moonlit bareback rides. "How on earth did Mom get on the horse with her nightgown on?"

"She just hoisted it up around her legs and it all worked. If I was an artist I'd paint a picture of them racing through the summer night that way. They had the romance of the century, you know."

Sabrina smiled at the tall rider. Chantry was easy in the saddle and easy on the eyes. She fought the temptation of envisioning him in war paint and a breech cloth, but he was equally as alluring in his Wranglers and denim shirt. "Did you ever play Cowboys and Indians when you were a kid?"

Chantry grinned. "Yes, as a matter of fact I did."

"Which side were you on?"

"You are the only person I know who would ask that question! You are never politically correct."

"Well?"

"Whichever side was winning, of course." Chantry leaned ahead in the saddle and clicked to Rio to hasten his pace. Sabrina had to nudge Rosie just to keep up. They loped up to a shady spot where wild strawberries grew near the creek. Chantry gathered dozens of berries in his hat. He and Sabrina sat near the water and ate them. They were tart and juicy, and Sabrina's jaws spasmed at the shock. Chantry laughed at her expressions. He leaned against the trunk of an aspen tree and watched as she kicked off her boots and trailed her feet in the icy waters of the rushing creek.

"This is my idea of a perfect day," Sabrina said, churning bubbles with her feet.

Chantry chewed on a piece of grass. "Better or worse than swinging through the jungle with Tarzan?"

Sabrina couldn't resist smiling at the man. "Different."

"Mmm…that's all? Just different?" Chantry plucked the grass stem from his mouth and threw it into the creek. "Perhaps I should have served these strawberries on little blue dishes."

CHAPTER TWENTY-SEVEN

Chantry stopped in Evanston to fuel up. A carload of girls pulled up to the side of the candy-apple red pickup, catcalling and whistling. "Thank you ladies," Chantry said smoothly. The girls peeled away giggling and screeching obnoxiously. "See what I mean? This truck *is* a chick magnet."

Sabrina leaned her head out of the window. "They weren't talking about your *truck*! They were talking about *you*!"

"Naw, I heard them. They said, 'Nice Wheels. Nice Bumper.'"

"You'd better get your hearing checked."

"They liked my wiper blades," he continued. "And my exhaust system."

Sabrina was lightly drumming her fingers on the steering wheel, listening to his absurd, twisted little observations. She had discovered in the last couple of days that Chantry Cantrell was a complete treasure of humor. He had a well-rounded scope of knowledge and he had entertained Sabrina with interesting bits of information. He would make an excellent history teacher! The two had visited all day long while riding horses and Sabrina was sorry to see the sun set on their time together. Of course Chantry could push her buttons by being stubborn, difficult, and maddening, but even the provocations were mostly enjoyable.

Honk! Honk! The noisy car was returning. Sabrina counted seven girls leaning from the windows. This time, in addition to whistling and calling they tossed little bits of paper. The papers fluttered in the air like confetti. Sabrina snatched one. *"Call Ginger,"* it listed a number.

Sabrina held the note up to Chantry's face. "Must be the name of a good mechanic…it's awfully nice of them to be so concerned about my truck."

"Listen *Dipstick*, they're not interested in changing your oil! I'm just grateful your license plates say *First Base* instead of *Home Run*."

Chantry hung up the fuel-hose and stepped into the truck. Sabrina quickly slid back into her seat.

"Are you hungry Breezy?"

"Um…"

"Because I am."

"Then yes."

Chantry grinned. "What is it with you women? You could be starving to death but you won't mention it until we admit to it first." The Dodge rumbled across the road to Arby's drive-thru window.

"Bet you didn't eat anything this fancy in California."

"Are you sure you want me eating in your truck? What if I spill?"

"Do not defile my truck," he warned, slowly annunciating each word.

Sabrina giggled and ordered the most non-crumbly, non-greasy, and non-messy food she could think of. It was about an hour's trip from Evanston to Morgan. The Dodge ate up the distance much too quickly.

"Now the work begins," Chantry said, pulling into his apartment. "This place has sat vacant for a little while, so I'm warning you…it's a little dank inside. It needs some sprucing up."

"This is almost the first work I've even done in a whole month. I didn't even get one paycheck for the month of July. All I've done is play."

"I'll have to crack the whip."

Sabrina filled Chantry's kitchen sink with hot sudsy water and began washing out cupboards and polishing his counter tops until they fairly gleamed. She took pride in her work, filling just a little bit like she was playing house. She arranged his odd assortment of dishes neatly in the clean cupboards. "Nice china," she said as he walked by for another load.

His mother had sent him with several large boxes of food. Sabrina enjoyed cataloging the canned goods, imagining Chantry's self-prepared suppers. Tashina had sent home-bottled tomatoes, peaches, pears, cherries, and raspberries. Sabrina polished the jars until they shone and lined them up inside of a high cupboard. Cans of corn, beans, and chili were plentiful. Spaghettios and Chef Boyardee Ravioli made the girl smile. "You're going to be eating like a real gourmet."

"Me and Chef Boyardee are like *this*," Chantry said, crossing his fingers tightly. "That's survival food. I've lived off it pretty well the last four years."

"Captain Crunch?" Sabrina asked, pulling it from the box.

"*With Crunch Berries!* It's the best!"

"I'm finding out all of your secrets."

"That's okay...I already know all of yours."

"I don't have any secrets."

"You've got a couple or three," he wagered from the other room.

Sabrina didn't dare pursue the conversation any further at that point. There was still too much work to be done. She tackled the refrigerator next, scrubbing, cleaning, and disinfecting. It smelled lemony and fresh when she finished. Tashina sent a couple boxes of baking soda. Sabrina opened one of them and placed it in the fridge.

Cantrell's had also sent a cooler full of frozen meat. Sabrina dragged it inside and began stocking steaks, burger, and roasts in the freezer. "Gee, you've got enough food in here to last a while," Sabrina observed.

"At least a week, huh?"

"I've seen the time this much food would have lasted Mother and I for months…things have kind of changed though. I'm not sure we'll have such a tight grocery budget anymore."

"That's kind of lucky."

"Yes, but we never went without. We just had to be careful, that's all."

"Sounds like my mission. We rejoiced over dinner invitations but I often pretended to be fasting. Everybody always wanted to feed us tuna casserole. *Yuck!* I hate that stuff. I got so hungry for a dish of home-bottled peaches and a couple slices of homemade bread and butter, I can't tell you!"

"That would have been a typical supper for Mother and I. Too bad you didn't serve your mission here. Maybe I'll have to come cook you supper one night. I'm a good cook you know. What if it tasted so delicious that you saw it as a bribe and you flunked me in history?" Her bottom lip jutted out playfully quivering.

"You're crazy."

Sabrina filled drawers with consumable products like plastic wrap and tin foil, garbage bags, and light bulbs. It was fun. "This is probably how much fun my Mom had outfitting her new house."

"You're having fun?" Chantry seemed amused by that, so Sabrina let it pass.

"Guess what Chantry?"

"What?"

"I'm filling up your junk drawer."

"Already?"

"Yes. Every loose odd and end that I don't know what to do with is in this end drawer, okay?"

"I might have to call you a lot to help me find things."

"Okay."

Sabrina tackled the bathroom next, scouring twenty-years of hard water from the tiles and grout.

She hung fresh bath towels, making them look pretty with a hand towel and washcloth draped over the top. She retrieved a baseball mug from the kitchen and placed a toothbrush and toothpaste in it. She filled the medicine cabinet with other items and toiletries which were neatly packed inside a box. She took the lid off of Chantry's deodorant just to smell it. It made her feel tingly inside, remembering how well he smelled when she rode on the back of the four-wheeler with him. She blushed at herself in the mirror then quickly clapped the lid on and put it in a drawer.

Chantry was shampooing carpets; he pushed the steaming hot machine by the bathroom door then quickly shot a double-take. He turned off the noisy monstrosity. "Sabrina this looks great! You've got everything looking so nice I won't dare use any of it. Really, you should have seen my apartment in college. It didn't look this nice. Of course I had four other slobs to deal with. Now I'm in your debt again. I didn't do nearly this much work for you."

"I'm having fun. It's kind of like playing house."

Chantry's brows shot up and a smile twitched against the corners of his mouth.

"I mean--um, don't get nervous or anything."

"Who's nervous?"

"You are."

"You're the one babbling explanations. I didn't ask for any. I agree with you! Girls are very good at playing house. You've got my kitchen looking so nice it will have the Tashina Cantrell stamp of approval."

"That's good."

Sabrina lugged a laundry basket of bed linens and quilts into the bedroom. It was a dark little room, screaming for sunlight. She raised the blinds and opened the windows, giving the room a good airing. She took extra pains to make the bed neatly. She didn't tuck any covers in at the bottom for she had a sneaking suspicion Chantry's feet would poke off the end of the bed. No sense giving the poor man claustrophobia. She chose a blue denim camp quilt as a bedspread. One chair sat in the corner of the little room. Sabrina tossed an afghan over it, dressing the corner up a little. Chantry heaved another box into the room. It was full of trophies, pendants, medals, plaques, and awards. Several large framed photographs of Chantry were in the box.

"These are cool!" Sabrina rifled through the items. "My heck, you've earned a lot of awards. Do you have a hammer? I'll start tacking some of these up."

Chantry retrieved a small toolbox from his truck. Sabrina began hanging his stuff. "This room is going to look like a shrine to the sport of baseball." She studied a photograph of Chantry making an out at first base. He was stretching way off the bag to make the catch. It was an impressive stretch! "Are you sorry you're not pursuing this career?"

"Not the right life-style for me, Sabrina. I think I can do more good by working with young people. I feel fairly confident I wouldn't have been in the minors very long before being called-up to the majors but like I said, the lifestyle's pretty rough. Even on college level the partying is unbelievable. Besides somebody needed to check up on you."

"Do I require being checked up on?"

"I don't know, do you?"

Sabrina didn't quite know how to answer that so she remained silent. *Chantry is probably just pushing my buttons, anyway!*

A copy of *Sports Illustrated* was in the box. Sabrina picked it up and started thumbing through it. "Did you make it in *Sports Illustrated*?" Chantry sat beside the girl on the bed. He took the magazine and flipped it open to a full color, two page spread. Chantry was slamming the ball with a bat. The intensity on his face was amazing.

The headline read, *"6' 7" First Baseman Chantry Cantrell, Powers His Way to the Top!"*

A three page article followed. Sabrina was dumbstruck!

"This is what I liked about this picture," Chantry said, pointing past his own image to a man in the background. The man was standing behind home plate, wildly cheering at the crack of the bat. Both arms were raised above his head in a triumphal gesture. It was Joseph Ashley. "That was the first thing I saw when the magazine came, Joseph standing behind me, cheering me on."

Sabrina nodded. She read the article through. The writer highlighted again and again the work ethic of the Idaho farm boy. Statements from coaches and teammates praised Chantry's integrity, determination, and athletic prowess. The final paragraph of the article read,

"In the midst of chaos and scandal in professional sports today, America needed a real hero to step forward, even at the college-level. Sure Cantrell can throw, hit, and catch, and he can do it without the use of illegal, performance-enhancing drugs; but what really makes this charismatic young athlete stand apart? The answer is simple: his commitment to excellence. He lives and plays by a moral code. Virtue and honor are not disregarded as foolish myth. Instead his life and career seem to be built upon the foundation of these standards. The strength he gleans from adhering to a strict moral code seems to be propelling him toward the top. Good news for baseball fans? Yes, for a new star is rising."

Sabrina sat the magazine down carefully. She felt lucky to know someone so extraordinary. She continued helping until the sunlight faded and lights had to be turned on. Sabrina stretched out on the sofa. "I'm bushwhacked! I need another vacation."

"You deserve one. Thanks for all of your help."

"You're welcome. Chantry, can you run me over to the shop real fast?"

"Did you need to get something?"

"Yes, a violet for your windowsill."

Chantry laughed. "What if I kill it? I'm not over-endowed with a green thumb you know."

"Anyone who can raise hay can surely keep a little plant alive."

Sabrina's phone jangled. She took the call. "Chantry, Mom wants to know if you'd like to come to dinner at our house?"

"Are you having tuna casserole?"

Sabrina giggled. "We never have tuna casserole. I don't like it either!"

The glow pouring from the dining room window revealed Amanda had the table all set when Sabrina pulled into the driveway. "Thanks for letting me drive this hot truck again!"

"You just like to drive so I have to reset my seat and mirrors when I get in next time."

"I like to drive it because it's almost as nice as Old Blue."

"I remember one summer when you were staying with Joseph and Juliet. I had to take Old Blue to Preston to get some swather parts. You wanted to ride with me."

"Yes! I was eleven. I thought I was pretty smart getting to go with you. You bought me an ice cream cone before we came home. You remember that?"

"I do. That was right before I left on my mission. I remembered you being a little girl, but when I came home..."

"What?"

"No more little girl. You'd blossomed while I was gone, and I do mean blossomed."

"I didn't think you even noticed me that day."

Chantry's brows shot up in his classic 'You've got to be kidding, right?' expression.

"You did notice me?"

"When have you ever existed beneath my notice?" The statement made Sabrina's heart skip a beat. For some reason the message infused her soul with joy. She felt radiant, and flashed a beaming, gleaming smile at this life-long acquaintance, this man whom she was now truly just beginning to know.

That night, after goodbyes and goodnights were said, Sabrina pulled her sketchpad out and worked on a drawing. She smiled and hummed as she worked, her mind wandering in a myriad of different directions. She sketched and shadowed, and finally smiled at the finished product, wondering what kind of flowery phrases Haskel would have made about it. Sabrina signed her name in the bottom corner. She leaned the depiction against her lamp. A cowboy hat full of wild strawberries was nested in a mat of grass near the base of an aspen tree.

Chapter Twenty-eight

Dorian looked up from his breakfast. "Brad will be home today."

"Already?" Sabrina was surprised at just how quickly two weeks could pass. "If time keeps racing like this I'll be graduated before I know what's coming."

"We're going to pick him up at the airport this morning, so hurry Sabrina."

"Why am I going? I thought I was working."

"Vandaline and Vidalia are. We're taking you kids school shopping."

"Why?"

A flicker of annoyance shadowed Dorian's face. "Because we're running out of days, that's why. Honestly, I never heard of a teenage girl brooking an argument over going school shopping."

"I'm sorry, I didn't mean to be difficult, I just...I haven't made very much money this summer. I'm not sure how much I can afford today, but I'll be happy to look."

"Sabrina, am I to understand that you feel responsible to buy your own clothes?"

"Of course. You have spent so much on my room, and our trip, and stuff. Usually I help Grandpa Ashley for a couple of weeks in the summers, then he'd give me five hundred dollars for school clothes, but I didn't help him this year. He offered to give me money before

267

I came home the other day, but I didn't feel right about taking it. I told him I was fine."

Amanda was patiently listening, tracing the top of her juice glass with a finger. "Go get showered, dear. We want to leave in plenty of time."

Sabrina rinsed off her dishes and stuck them in the dishwasher, then scurried upstairs. She wasn't sure what to expect when she saw Brad. She'd felt apprehensive about him coming home. They hadn't talked, or even texted since Sabrina left California. It had been easier as he entered her thoughts less and less.

The airport was manic. Sabrina wasn't a well-seasoned traveler, so every trip to the airport seemed that way to her. Brad's plane had already landed, and he was waiting like luggage to be picked up. Dorian loaded his bag in the trunk, and then Brad piled into the backseat. "Hey guys! Did you miss me?"

"I should say we have," Amanda said. "How was work? Did you eat well enough?"

"Work was great and I'm amply well-fed, thank you," Brad said, fastening his seatbelt. The car suddenly filled with the musky, spicy scent of the boy. It instantly renewed shared memories and old feelings. Sabrina caught a breath at the sight of him. He was even tanner, which made his eyes seem bluer. His hair was longer, spilling well over his collar now. Sun-kissed golden streaks highlighted the rich brown tones. "Hey Sis, how have you been?"

"Good," Sabrina answered briefly. She was trembling inside.

"Son, you need a haircut," Dorian observed in the rear-view mirror. "You look like a Golden State surfer-dude."

"I know, right?" Brad ran a hand through his hair. "I was working on my own Tarzan hair. That weave gets too itchy."

"I don't think so," Dorian said.

"Have you been lonesome the last few weeks?" Amanda asked, turning in her seat to look at her new stepson.

"No, I've had all kinds of fun. I went to Catalina on Sunday and spent the day with my friend, Tony. We took a couple of chicks parasailing. It was fun."

Sabrina couldn't help asking, "What chicks?"

"Morgann and Naya, remember them?"

"Oh yes, the *models*. Did they wear their seashells and mermaid tails?"

"No, on this occasion they happened to have shimmied out of them, but let me tell you! They still managed to make quite a splash!" Brad grinned at his tale and Dorian chuckled. "They knocked Tony out; I can tell you that right now."

Sabrina felt defensive but she'd better get used to it. There would be other girls, and other dates. That was the one weapon Brad had used against her best reason, on the day he'd proposed just running away together. He had said, "Sabrina how can I possibly watch you dance at Homecoming and not have it be with me? How can I bear to watch you go to prom or even ball games, and not have it be with me? Won't it bother you to see me go out with other girls?" Sabrina admitted it would be an excruciatingly painful process to bear yet she felt firm in her resolve. Now he sat bragging about parasailing on Catalina Island with girls who passed for flirtatious, mischievous mermaids while on the job! What could they do at the beach while having fun? Jealousy prickled like a myriad of hot little pokers. She fidgeted with a hangnail.

"I also went sport fishing with a couple of my friends. That was fun."

"Nate and Cody?" Dorian asked.

"Yeah. Cody reeled in a swordfish. It was awesome."

"Nate's father has quite a nice boat," Dorian explained to Amanda. "Nate also has a very cute little sister; a petite, darling blonde. Was Shayna there?"

"Yeah, both she and Jen came along. It was a party!"

"Sounds great!" Sabrina mumbled while scowling at a carload of girl scouts from her window.

"Who's Jen?" Amanda asked.

"She's Cody's younger sister," Dorian explained. "Her baby browns are stunning! She's just as pretty on the inside as the outside though--a real gem."

"If you guys would have left Sabrina in California with me then I could have had a cute sister to brag about, too."

"Sabrina was busy with her own activities," Dorian said.

"Oh yeah?"

"She's been riding horses, four-wheelers and all kinds of good stuff."

"With your cousins?" Brad asked hopefully.

"Yes and no," Sabrina answered briefly.

Brad's head drifted to gaze at traffic streaming by his own window. They rode in silence for a moment or two. "Did Vidalia ever make it home?"

"Yes, she and Phillip rolled in last Thursday." Amanda smiled, "I'm afraid she wants her own Harley now. I may well have lost my dear employee!"

"She's hooked huh? On the Harley or the guy?"

"Both!"

"Is Phillip going to move to Utah?"

"He's on his way to San Diego as we speak, to clean out his apartment and move back. He's got plans to renovate the old farmhouse and stuff. He's a great guy. I immediately felt comfortable with Phillip." Dorian explained.

Brad's elbow nudged Sabrina's. "Will he marry Vidalia?" Sabrina shrugged. She felt broody and cross.

"Guess what Brad?" Amanda asked pleasantly. "Our dear friend, Chantry Cantrell is going to be the new history teacher at the high school. Sabrina's been helping him get his classroom ready. She's made the most stunning bulletin boards! Sabrina should consider going into education with bulletin board skills like that."

Sabrina's eyes rolled. "There's more to teaching than making attractive bulletin boards.'

"Your schedule came," Amanda continued. "You and Sabrina both have history and English composition together."

"That's good. Just for the record, nothing excites me like a good bulletin board. Where are we going?"

"School shopping, so I hope you brought your piggy-bank."

"Oh Sabrina, you're kind of cute," Dorian said, pulling into the South Town Mall. "Amanda and I have some errands to run. We'll meet you right here at three then we can see where else we need to go to finish up." He handed Brad and Sabrina both visa cards.

"What?" Sabrina asked, staring at the card. "I can't use this. Here," she pushed the card back to the man.

Dorian put his hand up. "Sabrina! Are you part of this family or not?"

"Yes, but..."

"Then please allow me to do certain things. You are not required to earn every ounce of your existence. It's okay to let me provide. Your Grandpa Ashley took pleasure in helping you just as much as he could, and he let you help him in return just to take the edge off of your stubborn pride. It's important for me to do this."

Sabrina looked from Dorian to Amanda. Her mother smiled at her. "I'm sorry Bree, you inherited the stubbornness from me--but just take the card. Have fun! We'll meet you kids here at three."

Sabrina ran a finger across the raised numbers on the plastic card. An amount in the upper corner indicated she had two thousand dollars in her hand. Tears stung her eyelids as she watched her benefactor's pull back onto the busy street.

"What's wrong?" Brad was looking suspiciously at the girl.

"I've never had such a big budget to do school shopping."

"How are you? I mean, how are you, *really?*"

"I don't know," she said, hurrying toward the mall door.

Brad caught her arm and flung her around. "What's your problem?"

Sabrina jerked her arm back. "Nothing! I don't have one! Except maybe one phone call might have been nice, *just one.*"

"I thought you wanted to break up, sever the ties, and get it over with. Honestly Sabrina! You give me so many mixed signals I can't keep up!" He was returning the fire, his eyes blazing black. "You can't have it every direction! I'm dizzy trying to figure out which angle I'm supposed to come from." Brad took a step closer, again grabbing Sabrina's arm. *"Don't touch me! Please kiss me! Don't tempt me! I love you! You can't have me,"* he mimicked. "You are driving me mad!"

Sabrina felt a sob tear in her throat. Each word sunk like a sharpened arrow. So much of what he said was true. "I'm sorry." She unclenched the grip on her arm and walked past him, allowing herself to be swallowed up by the sale-frenzied shopping mob. She stumbled dumbly forward not seeing anything but a hot mass of tears. She made her way to a dressing room and wept privately for awhile. At the end of one whole hour she had only purchased a package of socks. Dorian would not be impressed.

Sabrina bought a hot buttery pretzel, hoping the salt would jolt her into action. She sat at a table, mindlessly stuffing little bits into her mouth. She wished Vandaline was with her. The classy dressing Vandaline would have been a big help. She dialed the shop's number.

"Ashley Floral, this is Vandaline. May I help you?"

"Hi, Vandaline, this is Sabrina."

"Yes?"

Sabrina pictured the nervous little woman, taking this phone call with eyes wildly darting everyplace at once. The image made

Sabrina smile. "I'm school shopping. Dorian just gave me two thousand dollars and all I've bought is a package of socks. I need some guidance."

"Did you need socks?"

"Yes."

"Then you can't feel badly about your purchase. I wish someone would hand me two thousand dollars and tell me to go shopping. I wouldn't need any help spending it. What do you want of me?"

"I wish you were here. I'm in a bad mood today, for one thing. I don't know where to start and I'm very overwhelmed."

"Snap out of it! The first thing you need to buy, since it's in your budget, is a *Wow* outfit! You know--something completely stunning that you can always have ready if you need it. I'm talking *class* here--sophistication yet flirtatious and fun. Sabrina, I'm talking about your own personal style of a little black dress. It really is a must you know. Now it's important that you get the whole package: shoes, jewelry, underwear, bag–I'm talking the *whole* deal."

"Where would I ever wear a little black dress? I'm supposed to be school shopping."

"You'll be dating! Opportunities always present themselves and it helps if you have a dazzler in your closet, ready to go at a moment's notice. Call me back after you've gotten that much done."

"Okay, bye."

Sabrina's eyes shot up and down the mall, looking for a fancier type of a dress shop. She spied one and sauntered in. A very chic sales woman accosted her at the door. "My name is Marcienne. Can I help you?"

Usually Sabrina would have said, "No I'm just looking," because she hated people fussing over her, but today she gathered her courage and said, "Yes, I'm looking for a *Wow* outfit–the whole package, do you know what I mean? I need a real dazzler to be all ready in my closet just in case I need it."

The woman tossed her dyed magenta locks. "Darling, I get it! Come with me and we'll totally find you the *Wow* statement you're looking for."

These fashionable women all speak the same language! Sabrina smiled and followed Marcienne to a fitting room. Sabrina was confused since she hadn't selected any dresses yet. The woman whipped a measuring tape from her pocket and began sliding it here and there and in some areas that Sabrina wasn't entirely comfortable with. "Have a seat Darling. I will go select a few pieces for you."

Sabrina sat on a little tufted stool, surveying the dressing room. It was quite a bit fancier than any she'd been in before. She studied her face. It was a mess of swollen red blotches. Sabrina grimaced at the girl in the glass. Marcienne entered. "I need to ask if modesty a big issue with you?"

"Yes Mam."

Marcienne's lashes fluttered impatiently, "What a pity." She returned with several selections. "Get your clothes off."

"You need to go out first."

"P'shaw! I need to help you dress to make sure there's a good fit."

Sabrina was embarrassed and pink cheeked. *I'll never ask for help again!* Amid humiliation

Marcienne pinched, poked, and prodded, but one after another the dresses slid on and off.

"This one is a quarter of an inch too wide through the shoulders," or "You need an extra inch in the waist." She was obviously perfect at her work.

In the end Sabrina selected two *Wow* outfits; a flirtatious black ensemble with a fun handkerchief hemline, and a lovely elegant number in red satin. Marcienne had paired each dress with coordinating jewelry when Sabrina had tried them on and had also selected appropriate footwear for each dress. She was a good sales lady, as Sabrina left more than a quarter of her total sum behind. She'd never spent so much in one place before, yet the purchase made her feel a little bit heady and excited. "Leave your things here, Darling," Marcienne said. "You can pick them up when you're done shopping. I'll have your shoes, bras, panties, jewelry, clutches, and everything all boxed and ready for you."

She phoned Vandaline to report. "Oh, I'm so glad you let the associate help you coordinate! Give me the name of that store! I'd love to shop there sometime. Now, Sabrina, I'm sure you can handle jean shopping, but make sure you select the best fitting ones. I'd rather have two or three expensive pair that fit properly than ten pair of cheap, ill-fitting pants. You can get a bigger bang for your buck with tops. Don't spare anything on your accessories! They are very important and you can always change up your look with a well-selected scarf."

"I don't wear scarves, but I'll see what I can do."

She actually had fun getting jeans, tops, hoodies and sweaters. She'd never been at liberty to make so many choices before. Sabrina totally knocked herself out shoe and accessory shopping. She had always had a fondness for cute belts and found several. Bangles, earrings, hair clips, and bags--Vandaline would be impressed! *It's a good thing I have an enormous closet!* She felt a little bit guilty lugging so many sacks around with her.

Sabrina's phone jangled. "Hello?"

Vandaline's voice whined in Sabrina's ear. "Did you remember perfume? You need a *Wow* fragrance that's a little heavier than your usual scent. While you're selecting it check out some makeup. A department store clinician will happily give you a trial make-over just so you can test the product. You should consider trying it."

Sabrina felt Vandaline was right. *This would be a good day for makeup.* Sabrina sauntered toward the makeup counter, wishing the fantastic Simi would suddenly appear. No such luck but a man named Rahul was happy to assist her. He smeared magical creams and foundations onto Sabrina's face all the while fussing over the glorious beauty of her hazel eyes.

"Here's my card," he chimed, "Let me know if you'd like to get started with a basic cosmetic kit. You'll feel just so *Uh-Uh* sexy today!" His hips gyrated around in a strange motion. "I know you'll just love it, love it! Boom, bam d' mama, hey-oh, all-a-yo! You can give Rahul a call for some more."

Sabrina gulped. "Now I need some *Wow* perfume."

"Have I got a signature fragrance for you!" Rahul bustled around the counter. "Sniff this and sigh. Tell me you don't love it, *love it*, and I'll have you arrested for perjuring yourself."

Sabrina tried it and was surprised. It was actually very nice and didn't give her a crushing headache which most perfumes did. "How much?"

When Rahul told her the amount she suddenly understood why Vandaline referred to it as *Wow*.

It was in fact, Wow-ee-wow-wow! Rahul watched her countenance, petrified that she'd turn and run. "But Rahul is willing to cut you a little deal on the cosmetics and perfume *together*," he said, wrinkling one brow and drumming his fingers together madly.

Sabrina weakened and made the purchase. Rahul threw some extra cosmetic samples into her sack. "Here, let Rahul sprits you once more from the tester. It's like a ten dollar free gift!" Sabrina thanked him and scurried away before he could possibly suck another two hundred dollars from her. Her phone rang while she was escaping.

"Hi Honey! We got done a little quicker than we thought we would. I want to come and shop with you. Where are you? Dorian will carry your packages to the car." Sabrina was ever grateful she had some for him to carry

Dorian smiled brightly when Sabrina came into view. "Are you having fun?"

"Sure," she lied. "It's been so fun! I have even more packages waiting down at The French Hen. "I splurged and bought a couple of dazzlers."

Dorian trucked one load out to the car then trailed his wife and new daughter to The French Hen to see exactly what a dazzler was.

Marcienne was thrilled to see Sabrina return. "I have your things ready, Darling. Are these your parents? Would you like to try the dresses on for them?"

"I would love to see them," Amanda said.

Sabrina grudgingly reentered the posh dressing room with the aggressive sales lady.

"Your makeup looks fresh! I didn't realize you were such a gem. You looked a little bit splotchy before. I feel fairly certain we need to try the midnight party dress on again..." Marcienne pinched and pulled, zipped and fastened.

Amanda applauded both dresses. "You look astonishing! These are great. I can't believe you made yourself shop this seriously." She dug her camera from her bag and snapped a couple of photos of each dress.

"There's another little number she *must* show you," Marcienne purred. "She decided against it in the end...but it's so luscious on her."

Sabrina donned the midnight party dress. Little tiers of crescent pleats in hammered satin tumbled playfully beneath a shirred bodice. Of course Marcienne also outfitted the girl with dripping earrings and a deep blue, crushed velvet choker to match. When she stepped from her dressing chamber, Amanda's mouth drew into a tiny O while Dorian nodded his approval. "She'll take that outfit as well," he said to the happy, yet hardly shocked, sales associate.

"The *whole* package sir?"

"The whole thing."

"I'm not sure how much I have left on my card..." Sabrina called from the dressing room.

"It's on me," Dorian said cheerfully.

"It's all been on you! I'm sure there's still enough on my visa, it's just that I didn't get a coat yet. I know I'll need one."

"Then get one. Lavishing you with little things is almost as much fun as doing it for your mother. You're very deserving and so completely unspoiled and undemanding."

"Sugar Daddy," Marcienne purred softly, unzipping Sabrina from the dress. She was very pleased with her successful sales tactic.

Sabrina resented the comment. "He is a very good man! He just wanted to do that for me."

"Darling, they all want to."

Sabrina was grateful to have her own clothes back on just to get away from the pushy woman and her coy little comments. In Sabrina's mind a *Sugar Daddy* was a sucker and Dorian definitely wasn't one of those. He was generous to a fault and very kind. She remembered her own foolish thought processes when she'd first met Dorian. She had determined to never like him but she now felt that he was genuinely good. Sabrina pictured him in forty-five years, feeding little great granddaughters cucumber sandwiches on miniature blue dishes. There was definitely a streak of dear Haskel in him!

"I'm ever so happy to have learned what a *dazzler* is," Dorian said, balancing an unbelievable tower of packages in his arms.

Sabrina laughed at him. Shopping was definitely improving now that she wasn't on her own! She had needed her mother. They had a fun time finding a coat and Amanda demanded Sabrina get some new pajamas and a robe. "We can't just clod around as sloppy as we always have."

When Dorian met up with the girls next, Brad was with him. Sabrina smiled sheepishly at the boy, hoping he would forgive her. She didn't want to fight and she certainly didn't want to drive him stark-raving mad. He returned the smile. His eyes sparkled brightly and Sabrina felt that their truce was sincere. She would take extra pains not to send mixed signals anymore. The family walked along, laughing and happy. Sabrina felt lucky since ninety-eight percent of the folks who passed by looked miserable and raunchy. She recalled how suicidal she probably looked, earlier in the day, to other passers-by.

Brad's voice stirred her from her internal reverie. "Sabrina, can I ask you a question--what scent are you wearing? It's pretty good."

Dorian nodded. "It really is. I noticed it right away and so did those sixteen poor boys we just passed. You're a little bit lethal."

"I stink?"

"No, you don't stink. Trust me, you're very alluring." Brad gulped loudly, bringing laughter to the group once more.

"I'm going to suggest your mother buy some of it," Dorian teased.

Sabrina handed her mother Rahul's card. "It's called *Dumbstruck*. Rahul will be happy to sell you some. He gave me one final drenching from the tester bottle as a parting gift so I'm sure I smell a little strong. Hey, I hope we fit in the car." Sabrina was worried about how many packages she sent out of the mall with Dorian. She could see them piled high in the backseat. Brad's purchases were stuffed in the trunk.

Dorian fired one quick smile at Amanda, saying "I'm not sure what to do...I don't think you kids are going to fit." He looked puzzled and rubbed a hand across his mouth. "I have a plan."

He trailed the family through a serpentine of automobiles in the parking lot. Sabrina couldn't imagine what they were doing! Suddenly Dorian stopped. "Here you go kids--I hope you like them."

Two brand new Jeep Wranglers sat side by side. Large bows wrapped around their sides. Brad leapt vertically, letting out an incredible whoop. He danced maniacally around the metallic blue jeep, calling for it.

Sabrina was frozen. "We can't possibly *both* have one."

"Do you like it Sabrina? I wanted to get you a flaming orange Pontiac Solstice but your mom disagreed. She thought you'd like to go trailing along in the hills too much. If you don't like this we'll go trade for what you do want."

Sabrina's lip quivered. She couldn't see the zippy yellow Wrangler any longer because her tears were too blinding.

"Is the color okay?" Dorian asked, still trying to decipher the girl's reaction. "Amanda thought you'd like the yellow one but Honey, we can go trade."

"It's called *detonator yellow*, isn't that perfect for your personality?" Amanda asked playfully.

"We can do whatever you'd like us to do. I'll be happy to take you to look at the Solstice. We just wanted to surprise you."

"You shouldn't have!"

"I didn't," Dorian said, pressing a key into her hand. "These are compliments of Grandpa Haskel. He sends his love."

"Grandpa?" Brad asked incredulously.

"I love him!" Sabrina wailed. "He's the most amazing little man."

"Apparently he was smitten with you, too. He said, 'Dorian, I want you to pick out a couple of autos for the kids. They should have a little something special to begin their senior years. Tell them that I aspire to be a just the smallest bit like the Lord; showering blessings, every now and then...' Doesn't that sound just like him?"

"It does." Brad popped his hood, to see what was underneath. "V6."

Sabrina was still trying to gather herself together well enough to see. "How can I ever repay Haskel?"

"He said to keep nurturing your talents and that's payment enough. He knew you would ask." Amanda explained. "He said he might never have captured an angel if it wasn't for you."

CHAPTER TWENTY-NINE

Sabrina dialed Chantry. "Guess what! I just got a brand new Jeep Wrangler! Brad and I both got one! Mine's detonator yellow...I know--I can't believe it either! Please come see it...Yes, I'll let you drive it. I'll be home in fifteen minutes...bye."

Chantry was leaning against the Dodge when the Manning procession pulled into the driveway. He smiled pleasantly at Sabrina as she unfastened her seatbelt and bounced out. He patted her shoulder affectionately, conveying his happiness at her surprise. Dorian, Brad, and Chantry popped the hoods once again to examine every angle and talk car.

"Stay for dinner Chantry," Amanda requested.

"That sounds more appetizing than Chef Boyardee."

Sabrina began unloading all of her purchases and carrying them up to her room. As she was thundering down the stairs for a second load she met Chantry. His arms were full of bags and boxes. "Where to?"

She wheeled around and led him to her large closet. "Just put them down in here."

"My heck, Breezy, did you buy out every store?"

"It looks like it, huh? Ah! This has been an amazing day. I've never gotten so much stuff in my life!" She spied her three new dazzlers zipped inside garment bags. "Look! I have to show you my dresses." She unzipped each dress, hanging them on her closet rod. "I really can't decide which one is my favorite."

"Me neither. Of course, I'm no expert."

"Am I boring you?"

"When have you ever bored me?" Chantry seemed amused.

"I don't know but tell me if I start, okay?"

"I am the very opposite of bored."

"That's good! I'm going to show you every single thing I bought today." She began pulling items from boxes and bags, hanging them up as she went. In the middle of show-and-tell Chantry stopped Sabrina mid-sentence.

"I'm sorry but my mind keeps wandering. Can I ask what you're wearing? You smell *good.*"

"Isn't that lucky?" she teased, echoing his previous answer.

Chantry arched one brow. "Breezy I have a question to ask you."

"Shoot."

"After dinner, okay?"

"Alright." Sabrina felt apprehensive and bit her lip.

Chantry laughed. "Don't worry--it's nothing too scary."

"Guess what? I even got matching clutches to go with my dresses. Want to see?"

"What's a clutch?"

"A dainty purse." She dramatically pulled the lid off of a box. "Ta-da!"

Chantry's chin dropped.

Sabrina quickly peered into the tissue paper to see why the clutch had caused such a reaction. A bra and panty set in lacy midnight blue peeked out. "Oh no!" she cried, quickly clapping the lid back onto the box and shoving it far under a shelf. Embers of embarrassment lit her cheeks. "I forgot about those…" Uncomfortable spastic giggles shook her body, accompanied by ragged hysterical breaths.

Chantry shook his head, laughing with her. "You really are related to Joe aren't you?"

Sabrina tossed her head with dismay at her folly. "I'm so dumb!"

"Although, I must say...that's the most titillating little *clutch* I've ever seen."

Sabrina climbed to her feet. "I'd better go help Mother with supper."

"Don't go," Chantry muttered sulkily. "I was hoping to see the other dainty purses. You only showed me *one*. I'm assuming there's a red one and a black one around her someplace."

"You're awful," Sabrina accused, shaking her finger at the handsome face.

He caught her hand, quickly lacing his fingers through her own. The action startled Sabrina. Chantry's movements were always so lithe and quick she usually failed to see them coming. His touch infused a warm rush of tingles up her arm. "Well...maybe you're not *so* awful," she stammered. She felt small and delicate next to him. His large hand dwarfed hers.

He stared intently at her for a long moment not saying anything. His eyes were black and searching. Sabrina gazed back, trying to interpret his emotions. He reached out with his other hand, entwining his fingers through hers in the same fashion. "Your perfume," he said huskily, "I'm thinking it may have opium in it...very addicting you know."

"Perhaps it's worth what it cost me then?" Her voice was shaky and she was afraid he could read her like an open book.

"I'm not sure. You were fairly addicting all on your own."

The words shot a thrill of delicious tremors through her system. Sabrina had wondered a few times in the last week if he might possibly be indicating a tad more than friendship, but he was hard to read. Yet here she now stood with both hands laced through his, and he was staring at her so intently she could scarcely breathe beneath his gaze. "That's good then."

"Little girls who aren't interested in fishing shouldn't bait their hook so temptingly."

Sabrina smiled at the cryptic riddle. "I was hoping to reel in a trophy before I ever cast my line." *There! Let him untangle that one!*

An interested spark lit Chantry's eyes as her sentence settled in. He gave her hands a firm squeeze, releasing her. "We'll talk later. I'm taking your jeep for a drive." As Chantry was turning to leave he saw the sketch pad resting near Sabrina's bed, and he walked over to it, studying the picture. Smile lines creased his cheeks and he telegraphed his approval with a searching look in Sabrina's direction. Her heart pounded at his reaction. "Do you like wild strawberries Breezy?"

"In the right setting I do."

"What about this setting?" He motioned toward the sketchpad.

"Those were the sweetest strawberries I've ever tasted."

"I thought so too." Chantry was still smiling as he left the room.

Sabrina watched from the window as he emerged from the house to the driveway, talking easily with Dorian and Brad. Chantry said something and Brad nodded. Dorian jumped into the blue jeep with Brad and Chantry followed them from the driveway. Sabrina estimated they were taking the vehicles out to see what they could do. She took a deep breath, wondering if she was fickle. She was certain she had loved Brad so much that she could have easily run away with him when he'd suggested it. She still loved him, but now...something even more euphoric was beginning to swell inside of her.

She floated down the stairs to help her mother with dinner. She took great pains to set the table prettily. "I wish I knew Vandaline's napkin tricks."

"The table looks fine just as it is."

Sabrina sighed. Chantry's words waltzed around in her head. *"You're fairly addicting all on your own..."*

284

Dinner was interesting! Several times Sabrina felt caught in a crossfire of imploring blue eyes and searching deep black ones. She tried to focus on her pork chop and mound of fluffy potatoes and milk gravy.

"I think I'm going to like having you for a mother," Brad said to Amanda. "This is the best gravy I've ever tasted."

"Thank you." Amanda was happy to have pleased the boy. "There's plenty," she suggested, passing more potatoes in his direction. Brad gratefully heaped his plate with seconds.

"So Brad," Chantry asked. "Are you going to play baseball?"

Brad shook his head. "No, I'm not going to get wrapped up in sports. My work is too sporadic. I'll be working most of spring break and too many weekends. I just couldn't commit to it."

Chantry nodded. "That's too bad. I'd like to have a sturdy guy like you stand up for me."

"Thanks, but...I really haven't ever played baseball."

"No? You're probably a natural. We'll have to round us up a game sometime huh? Maybe we can change your mind."

The conversation was pleasant and carried through dessert. Brad's phone jangled. "Hey Tony! You'll never believe what happened to me today!" He excused himself from the table and jogged upstairs to tell his friend about his new jeep.

Sabrina cleared the table, rinsing dishes and loading the dishwasher. Dorian and Chantry talked baseball while the women tidied up. "Is it okay if I talk with Chantry for awhile?" Sabrina asked her mother.

"Yes Honey, but don't be out late, in by eleven. It's been a big day."

"I'll say! I'm so excited with everything. I think tomorrow I'll invite Danforth and some of the kids over to meet Brad before school starts."

"That's a wonderful idea! We'll have a party." Amanda instantly began scheming her next meal and teen-age appropriate snacks. "I'll ask Brad if that would be okay with him. I'll kind of let him decide what he wants to eat, okay?"

"Sounds good." Sabrina eased her way into the dining room, standing near the table.

"Ready?" Chantry asked.

"Sure." Sabrina grabbed a jacket and the two headed outside.

"Your outfit or mine?" Chantry smiled and Sabrina's breathing picked up a notch.

"Whatever, it doesn't matter."

Chantry opened the Dodge door and Sabrina climbed in. "Where's a good place to talk?"

"My Thinking Place?"

Chantry laughed. "Oh you and your Thinking Place," he chided gently. The Dodge rumbled toward Commercial Street and pulled into the driveway of the old house.

Sabrina unlocked the back door and called for her kitty. Mia came running. "Mind if Mia comes? I haven't got to spend very much time with her lately."

"Of course not."

The willows along the river smelled sweet and mellow. Sabrina sat down in her favorite spot and patted the ground for Chantry to join her. Mia purred loudly from the girl's lap. A fish jumped, sending moonlit ripples across the languid surface. "Too bad I don't have that hook all baited," she said, waiting for some kind of reply.

"How serious are you about Brad?"

The question startled Sabrina. "Why?"

"I just need to know."

There was obviously no reason to deny anything. Sabrina wasn't sure what he knew already or if Grandpa and Grandma Ashley had said something to him when Vidalia invited them to fast with her. Vidalia had alluded that Chantry had known about it previous to that however. *No, I won't deny anything.* "What do you think?"

"I know he's been more to you than a brother."

Sabrina inhaled deeply. "I met Brad the first day of June. I liked him instantly. He's really easy to like. We started going out and it didn't take very long before I liked him—I mean, *really* liked him."

"You love him, you think?"

"Yes."

Chantry arms hugged his knees. His face was turned toward Sabrina, listening. "Go on."

Sabrina shrugged. "I had no idea that his dad was dating Mother. *None.* I found out the day before you showed up and helped me move my stuff over to the other house."

"And?"

"What? That's all."

"No it isn't all. What's your current status?"

"Brother and sister."

"You're so innocent, aren't you? What about California? How did that shake down?"

"Well...I was resolved at first but the ocean was so amazing, and the moonlight, and..."

"You kissed him?"

"Yes."

"A lot?"

"Enough." Sabrina felt her honesty was brutal to say or hear. "Why are you asking me these questions? Chantry--I don't like telling you any of this stuff."

"Why?"

"I don't know. I just don't." Sabrina's voice cracked and she wanted to cry.

"Are you still kissing him?"

"No! The night of the parade at Disneyland was the last. I talked to you on the phone the next morning. I don't know if *that* did something to me, or...well, actually it *did* do something–it made me hope..." Sabrina shrugged in the darkness. She sucked in a breath and continued. "But we kind of broke off the romance that night. It had to happen! It was inevitable."

"Can you pull this off, going from hot to cold? Can you do it?"

"I'm trying. We're both trying! Now I've been as honest with you as I could possibly be. You know everything. Why are you asking me these questions, knowing full well I didn't want to answer them?"

"I just needed to know the score."

"Why?"

"Before I played any game I always knew what to expect. I'd study the pitcher, the catcher, and the fielders. I knew each of their strengths and weaknesses. I needed to prepare myself--steel myself up for the challenge. I would adjust my game to compete with theirs."

"Are we talking about baseball?"

"Yes you maddening little creature! And no."

"Enlighten me."

"I'm adjusting my game! Sabrina, I thought I would let you grow up before I started anything. Just as I was feeling confident about my game plan I found out I nearly missed out entirely."

"What do you mean?"

"I mean I wasn't prepared to see you had already fallen in love with Brad when I came to Morgan last month! I'd calculated things fairly well, my graduation, etcetera. I tried for the Morgan job knowing it would bring me closer to you. I planned on patiently biding my time through nine months of the school year before asking you out, but I feel really pent up and edgy knowing you are now living with the boy you've been kissing all summer. I no longer see you as just a kid, Sabrina."

"Oh." The light was beginning to turn, and the illumination was astonishing and wonderful!

"But if I don't step things up a bit I'm afraid you'll go skipping off with that boy--or another one. That complicates things because now I'm your stupid teacher and I don't want to be perceived as a cradle-robber or some perverted child-predator."

"I would never see you that way."

"I've talked to your mom and Dorian. I have their blessing and now I'm asking you. Is it okay with you if we see each other?"

Sabrina's heart began trilling like the wings of a hummingbird. "Yes."

"It will be strange because it's got to be on the sly. I don't want you being heckled because of me. I understand you're young and I want you to go to all of the dances and parties at the school when you're asked, but..."

"I said *yes*."

"Next weekend I'm flying to Portland then driving down to Corvallis for an award ceremony at Oregon State. I'm receiving a fairly prestigious award from the Pac-Ten Conference. It's a formal affair with dinner and dancing. I would like you to come with me. I have permission from your mom if that helps."

Sabrina's heart was hammering. "I'd love to come!"

"Promise? You're not just saying that?"

"I want to."

"You'll want to bring one of those new dresses...and I know you have the most perfect *clutch* for the occasion!"

Sabrina giggled at her latest blunder. "I'm excited!"

"Me too. I'm ready to show you off. Vandaline was right--you can't spare anything on the accessories. You'll be *my* accessory for the evening. I'd like to show some of those old teammates just what I was holding out for...*perfection*."

The word sizzled in Sabrina's ears. Her breathing was erratic as she focused her scope on new horizons. She felt haphazardly giddy at Chantry's confessions of game plans and well-laid intentions.

"You do understand what *on the sly* means, right? Our time spent together won't be anything to titter about in the girls' bathroom with your friends."

"I understand. I've only had relationships on the sly, remember?"

"But you didn't fool me for one second. You'll have to do better than that."

"How did you know?"

"You two kept texting each other—right in the same room. It was so obvious! Plus, Brad was positively love-struck with your every action and reaction. I drove home from Morgan, after that day I helped you move in, and I was so edgy! I paced ten trails in Mother's carpet worrying about you two knot heads in California. I kept tabs through Vidalia pretty well but I knew you were smitten. I didn't like it! I still don't."

Sabrina smiled at the thought of Chantry pacing over concerns about her! "I'm sorry."

Chantry stood, pulling Sabrina to her feet. He laced his fingers through hers as he'd done earlier in the evening. His expression was once again eager. The depth and intensity which burned in his eyes sent little shivers rippling through Sabrina like shock waves. "Sabrina, *Breezy*," he said lowly, "I'm asking you to separate the men from the boys. Can you do that?"

Sabrina nodded, keenly aware of every finely-carved detail of Chantry's face. She liked the way she felt when she was near him— protected and secure. He was a man and he made her feel like far more than a school-girl. "Thanks for finally not treating me like a little kid!"

"You've haunted all of my thoughts lately."

"I didn't mean to."

"As usual, you're clueless." Chantry's hands released hers but his arms slid around her waist. The movement was like striking a match to the adrenaline coursing in Sabrina's veins, igniting them into pulsing, flaming flickers of emotion. She lifted her own arms around his neck, stunned by the lean sinews of his chest and broad shoulders. She was overwhelmed by the sheer strength of him, yet he was gentle, as always. She leaned her face against his chest. She could hear his heart pounding and loved the sound of it. For some reason this whole situation felt brand new to her. She had embraced a boy before but never a man.

Chantry's face rested against her head. She could feel his ragged breaths stirring against hair. It tickled and thrilled. "How much older was Ben than your mother?"

"Eight years."

"Joseph than Juliet?"

"Eight years."

"How much older than you am I?"

"Eight years."

"Exactly." One hand tilted her chin upward. His hand rested against her throat, his fingers softly tracing the outline of her neck. Chills sprung to the surface of her skin beneath his touch. His face bent near, his mouth caressed hers briefly. The kiss, although just a whisper, left Sabrina's legs weak. "I'll try to discipline myself so that we can survive nine months of each other. You've still got a lot of growing up to do." Sabrina stubbornly threw caution to the wind, leaning up and catching his mouth with hers once more. The kiss was lingering and reckless. "Or not," Chantry stammered, surprised by the fury of the girl's kiss. "Maybe I'm the one who has to catch up." He gently pulled her back toward the shop. Sabrina let Mia inside the house before climbing into Chantry's truck. Chantry prevented her from sliding all the way over to the passenger seat.

He draped his arm around her, holding her tightly at his side. "I've wanted to do that all week! The whole way from Raymond, I wanted you right here next to me."

Sabrina giggled. "I wanted it too. I'm really excited about going to Oregon with you. I've never been there."

Chantry kissed her hair. "It will be good. There's a lot of stuff I want to show you. I used to wander around, thinking about taking you there someday."

"Really?"

"Yes. I've had a few odd dreams that turned my thoughts in your direction."

"Dreams--like what?"

"Oh, I've had several, but in the most recurrent one, I'm riding my horse down this road and your Dad stops me. He says he has something for me, and then he hands you up to me in the saddle. He tells me to ride slow because you're young...I guess that sounds pretty crazy to you."

Tears sprang to Sabrina's eyes and renewed shivers splashed down her neck. "No it doesn't sound crazy to me at all. I had that *exact* dream while I was in California. It felt *so* real! I didn't want to wake up but when I did I realized that I couldn't wait to see you again."

"Not really Sabrina? That's more than a coincidence."

"Yes, it sounds like Dad's way of arranging things to *his* liking."

Chantry nodded, "Still taking care of his little girl. His liking is my liking." His arm gave her an extra squeeze. Sabrina took his hand, lightly running her fingers along his. There was something about his hands, and wrists, and...Sabrina's mind trailed to all of the delicious details that made Chantry special. Sabrina hoped Chantry would kiss her once more before leaving her at the door but he didn't. His smile, however, made up for it. "See you in class, Breezy," he called before rumbling away.

Chapter Thirty

Just as Sabrina had predicted, Brad and Danforth Wycliff MacL'main hit it off, becoming buddies immediately. On the first day of school Brad stopped by MacL'main's to pick up both Danforth and Binny Jo. Three other guys also begged a ride so the new blue Jeep was filled to capacity as it pulled into the school parking lot. Brad parked his Wrangler right next to Sabrina's. They had personalized license plates which read *Brad* and *Bree*. Danforth again inspected the outfits. "Gee whiz Sabrina; did you win the lottery or what? What a summer this has been for you."

"Not really…"

"Oh, I think so. Your new house is nice--and these twin jeeps…I think you're gall-dang lucky."

"Sabrina!" Lyndi hollered, dodging her way through the parking lot. "I haven't seen you all summer!"

"How have you been?" Sabrina was happy to see her athletic friend. Lyndi was an incredible volleyball and basketball player. Between Lyndi's practices and camps and Sabrina's work at Ashley Floral, the two didn't get to spend enough time together.

"Not as good as you," Lyndi said, inspecting the new yellow vehicle. "I call shotgun during lunch!" She stared at the crowd of kids, isolating a handsome face with a deep tan and blue eyes. "Are you Sabrina's brother?"

"I'm Brad. I'm assuming you must be Lyndi. Sabrina's told me about you."

"Yes but I'm ticked off because she obviously hasn't told me *enough* about you!" The group of kids laughed.

"Lyndi is our resident comedian," Sabrina informed. "She's always cracking us up! With us kids she's like funny and regular, you know? But when adults talk to her she clams right up and just stares at them like they really aren't there. It drives them nuts!"

Danforth interjected, "Boy I'll say! She makes my mother as nervous as a cat."

Lyndi wrinkled up her nose. "Well your mother makes my cat nervous." The group laughed again.

"See what I mean? She's the funny one. We never plan anything without making sure Lyndi's going to be there."

"She wasn't at our party on Saturday," Brad stated grimly.

"That's because my Aunt Matilda got her gall-bladder out. I got stuck baby-sitting her bratty little brood. I would rather have come and made you all happy."

The group jostled their way toward the school. Brad was getting stares from every direction. He handled it with confidence. Danforth was a big help, calling out, "Make way for the new student--make way for Brad!"

Sabrina tossed a wave in Brad's direction. "Good luck!"

Danforth hollered, "With me around he won't need it, Sabrina! We're on our way to the office right now to get my mother to fix his schedule so he can take seminary with me!"

Sabrina smiled, wondering if the boy really did want to take the class. She hoped he would enjoy it. A pale blond girl named Delphinia Blue was hobbling around the hallway. "I have new shoes," she said to Sabrina.

"Yes you do! So do I..." Delphinia clapped her hands and danced around, happy for Sabrina's good fortune. Delphinia had Down syndrome and she was clearly the kindest, most guileless girl in the school. Everybody liked Delphinia because her friendship was unconditional.

"There's a new person in our school," Delphinia said to Lyndi. "He is over there."

"That's Sabrina's new brother," Lyndi explained.

"Oh," the blond head bobbed.

Lyndi smiled at Delphinia. "Would you like to meet him?" Delphinia nodded.

"Hey Danforth Wycliff MacL'main!" Lyndi's voice peeled. "*You'd better be afraid!* Bring Brad over here, pronto!" The boys obediently ambled over. "Brad this is Delphinia Blue. She noticed you were new here because she notices everybody."

Brad smiled at the girl. "Hello."

Delphinia's eyes suddenly hit the floor. That wasn't common. Sabrina was startled to see her looking embarrassed. Brad leaned over, tipping himself sideways until he caught her gaze. "Hello, Delphinia," he said again.

"I have new shoes."

"They're good ones."

Sabrina was impressed with his ease at talking with her. Delphinia was blushing when he left.

Halsey Redding came tromping by and shoved Delphinia sideways. "Move, you *idiot!*"

Brad caught Halsey's arm. "Apologize!"

"I was talking to *you*," she seethed. "You and your *sister* are a couple of freaks! Hey everybody! I've got a story on these two!" Sabrina winced for she had expected a firestorm of gossip to ignite from the lips of Halsey Redding. "Brad and Sabrina are lovers! Isn't that convenient?"

Danforth intercepted her boldly. "Nobody cares Halsey. How about you go slither back under your rock?" The girl flipped her shoulder and stomped away. Nobody was sorry to see her go and nobody even batted an eye at her juicy secret. Apparently everyone was immune to her nasty tales and opted to not pay attention.

Sabrina was happy to learn Lyndi had several classes with her. "Wait until you meet the new history teacher," she said. "He's an old friend of ours from Idaho."

"Is he cute?"

"I think so."

The bell rang and kids bustled into their classes, new schedules in hand. Sabrina was excited to begin her day with her favorite subject *and* with her favorite person as teacher. She hadn't seen Chantry since Friday night but their conversation had played over in her mind a million times. The memory of his touch sent shivers shooting down her spine.

Chantry was leaning casually against his desk as the students filed in. He was wearing his Tony Lamas, black Wranglers, and a pale yellow button-down shirt with a black tie. His sleeves were rolled to his elbows and Sabrina noticed the veins in his wrists and arms. *Why is that so appealing to me?* Sabrina heard many delighted gasps from girls and impressed awes from boys. Sabrina smiled at the new teacher. He returned the smile and his eyes locked with hers, shooting sparks into her, making her adrenaline surge. She took her seat behind Lyndi.

Lyndi whipped around and faced Sabrina. "Oh my gosh, he's *hot*! If that's what Idaho's producing these days I might consider sneaking across the border for some spud smuggling."

Sabrina grinned at her friend. "I know me too."

When the second bell rang Chantry stood amid a tiny flutter of collective oohs and awes. "I am Mr. Cantrell. I'm excited to teach American history to you. I'm also the new varsity baseball coach. Are there any prospective players in this classroom?" Several hands shot up, Danforth's was among them. "Stand up," Chantry said, "and let me get a good look at you." The boys did. Chantry strolled up and down the aisles, looking down at the prospective recruits. "You're a good looking bunch! Now I'm expecting you to step up and lead out in this classroom. You won't be given favoritism but

I'm now expecting more from you than the other students." A groan hissed among the players. "You may be seated."

Sabrina watched, completely fascinated. In one paragraph, he had shaped his expected discipline level, pinning the most rowdy students in the class for his leaders. *Brilliant!*

"Now why do we care about history?" he asked the class. Kids stirred in their seats uncomfortably. "Anybody?" No one moved. "In that case I'll call on my leaders...*You*," he said, pointing to Danforth. "What's your name?"

"Danforth Wycliff MacL'main."

A tiny smile tugged against Chantry's mouth. Sabrina forgot to tell him about the boy. "That's a tremendous name...am I wrong or is there a story there?" The class laughed and several hands shot up. Sabrina was stunned to see Lyndi's hand fly in the air. "What's your name, please?" Chantry asked, calling on Sabrina's dear friend.

"Lyndi." The whole class seemed surprised by her ready participation. Lyndi never talked to adults.

"Lyndi would you like to fill me in on the story of Danforth Wycliff MacL'main?"

Lyndi proceeded, recounting the story of the ice ball even more humorously than it had originally occurred. Sabrina noticed Brad grinning sideways at the girl. He then flashed a quick smile at Sabrina. Mr. Cantrell listened with interest, laughing with the class when appropriate.

"That's interesting! Lyndi just delivered a little bit of history to me. She told me of something which had happened in the past that sheds light on a situation today."

Mental light bulbs were turning on all over the classroom. Students began nodding their heads. Sabrina was proud of the first-time teacher! Her heart pounded when she remembered that she was flying to Oregon with him in only four days.

"So, Danforth Wycliff MacL'main, why do we care about American history?"

Danforth beamed with pride as if he had a good answer. "Because *Coach*, we can learn from the past."

"That's right. We can learn from the past. What can we learn-- just boring facts?"

Someone suggested that they could learn funny things as well. Someone else said there were no boring facts, that it was just a matter of attitude. Chantry smiled and nodded encouragingly to each student's comment. Before the first twenty minutes of class had gone by, Chantry had learned each student's name. Sabrina was impressed.

"Miss Ashley, would you please come up here." Chantry smiled so winningly that she couldn't be angry although she felt apprehensive being put on the spot. "Miss Ashley is an old friend and neighbor from Idaho. I used to work for her Grandpa on their ranch. She used to come up for visits and she was always prattling about historical facts. I'm going to grill her and see how much she still remembers. Are you game, Sabrina?"

Sabrina nodded. "I guess."

"Danforth, would you mind coming up to the board and keeping score? For every question that Sabrina answers correctly, each student in the class will receive five extra credit points."

Cheers shot from the students. Lyndi was hunkered down in her seat, looking at Sabrina as if she was standing at the foul-line, shooting free throws with a tied score and only two seconds remaining on the clock. It was quite humorous!

"I'm starting off easy, okay?"

"Shoot."

"When did Columbus sail the ocean blue?"

"Fourteen hundred and ninety-two." The class applauded and Danforth marked a big check on the board.

"When did the pilgrims come?"

"Sixteen hundred and twenty."

"Correct. How many years expired between Columbus and the Pilgrims?"

"One hundred and twenty-eight."

"Right again," Mr. Cantrell said, waiting for Danforth to catch up the tally marks. Sabrina was answering questions faster than Danforth could write. Students cheered. "What were the skirmishes called between the colonists and the Indians?"

"French and Indian War."

"When did France sign the peace treaty?"

"Seventeen hundred and sixty-three."

"Correct. When did our forefathers sign the Declaration of Independence?"

"Seventeen seventy-six."

"Don't count that one, Danforth. It was too easy." Students groaned about the injustice.

Chantry's eyes smiled at Sabrina, challenging her. "When did England sign the peace treaty?"

"Um..." Sabrina wavered. Lyndi was gripping her desk like a state championship was on the line. "Seventeen eighty-thee."

"Correct!" Chantry smiled at the girl. "What do you think class? Does Sabrina know her stuff?"

The class cheered, calling for more. "How many years existed between the peace treaty and the draft of the Constitution?"

"Three. The Constitution was signed in seventeen eighty-seven."

"When was General Washington elected?"

"Seventeen eighty-nine."

"When did the famous expedition of Lewis and Clark begin? Be specific."

"August thirty-first, *I think*, eighteen hundred and three."

"Yes. What were their names?"

"Captain Meriwether Lewis and William Clark."

"Correct. Who commissioned their expedition?"

"President Thomas Jefferson."

"That's correct; you may take your seat. Okay students give Miss Ashley a round of applause. She just earned you about fifty-five extra-credit points. Is that boring?

"No!" Students called.

"How many points can you award your classmates when it's your turn to be in the hot seat?" The room was silent as mental wheels turned furiously. "Do you know enough to garner extra points? How many of the questions I asked Sabrina could you have answered? I'm sure you could have gotten some of them," Chantry paused, giving his class the benefit of the doubt. "It's interesting isn't it? What's interesting to you Danforth? Is there anything about history that excites you?"

"I like old guns," Danforth said.

"I do too," the teacher agreed.

"Binny Jo? Does anything interest you?"

"Native Americans." The classroom tittered nervously, not knowing what Mr. Cantrell's reaction would be.

"I'm glad you said that. It interests me too. My mother is Native American, a full-blooded Shoshone, but my father is a descendant of English immigrants. Should I be interested in history?"

A cacophony of yeses echoed around the room. "Lyndi? Anything excite you?"

"Mountain Men." Sabrina couldn't tell if she was serious or not but the classroom burst into laughter anyway.

"Kara?"

"The development of technology."

"Good answer. Trey, what about you?"

"Mr. Cantrell, I'm interested in the Civil War."

"Good because we're going to get into that. We're going to touch on all of these subjects. How about it Dawson?"

"World War II, Pearl Harbor, and dropping the A-bomb on Hiroshima."

Chantry nodded. "Brad? You're extra quiet. What interests you?"

"The amazing accomplishments of certain individuals."

"Such as?" Chantry prodded.

"Walt Disney." Some students chuckled but Brad was serious, and Chantry nodded thoughtfully.

"That opens up a whole different scope of history, doesn't it? The individual accomplishments of great people have shaped and molded our culture and our identity as Americans. Think about it! Your assignment for tomorrow is to write an eight hundred word essay on one such person." Groans shuffled around the room. "What?" Chantry asked incredulously, shushing every murmur. "I can't believe I'm hearing complaints when you've clearly illustrated to me how fascinating history can be. Think about it! I want to know who inspires you. You may take your information from a family member, or a family history. It could be a famous person, an entertainer, or perhaps an inventor. Have fun with it." The bell rang. "Class dismissed."

Sabrina filed past the teacher, keenly aware of him. "Good job," she mouthed.

He fired the quickest wink at her. "Thanks for your help Miss Ashley."

"I wish he was my old neighbor," Lyndi confessed when the girls were beyond ear-shot.

Danforth, Trey, and the gang gathered around Sabrina, giving her lots of high-fives for scoring them some extra credit. It made her smile. She fumbled with her new locker combination then grabbed a binder for English.

"I'm Miss Clisp. Michelle Clisp actually, but you may call me Miss Clisp." A mousy washed-out teacher called. She appeared to be about the same age as Chantry but Sabrina wasn't very impressed.

"She's not nearly as much fun to look at," Lyndi whispered.

"Speak for yourselves ladies," Brad said. "I think she's okay." Brad's comment annoyed Sabrina. Was Miss Clisp attractive? She stared at the woman, trying to decide.

"Welcome to English Composition. We're going to write, and write, and write in this class, and when you are tired of that, we'll just take out our notebooks and write some more." The class moaned and Sabrina groaned with the rest of them. "I'm going to be working very closely with Mr. Cantrell. We are teaming up. Some papers that you write for history will be co-graded in this class on a literary basis."

How closely are you working with Mr. Cantrell? Sabrina felt defensive. She didn't like Miss Clisp.

A smart-aleck on the back row raised his hand.

"Yes?"

"So what are we going to do in here?" Kids laughed.

"Write! Let me make that perfectly clear. We are writing. Let's get started right away. Take out a notebook or a piece of paper. I want you to compose a poem about something that happened to you over the summer. These poems will be due at the end of the class period."

"Do these have to rhyme?" Trey asked.

"No. This is a basic evaluation of your skills. I will know where and how to proceed after reviewing your work. Feel free to be creative. You may begin."

The smart aleck attacked again. His name was Bryce. "I had a pretty exciting summer. How R-rated can our poetry be?"

"Just write, *Mr. Whoever You Are.* I'm certain your life couldn't be *that* juicy." More laugher. *Chalk one up for Miss Clisp.*

Sabrina stared at her paper. She had a heavy arsenal of subject matter, as her summer had been very interesting. She wondered what Brad would write about. She shot a look sideways at him. He didn't seem to be struggling as his head was down and his pen was scratching away.

Lyndi raised a notebook over her head. Bold letters scrawled, "THIS IS DUMB, THAT RHYMES WITH BUM. THE <u>END</u>!" Sabrina drew in a sharp breath, trying not to giggle but raucous laughter bellowed from further back in the row. Lyndi quickly jerked her notebook down appearing innocent and spellbound on her assignment. Miss Clisp eyed the students suspiciously.

English wasn't Sabrina's favorite subject but she was happy to see Brad seemed to be handling it so well. Perhaps a live-in tutor would come in handy. She'd gladly trade him for tips in history. She began writing words about dolphins but easily became discouraged. There were only so many words that rhymed with splash.

Precious class time ticked by without a single stanza on Sabrina's paper. She felt panicked to produce *something*. She drilled her mental reserves and finally managed to get some words down on paper. She was actually grateful for the bell. "That was fun," Brad called cheerfully, exiting the classroom.

"Just like hemorrhoid surgery," Lyndi said. "The procedure was irritating but it feels good when it's over."

Brad smiled and turned for his locker. Delphinia Blue stood in his path. "You are Sabrina's new brother. You like my shoes."

"My name is Brad, Delphinia. Can you remember that?" The girl smiled at him.

Trigonometry was the most painful part of the day. Sabrina didn't love math. Somehow Sabrina lucked out and got Lyndi in this class too. "Mr. Middlemiss is a Number Nazi," Lyndi declared.

"Miss Wesson, did you have something to say?"

Lyndi stared ahead. *Silence.*

"Answer me!" the balding man thundered. "You had a comment to share with Sabrina. Share it with me."

Patiently Lyndi stared forward, as if catatonic. Ignoring adults until they went away was her usual policy.

"What?" He hollered. Mr. Middlemiss was growing red in the face and beads of perspiration dampened his brows and upper lip. Sabrina felt petrified for her friend. He slammed a fist down on Lyndi's desk. The girl did not even jump. Sabrina wondered if she blinked. The classroom felt like a morgue, the silence was so deathly. The students seemed to be holding a pensive, collective breath for their classmate.

In sheer frustration Mr. Middlemiss grabbed the girl's shoulders, shaking her once. "Lyndi! Are you *on* something?"

"Yes!" Lyndi thundered back.

Mr. Middlemiss released his grip on her shoulders. "Aha!" he triumphed. "What are you on?"

Nothing.

He grabbed her and shook her again. "I asked what you were on!" Sabrina was trembling inside, frightened for her friend but aching to see how the scenario would play out.

"I'm on my *chair!*" Lyndi bellowed. Her voice was dripping with disgust and loathing for the purple-faced teacher. Laughter exploded like cannon fire on the Fourth of July! Mr. Middlemiss had lost the war of wits with Lyndi Wesson. Sabrina was sorry Brad had missed it, but news of the altercation had circled the school by lunchtime.

"We've gotta get cracking on Homecoming dates," Danforth said. A group of nine or ten kids had ridden to the drive-in for lunch in Brad and Sabrina's new jeeps. "We've only got a three weeks and it will be here."

Brad nodded.

"Met anybody you'd like to take?" Danforth asked.

Brad's eyes studied Sabrina thoughtfully. "Maybe."

"Who?" Danforth hunkered down for the details.

"Delphinia Blue."

Shocked silence rippled across both tables of students. "Why?" someone finally asked.

"Because she deserves it," Brad said confidently. "But don't say anything. I want to surprise her."

"You're not serious, man?" Trey asked.

"Why not? I am."

"But Dude, it's your senior Homecoming. It's the best time for making memories."

"What grade is Delphinia in?"

"Ours, but..."

"So which one of you big, brawny guys took her dancing last year?" No one spoke. The drive-in corner was nearly as silent as the Number Nazi's class room had been during Lyndi's interrogation.

"What about prom last year?"

Silence.

"So..." Brad continued, "Doesn't Delphinia deserve some fun senior memories? Or are they exclusive to the football team, and the drill team, and the honor society?"

Danforth cleared his throat, "Okay Man, point taken. You're stepping up and leading out. You're making me feel guilty here...I feel like I need to call a reporter from *The Church News* to come and cover your story."

"Not only am I going to ask Delphinia," Brad continued, disregarding Danforth's sarcasm, "I'm going to make sure she gets asked before anybody else in the whole school." He quickly whipped his phone from his pocket and punched a number. "Hello, Amanda? How much do you love me? I need to ask a girl to Homecoming. Could you bring me a dozen roses right away? Just leave them at the front office...Thanks! You're the best. No wonder my old man is crazy about you...Bye."

565536566

Sabrina stared at her brother. His character was faultless.

Lyndi looked sideways at Brad. "Well whoopity-do for Delphinia Blue! What about the rest of us? I'm feeling a little jilted. I was hoping to go to Homecoming with the Californian." She was teasing of course but Brad grinned warmly at her.

"Oh yeah?" he asked the funny girl, who was pretty cute in her own right. "Then come with me to the Back to School Dance this Friday. We'll have a blast." His grin was charming and Sabrina felt Lyndi soften like butter in the sunshine. "Is it a date?"

"It absolutely *is* a date!" Lyndi agreed, flashing a radiant smile at Brad.

"Oh my heck," Danforth muttered to Trey. "I'm going to move away just so I can be the new kid for a change."

"This guy is phenomenal--completely smooth, a legend. In less than one minute he's just purchased a dozen roses to ask out one girl and captured another eligible female for the dance on Friday. I'm stunned."

"I think I might write about him for my history essay," Danforth said sarcastically. "He's got Babe Ruth beat."

By the time Seminary rolled around the whole school was buzzing about Delphinia Blue's yellow roses. The girl stumbled into seminary carrying them. "I'm asked out," she said to Brother Delenbaugh.

"I'm asked out the first in the whole school, *and* I've got new shoes."

Brother Delenbaugh looked intrigued. "Let me see your roses."

The girl handed them to him. "They're from Sabrina's brother. His name is Brad. He's taking me dancing. I'm asked out. I'm asked out before anybody!"

Brother Delenbaugh's eyes searched the room. They looked misty. "Is Brad here?"

Danforth waved a hand in the air, pointing at the new student. "He's not even a member, Brother Delenbaugh. He's a good kid though. I talked him into joining seminary."

Brother Delenbaugh darted down the aisle to shake Brad's hand. "Welcome! You've taught us our first lesson in living the gospel."

Brad looked strangely at the man. His eyes trailed to Delphinia who stood smiling brightly in the center of the room, cradling her flowers, rocking from one foot to the other. "Sir, I can't help it if I'm the lucky one. I got to Delphinia first--before the others could ask."

Sabrina could hear the sincerity in Brad's voice. He wasn't putting anything on. He was genuine and confident enough in life, and in himself, that he was completely comfortable with his choice of a Homecoming date. Haskel would be eager to hear about this! Sabrina would write him and tell him all about it. At that moment she felt as if she'd been blessed with two angel brothers.

That was the beginning of an incredible year for Delphinia Blue, who waltzed around the seminary room, smiling dreamily and feeling the magic of new shoes.

CHAPTER THIRTY-ONE

The next morning Sabrina dressed carefully for school. She wanted to look her best for history. She had taken the arrowhead Chantry had given her to a jeweler and had it fastened to a chain. She clasped it around her neck. The obsidian point shimmered near her throat where Chantry was sure to see it. She carefully arranged her history essay in a neat cover and slid it in her back pack.

"Remember your essay?" Brad asked when they met in the hall.

"Got it," Sabrina said. The two had proof-read each other's papers. Because of Brad's brilliant writing style and personal quotes and experiences from Haskel, his report on Walt Disney seemed much superior to Sabrina's essay on Sacajawea. Brad shouldn't have any trouble with Miss Clisp's aspiration to write, and write, and write, and write.

Chantry was writing on the board when Sabrina entered the classroom. When he turned around she noticed his eyes quickly fired around the room until they found her. A touch of a smile lit his features. She reached up and fingered the arrowhead at her throat. Chantry rocked back on his heels. The smile spread larger as he recognized the ancient relic. "Good morning!" he greeted his students cheerfully. "How were the essays? Did you learn anything?" Different answers echoed around the room. "Brad would you like to read your essay this morning? You've become somewhat of a local celebrity overnight. I'd be interested to hear who inspires you."

"I'm no celebrity but I'll be happy to read." Brad cleared his throat and launched into his paper. It was anything but a boring historical account. Kids applauded and cheered when he finished.

Several other students volunteered to share their essays but Sabrina was content just to listen. The period went much too quickly and the entire class actually seemed disappointed when the bell rang.

English Composition proved to be an interesting hour. It began with Miss Clisp's shivery voice; her soul was obviously rent with emotion. "Class, every once in a while a very gifted student comes along. Do you agree with me?" She paused for dramatic effect but didn't get the rousing response she was expecting. "After reading your poetry yesterday, I quickly recognized a few very talented writers are in our midst. I want to read you a poem. This one was my very favorite. I actually shared it in faculty meeting this morning.

Tremble

Reckless and carefree, two souls flickering like fire,
stood breathless and trembling near the sea of desire.
The skies and waters boiled black
as I stared at her and she gazed back.
Her eyes were wild, and as dark as the sea
while she stood trembling, just looking at me.
Alas, summer love is fleeting and fast,
and the embers are dying and the kisses are past,
but I'll never forget the moment that we
stood trembling and breathless by the side of the sea.

For a moment the class sat in shocked silence, whether moved by the literary genius or stunned at the subject matter, Sabrina couldn't tell. She realized her knuckles were white from gripping the desk. She had scarcely breathed through the poem, reliving the sweet, drunken moment. Of course she knew who the author was! It sent a small thrill knowing he had been thinking of her as he wrote the words.

Sabrina considered the implications, however, of Miss Clisp's sharing it in faculty meeting. *What did Chantry think?* Sabrina could only imagine.

"What the—"Danforth blurted. "Somebody sure as heck had a more exciting summer than I did!"

Several boys leapt to their feet, stomping and cheering for the unknown author. Girls were twittering and fluttering over the sizzling moment. Lyndi mirrored Danforth's sentiments as she threw her hands over her head exclaiming, "While I've been sweating my guts out at sports camps, *somebody* has been romping on the beach and I dare say they've had more fun!"

Miss Clisp held her hands up, requesting order in the classroom. "Isn't it wonderful?" she cried. "I'm very happy to see you appreciated the emotion which the author captured in his text."

"I'll say he captured emotion," Lyndi charged. "That was a zinger!"

Sabrina's eyes stole sideways at Brad. He felt her gaze and answered it with the faintest wink.

"I have already submitted this poem for consideration in a student poetry contest, as well as for publication in the school paper."

*Great! Now Chantry can read it over and over again...*Sabrina felt such a mix of emotions. Her feelings were harrowed up by the reflection of her first night in California; she felt proud of the writing skills of her new brother yet complete mortification that Chantry had already been privy to the words.

"Who is this writing whiz? Stand up Brad Manning and take the credit due to you." Miss Clisp said. Brad grinned easily under the pressure and obediently stood amid whistles and cheers from his classmates.

"Oh why am I not even surprised?" Danforth hooted. "Of course it would be Brad! Manning buddy, you've got to tutor me and I'm not talking about writing either. Miss Clisp, he should get extra credit for using the word *alas* in his poetry! I'm not even sure what alas means, exactly."

Lyndi wheeled around in her chair, facing Sabrina. "I get to go out with him on Friday! Alas, I'm going to suggest the beach..." Sabrina laughed with her friend. Brad wrinkled his nose playfully at his former flame before taking his seat.

"Okay Kids, settle down now. I have another poem I'd like to share with you. I also read this one in faculty meeting, and it too will be published in the school paper. It's oddly similar yet you will notice an entirely different writing style and iambic pentameter--but a person almost can't help but wonder if these two writers weren't writing about each other."

Oh no! Sabrina's heart sank and she wanted to hurl. *Please don't let it be my poem, please!* She also noted a momentary streak of panic cross Brad's face.

Summer's Dance

When I get a chance I remember the dance
and the memory makes me glow.
To our own private tune we swayed with the moon
while the surf crashed loudly below.
It was romantic and sweet just moving our feet
with no other souls in sight.
Together we swayed while the melody played
under stars that twinkled so bright.
Oh say it's not so! Was it time to go?
I wasn't ready to leave the ball!
But the spell had to end; soon I'd call him just friend
when summer bled into fall.

Ripples of excitement stirred around the room amid hearty applause. Brad's hand smacked his forehead and Sabrina's mouth felt dry. *Whoosh, whoosh, whoosh* began sounding in her ears. *Please don't make me stand up, Miss Clisp!* She prayed like a saint for a way out. *If only I could just have a stroke or something...*

"Would the author please stand?" *Whoosh, whoosh, whoosh.* Miss Clisp waited. Students looked curiously from one to another. The second hand ticked loudly on the clock. Sabrina was trembling inside and she felt immediately sick. Just as she was finding her footing to stand a collective gasp escaped the mouths of many for Halsey Redding stood, smiling smugly. Brad threw his pen down on his desk, huffing a disgusted sigh. Lyndi looked defiantly at Halsey and then she also stood. Miss Clisp's eyes popped open widely, seeing that two girls were claiming authorship of the poem. Halsey scowled furiously at Lyndi. Sabrina was decidedly thrilled by this new chain of events as the spotlight was now taken from her. She stood then to support Lyndi's defiant stance of Halsey Redding. Impressively, Kara, Melody, Tahnee, Janice, and Shan all simultaneously rose from their seats as well.

"What the–" Danforth thundered. He shrugged his shoulders and jumped to his feet with the girls. His shoulders were rolling with laughter. Brad again leapt up, followed by Bryce, Justyn, and all the others. Every student in the class was claiming Sabrina's poem! *My prayers have been answered!*

Miss Clisp massaged her temples, looking as if she suddenly had a dire headache. The class was completely out of order. "That's enough! That's enough!" she shrieked. "I couldn't submit this poem for the poetry contest because the author forgot to put their name on the paper. I need to know who really wrote it! Quiet Down! Who wrote this poem?"

"Me!" Halsey hollered.

Lyndi stomped her foot. "Miss Clisp, Halsey lies! She can't even spell."

"Fine!" Miss Clisp finally stated. Her voice was uncommonly shrill. "No one will get credit for this poem. They shouldn't be recognized anyway if they are so illiterate as to forget to put a name on their paper!" The bell rang before Miss Clisp could relieve her headache. She looked happy to see the students funnel through the door.

Lyndi leaned closely to Sabrina's ear. "Nice poem Sabrina."

"How did you know?"

"I heard your breathing start to go haywire. Alas! You were having one of your spells. I figured I needed to do something to save you."

Sabrina hugged her friend. "Thank you."

"But you've got to tell me about California some time!"

"Okay," Sabrina laughed. "I'll see you in class."

Chantry was standing near the drinking fountain when Sabrina breezed by on her way to trig. She felt her cheeks flush and she tossed her head in an awkward manner. Chantry arched one brow. "Really Breezy? Dancing with the moon?"

Chapter Thirty-two

Sabrina worked at the floral shop that evening after school. It had been a long, crazy day. A blizzard full of rumors swirled around the school about the unknown poet of Morgan High School. It was so ludicrous Sabrina had to laugh. Brad's status really had neared celebrity level. Students, teachers, and administration all seemed to love the boy. Asking Delphinia Blue to Homecoming was a brilliant ice-breaker, socially speaking; although he didn't do it for any personal gain. Brad didn't think like that.

Sabrina spritzed plants on shelves with a spray bottle. Happy thoughts tumbled in her mind as she thought about the ripple effect of doing good. Brad never estimated what kind of an influence he would have over the other boys in the class. At lunchtime Trey was happy to tell Brad that he'd asked Meggie Richards to Homecoming. "Meggie's a recluse," he informed Brad. "She's never been to a school party or dance in her life, but I asked her. I figured she might want to make some memories." Other boys were quickly clamoring to ask out any other previously invisible girls. Brad had single-handedly begun a dating revolution. Brother Delenbaugh was overjoyed.

Brad seemed to be enjoying Seminary as well. Amanda had given him a set of scriptures and he and Sabrina had set a goal to read a chapter together each night. Whitlee was happy to receive the news via a quick e-mail. Both Dorian and Brad had accompanied Amanda and Sabrina to church. Brad signed up for the ward choir, saying, "What a rush! This will look good on my resume." Enthusiasm for the simple things in life is what set the boy apart. His attitude was nearly faultless.

The afternoon was slowly winding down. Sabrina turned the *closed* sign then fed and watered Mia before locking up. She was thrilled to see the red Dodge waiting in the driveway when she got home. She was hungry for some personal time with Chantry, despite the morning's tangled-up poetry scandal. Phillip's Harley was also parked in front of the new home.

Sabrina quickly slipped upstairs to tidy up. She made sure the arrowhead was still visible beneath her collar, brushed her teeth and applied fresh gloss to her lips. She gave her hair a quick teasing with a pick then bounded down the stairs looking fresh.

Her eyes scanned the room for Chantry. He smiled knowingly at her from across the room. Her pulse quickened. He was casually leaning against the sofa, visiting with Phillip and Dorian. The three seemed to be fast friends. Vidalia and Amanda were setting the table in the dining room.

"Where's Brad?" Sabrina asked.

Amanda looked up. "Hi Honey. He was invited over to the Blue's for dinner. Dante and Tiffany Blue are ecstatic over his asking Delphinia."

"He's a charmer, that Brad," Vidalia concurred. "I just fell in love with that boy in California. I nearly ran off with him."

Sabrina smiled at Vidalia's exaggeration. She had wondered if Vidalia was ever going to rat them out to Amanda and Dorian for Sabrina hadn't heard one word about the affair since returning to Utah. Brad, however, had informed her the night before, while they were proof-reading history essays, that Vidalia had discussed everything with them, in detail before leaving California.

"Mother's never said a word to me." Sabrina was shocked to learn that their parents were now in the loop.

"Well, Dad said plenty to me! He railed something eloquent and I was told, in no uncertain terms, that if any funny business continued between us he was going to pack me up and send me to live with Grandpa Haskel."

"Oh no! Why didn't they say anything to me?"

"Because Dad figured the problem would be settled if I straight-ened up."

"But I was just as involved as you were!"

"Well Dad figured that since I was staying in California for two or three weeks, away from you, the problem would resolve itself. Then of course, Chantry informed him of his intentions...way to reel 'em in, Sabrina." Brad looked a little bit chagrined.

"You know about Chantry?"

"Yes. Dad told me on the phone. I'm not to interrupt or intrude into your future. I'm also not supposed to say one word about it anyone but Sabrina, your secret is safe with me."

"I know. You're awesome at keeping secrets and following the rules. I'm sorry though."

Brad shrugged. "We knew it was coming. My life is great here and I'm happy. I like school and I *love* your mother. I'm going to start calling her *Mom* if it's okay with you. I love my new sister, too. I'm adjusting to loving you in a different way. In some ways it's even better."

"Where the hell are you?" Vidalia asked, snapping her fingers at Sabrina.

Sabrina flinched, shaking herself from her thoughts. "What?"

"She's useless," Vidalia muttered in Amanda's direction. "I'll just do it myself."

"What?" Sabrina asked again.

"Vidalia wanted you to go round up the guys from the other room. Dinner is ready."

"Sorry, I didn't hear."

Amanda smiled at her daughter. "You seem happy, are you?"

"I've never been more so," Sabrina said confidently.

"Excited about this weekend?"

"You'll never know! Thanks for giving me permission to go."

"There's not a man in the world I'd let you fly away with *except* Chantry Cantrell. I just want you to know that."

It occurred to Sabrina as everyone took their places at the table that each couple was seated in pairs. It tickled Sabrina to think she was paired with the tall and painfully handsome Chantry. Sabrina peeked at him during the blessing but he cracked one eye open and caught her looking. Both heads ducked with sheepish grins. Chantry's boot nudged her ankle.

Half way through dinner Brad returned home. He pulled up a chair to feast again on Amanda's cooking. "This roast is good, Mom."

Amanda's head jerked up. Dorian's brows raised and he quietly patted Amanda's hand and resumed eating.

Brad never looked up, but he smiled all over when Amanda said, "Thank you, *Son*. Just wait until you bite into Vidalia's homemade apple strudel. It's to die for."

"Vidalia's my girl," Brad said with a wink.

Phillip grinned at the boy. "Want to make a bet?" Vidalia's cheeks colored prettily.

"You look great Vidalia. I think you've lost even more weight."

"I have! Another ten pounds has run away. That makes twenty totaled and I'm down three pant sizes."

"You'll be a size six by the time I ask you to prom, Vidalia," Brad teased.

Vidalia's laughter rang heartily. Phillip's lip curled pleasantly beneath his mustache. "I have something I'd like to say. I've been happier these last three weeks than any time in my life. Vidalia," he began earnestly, "will you marry me?" He pulled a ring from his shirt pocket. It was a red ruby and diamond encrusted band. It glinted expensively beneath the glow of the red chandelier.

Vidalia's chin began to quiver and her hands trembled helplessly. The room was silent and hopeful. Phillip slid one arm around her shoulders, steadying her hand and sliding the ring on her finger. "Marry me Daisy." Phillip's steel blue eyes focused solely on the woman as if the others in the room ceased to exist.

After a silent minute's worth of composure she said, "Well hell, I guess I will!" Happy tears coursed into her plate, marinating a pile of roast beef.

Cheers and congratulations filled the evening. Phillip and Vidalia left before the apple strudel was even served. "They have a lot to talk about," Dorian said. "I am so happy for Vidalia! Phillip is a first-rate guy."

After dessert Brad said, "I'll help you clean up dinner Mom...if you'll play a game of Battleship with me."

"Do you cheat?"

"Sometimes," Brad confessed.

"Me too. You're on!"

Chantry gently slid an arm around Sabrina's waist and guided her to the coat closet for a jacket.

"I'll have her home before too long," he promised.

It was the first private moment they'd had alone in nearly a week. Sabrina was aching for his arms to slide around her! Chantry opened his truck door and she slid in, wondering if she should stop in the middle. While Sabrina was fidgeting, trying to decide what to do, Chantry climbed inside, reaching one arm around her. Sparks ignited instantly beneath his touch. He pulled her around to face him. His eyes were black and brooding. "So Breezy, it's a nice night. There are no beaches around here and no pounding surf, but there sure as hell *is* a moon. Would you like to go dancing?"

"I'm sorry about the poems. It's Miss Clisp's fault."

Chantry's head bobbed. "Oh that's a good one! I accidentally snapped a pencil in half while Michelle read the love sonnets in faculty meeting this morning. I didn't enjoy them very much. Guess I'm not much of a poetry connoisseur."

"Maybe I'll have to write one about you then. Maybe that will change your mind."

Chantry looked intrigued. "Oh yeah?"

Sabrina stared boldly at the jealous man. "Perhaps I should write about the crazy hot flutter which stirs in my stomach every time you look at me." Sabrina had never been so brazen in all of her life but she enjoyed the ripple of shock which registered on Chantry's face at her statement, so she continued, "I guess I could write about the way I can't get enough of thinking about you. I lay awake and pretend I'm tracing the hard lines of your fingers, your wrists, your arms, your shoulders...maybe I could write about all of that."

Chantry looked stunned at her fortitude. "You've completely caught me off base," he said, again drawing a comparison to baseball.

"For your information Chantry Cantrell, I don't need the beach, or the ocean's surf, the stars, or even the moon to feel the way I feel when I'm next to *you*. My heart's already dancing and I can't even *see* the moon!"

Chantry swallowed hard. Sabrina had blind-sided him with such straight talk. His eyes smoldered. His arm pulled her even closer, his hand gently pressed against her head until it lay against his shoulder. His other hand cupped around her chin. Lightly his finger traced the shape of her mouth. He kissed her hair, breathing in the very essence of her. Sabrina smiled in the darkness.

Chantry straightened back in his seat, quickly starting the truck and barreling out of the driveway. Sabrina didn't have a clue where they were heading. "Isn't it lucky we have one whole school year for *me* to grow up?" he asked playfully. "Seems like I'm the teacher at school and you're the tutor when the sun goes down." He drove to his apartment then led Sabrina quickly through his back door and into the kitchen. He never bothered to turn on the light. Suddenly he pulled Sabrina against him roughly. His lips pressed against hers again and again.

"Girl, you've got me so crazy I don't know if I'm coming or going." Chantry played with the arrowhead at her throat. The touch sent chills down her arms.

"Day after tomorrow is our trip...I'm still invited aren't I?"

Chantry's hands then locked behind Sabrina's head, his fingers combing through her hair. "What do you think?" His voice had a raw tenor to it.

"I think that's a *yes*."

Chantry lifted Sabrina until her feet were standing on top of his boots. He began dancing in the dark kitchen with her riding on the tops of his Tony Lamas. She had often done that with her dad when she was little. Chantry's arms held her tightly as he whirled her around and around. Dizzy laughter filled the apartment. "I've got to take you home. It's a school night remember?"

"School's more fun than it used to be," Sabrina confessed. "I love first hour. By the way, you seriously are the best teacher I've ever had."

"Bet I'm the only one that ever did *this*." He kissed her once more before leading her back outside. Chantry deposited her safely on her doorstep at ten fifteen. Sabrina watched him saunter to his truck. He kicked a rock with his boot. "So much for my discipline," he called over his shoulder. "I've got a crazy hot flutter stirring in my stomach too. See you in class Breezy."

Chantry's sultry words softened Sabrina's legs to jelly and she had to keep a tight grip on the stair railing as she climbed the steps. She tossed her head from side to side to clear her mind. Brad was waiting in the upstairs hall, scriptures in his hands. "Ready to read?" he asked hopefully.

CHAPTER THIRTY-THREE

Sabrina felt liberated and a little bit heady when the Dodge pulled into the driveway on Friday morning. While her friends were buzzing with anticipation over the Back to School Dance, Sabrina had been planning her wardrobe for the weekend trip. It had been such a delicious secret!

The flight was pleasant. Chantry and Sabrina filled the time with easy conversation. The more Sabrina learned about Chantry the more endearing he became. She felt proud sitting next to him as other lady travelers and even the flight attendant, seemed mesmerized by Chantry's height and good looks.

"So what's the deal with Lyndi?" Chantry asked. "Middlemiss is convinced she's trouble. He was pitching a fit about her in faculty meeting. I was a little bit surprised since she's been a joy in my class."

Sabrina's gaze shifted from the tiny patchwork of land spread beneath the plane's window to Chantry. Sabrina smiled. "Lyndi *has* been good in your class. I was a little bit surprised. She and Mr. Middlemiss did have a scuffle on the first day of school. He should have just left her alone. That's the best way to handle her if she ever goes catatonic on you."

Chantry nodded. "Danforth seems like a really good kid. He's been fun to get to know. Justyn's easy to get along with. I've actually enjoyed all the students--except for a girl named Halsey. Do you know her? She's in my fifth period class."

Sabrina's eyes rolled. "Ugh. She just lives to cause distress. She's a mess. Her parents are really nice though. I know Brad can't stand her!"

"No? Brad's a gem! I know it shocks you to hear me say that but it's true. He has a rare leadership quality that's pretty amazing. I'd love to have him on my baseball team just for his attitude alone. His essay was good and he's just plain kind to others. I wish I would have been more aware of other people when I was seventeen. I only thought about baseball and breaking broncos. Do you know what he's done for Delphinia Blue? Did you hear that Dawson asked her to the dance tonight?"

"I hadn't heard. Delphinia is turning into quite the debutante."

"They're all going as a group; Brad and Lyndi, Danforth and Tahnee, Dawson and Delphinia, Justyn and Kara, Trey and Binny Jo."

"They'll have fun, but not as much fun as I'm going to have!"

Chantry smiled and laced his fingers through hers. It was a pleasant flight.

Sabrina followed Chantry through the maze of people at the airport. It was hectic, being Labor Day weekend. He had an advantage as he could see well above the heads of most of the crowd. Chantry rented a car and easily maneuvered Portland's tight network of roads. He took Sabrina to see a few sights; Lake Oswego and the International Rose Garden. Sabrina was swept away by more than sixty-eight hundred rose bushes in five hundred and fifty-seven different varieties of the blooming beauties. Again and again she would squeal delightedly at the specter. The air was rich and draped with majesty's perfume. "Turning me loose in a rose garden is like taking a drunkard to a brewery. I've got to bring Mom to see this place!"

"I knew you'd like it. Well Breezy, we'd better get down the freeway to Corvallis. The banquet starts at six but there's a Meet and Greet an hour before and I know you'll want time to primp and fuss--even though it's not necessary."

The words thrilled the girl! "That was a nice thing to say!"

"What? It's true. Every rose in its splendor can't compare with you." Chantry smiled, lightly tweaking Sabrina's nose. He tugged her by the hand, weaving through the blossoming pathways until they reached the car. His cat-like movements were agile and smooth and Sabrina's feet felt as if they too, just glided gracefully along in his stride.

"This is a pretty city," Sabrina mused, watching the scenery fly past her window. "There are actually roses *every*where."

"Portland is known as the City of Roses. You'll like Corvallis, too. It's a pretty place. The low elevation makes it perfect for raising things. This land had to be worth the sacrifice and deep ruts carved by the Oregon Trail. Every pioneering settler who made it here deserved a rich, fertile piece of this soil." Lush farms and fields blazed past Sabrina's view. She was a long way from Morgan.

It was three in the afternoon when Chantry and Sabrina pulled into the Hilton Garden Inn, in Corvallis. It stood across the street from Reser Stadium. Chantry pointed out several buildings on the historic campus. "This is the oldest university in Oregon."

"You sound like a history teacher. Would you like me to call you *Mr. Cantrell* on this trip?"

"Only if you'd like me to call you *Miss Ashley*." Chantry grabbed their bags and Sabrina followed him into the ritzy lobby. "I have a reservation for two rooms," Chantry said at the desk. A swooning desk clerk named Irene handed him the room keys.

Sabrina and Chantry walked down a long tunneled hallway until they found their rooms. They were straight across the hallway from each other. "You have an hour and thirty minutes, Breezy. If you shower please keep track of the time."

Sabrina entered her room. It was nice but only half the size of her Morgan suite. It was strange how different her life was from a year ago. She bathed quickly. *Ha! I should call everyone I know and tell them that I can hurry.* She wanted to take pains with her skin and hair. Sabrina used the special cleansers and moisturizers which she'd purchased from Rahul. Painstakingly she followed each step until her makeup looked perfect. She applied more eye makeup than usual for a dramatic evening effect. She was pleased with her results. Studying Simi, and strangely enough, even Rahul, had benefitted her cosmetic abilities.

Sabrina retrieved a corsage box from her travel bag. She had made herself a hairpiece of fresh red roses. Luckily they seemed to have fared well through the flight. She often made floral clips for brides, and thought tonight would a good time to try one for herself. She swept her hair up and fastened the clip. Scarlet velvety roses cascaded through dark curls. The look was very Victorian, soft and romantic.

After serious deliberation Sabrina had finally chosen the black party dress. She was ever thankful to Vandaline for her advice. *Having a dazzler hanging in the closet can be helpful!* The bodice was silky and the fabric was shirred, making Sabrina's waist appear extra small. A flirtatious skirt draped over her hips nicely, accentuating her figure and the handkerchief hemline felt swingy and fun. It was a great dress!

Her shoes were black patent strappy heels. Shimmery rhinestone buckles fastened at Sabrina's ankles. Drippy black rhinestone earrings swung delicately from her ears and she fastened a matching choker of sparkling gems at her throat. Sabrina admired herself in the glass, turning this way and that.

"This is surely bound to ruin everyday life for me," she said to the girl in the mirror. Sabrina grabbed her alluring new fragrance and misted it lightly against her throat and wrists. She retrieved her clutch and tossed her phone and lip gloss inside. Her phone jangled. "Hello?"

Brad's voice sounded in her ear. "Hi Cinderella I'm just on my way to a different ball with another princess but I called to wish you luck Prince Charming."

"Thanks Brad. You have fun tonight. I know you will because Lyndi is a card! She's lucky too because you're the best. Thanks for calling."

"Sabrina? Remember what Vidalia said..."

Sabrina giggled into the phone. "Like I could forget *that* advice!"

"I half expect her to show up in Corvallis at any moment to protect your honor. Just in case she doesn't, you work on it yourself okay?"

"Thanks Brad. You're a super brother." The phone clicked. Sabrina stared at the empty screen for a moment, replaying Brad's interesting words. *I'm on my way to a different ball with another princess.* It made her smile.

Knock. Sabrina glided to the door and swung it open. Chantry stepped into the room. The two gawked at each other. Sabrina's eyes beheld a vision in deep charcoal Italian silk. Chantry's suit was suave to say the least. His shirt was scarlet, the color of Sabrina's roses, and his tie was a snazzy swirl of blacks, reds, and silvered grey. His raven hair was still wet and neatly tousled. Gone were his boots. Sabrina didn't even know the correct term for guy shoes but they were definitely spit-shined and polished. "Chantry, I see you have a *dazzler* in your closet too. You look like you slid off the cover of *G.Q. Magazine!*"

Chantry smiled. "I manage to leave the farm once in a while." His eyes continued to sweep her. He covered his mouth with one hand. "Girl, you are one lethal little vixen! When I said you'd be my accessory for the evening you really took me at my word. I'm going to have to fight all the guys away from you."

"I look okay then?" Sabrina fished for one more compliment since hearing them was so much fun.

"You shame every other creation. How's that? And the smell of you is driving me wild. I hope I can make it through the evening without ripping you to pieces like a ravenous wolf." A fiery chill splashed down Sabrina's neck. "You'll probably make me forget the words to my speech."

"You have to speak?"

"Well *yeah...*"

"Wow! This really is a big deal for you huh?"

"I guess we'll see." Chantry smiled above Sabrina's head as he guided her from the room and down the hall. The walk from the hotel to the conference center was a couple of blocks. Usually heels would make Sabrina's feet ache but tonight she felt like Delphinia Blue and her new shoes skimmed magically along. Chantry's hand pressed against her back as they walked. Several people stepped aside, watching as the couple drifted past.

Chantry gave Sabrina a little squeeze in the elevator. "Don't be nervous, Breezy. Just be yourself and you'll knock 'em dead." The elevator doors opened with a chime. Sabrina stepped into another world. Clusters of athletes and their dates socialized in pockets around the room. Sabrina felt the eyes of many men trailing her. It was an odd sensation yet she felt so protected and secure with Chantry's hand pressing gently against her waist. He always kept in physical contact with her even while shaking hands with buddies and acquaintances.

"You're a sly dog, Cantrell."

"Hello, Valdego. Looks like you've already found your way to the bar."

"It found its way to me first," he stammered, laughing as if he were very funny. "Who's the *Betty*?"

"This is Sabrina Ashley. She's a lady and so I'll ask you to watch your mouth around her. She's a little more refined than the average vamps who keep you company." Sabrina was surprised by Chantry's curt words but they rolled like water off a duck's back to Valdego.

"Baby, you're deep dish," Valdego slurred. "You might be too much woman for Chief."

Sabrina tried to keep track of Chantry's old teammates as she was introduced to them one by one. They all had nicknames and Sabrina wondered if she could ever keep them all straight. So far she'd met Diesel, Knight, Mickey Jax, Metzger, Newmeyer, Davis, Jazz, Johnny Rolaids, and Valdego. Obviously she was attending the soiree with *Chief*, as many of the players had referred to Chantry that way.

Most of the women in the room cradled a wine glass in one hand and looked suspiciously at Sabrina. She saw a lot of beautiful dresses but none of them did she like as well as her own. Sabrina felt comfortably covered up while some of the gals had left very little to the imagination.

Johnny Rolaids was bold! He winked at Sabrina and blew her a little kiss from across the room.

Chantry caught the action and wrapped his arms around Sabrina in a protective manner, shielding her from the flirtations. Several of the teammates laughed. "You'd better keep her wrapped up," Johnny called. "She's one hot number. I didn't even think you liked girls."

"Well unlike the rest of you fools I kept my mind on the game." The guys laughed and hooted.

"Is his name really Johnny Rolaids?"

"No, he's just called that because he's the *relief* pitcher. His name's John Roland, but Johnny Rolaids is much more fun to say. He was one of my roommates, along with Mickey Jax, and Valdego."

"You don't like Valdego much."

"He lacks every form of self-discipline. He's on a road to self-destruction. His baseball career won't last very long if he doesn't get some help. Coach is getting fed up and I don't know how he's even passing any of his classes. I don't have too much respect for a guy like that."

An older man approached. "Chantry Cantrell, you're the man of the hour."

"Mr. Blitzer," Chantry nodded.

"Can we talk? Let's go out in the hall where it's quieter."

Chantry followed the man to the door.

Mr. Blitzer smiled at Sabrina. "Hello Honey, I'm Ralph Blitzer with the Cincinnati Reds. I've been trying to reel in this guy for two years. You'll help me won't you?"

Sabrina's jaw dropped. The Cincinnati Reds were no minor league team! "What?"

"I'm coaching baseball Mr. Blitzer. That suits me just fine."

"You can't be happy making peanuts when I've offered you millions! You can always coach after your ball career is over. You've only got about eight or nine years left in your baseball future, anyhow. What do you think Honey?" Blitzer asked Sabrina.

Sabrina only smiled. She thought it was better to let Chantry take care of his own destiny. Chantry listened patiently to the man for a few minutes then he reached out a large hand and shook Blitzer's. "Once again I really appreciate the offer. If I change my mind I'll let you know."

Blitzer's face turned red. He coiled back. "Foster hasn't gotten to you has he?"

Who's Foster? Sabrina studied Chantry's expression carefully. His brows were furrowed and his mouth was set stubbornly. The indentation under his lower lip seemed deeply shadowed beneath the hard, tense line of his mouth. The longer Blitzer pestered him the more defiant Chantry seemed. His black obsidian eyes were sharpening into points, making Sabrina think of her arrowhead.

"I seriously considered the Diamondbacks' offer but Foster's had the same luck as you have, Mr. Blitzer. I'll let you know if I change my mind." Chantry turned on his heel, wheeling Sabrina with him.

"Work on him Honey! Help me wear him down," Blitzer called behind her.

When Chantry and Sabrina retreated to a safe distance, Sabrina looked at Chantry. *"There are a few minor league teams squabbling in my ear,"* she mimicked his earlier words to her. "What's going on?"

"Well that's been my story," Chantry said, grinning down at the girl. "I haven't told anybody about these offers because I don't want people riding me to sign. Everybody would think I was crazy to walk away."

"Why are you?"

"I don't want to live on the road. I'm ready to settle down and enjoy my life. I want to teach, coach, and help hobby farm Dad's four hundred acres in the summers. I'm also walking away from baseball at the pinnacle of success. Maybe I'm too proud to see my-self age and decline in the sport. I couldn't bear to sit and rust on the bench." Sabrina listened, nodding. "But if you want me to sign I'll be glad to take Blitzer's money. I'll be gone most of the time, living out of a suitcase."

"It doesn't have anything to do with me," Sabrina said defensively.

Chantry looked intently at the girl. "It has *everything* to do with you, Sabrina!" The words knocked Sabrina back a step. *What does that mean, exactly?* Her mind reeled with possibilities. "We'll talk later. We'd better head into the banquet room."

Sabrina was surprised by the sheer number of attendees already seated for the dinner. She estimated at least three hundred people in attendance. Lush autumn foliage draped the centers of the tables. It was an elegant spread! Votive candles flickered from hurricane globes. Three large screens were mounted in the front of the room. Impressive floral arrangements hugged both sides of the podium.

Several important looking officials rose from their chairs to greet Chantry. Sabrina was introduced to Chantry's coach, the dean of the university, and the Pac-Ten Conference chairman. Chantry's coach grabbed him in a rough embrace and hard slaps to the back. *Men are so rough.* "I'm going to miss you Chief," Coach Clayson said.

"Follow me and I'll show you to your seat as Guest of Honor," Commissioner Hansel offered. The group moved through tightly clustered tables to the front of the room. Sabrina's eyes were wide, taking it all in. She was mentally calculating what the floral arrangements alone had cost. Elegant champagne table cloths with black lace overlays looked classy beneath the handsome centerpieces. Champagne chair covers were tied with black satin sashes. Sabrina had catered enough events to appreciate all of the work which somebody had put into the evening. Chantry's right arm was around her waist, her left hand in his. Sabrina felt like the luckiest little accessory in the room! The group was halted a myriad of times by people standing, reaching out to shake one, or all of the men's hands.

When at last Chantry whisked Sabrina to her seat she noticed four familiar faces smiling at her. Her chin dropped and her eyes sprung open with the pleasant surprise. Randy and Tashina Cantrell, and Joseph and Juliet Ashley were grinning at her. Her cheeks colored as she realized they had been studying her for a long time, as she floated through the room on Chantry's arm. "I didn't know you guys would be here!"

Grandpa Ashley winked and shook his head slightly. "Hello Bree, you're a long ways away from home. Good thing it's not a school night."

Grandma began fussing about Sabrina's dress. "You look so grown up," she said, reaching across the table and hugging her only granddaughter. "Your hair is scrumptious and I *love* the roses!"

"Thanks, Grandma."

She felt Tashina's brown eyes silently sizing her up. The white-hot flame of a mother's scrutiny was upon her. Sabrina fiddled with her clutch clasp for a moment, feeling uncomfortable before a soft bronze hand reached out and patted hers. She looked up. Tashina Cantrell was smiling kindly. "I'm glad to see you Sabrina."

"I'm happy to see you, too."

Randy was grinning at Chantry with one eyebrow raised. "Son, it looks like you scored a date for the evening," he commented wryly.

"Certainly that's not the little gangly girl who used to pedal her bicycle past our house every day."

Sabrina wondered if Chantry would shy away from her under his father's teasing but he continued to keep his arm around Sabrina. Chills thrilled her arms at the thought. He was not embarrassed about bringing her—he was proud!

"Thank you for helping Chantry get settled into his new apartment so nicely. He tells me you were a tremendous help." Tashina said. "How's school going?"

"Great. My history teacher is especially good."

"Really?"

"Yes! All of the kids think so. He's definitely the most popular teacher." The Cantrell's and Ashley have seemed pleased with the report.

"And is our Sabrina quite well-behaved in class?" Joseph asked Chantry.

"She's my star pupil. I couldn't be more pleased." He kissed her against the side of her head. It was impulsive and quick but Sabrina noticed four sets of eyebrows quickly rise. Her heart began hammering under the observing eyes and Chantry's obvious determination to claim ownership of her. She couldn't contain the smile which spread across her face or the crimson flushing of her cheeks. After a moment she dared cast her eyes in Chantry's direction. He was looking at her, his gaze was penetrating. He smiled at her. Every nerve in Sabrina's body jumped beneath his sultry expression. A renewed surge of adrenaline slammed her bloodstream. She would have to concoct an adrenal-supporting remedy for herself, if these thrilling emotional surges were going to persist.

Dean Hamilton strode to the microphone and bid the ceremonies begin. He welcomed many university dignitaries and officials from the Pac-Ten. Many important sounding people stood and waved at their introductions. An army of waiters then invaded the large hall, wheeling carts of food. A pineapple spear and shrimp cocktails started off the seven course meal. Sabrina savored the obvious sophistication of the occasion. Different servings of wine and champagne were poured in dainty fluted glasses but no liquor was poured at Chantry's end of the table. Coach Clayson had requested non-alcoholic beverages for the Cantrell party. Sabrina smacked her lips on a fizzy watermelon punch. It must have been too tart for Grandpa Ashley because he screwed one eye shut after tasting it.

A bite-sized morsel of smoked salmon was served on top of a French crouton. A wedge of lemon and a sprig of parsley garnished the plate. Chantry's father bent his head toward Joseph's. "I hope they feed us more than this." Little dollops of raspberry sherbet in silver dishes came next. Grandpa Ashley looked disappointed. "I hope you enjoyed the last course Randy, for dessert is already here."

Sabrina wrinkled her nose at her Grandpa. "The sherbet is supposed to cleanse your pallet," she said. "It's usually served in the middle of dinner to prepare your taste buds for the rest of the meal."

"Oh," Grandpa said. "My taste buds are amply well prepared for some real food."

The group laughed quietly at his comment.

When the next course was served it was indeed a feast! Pheasants-under-glass and steamed vegetables filled an entire serving plate. Sabrina stared at her whole bird. "I can never eat all of this."

"It's a daunting task," Grandpa agreed. "They should have sawed that bird in half and served it up with the salmon. Then we might have enjoyed two moderate dishes."

"Use your best table manners," Chantry advised. "The reporters are here." Sabrina noticed a wall of cameras and crews filling a back wall. "The first set is from ESPN," Chantry explained. "I noticed two local stations as well. The *Sports Illustrated* reporter who covered my story last year is standing over there." Sabrina's eyes were huge. She felt nervous and was grateful she didn't have to speak in front of such a large and auspicious gathering. She hoped the cameras would leave her out of every shot.

Fancy French cheese and strawberries followed the main course then crème brulee capped off the meal. Sabrina was so stuffed she couldn't eat another bite and Chantry must have been nervous because he scarcely touched his dinner.

Commissioner Hansel kicked off the night with a humorous and rousing speech. He highlighted America's need for believable, sustainable heroes with a firm commitment to success. "We've decided to honor one such recipient tonight with an award symbolizing strength, dignity, humility, and honor in America. We want to establish the Pac-Ten Conference *New American Hero Award* as a highly sought-after prize. Tonight begins a new tradition in moral, academic, and athletic excellence. Every coach in the Pac-Ten Conference, as well as the university deans were allowed to nominate one potential recipient from each team. The nominees were then voted on. Our winner tonight received a clean sweep of votes, being chosen unanimously! It is my pleasure to award Oregon State's Chantry Cantrell with this prestigious award." *Applause, cheers, whistles.* Commissioner Hansel held a hand out to Chantry, extending a beautiful crystal trophy, wall-plaque, signed certificate, player's autograph book, and a check for ten thousand dollars to be used as a post-graduate head start. "We have to dangle the money to entice up and coming student athletes to step up to the plate and raise the bar of excellence! We invite them to follow in Chantry's footsteps."

Chantry's arms filled with the many honors. He returned to his seat and the lights dimmed. A DVD presentation lit the three jumbo screens, highlighting Chantry's golden moments in baseball, interspersed with interviews of Coach Clayson, team members, opposing coaches and players, and even a few sports commentators and umpires. College professors, Dean Hamilton, and Chantry's parents were interviewed for the documentary. It was professionally put together and depicted four years of amazing success. Sabrina was surprised to learn that Chantry was a 4.0 student, donating more than five hundred hours of charitable work at a nearby children's hospital during his years at Oregon State. Personal experiences were shared which spotlighted both the humorous and touching moments.

"He has the heart of a champion," Coach Clayson said. The jumbo screen showed actual game footage while the beloved coach narrated the event. "It had begun to rain and the field was slippery. Chantry snagged Morrison's hard line drive off of a bounce, but as he was hustling back to his base, he slipped down a couple yards from the bag, all sprawled out on his stomach. I don't know how he did it, but somehow he stretched his long ole' arm out, tagging the base with the ball just as Morrison hit the bag. The umpire called the runner out and the whole crowd went ballistic. Cantrell pulled himself up to his feet, still holding the ball. I saw bloody trails streaming down his arm. Morrison's cleats had caught the flesh of his forearm, ripping it to mincemeat, but Cantrell never dropped the ball. I took one look at that bloody baseball clenched in his fist and raised over his head to quiet the hometown's disputes, and I *knew* I was looking at a champion! Cantrell earned the nickname of *Chief* that day. He became leader of our tribe." Applause erupted in the banquet room. Teammates and opposing players alike stood cheering at the memory. In unison the whole crowd began chanting, "Chief! Chief! Chief! Chief!"

The presentation lasted forty minutes. Sabrina sat in silence, witnessing perfection and wondering how she ever managed to gain favor in the sight of such a man. He had accomplished so much! One dazzling play after another danced across the screen. It was an indescribable honor to be part of his circle, part of his life. Sabrina thought of Brad's earlier query in history class, about studying the amazing accomplishments of certain individuals. Sabrina knew she was sitting by one--a *most* incredible individual.

Chapter Thirty-four

People swarmed around Chantry, congratulating him on his honor as well as his perfectly-articulated acceptance speech. He spent about an hour posing for photos and answering reporters' questions. Sabrina watched from the sidelines, contentedly visiting with her grandma and grandpa, and Chantry's parents. "Are you guys staying to dance?"

"Not me. It's past my bedtime," Grandpa said. Randy agreed with his neighbor.

"We're all going to drive out to the coast tomorrow, Sabrina. We'll pick you two up at eleven- thirty for brunch. How does that sound?" Tashina asked. "I know you're in for a late night of it."

It's fine with me." She smiled at the woman who had raised such a son. Tashina was lovely with large brown eyes and straight black hair which hung down her back. She was quiet, dignified, and very hard working. She wasn't very tall. Chantry's build was inherited from his father although Chantry easily towered above him as well.

"We were...surprised to see you tonight," Tashina said, pausing thoughtfully in the middle of the sentence.

Sabrina smiled. "You were?"

"Yes, but...relieved as well. Chantry's been quite worked up about you lately. His nerves seem much recuperated with you on his arm. It's a nice change seeing him so happy."

"Do you need to stay with us tonight?" Grandma asked.

"No, thank you. I have all my things in my room. That way I won't wake you when I come in. Sabrina could see wheels turning in her Grandma's mind. She knew she wanted to impose a curfew but didn't.

Chantry finally strode across the room, saying goodnight to his folks and dear friends. "Mom, will you take all of this stuff with you?"

Tashina sighed, "What else is new? Once a mother always a maid."

"Thanks! See you tomorrow," Chantry said with a smile. He slid one arm around Sabrina's back and whirled her onto the dance floor. He held her closely. Sabrina felt a little bit star-struck after his big night. "I want a copy of that presentation."

"I've ordered one for you."

"Chantry, thanks for bringing me here."

He didn't answer but kissed her hair, nuzzling his face against her head. Around and around they whirled, alone in the crowded room, disrupted only occasionally by well-wishers and acquaintances. Finally Chantry tugged Sabrina by the hand and they quietly slipped away from the party and out of the building into the night. The air was balmy and fresh, and the quiet felt good to Sabrina's ears.

Chantry guided her to a wooded area with benches. Nobody was around after midnight. He leaned against a brick retaining wall and pulled Sabrina to him. He studied her carefully. The familiar hot flutter skittered and jumped in her stomach. His hands closed around her throat and he kissed her wholly. It was a long, delicious, satisfying kiss. Chantry lifted Sabrina's hands to his lips, whispering kisses against her fingertips. "I love you Sabrina."

The words were strange and beautiful, as if Sabrina had never really heard them before, nor understood their meaning so fully. A symphony of brilliant notes trilled throughout her consciousness, lighting her being with unimaginable, exultant joy. "I love *you* Chantry Cantrell, and you know I always have, but I...I don't understand how I've ever merited a second look from you. You're so incredible! I think I must be dreaming this whole thing."

"Sometimes our dreams are the same, remember?" His lips found hers again as an encore performance. "I need you Sabrina. I'm going to marry you. I wish I could marry you tonight."

"You want to marry me?"

"Why do you think I'm hanging around?" Chantry smiled at the dumbstruck girl. "Of course I want to marry you. I'm going to if you'll let me."

"When?"

"The day after school gets out--the day after you graduate and not a second longer."

Sabrina's nerves began to tremble. She knew with all of her soul that she could want nothing more. She threw her arms around the man, hugging him tightly. "That happens to be my birthday."

"Happy birthday."

"What if you change your mind?"

"I won't. I can't! I've already tried but I'm hooked."

"This has all happened kind of fast," Sabrina said shakily.

"No it hasn't. I've been waiting for a while now. Sabrina, here's the thing; if you say the word, I'll sign with Blitzer for twelve million dollars. That's not a bad wage for a rookie! The Reds will own me for at least four years. I'll get to see you a lot but mostly I'll be gone. That might not be a bad plan if you want to graduate in peace and go off to college, as I wouldn't be hovering around and getting in your way. I'll be living out of a motel room, having strange women thrust their room keys in my face night after night. I'll turn every one of them down but you need to know there's a lot of pressure. Is that the kind of lifestyle you want? We could live big, celebrating fame and fortune. We'd never have to worry about money."

"So what's my alternative option?"

"I come home from coaching ball practice in the evenings and you and I hold hands across the kitchen table while we dine on bottled peaches and toast for supper. We face life in the real world, complete with general mundane worries, yet beneath the radar of public detection and scrutiny. We'd sort things out privately and away from the spotlight. We would go to bed together every night."

"So what's the question?"

"What do you want?"

"*You*, Chantry! That's all that matters to me."

"No twelve million dollar starting salary?"

"I'm not sure there are enough benefits."

Chantry laughed. "I'm glad you see it my way, Breezy. You're beautiful!" He drew her into his arms again, dancing slowly to the rhythm of the faint bass beat pounding from the crowded building.

Chantry and Sabrina walked together in the moonlight. He pointed out different buildings and areas of interest as they strolled along. Eventually he led her to Coleman Field and Goss Stadium, where he had practiced and played so many games. "Here it is…my old home away from home." He fiddled with a latch on a gate and the two walked in.

"Are we going to get in trouble for being here?"

"I never get in trouble." Chantry pulled Sabrina toward the Beaver's dugout. He sat down, studying the field. "This place holds a million memories." He reminisced and entertained Sabrina with tale after tale. She was thrilled to hear him open up so much. She wanted to know and understand every aspect of him.

"Thanks again for bringing me here."

"I needed you with me."

Sabrina's pulse quickened, hearing the words. *How could Chantry Cantrell ever need me?* She didn't mean to be dense about things--it was just so difficult to comprehend that *she* was the object of his desire. "I'm glad, but I still feel unworthy to eat wild strawberries in your company."

Chantry shook his head. "You know the story of *Johnny Lingo*? He was willing to pay eight cows for a wife. Well, you can brag to your friends that you're worth more to me than twelve million dollars."

Tears pooled against Sabrina's eyes. Chantry's brows furrowed with concern when he saw the emotion which his statement had caused. He quickly reached out and caught a stray tear. "Are you okay?" His voice was soft and genuine.

"It's just all hard to believe. I'm having a hard time taking it in-- that you could love me so much."

"Why?"

"Because I'm just me, and you're something *really* special, and– well, just like tonight! Who gets an award like that?"

"You think you're not special? Oh Sabrina! If only you could see yourself from my view. You were *born* special: spunky, stubborn, strong, maddening, frustrating, adorable!" Chantry paused only to draw an exaggerated breath, "Quick, bright, precocious, willful, spirited, and *real*. I want a *real* person in my life. I'm sorry if I've leveled too much at you tonight. My game plan just keeps tweaking itself. I wasn't going to mention marriage until at least April, but my feelings are rushing along ahead of schedule. I don't want to frighten you."

"I'm not afraid."

"Well I'm petrified! But my need for you is burning like a fever, and the more of you I get the more of you I want. I'm ready to play house."

"You wouldn't play house with me eleven years ago. Remember? I always used to beg you to."

Chantry's head cocked back as a laugh rolled from his throat. Sabrina found the cords in his neck to be very alluring. "Yes, I remember. What a pest! There's not a fourteen year old boy alive who wants to play house with a six year old!"

"You were a poor sport not to indulge me."

"I'm sorry. I'm ready to indulge you now."

"I thought you were mean." Sabrina jutted her bottom lip out in a fake pout.

Chantry's head moved closer. "Shut up," he murmured, kissing her. The kiss, although playful at first, crescendoed in fervency. Sabrina leaned harder and hungrier against Chantry until she knocked him off balance and he lay back on the bench with her pressing against him. Sabrina felt that she would be consumed in the blazing flames of desire. Vidalia's advice circled somewhere in the outer perimeters of her consciousness. Sabrina drew away, trembling, and very much awakened to a powerful storm of emotion which was howling against her best defenses and reserves. The kid stuff was past. Sabrina yearned with the dangerous, delicious, grown-up desires which drew men and women together. She pulled herself upright and extended a hand to Chantry, pulling him up also.

Chantry's inner fire extinguishers were laboriously fighting to control his raging inferno. His brows rose and a grin turned the corners of his mouth. His eyes softened from blazing to black. Sabrina loved watching him and studying his features. He seemed content to return the gaze. "Your eyes were blacker than mine a second ago."

"They were?"

"Yes. Brad was right," Chantry teased. "He really is a very descriptive poet."

"Shut up." Sabrina smacked his arm.

"Seriously, what am I going to do with you? I warned you about the ravenous wolf Breezy, but you invited it out to play anyway."

"Did I instigate that? I didn't mean to if I did."

"You just have a great capacity to love and you open up and let it flow. It's a wonderful quality Sabrina, and someday I'll be lucky enough to take a full measure of it."

Sabrina nodded, pondering Chantry's statement. She looked around the darkened shadows of Coleman Field, mentally replaying scenes of game footage from Chantry's award presentation. "How many times did you score in this place?"

"A lot--and I'll bet I've knocked at least sixty home runs over that fence, right there," Chantry said, pointing over left field. "I used to hate being left on base when the inning finished."

"I'll bet."

"But tonight I'm left standing on second with such a clear view of home plate that it hurts."

Sabrina laughed. "You and your baseball analogies! You're going to be the best coach in history."

Chantry stood, pulling Sabrina up with him. "We'd better go."

Sabrina was surveying the infield near first base. "I can't believe you got cleated in the arm and never dropped the ball! That was impressive. It was cool tonight after Coach Clayson told that story and everyone in the room started chanting, "Chief! Chief! Chief!"

"The crowd used to chant that whenever I'd smack a home run. It sounds egotistical but I kind of liked it."

"Are we really getting married, Chantry?"

"Yes, Breezy, we really *are*...unless you flunk history. That would be a deal-breaker."

"This all sounds good to me and you can be the chief, but I will be the boss."

Smile lines creased the handsome face. "Yeah, I kind of figured that's just how it will be."

"Do I have to go to Homecoming with stupid Bracken Spicer?"

"I'll get you out of it if you'd like."

"I'd like."

"Who would you rather go with?"

"My history teacher of course."

"Uh uh! That would be taboo. We'll sneak out of town and have a midnight picnic on some mountain top if you'd like."

"I'd like!"

"Maybe we'll take a leaf out of your dad's book and take a moonlit horse ride."

"That sounds romantic and I'm game, as long as I don't have to wear my nightgown. I'll tell my friends I'm going to Raymond to see my grandparents."

"We could dance with the moon to the sounds of water splashing over the rocks of Raymond Creek, and then sharpen our pencils and write anonymous poetry about it."

The couple giggled and talked as they walked back toward the hotel. Chantry's necktie was undone and his top button was open at the throat. Sabrina's strappy shoes were off and she toted them along barefooted. Irene looked miffed with them when they finally sauntered back into the lobby.

"Fun night?" she inquired jealously.

"Oh Irene, it was so good you wouldn't believe it," Chantry answered to Sabrina's delight.

CHAPTER THIRTY-FIVE

Early November winds were blowing colder and Sabrina felt a little chilled as she drove her snazzy yellow jeep inside the garage. It had been a long day at school followed by floral deliveries. She trudged up the stairs to her room. Tonight merited a long hot bath in her sunken tub. She would climb in and soak, immersed in the surrounding mural of her Thinking Place. Sabrina always felt as if she were actually just bathing in the river.

Sabrina's phone jangled. "Hello?"

"Hi Breezy. You looked so super-cute in class this morning I had a hard time remembering who actually won the Civil War."

Sabrina snickered. "The South?"

"It doesn't sound like you learned very much today."

"I was too busy daydreaming about the teacher."

"How's your Mom doing? Was it the twenty-four hour flu?"

"It's been the twenty-four hour flu for about six weeks now and you can guess what I'm thinking."

"You're not serious? Breezy, not really!"

Sabrina shrugged even though Chantry couldn't see her body language. "Whatever, but I'm telling you, she's craving raspberries."

"So? She's a former Bear Laker. We all love raspberries."

"Raspberry helps alleviate morning sickness."

"Have you asked her about it?"

"No, I guess they'll tell us when they're ready. Brad's got it figured out, too."

"Really?"

"Yes, because his dad looks so shocked and petrified."

Chantry laughed. Sabrina savored the sound of it, peeling through her phone, tickling her ear. "So, are you going to come over here for Family Home Evening, or what?"

"I was making sure you were still having it. I didn't know if Amanda was too sick or something, but I really need to talk to you anyway."

"No, she's up. She's not cooking though. Meat makes her gag, like that's not a dead give-away. Dorian and Brad are flipping steaks out on the grill where Mom can't smell it. The Elders will be here at seven."

"How's that been going?"

"Good. Brad seems ready."

"What about Dorian?"

"I'm not sure about him. He really can't figure out how baptism could help him be any happier than he is now. He's pretty content but I'm sure Mom will keep working on him."

"I'll see you in a bit."

Sabrina lay back in the tub, her mind swirling like a familiar river eddy. Brad's involvement with seminary had been phenomenal! He'd instigated a seminary service project with Brother Delenbaugh, which had eventually included the whole school, and townspeople, too. He kicked off a big fund raiser to send Delphinia Blue and her family to Disneyland for Christmas.

During Brad's homecoming date with Delphinia, he learned of her fondness for Sleeping Beauty. Brad started scheming and he and Haskel came up with a cracker-jack vacation package. Delphinia's travel itinerary included a week's stay in the private story-book lodging at Sleeping Beauty Castle, which wasn't even open to regular tourists. She was to enjoy an intimate luncheon with all of the Disney Princesses; Cinderella, Snow White, Belle, Sleeping Beauty, Ariel, and Jasmine. Brad wanted her to feel like a princess too, so the fund raiser's goal was to also afford a beautiful ball gown, sparkly shoes, and a dazzling tiara for Delphinia to wear as she dined with the ladies in her fairy tale.

Grandpa Haskel had a production crew working on an animated short, featuring the Princess Blue, herself. Haskel was doing the major part of the animation but he was recruiting help with the technical side of things. *The Delphinia Movie* would be shown to the Blue's at a private screening. Morgan County was in frenzy over helping the dreaming, scheming, Brad to grant such wishes. He had successfully spearheaded the whole project which raised more than twenty thousand dollars. The locals were thunderstruck by Brad's ambitious plans and abilities to carry through his well-laid intentions. Of course Haskel's connections helped.

Principal Hodges and Superintendent Casey nominated Brad for a national service award, as well as several Utah citizenship recognitions. Just as Sabrina predicted, he had taken Morgan by storm! He had even been elected Homecoming King and the queen was none other than Delphinia Blue. The royal couple reigned over the week's festivities with sweet enthusiasm, whipping up school spirit and county-wide unity. Dante and Tiffany Blue remained teary-eyed and shocked over the opportunities now streaming Delphinia's way.

Through his actions, Brad had taught the community more about living the gospel of Jesus Christ, Sabrina felt, than any church members had been able to teach him in return; yet he remained impressed with his new friends and associations with the church in general. His conversion process was donning excitement among his peers and building testimonies to everyone around him, especially in their seminary class.

"Why are you doing so much for Delphinia?" Sabrina asked Brad, one evening after scripture study.

"It helps me cope with the cold hard facts about you and Chantry, for one thing. I've just had to keep myself busy to keep from going mad. Plus, Delphinia is a sweetheart! Isn't she beautiful?"

"Brad, you see the beauty in everybody and everything. I've never quite known anyone like you." In Brad's mind all women were princesses.

"Delphinia seems to have a special link with Heaven."

"In what way?"

"The day of our Homecoming date she was out in the front room with me. We were waiting for everyone else to get here. She was staring at the portrait that you drew of Brian. She kept smiling at it so finally I said, 'That's Sabrina's brother, Brian.' Delphinia said, 'I know. He moved to Morgan with Sabrina in the second grade, but I'm the only one that ever talks to him.' Sabrina remembered the chills which swept across her neck and shuddered down her arms when Brad shared the incident. She shivered again at the memory. Brad continued, "I said 'What do you mean, Delphinia?' She just smiled, rocking back and forth, and said, 'Well he's always been nice and talked to me. He told me you were bringing me flowers and that I'd be asked out before anybody.' Tears streamed down Brad's cheeks after sharing Delphinia's declarations to his sister. "How can any of it be, Sabrina?"

"Delph's obviously very close to the veil." That comment sparked a lot of questions and Sabrina had answered them as simply as she could but Amanda felt it was time to call the missionaries. Tonight would be Brad's third discussion.

Sabrina pondered Delphinia's claims of talking to Brian since the second grade. It didn't really surprise her for Brian himself, had declared that he'd always been near, but she felt envious of Delphinia's conversations with her angel brother.

Sabrina climbed out of the tub, wrapping herself in a fluffy green towel. Her phone jangled. "Hello?"

"Breezy, are you ever going to come downstairs?"

"You're here?" How long had she been in the tub for crying out loud?

She quickly dressed and scurried downstairs. The Elders had arrived and Dorian was serving steaks and Dutch-oven potatoes to the guests. Chantry shook his head at Sabrina when she sheepishly made her appearance. "Sabrina should never have been given a sunken tub. An old galvanized wash-tub like the pioneers used to splash in would have encouraged her to be more prompt."

Amanda nodded at Chantry. "I know right?" Brad was definitely rubbing off on her!

Brad noticed her answer and happily touched his fist against hers. "Good job, Mom! You're getting cool like me."

Elder Davidson and Elder Walton seemed intrigued by the young investigator. During dinner the topic of the Word of Wisdom came up. Elder Davidson asked Brad if he understood the principals of it. "Yes I do, Elder. Mom confiscated all of the beer before Dad could marry her. Of course she strictly prohibits cigarettes and Sabrina has outlawed cigars in no uncertain terms. She claims they tend to make a jackass out of a person. Drinking coffee just makes me feel hot and tea tastes like the giraffe barn smells at the zoo. I don't do drugs, preferring to get my highs from singing in the ward choir. I think I'm good with it, Elder."

Laughter shot around the table. "I wish all of our discussions were this easy," Elder Walton said.

Elder Davidson studied Dorian. "What about you, Dorian? Are you good with it?"

"Ditto for me. Amanda rules the roost around here. She says we don't drink coffee so we don't, especially since it's nowhere to be found in the house. We own every kitchen appliance known to man *except* a percolator! It wasn't much of a fondness for me anyway. It always made me feel hot too."

Sabrina sawed a piece of steak with her knife. She went to spear a tender chunk with her fork but Chantry nudged her with his elbow and her fork skidded off her the plate. She laughed and tried again but he repeated the trick. The missionaries were amused by Chantry's sport.

"Do you mind?" Sabrina asked, sounding annoyed.

"Not very often."

Again laughter echoed around the table. Sabrina gave Chantry a *"you'd better straighten up"* stare but it didn't help, for as she was nearing her lips with the juicy morsel, he bumped her again, and the meat smeared across her nose. She dropped her fork in exasperation. "Really? Are you going to let me eat or not?"

"The Word of Wisdom warns us against the over-consumption of meat."

"Yes, well I'm in no danger of that, am I?"

Chantry smiled and tweaked her nose. "You've got a little bit of something right there," he said, rubbing a smear from her freckles.

"I can't imagine how it got *there!*"

Amanda cleared her throat. "One thing that really impresses me about Brad is his clean language. I've never heard him swear," she boasted to the missionaries.

"Me neither," Sabrina agreed. She cast a sidelong, shaming, glance at Chantry. "*You*, however, I have heard swear."

"That's because you provoke me."

The missionaries leaned forward in their seats. They were finding Sabrina and Chantry's friendly fire to be most amusing.

"Spending the last four years in the locker room and dugout, it is amazing Chantry remembers any good words at all!" Dorian defended.

"And rooming with Valdego," Chantry said. "He only knows twelve words which aren't vulgar. He needs a vocabulary coach."

Brad scooped up another serving of potatoes. "Chantry's my hero."

Dorian's face looked somewhat surprised. "Oh?"

"Yeah, I want to be just like him. That's why I've started dating a fourth grader." He smiled smugly, obviously feeling very pleased with himself. Sabrina shot a few daggers in his direction, wishing he would shush up in front of the missionaries.

Chantry smiled pleasantly at the youth then smacked a verbal home run. "At least I never dated my sister."

Sabrina closed her eyes so she couldn't see the Elders' reactions. She jutted an elbow into Chantry's ribs and kicked Brad under the table. Dorian choked on a bite of steak and Brad turned forty shades of red. "You're rather quick for an old guy," he mumbled. Chantry laughed heartily and Dorian joined in just as soon as he could clear the meat from his throat.

"That's enough you two," Amanda scolded softly. She looked pale.

"Inside joke?" Elder Walton asked.

"It used to be," Sabrina stated glumly. A shot of irreverent laughter erupted once more.

Sabrina was in charge of the lesson for Family Home Evening, and she had chosen to surprise Chantry by playing his baseball DVD. "We are going to watch something *very* inspirational," she announced. The missionaries leaned forward, thankful to be watching anything at all.

When Chantry saw what was playing, he winked at Sabrina and slid an arm around her. The family was spellbound. Respect for Sabrina's beau hit an all time high during the treasure of highlights. Dorian, Brad, Amanda, and the Elders kept looking over at him, making sure he was real. "Dude, you're awesome," Elder Davidson said.

"Why haven't you shown us this before?" Brad asked.

"I ordered copies in Corvallis," Chantry said, "But they just came the other day."

"We need to see this in school, as an assembly," Brad piped. "I'm going to work on it."

"Well, I guess we'll end up having an assembly then. It seems like you usually achieve what you set your mind to."

"Thanks Chantry. I really don't think you're *too* old of a guy."

Amanda was extra emotional. She wiped her eyes again and again. "I just love you Chantry Cantrell! Ben always knew you had it in you. He loved watching you play! I'm just so proud of you. I would like my own copy of this DVD. I'll be happy to pay for it."

"I'll see that you get one."

The Elders meshed their discussion in with Family Home Evening. It was a better-than-average Monday night. After they left, the family wandered into the cozy sun room. Dorian and Brad both seemed a little star-struck with the athlete; as if their respect for him had been renewed. "You've done amazing things," Dorian said. "I knew you had, but when you see it visually like that...it's very impressive."

Chantry and Brad stretched out on their stomachs to play a game of Battleship. "What is it with you and that game?" Sabrina asked.

"It's just fun to have somebody to play it with. Sometimes I played by myself when I was younger. It's not the same."

"I guess not," Chantry agreed, shaking his head.

"I always wanted a brother or sister," Brad went on, hopefully baiting a family discussion on Amanda's current status. It worked.

"Well, Son...better late than never."

Sabrina was expecting the news but she didn't think they'd fall for Brad's trap, so her head snapped up, along with Chantry's and Brad's. "What?"

"I'm going to have a baby," Amanda said. She was smiling and radiant with a touch of pink coloring her recently pale cheeks. "I can't believe it but I went to the doctor this morning, and it's true. I didn't think I could ever have more children after the twins. I tried for a long time with no success, so the possibility that I *could* get pregnant now never even entered into my mind."

"Good job Dad." Brad offered. Dorian sighed pensively but didn't comment.

"Your poor father's in shock. I think it's because he's remembers how difficult it was, raising you all alone, and he feels overwhelmed by it. I've tried to reassure him it will be different this time."

"That's right," Brad said. "Dad, this one will have a mother who will love it. Heck! Can you even imagine the way Amanda will cherish the baby? What a lucky kid." Brad's voice cracked as he said it. Sabrina was moved with tender emotion for the boy who had always yearned for a mother and finally had one after so many years of waiting.

Sabrina didn't really know what to say, for sure. It was so odd, hearing that she'd have a baby brother or sister, but by the time the child arrived, Sabrina would be married. "Well...Mom...you need to get on some raspberry leaf. It's very healthy for pregnant women. Midwives love to use it. It prevents nausea and anemia in most cases. Make sure that you take folic acid, as well. You also need a quality, whole-food supplement. Don't take a synthetic prenatal vitamin; they don't assimilate very well."

"Thank you, Doctor." Chantry said, studying the grid pattern on the Battleship unit.

Sabrina scowled at the perfectly handsome face. "You're just jealous because I'm a better medicine man than you are! Brad, his little boat is on the J column."

Chantry looked annoyed. "Breezy!"

"Thanks, Sabrina! Hey Chantry, how about J nine?"

"Hit. B four?"

"Miss! J ten?"

"Sunk." Chantry glared back at Sabrina. "I hope you're satisfied," he said, climbing to his feet. "Well, you win Brad. I guess I'd better be going. Congratulations, you two," he offered, shaking Dorian's hand and giving Amanda a hug. "I didn't see that one coming."

"That makes two of us," Dorian answered stoically.

"I'll walk you to your truck," Sabrina volunteered.

"That means Sabrina wants to make out for ten minutes before you go home," Brad piped.

"*Jerk!*" Sabrina hissed, kicking him in the arm as she walked by. "I should have told Chantry where *your* dumb little boat was instead! Then he would have won."

"That's okay, he's won everything else," Brad mumbled, cleaning up the game. Chantry shot a smile at Brad then slid an arm around Sabrina.

The air was chilly so Sabrina hopped inside Chantry's truck with him. "Thanks for coming over tonight."

"You're welcome. Thanks for calling my DVD *inspirational.*"

"Thanks for *being* inspirational!"

"Sabrina, your mom isn't going to feel up to a wedding when we've planned one."

"She'll have to stay home with her feet up."

"Breezy, we can't do that to her."

"She has a knack for messing up all of my plans! It's not fair."

"I'm sure as heck glad she tripped up your last one." Chantry's onyx eyes glinted in the shadows.

"You are?"

"You know it! I love you." He pulled his phone from his pocket and punched a number sequence. "Hey Dorian, I'm taking Sabrina with me for a while, okay? Thanks." Chantry started the truck and drove quickly into Morgan. "We need to talk," he said, helping her from the truck and into his apartment. He turned on the lights and pulled the shades. Sabrina always felt perfectly comfortable at

Chantry's. Instead of smelling musty and dank, the apartment now smelled like him and Sabrina relished the scent.

"Want some hot chocolate, Breeze?"

"Sure." Sabrina grabbed a couple of mugs from the cupboard while Chantry put water on to boil. "Hey Chantry, did you know I purposefully hid some of your things when I helped you move in here, just so you'd have to call me and ask where they were?"

"So that's why I found the spatula in the freezer! I have a confession to make, too. Remember when I called looking for my pizza cutter?"

"Yeah?"

"I was holding it in my hand when I dialed your number."

Sabrina smiled. Sometimes the very sight of Chantry would steal her breath. "You're beautiful! Men probably don't like hearing that word, but Chantry, you are! You're the most beautiful person I've ever seen. I love your smile and your teeth. I love your mouth, nose, and cheekbones. I totally dig that indentation under your lower lip. I love your eyes, and I'm wild about the delicious color of your skin. It reminds me of burnt caramel or something, and frankly it teases my appetite."

Chantry was leaning against the counter with his arms folded across his chest. He listened to the girl, seeming both startled and intrigued by her ready acknowledgment of his so–called *beauty*. A playful smile tugged against his mouth as she spoke. "You're a funny little bird, twittering away about me. You're the beautiful one! Look at you, with your spicy nutmeg hair, and sprinkled cinnamon freckles; dancing, passionate eyes, and soft, kissable mouth. I love your adorable, mischievous dimples and bright smile. You are the beautiful one!" Sabrina tossed her head. "Don't argue with me!" Chantry grabbed her by the hand and jerked her into the bedroom where he turned her to face a full-length mirror. "Look at yourself!"

She tried to stare but her eyes were more drawn to his dark, brooding, and luscious image standing above her in the glass. His expression was intense, his black eyes smoldering as usual. His mouth was pulled into a hard line, and his brows were furrowed. Strong arms reached around her, holding her steady before the mirror's reflection. "Look at *your* skin," he whispered. His voice sounded husky and raw. Chantry raised a hand to Sabrina's neck, lightly tracing the contour of her throat and collarbone. The hard bronze lines of his hand and wrist against Sabrina's own delicate bone structure and pale skin made her shiver. Her breath caught and she felt mesmerized by the contrast in the glass. Chantry's hand felt hot against her flesh.

His head bent against her neck, moaning softly as he kissed her throat, trailing kisses along the same line his fingers traced against her skin. Sabrina once again began to tremble beneath Chantry's touch. Her pulse was racing and her breathing was ragged. She pivoted away from the mirror, turning into Chantry's embrace, burying her face against his chest. She clung to him tightly, trying to calm her inner quaking. "I love you Chantry." His arms were strong and steady, supporting her. One hand tilted her chin upwards and his lips crushed against hers with savage passion. Sabrina's legs were so shaky she didn't think she was even standing on her own power; obviously Chantry was holding her up.

The kettle whistled. *Time out!* Chantry drew back. His eyes continued to search Sabrina's. He ran one hand through his raven hair. "Great, the hot chocolate is ready. I want a honeymoon, but I have to settle for a cup of cocoa. What a rip off!" He kissed her once again then turned for the kitchen.

Chantry stirred chocolate in a mug and passed it across the table to Sabrina. "Here Breezy," he said, heaving a long sigh. "I want you. I'm starting to feel like June's a long way off." Sabrina nodded, her tremors were subsiding, but she still hadn't found her voice. "I light of your Mother's condition, what if we got married during Spring Break?" Sabrina gulped her chocolate audibly. She wasn't certain Chantry was serious, but his solemn, piercing gaze said he was. She still couldn't manage to speak. Chantry waited patiently, watching the wheels turning in her head. "Or better yet, Christmas vacation?"

"Yeah, right..."

"Thanksgiving?"

Sabrina's eyebrows shot high at the impatient suggestions. "I thought we were supposed to be seeing each other on the sly."

"Yeah, that's what I needed to talk to you about." Chantry walked into his living room then returned carrying a new issue of *Sports Illustrated*. "Breezy, I'm afraid our secretive days are over. I couldn't believe it when I saw it, but take a look at page forty-two." He plopped the magazine in front of Sabrina. She quickly flipped the pages until she found it. There, in living color, was an article covering Chantry's award ceremony. There was a rather large write-up and many stunning pictures of the event, but the one that drew Sabrina's immediate attention made her eyes bulge and her jaws drop! She stared at the photo. Chantry's arm was around her and he was kissing the side of her head. Her cheeks were a lovely shade of pink and she looked happier, and prettier, than she'd ever seen herself.

"This is a good picture of us." She remembered the exact moment it must have been snapped, as they had just taken their seats at the table with the Cantrell's and Grandpa and Grandma Ashley.

"Sabrina, everybody is going to see this!"

"Are you sorry?"

"No. Read the caption."

"Is this mystery girl responsible for Cantrell's decision to walk away from several major league offers?" Chantry grabbed the article. His eyes scanned down printed columns, searching for something. "Listen to this: *"Former team member, and roommate, Kenny Valdego, reported Cantrell's date to be a hot dish, and worth pursuing. Valdego claims Cantrell wants to settle down and start a family, away from the spotlight..."* Chantry paused. "I didn't think Valdego was sober enough to ever know what I wanted. The article ends this way, *"Wipe your*

eyes baseball fans, for the new star rising has chosen to blink out; preferring to twinkle in less exalted skies. Cantrell has taken a position, coaching high school baseball in Morgan, Utah. Surely major America's loss becomes the small town America's gain. Farewell, Chantry Cantrell, and good luck! Surely you will touch the lives of young people with the same fiery passion that lit the fans of collegiate baseball." Chantry dropped the magazine again to the table.

"That was actually very nice."

Chantry nodded, taking a sip from a steamy mug. "My complimentary copy came today. This won't hit subscribers' hands for another day but are you ready for what's coming?"

"I'm proud to own up to being your girl, but what are the implications for you?"

"I went into Mr. Hodges' office this afternoon. I plopped the article down on his desk and let him read it. He was so impressed, he requested the DVD for a school assembly. Won't Brad be surprised when the student body gets called in for an assembly tomorrow?"

Sabrina nodded, smiling. "Before he gets a chance to use his own charms to convince the principal?" She chuckled at the amusing thought.

"I pointed out the picture of us and explained to Hodges that you were the reason I even came to Morgan in the first place. He didn't seem very alarmed about anything. He was feeling too flattered and star-struck to be very affected by the fact that I was dating a student. He said, 'Well if her parents don't have any objections, and there's no funny business taking place in school, I fail to see that any of this is relevant. Miss Ashley's academic performance has been unsurpassed and most exemplary. We can't even quibble with her grade in history, nor make favoritism claims, as she's never received less than an A in any other class, either. Some may see this as scandalous--there are always wagging tongues, but rest assured, I do not see it in that light. On the contrary, Miss Ashley should be thanked for bringing you to us. I'll gladly talk to Superintendent

Casey and make any necessary explanations so that he's not caught off guard.'"

Sabrina nodded her head. She'd drained her mug and walked to the sink to wash it. She grabbed a dishtowel and wiped it dry. When she turned back from the cupboard, Chantry was standing right behind her. "Sabrina, my best defense has always been a good offense."

"What do you mean?"

"We won't let the article force us into anything. We'll beat it to the punch." He clasped Sabrina's left hand, sliding a dazzling platinum and diamond ring onto her finger. Sabrina's jaw dropped and her breath became trapped in her throat. Tears instantly sprang to her eyes, clouding her vision as the realization of the moment settled in. Her heart trilled in her chest and joy tingled from the top of her head, rushing through her entire body like a warm, drenching rain. She blinked through her tears to gaze at the brilliant diamond on her hand and then she looked at Chantry. He was playfully kneeling before her. "Marry me, Breezy. This is official. I want you to wear this ring and show it off as much as you'd like to." His eyes were searching, yet gentle, and his expression was soft and sincere.

Sabrina tried to answer, but the only sound that could escape her throat was a twisted, triumphant sob.

"So that's a yes?" Sabrina nodded, laughing and sobbing. Chantry gathered her in his arms. "Remember how I said I wanted you to go to all of the dances and parties at school?" Sabrina bobbed her head but didn't move from his embrace. "Well, I take it all back. From now on you'll attend them all with me. I'll take you to prom. I'm a class advisor so I have to be there, anyway. It serves me right since I never bothered going to my own high school dances. Can you handle being so tied up? Do you really want to be engaged?"

"More than anything."

"We'll toss around possible marriage dates with your mother. I'm still thinking Spring Break would be good as I wouldn't be too far into baseball. Well, Little Bird, my Breezy, my girl, I'd better get you home before Dorian comes hunting me with a shotgun."

Sabrina chuckled at the mental picture. She made Chantry drive with the dome light on in the truck so she could stare at her diamond. "I don't think I'll be able to sleep tonight. When did you get the ring?"

"Breezy, that ring was in the glove compartment the day I helped you move into your new house."

"You're kidding?"

"No! I offered to let you drive so you wouldn't start fiddling with things and find it."

"I can't believe that."

"Well…believe it. I told you I came to Morgan with a purpose and you were it! The ring was my insurance policy to force me to stick to my guns. Those dreams I had were too real and too persuasive. I went to the temple a lot too, and that only validated my feelings. I was pretty confidant of my course. I'm just glad I was able to convince you."

Sabrina wrapped her arms around his neck and kissed his cheek while he drove. "I love you, Chantry. I'm ready to be your wife."

"I'm going to break the news in first hour tomorrow so prepare yourself. News will spread like wildfire all over the school. By lunchtime the whole town will be talking about it. By the time *Sports Illustrated* shows up in mailboxes, the fresh tinder will be already burned up. People will see our photograph and say, 'Yeah, we already knew that. They're getting married.' Hopefully they'll realize my intentions toward you are honorable."

CHAPTER THIRTY-SIX

Just as Sabrina predicted, she didn't sleep well. She kept turning on her light to make sure the ring was still on her finger. She was apprehensive about the up-coming announcement in class, yet eager as well. She was tired of secrets.

Something was bothering her. She walked into her dressing area. Brad's bracelet was coiled up on her vanity. She examined it, running a finger across the engraving, *Summer Love*. It was a great reminder of important days gone by, and a keepsake, but to wear it now felt like a betrayal to Chantry. She pulled her treasure box from a shelf then knelt on the floor and removed the lid. She rifled through her things until she found the tiny box which had housed Chantry's arrowhead for so many years. She set the gold bracelet into the aged folds of tissue paper and laid it back into her box. An envelope peeked up at her. Sabrina stared at the item for several long minutes. She pulled it from the box, inspecting it.

Her nerves jumped at the touch of it. *Ben* was scrawled across the front of it in careless cursive. She turned the envelope over and studied the closed seal. *What was inside?* Sabrina often wondered. She flinched against the temptation to open it. Surely the ugly words would leak their poison if disturbed. No, the envelope must forever remain sealed, for its contents felt as lethal as anthrax.

"Tears began spilling. Sabrina tossed the envelope back into the box, burying it deeply beneath her dearest treasures. She roughly jammed the lid on and put the box back in its place on her shelf. She walked back to her bed, trying to shove unpleasant memories from her mind, but the tears continued to wet her pillow. "Chantry listened to his dreams, Dad! I know you'd be so happy that we're getting married. I love him, Daddy! He makes me happy and I wish you were here to see. I know I'm young, but with all my heart I know I'm ready."

Sabrina lay engulfed in so many varied emotions she felt as if she'd go mad. Sometime after two o'clock she drifted off to sleep, her mind reeling through one strange dream after another. At first she was at work but none of the flowers would fit into vases. She ran outside to see if there were any extra vases in the garage. Chantry's truck was parked inside and loaded to the brim with them. She rejoiced at the sight!

That dream melted into one about Mia having kittens in Grandma Ashley's cupboard. Grandma handed her a box and demanded that Sabrina load the cat and kittens inside, and take them away. Sabrina reached into the cupboard, first retrieving Mia, and then a whole handful of tiny, bleating kittens. Every time she reached her hand into the cupboard she drew out more and more. The kittens at the back of the cupboard were bigger and already had their eyes open. The next animals she pulled from the cupboard were not kittens at all, but puppies and bunnies. Sabrina felt upset about putting so many animals in the box with Mia and her tiniest, nursing babes. She ran out of the house, looking for another box. As she stumbled across the back yard to Grandma's garage, a dust-devil whirled across the road, carrying a swirl of fluttering leaves and debris. The miniature tornado engulfed Sabrina, trapping her inside. As the leaves whirled and twirled manically around her they morphed into sealed white envelopes. Sabrina tried to snatch them all up. Her hands flew at lightning speed, grabbing them one by one and stuffing them inside of her pajamas. One last envelope fluttered and danced on the naughty air draft. It whirled around and around, high above Sabrina's reach. She jumped and strained, but the envelope darted and hovered, taunting elusively on the breeze. Sabrina hollered in sheer exasperation. A bronze hand then plucked the envelope from the air, as if picking an apple from a tree. Chantry stood smiling down at her, extending the envelope. "For you, Breezy." The wind and debris died down and everything was calm.

Sabrina was so ecstatic to see the man. She threw her arms around his neck, kissing him again and again. "I need a box."

"I have a whole truck load of them."

Relief! Chantry helped her carry several boxes into the house. They sorted the animals as best they could. "Kittens, puppies, or bunnies," Chantry said pleasantly, "together we can surely sort them out."

Sabrina startled awake. Her pajamas and sheets were damp with sweat from the restless dreams which had been both disturbing and weirdly wonderful. The clock said five-thirty and Sabrina was happy to see that morning was here. She decided not to wrestle with another hour's sleep so she quickly stripped the linens from her bed. Using her favorite sheets she then made it up fresh and headed for the shower.

Her ring sparkled brilliantly from her finger, reminding her that Chantry had officially staked a claim on her. The realization was zinging and delightful! She waited until six-fifteen then called him.

"Chantry? I'm sorry if I woke you."

"Breezy, I wasn't asleep. I was laying here thinking about you. Are you happy?"

"Utterly."

"So you're willing to go through with our plans today?"

"Are you?"

"It almost makes me laugh now that I thought we had to tip-toe around in the first place. I'm kind of glad that reporter snagged a photo of us. This is a better way."

"I love my ring! I couldn't have picked one that I liked any better."

"Just wait until you see the wedding band! It's a gorgeous set."

"Will you show it to me? *Please!*"

Chantry's laughter tickled Sabrina's ear. "Oh Breezy, you haven't changed very much. You still think *please* is the magic word. How about we come back here for lunch today? Then you can see it and try it on."

"Now that's what I'm talking about! I'd love to have lunch with you."

"I love you, Sabrina. I'll see you at school. I'm praying for us, hoping this works out according to plan."

"It surely will then--and I love you too. Bye."

She sat the phone down with a smile. She had decided to power dress for school. She followed every step of Rahul's beauty regime and took extra pains with her hair. She swept it up, carefully leaving strategic wisps here and there to curl against her face. She sprayed her fragrance against her throat and wrists. She pulled on her favorite, best-fitting jeans. They made her legs look thinner and longer. She wove a hot pink belt through the pant loops. The buckle was shaped like a large, silvered butterfly. Smaller butterfly rivets were inset sporadically along the length of the belt. It was both feminine and edgy. Sabrina layered a figure-flattering black shirt over a lacy, hot pink tank top. A snug-fitting, light-weight, denim jacket added another layer. She rolled the jacket's sleeves up a couple of turns. Her black rhinestone choker sparkled at her throat. She employed Vandaline's bracelet skills, pairing two or three simple bangles on each wrist. Vandaline was able to layer jewelry without ever looking gaudy and Sabrina had been silently taking notes. She then pulled on her Ariat fatbaby boots in pink and black. She studied her reflection in the glass.

Brad whistled when she stepped into the hall. "What the--" he said, parroting Danforth's usual comment. "You look good Sabrina."

"Thanks. You were asleep when I came home last night."

"I know! I finally read scriptures by myself, thank you very much."

"I'm engaged."

"Not really?"

Sabrina thrust her hand out for inspection, studying the boy's reaction. He paled significantly and his eyes squinted into slits. He chewed nervously against the inside of one cheek for a second or two. "I guess that's that, then. I thought you were the high and mighty one who would *never* dream of getting married in high school. Perhaps it was just my offer that was so revolting to you."

"Brad, I'm–"

"Save it! I don't need to know any of the details. You were snatched up before we ever even left California! You've never had to suffer for fifteen seconds over me. I've just had to endure watching Chantry waltz you into his world. Well go ahead! I don't need you anymore."

"I'm sorry," Sabrina whispered fiercely. "I still need you. We're family now, remember? I'll always need you." She turned on her heel and retreated downstairs.

Dorian was flipping pancakes in the kitchen. "Good morning. How's the newly betrothed?" He sounded like Grandpa Haskel. "You're looking as lovely and radiant as any blushing bride ought to," he commented lightly. He loaded a plate with a fresh stack. "Would these pancakes pass your Grandpa Ashley's approval, do you think?"

Sabrina nodded and took the plate. "How's Mom this morning?"

"Unfortunately she's in worshiping the porcelain throne. That usually doesn't let up until nine or ten, then she hurries around, making up for lost time the rest of the day."

"It will be okay Dorian."

"I guess we'll see. I don't figure there's another choice, do you? It's just that your Mom and I were both teetering on the brink of an empty nest. I had a lot of plans and none of them included Pampers or preschool."

Amanda breezed into the kitchen, still wearing her nightgown. "Good morning. How do you feel about that diamond ring sparkling on your finger?"

"I love it."

"It seems a little early," Amanda confessed. "Yet it feels right to me at the same time. I'm sure people will call me crazy for letting you jump into marriage so young. In fact I'm apt to be tarred and feathered in the town square."

"Marriage in general is no longer the politically correct form of living, haven't you heard?" Dorian remarked sarcastically. "You can't worry about other people! They may be masters of their own destinies but they have no jurisdiction over yours. Remember that. You're young in years Sabrina, but some people have older spirits, I swear that is true. Maturity is relative and I think your head is fastened on your shoulders well enough."

"Brad's angry with me."

Dorian shrugged his shoulders. "He'll bounce. Give him a little bit of space. I personally think that your engagement to Chantry Cantrell solves everything! Now I don't have to worry about Brad trying to run off with you during the holidays."

"I wouldn't have gone. I already told him no. I was dead set against Brad's plan, yet here I am, engaged to Chantry and eager to go. It's crazy! I swore up and down I would never get married this young."

"Chantry's the one. Why quibble over four or five months? You're a mature, capable, intelligent girl who obviously knows her mind."

Amanda looked annoyed at her husband. "You're not helping! I think Sabrina should at least graduate first."

"Chantry's getting jittery. He looks like I felt last June--totally frustrated! Women with morals have the ability to frustrate even well-intending gentleman." Dorian smiled, kissing his pale wife.

"Chantry has morals, too." Sabrina offered. "Although..."

"Ah-ha!" Dorian exclaimed. "It's getting tougher being good, isn't it?" Sabrina's cheeks flushed but she didn't elaborate. "What if it comes down to getting married in March, *in* the temple, or getting married in June, *outside* of the temple?" Dorian asked, playing the devil's advocate.

"Of course I want Sabrina to get married in the temple!" Amanda cried before turning and running back towards the bathroom, gagging as she went.

Dorian's nose wrinkled comically, in sympathy of his wife's nauseous plight. Sabrina giggled at the man. "Thanks for everything, Dorian."

He gazed affectionately at her. "I wish I could have met your Mom years ago. I would really have enjoyed raising you. I like your spunk and your spirit. You're definitely not high-maintenance. Sabrina, there's not a better man anywhere, than Chantry. I am very impressed with your choice. Keep your chin up today. If you know what you want, face it, own it, and savor it."

Sabrina leaned over the bar and hugged her stepfather, deeply appreciating his kindness. "I love you Dorian."

"The scandal of you marrying your history teacher is much more appealing to me than the scandal of you running around with your step-brother." He smiled and winked. "Good luck Sabrina."

When Sabrina got to school she checked her reflection in the jeep's mirror. She reapplied fresh gloss to her lips, uttered a silent prayer, and climbed out of her vehicle. She noticed a few appreciative looks being shot in her direction. Danforth whistled. "Hey Hot Stuff. How are you doing?"

"I'm fine, thank you. How are you, Danforth? Thanks for always being such a good *friend.*"

"Maybe we should go out sometime; like bowling tonight."

Sabrina was amused by his timing. If he had asked her out yesterday, she might have said yes. "Oh Dan, you don't want to take me out! I'm not athletic enough for you and besides that, Coach Cantrell wants your mind on the game."

"We're four months away from the season! My game is untouchable and cannot be deviated by one date." Just then a wayward football careened into Danforth's head. He let out a bellow and went in search of the offending thrower. Dawson Gregory took off running, and the two wrestled each other to the brown November grass, whooping and hollering. Sabrina opened the school door, leaving them to their play.

"You look nice today," Lyndi said. "I like your boots. So guess what?"

"What?"

"I made All-State in Volleyball!" Sabrina was thrilled for her friend's news and the two strolled to their lockers, heads bent. "Tahnee and Kara made it too."

Sabrina yearned to show Lyndi her engagement ring! She fiddled with her locker combination left-handed, hoping she would notice but she didn't. "Did you know I went out with Trey on Saturday? I was kind of surprised when he called. It's almost like one date with Brad and suddenly you're introduced to male society."

"That's funny. Where did you go?"

"He took me to Frightmares at Lagoon. I think it was the last weekend of the season. It was fun. We rode Wicked seven times."

Sabrina grimaced at the thought of the screaming amusement ride. "That's too much ride for me. I don't enjoy that one very much."

"We kept double-dog-daring each other. Trey won me a giant stuffed dragon by shooting hoops, so I won him a humongous Pink Panther. We buckled them into the backseat and you should have seen us driving back to Morgan! We looked like some deranged, alien family. It was so hilarious!"

"Did he kiss you?"

"Not directly, but his Pink Panther kissed my dragon at the door. It was kind of tender."

Brad strode toward the two. "Good morning, Lyndi! Would you care to go bowling with me tonight? I've invited a few couples to come with us so it should be a party. I've got a ten dollar bet going that I can beat Danforth's game." Brad cast an annoyed glance at Sabrina. "You're welcome to drag a date along, Sabrina."

Lyndi looked startled but accepted the offer. "When it rains it pours."

Two other girls scurried to join Lyndi and Sabrina in the hall. "Oh my heck! Somebody help me," Janice Jenkins gushed. "Mr. Cantrell is *so* hot today!"

Lyndi's head cocked off to one side and she took a fake swing at Janice's head. "Snap out of it already! Mr. Cantrell looks hot every day. It's nothing new! It's what we live for; it's why we crave an education! Don't you know we hunger to learn? Why else would we drool all over our papers?"

Janice peeled into giggles at Lyndi's words. "But he's totally gorgeous today."

Tahnee nodded in agreement. "Seriously, he is. I was in Miss Clisp's room, getting some help on an assignment, and Mr. Cantrell walked in and handed her something from Mr. Hodges. You should have seen Miss Clisp's face! She turned red and sweaty, right then and there. Her eyes trailed him all of the way out of the classroom. She saw me watching her and she got even more flustered! I was totally laughing at her. I said *"Whoo-whoo, Miss Clisp!"* She didn't say a word because she knew she was busted."

Sabrina listened to the tales of the hot and handsome history teacher with great interest. She looked down at her ring, cherishing the precious band and the delicious thoughts of all it symbolized.

She wished someone would notice but her friends were too giddy to see what they weren't expecting in the first place. The bell rang.

"See you three later," Tahnee said. "Have fun crunching on the history teacher! I'll get my turn in fifth hour but first I have to endure Mr. Middlemiss. Yuck!"

"That sucks for you," Lyndi lamented. "Try calling him *Miss Middlemister* and see what happens."

Sabrina grabbed her books and trudged after Lyndi and Janice. Chantry was half leaning, half sitting, against a corner of his desk. His eyes locked on Sabrina, taking a quick appraisal. His brows rose slightly and his mouth curled with obvious pleasure. Sabrina knew that look meant she'd passed inspection. She was sizing him up as well. *Did he power dress today, too?* A black turtleneck sweater stretched across his muscular chest and shoulders in a most flattering manner! He wore a caramel leather blazer, black Wranglers, and a western belt with a large buckle. *No wonder Miss Clisp and all of the girls were swooning!* Sabrina hoped today's announcement wouldn't earn her a failing grade in English.

Danforth dropped a folded note on Sabrina's desk, winking at her as he did it. Sabrina groaned inwardly but didn't touch the note. It would be better left unread, she was sure. Chantry caught the action, arching one brow in a very amused manner. Brad also saw the note fall and rolled his eyes, looking completely disgusted. He shook his head at Sabrina. "I can't believe you," he whispered belligerently. "You're like a scalp collector."

"Good morning," Mr. Cantrell called pleasantly.

"Good morning," the students answered back.

"Isn't it a beautiful day?" Heads nodded and bobbed around the room. Chantry always held the class spell-bound. "I was just thinking, as you were walking in this morning. You're a mighty good-looking bunch!" Danforth straightened up in his seat, feeling proud, and owning the teacher's ready observations. "You're an intelligent group of individuals," Chantry continued. "You're not little kids anymore, are you?"

"No," sounded the unified reply.

"What about you, Janice? Are you a kid?"

"No Mr. Cantrell."

"What about Sabrina? Is she a mere baby, peering over her cradle?"

Again the class stirred, "No!"

"Danforth?"

"Absolutely not!"

"No. You're all seniors, standing on the rim of your own horizons. Are you all choosing for yourselves what you want out of life? Are you busy thinking about colleges and careers? Some of you young men are contemplating missions. Are you grown up enough to handle so many big decisions?"

"Yes!"

Chantry smiled at his students. "That's right. You're intelligent, capable people and I'm proud to call you friends. I enjoy your participation in this class. What about me though?"

The students were quiet, wondering what the teacher was getting at.

"Am I over-the-hill? Ancient? Decrepit?"

"No!"

"Are you kids telling me that I'm not old and you're not young?"

"That's right!" Danforth blurted. "You're a cool teacher--you're more like one of us."

Chantry grinned at the stray comment. "I'm twenty-five years old. Do you think I'm old enough and wise enough to choose for myself?"

"Of course!" Binny Jo piped.

"Good," Chantry said, nodding at the group, quickly sweeping his eyes up and down the aisles, and carefully making eye contact with each pupil. "I've just made a big decision in my own life. Since you are all old enough and intelligent enough to handle the news, I'd like to share it with you." The butterflies on Sabrina's belt leapt into her stomach. She couldn't control their twisting and cramping movements so she just gave in, beaming at the teacher with heady anticipation. "I'm getting married."

Excited and disappointed murmurs hissed around the room, coiling and recoiling like whipping snakes. The girls looked sad. The boys just looked weird. "You're still going to stay and teach us aren't you? You're still going to be our coach?" Trey asked pensively.

"That's a good question. Listen up and I'll tell you the answer to that." The class quieted, instantly, as if it had been covered with a death shroud. "I received an offer to sign with the Cincinnati Reds, a four year contract, worth twelve million dollars."

A dull roar exploded along the aisles. "What the—"Danforth thundered.

"I considered the offer carefully but I turned it down, opting instead to take the coaching position here."

"Why?" Danforth demanded.

"Because of a girl," Chantry said quietly. The whole class shushed again, waiting. "I wanted to marry Sabrina Ashley."

Shocked, stunned, unbelievable silence. Danforth slapped his forehead. "What the—" he erupted, looking crazy-eyed at Sabrina. Brad leaned across the aisle and snatched Dan's note, then returned it to the author. "You turned down twelve million dollars to marry Sabrina?"

"I sure did. I wanted to marry Sabrina and coach you guys in baseball. That's why I said *no* to the Reds, and *yes* to the Trojans. Did you know you'd all be worth that much to me?"

Lyndi whipped around in her seat, staring holes through Sabrina's head. "You suck! You've never said one word to me. Alas, dear maid, not one!"

Sabrina's eyes met her friend's. "I wanted to Lyndi, but...I didn't. Please forgive me."

Lyndi scowled, considering Sabrina's request. "Let me see your ring."

Sabrina eagerly slid her hand forward and suddenly her desk was surrounded by every girl in the class. She was cocooned inside threads of envy, congratulations, disbelief, and good old-fashioned shock. A host of oohs and awes swirled around her. Chantry let the girls have their moment.

"Now since you've already declared to me that I'm not ancient and Sabrina's not a baby, I don't want to hear tales of cradle-robbing. Is that understood?"

"Yes."

"If you hear viscous reports about either one of us, as your friends, we would ask you to put them down. Sabrina's garnered enough extra-credit points for all of you in this class, by her amazing knowledge in history, to cinch the fact that she's an A student, correct?"

"Yes!"

"There hasn't been any favoritism in this classroom. Sabrina has earned every grade she's received. Can I count on each of you to deny any silly gossip which might imply otherwise?"

"Yes," again arose from the students.

"I knew I could count on you. By the way, next to Sabrina's parents and Mr. Hodges, you are the first people to know." The classroom applauded and whistled. "Now, let's get down to business. Kara, tell me five distinctive qualities possessed by Robert E. Lee."

Kara ticked them off, and the history lesson began. Chantry had steered them through their controversial announcement with the same ease that he seemed to play baseball. He was brilliant! Sabrina listened attentively but couldn't stop her pen from doodling, *"Mrs. Sabrina Cantrell"* over and over again on her notebook. She tried it different ways. *Mrs. Chantry Cantrell, Sabrina Lyn Cantrell,* and *Sabrina Lyn Ashley Cantrell.* Each one tickled her fancy as no matter how she wrote it, her name still ended with *Cantrell.*

As the period was nearing the end Mr. Hodges' voice sounded over the intercom announcing a surprise assembly for second hour. The class again cheered. When the bell rang, Sabrina gathered her books.

"Would you like me to save you a seat, or will you be attending with the faculty?" Lyndi asked sarcastically.

"Save me a seat!"

"Promise you'll tell me all about it."

"I will."

Brad paused at Chantry's desk, jutting out a hand. "Congratulations," he offered congenially.

"Thanks Brad. I guess we'll be brothers, huh?"

"I'm throwing a bowling party tonight to celebrate. I hope you and Sabrina can come since you two are the guests of honor. There will be a bunch of us." He sauntered out and Sabrina was alone with the teacher.

"You're amazing. I'm the envy of every female on the planet, I think."

"Were you really taking notes during class?"

"Kind of," Sabrina confessed. She flipped her notebook open to her doodles.

Chantry read through each of the titles. "That has a good ring to it."

"By the way, Chantry...you look incredible today."

"Right back at you, Breezy. You walked in this morning and rocked my world. Looks like you rocked Danforth's too! I guess we'd better take our places in the auditorium. I'll kind of be glad to shed the spotlight tomorrow. I'll meet you at my truck at lunch hour. Try to hurry."

"I'll be there."

Chapter Thirty-seven

A swirling wind of whispers blew around the auditorium as news about Chantry and Sabrina spread. Stunned stares and startled eyes followed Sabrina to her seat. She nestled between Tahnee and Lyndi. As soon as she sat down Tahnee grabbed her hand to inspect her ring. "I cannot believe this!"

"I know."

"You should have told us!"

"I wanted to, really I did!"

Tahnee's eyes were large and her features seemed incredulous that such a thing had happened to one of them. "Can I ask you a question?"

"Shoot."

"Do you call him Mr. Cantrell?"

"Only in class, usually I call him Chantry."

Tahnee squealed at the thought, rubbing her palms against her pants and shaking her head. "Oh, my heck--I just can't picture it!"

Lyndi was staring dead-panned at Tahnee. "Seriously? That was as juicy of a question as you could think of?"

"I wanted to know! Why? What would you have asked?"

"Is he a good kisser?"

"The best," Sabrina assured them.

Tahnee began shaking her head back and forth. "Oh," she trilled. "I can't believe it."

Lyndi began sending the questions out rapid fire. "When did he kiss you for the first time?"

"The day I got my jeep."

"You suck!" Lyndi said again, slugging Sabrina's leg. "Which one did you like better?"

"The kiss."

Tahnee's head tipped back dramatically. "Well, obviously! How did he ask you to marry him?"

"I was at his apartment last night washing my cocoa mug. When I turned around he was right there, sliding the ring on my finger."

"Oh, oh, oh," Tahnee said, shaking her head again, rubbing trails onto the tops of her jeans. "Did you just die? I would have fainted dead away."

"How weird is that—just being at his apartment, anyway?" Lyndi asked, dumbfounded.

"It's not weird at all--I helped him move in." Both friends leaned in, straining for the details before the assembly began. Sabrina saw Chantry smile at the gossiping trio. She knew he was happy that she could now clue her friends in on her life.

"How did he tell you he loved you? When did that happen?" Lyndi asked.

"You know the night of the Back to School Dance?"

"Yeah?"

"Chantry invited me to fly to Portland with him for the weekend. We drove down to Corvallis for this big awards ceremony. After the banquet and dance Chantry led me outside. We danced all by ourselves and then he told me he loved me."

Lyndi's hands were smacking against her forehead and Tahnee's pretty sing-song voice was trilling "Oh, oh, oh," again. Sabrina was happy to see their delighted and frenzied responses to her last two months' activities.

"You mean you flew away with Mr. Cantrell for the weekend? And *I* thought *I* was smart because I got to stay out with your brother until two in the morning!"

"I can't even tell you how awesome it was."

"But *how* did he say it?" Tahnee prodded.

"As soon as we left the ceremony and dance, Chantry kissed me. It was the longest, most delicious kiss you can imagine. Then he pulled my hands up to his lips and kissed my fingertips, saying, *'I love you, Sabrina.'*"

Tahnee's eyes were opened wide and her fists clenched. She was soaking up every juicy detail. Lyndi's foot was rapidly stomping on the floor in Thumper fashion. Her head was shaking back and forth. "Stop! You're making me crazy! Quick! Tell me more." Tahnee and Sabrina laughed at Lyndi's statement.

Mr. Hodges strolled to the microphone, recognizing Superintendent Casey and several members of the school board who had arrived for the assembly. He then recognized Kara, Lyndi, and Tahnee for making All-State Volleyball. The girls went up to the stage for their certificates. The students applauded heartily for their star lady athletes.

"I'm proud of our high school when we can award our young students for their outstanding achievements. Commitment to success begins at an early age. We have a very motivational DVD presentation that we would like to share with our student body this morning. I'm sure you'll find it very enlightening." The lights dimmed and Chantry's image illuminated the giant screen.

"Awe," escaped the mouths of many girls, creating a collective humming sound. During one close-up of Chantry slamming a home run, Tahnee leaned over and said, "I can't believe you get to kiss that face."

Danforth, Trey, Dawson, Justyn, Tyler, Bryce, and others from the baseball team all leaned in their seats, seeming mesmerized. They were excited to get practicing under the guidance of the new coach.

Several times Justyn leaned toward Trey, mouthing the words, "He's awesome." During Coach Clayson's interview the boys turned in their seats and saluted Sabrina. She grinned back at her friends, touching a hand to brow in a return salute.

Everyone shot to their feet, applauding and cheering raucously when the lights came back on. Star struck students and faculty members gazed in Chantry's direction. Mr. Hodges stood before the microphone again. He told the student body how thankful he was that one young Morgan High School student had brought the phenomenal teacher and coach to them. "I would like to thank Miss Sabrina Ashley," Mr. Hodges said, "and congratulate both she and Mr. Cantrell on their engagement."

An audible buzz lit the room. Those who hadn't heard the news yet were now in the loop. Sabrina noticed Miss Clisp slump in her seat, completely defeated and crestfallen. Mr. Hodges continued, "You can read more about Mr. Cantrell in this week's edition of *Sports Illustrated*. It should hit newsstands today. I knew we hired a qualified and dynamic person, with an impressive resume, but I never realized when we extended this job to Mr. Cantrell, just how lucky we really were. Did any of you realize that I'm staring at a twelve million dollar student body? That's what Coach Cantrell has given up to be here."

"That's what I'm talking about!" Danforth hollered, jumping to his feet. The other boys leapt to their feet in a rippling motion. Row by row students jumped and began chanting "Chief, Chief, Chief!" It was a replay of the scene in Corvallis.

"Oh my heck," Tahnee said. "This has been a weird day."

Mr. Hodges held his hands up, waiting for silence. "As you students head back to class I want you to remember one thing. Greatness isn't just bestowed on certain people. It's earned! It's a combination of talent, effort, respect, reaching out to other people, and determination. A person never has to achieve fame in order to be great in the lives of other people. Thank you. Go back to your third period classes."

Sabrina was slammed by a mob of students patting her on the shoulder as she tried to make her way from the crowded auditorium. Lyndi and Tahnee were comically playing the role of body guards. Kara, Janice and Shan clamored to hug their friend. A big hand clapped against Sabrina's shoulder. When she looked up she saw Danforth Wycliff MacL'main smiling down at her. "Coach Cantrell sure is lucky." Justyn, Trey, and Dawson agreed.

Sabrina was taken aback by the kind comment. "Thanks you guys. You're the best friends in the world. Thanks for telling me that."

"We mean it," Danforth said. He then grinned in Tahnee's direction. "Hey All-State," he drawled. "How about going bowling with me tonight?"

When the lunch bell rang Sabrina glided from the school without even returning to her locker. She didn't want to keep Chantry waiting. She beat him to the parking lot and casually leaned against his door. She noticed Miss Clisp sitting in her car. She was wiping tears from her cheeks. Sabrina quickly looked away and felt relieved when the Ford Focus sputtered to life and motored onto the street.

Chantry strode from the school taking long easy strides. He pushed his keyless entry button and Sabrina climbed into the truck. Chantry swung himself in and the red Dodge rumbled from the parking lot under the view of many curious eyes. "We did it! It's behind us."

At Chantry's apartment Sabrina quickly grabbed items from the fridge and started making lunch. She felt at home in his kitchen. She listened as he dialed his parents. "Hi Mom…guess what? I gave Sabrina a ring last night and she accepted it! How cool is that? Yes, that means we're engaged…no, it's all good…Amanda seemed okay with it…Here, I'll let you talk to her."

Chantry handed the phone to Sabrina. She was nervous and her heart was hammering when she said, "Hello?"

"Sabrina?"

"Hi."

"Did Chantry really propose?"

"Yes."

"I thought maybe he was teasing me."

"Well, the ring looks genuine and he made the announcement in class today."

"Oh my word...he *is* serious. Well...congratulations! Is your mom okay with all of this?"

"Yes."

"I guess I'd better call her...when are you planning on getting married? Surely not until school is out..."

"Um...I'm not sure. Tashina? Thanks for raising him so good. Well, here's Chantry."

She passed the phone back to him, grateful to have gotten that conversation over with. She quickly sliced celery into diced chicken and added a dollop mayonnaise. She peeled crisp leaves from a head of lettuce and constructed chicken salad sandwiches. She found a bag of chips stuffed into a high cupboard and divvied a handful onto each plate. She set the plates on the table.

"Well, I've got to go now Mom. We don't have very long for lunch. I'll call you later. Bye."

Chantry snapped his phone shut. "You've still got to call your Grandma and Grandpa."

"Yes, and Vidalia and Phillip."

"But we'll eat first. Actually, we'll do *this* first," he said, pulling her onto his lap. He kissed her several times. One hand caressed her throat near her necklace. "Breezy, you really do look hot today."

"So do you, so we're even."

"I love you, Little Bird."

"Is that my Indian name?"

Chantry laughed. "Yes, that's the one I'm assigning you, I guess... you used to pretend you were an Indian when you were little, remember? What did you call yourself then?"

Sabrina giggled at the memory. "Princess Tail-Feather."

"That's right. What a funny little girl you were. You were always so smitten with Native Americans and their ways. Remember how disappointed you were to learn my mom didn't make arrowheads?"

"I was even more crushed to learn she had never spent the night inside of a tipi, *ever*. I just knew deep down in my heart, that I was a better Indian than she was."

"You used to lug your doll around on that piece of plywood all strapped to your back like a papoose in a cradle board. I actually felt sorry for your doll."

Sabrina's cheeks colored at the recollection. "Her name was Princess Pussy Willow."

Chantry laughed again. "I rest my case! This is a good sandwich, Sabrina. Thanks."

They finished their lunch then Chantry shoved his phone across the table. "Wouldn't you like to make a few of those calls?"

Sabrina punched Grandma's number. Grandpa was in for lunch and happened to pick up. "Hello, Grandpa?"

"Sabrina, is everything okay? Aren't you in school?"

"I have some news..." She searched for the words. It seemed like a strange thing to tell her Grandpa. "And Chantry will tell you all about it," she rushed. She shoved the phone back towards the man, giggling at her own maligning behavior.

CHAPTER THIRTY-EIGHT

Sabrina was surprised by the sheer number of classmates stuffed inside of the bowling alley. Dorian and Amanda were there ahead of time, ordering pizzas and pitchers of soda. They had reserved every lane. Sabrina shuddered at the thought of what Brad's informal, congratulatory party was costing his dad.

Danforth and Tahnee arrived with Brad and Lyndi in the blue Jeep. Trey was bringing Delphinia, and Justyn sauntered in with the dark-haired Kara on his arm. They were all good friends and Sabrina was happy that they were willing to come and show support for her. Janice, Tyler, Dawson, Shan, Bryce and Binny Jo came honking noisily into the parking lot a few minutes later. Apparently Brad's dating revolution was still in full force.

Danforth and Brad had a big ceremonial handshake before they matched bowling skills. Lyndi was nominated to hold their bet money. "I'll gladly spend your ten bucks, Danforth," Brad mused. "I'll take Lyndi on another date with it." Trey looked slightly annoyed at Brad's comment.

"I'll take Tahnee to the movies on your money, you mean," Danforth challenged.

"How about I beat both of you?" Tahnee asked, grabbing her ball and throwing it down the alley. *Strike!* Pins flew in every direction.

Danforth looked smitten. "Hey All-State, I have a thing for girls who can throw like that."

"I'm here with an All-Stater, too," Brad blustered. "Should we make this a couple's challenge?"

"You're on! Okay, everybody on this lane, this is a team competition."

Sabrina looked sadly at Chantry. "I'm not much of a bowler, Chantry. We're going to lose."

"That's okay," he whispered against her hair. "We don't have anything to prove." Chantry flipped a ten spot from his wallet, adding it to the pot for sport.

Danforth barreled headlong, throwing a hard, curving ball. *Strike!*

"Okay Lyndi, you can do it!" Brad encouraged. He leapt to his feet, planting a quick kiss on her cheek right before she threw the ball. "That's for luck!" he crowed enthusiastically. From a couple of lanes away Trey's eyes rolled.

The kiss was unexpected! Lyndi was flustered and stumbled once then clumsily chucked the ball straight into the gutter, *kerplunk*.

Shouts of jubilation rose from the bowlers. "Nice going," Tahnee said with a grin.

"Shut up! Alas, there was a deadly spider in the gutter and I had to squash it."

"What was that Brad--the kiss of death?" Chantry teased.

"I'll just have to shut you all up," Lyndi muttered, approaching the lane with grim determination. Pins flew to pieces as she pegged a beautiful spare. Lyndi took her seat, grinning and blushing at Brad as she went. Sabrina clapped for her friend, laughing about her new-found usage of the word, *alas*. It had been inspired by Brad's poem, and was now an integral part of Lyndi's vocabulary.

Brad bowled with a lot of finesse and skill. Utilizing the strength of his upper body he rolled the ball with a precise delivery. *Strike!* He and Lyndi smacked a high-five.

Sabrina dreaded her turn. She had scarcely ever bowled and she'd be thrilled to break fifty.

"Want Brad to kiss you for luck?" Danforth teased.

"I'll pass. I saw how it affected Lyndi's first attempt." She rolled the ball and jumped for sheer, ecstatic joy when it actually managed to knock eight pins down.

The others seemed amused by her happy response. "Clean 'em up, Breeze," Chantry encouraged.

Sabrina gave it her best effort but the ball waned off target, missing both of them.

"Come on Coach," Danforth cheered. "Let's see what you can do with a sixteen pound ball."

Chantry's movements were catlike and fluid. He had the most unusual bowling style Sabrina had ever witnessed, but the pins exploded at the end of the alley. "You hit a home run," she squealed.

Lyndi's head cocked back. "Hey Sabrina, that's not a home run it's a touchdown. Anybody knows that."

"That was a rather forceful strike, Coach." Danforth was impressed.

Prospective baseball players cheered and whistled from several lanes away but the greatest applause sounded for the pins knocked down by Delphinia Blue. Trey was tender and affectionate with her throughout the evening, yet his eyes cast continually toward Lyndi.

Chantry leaned against Sabrina's ear. "Why do I feel like Brad's biggest challenge isn't against Danforth in bowling tonight, but against Trey for Lyndi's attention?"

Dorian and Amanda were quietly bowling on an end lane trying not to interfere. Sabrina disengaged herself from the noisy cluster on the middle lane and wandered over. "Thanks Dorian. This was really nice of you."

"I figured Brad would quit sulking if he had something fun to spearhead. You know Brad."

"How are you feeling Mom?"

"Evenings are the best part of my day."

Sabrina was summoned back to her lane to take her turn. She studied the scoreboard. "The competition is fierce around here." She released the ball again, hoping for something. She hopped excitedly when eight more pins toppled sideways. Chantry gave her a pointer about where to stand to clean them up. Her ball managed to nick one of them.

When it was Brad's turn to bowl again, Trey ran over from his lane. "I have something to help you bowl better Brad!"

"What's that?"

Trey threw an arm around Lyndi, kissing her other cheek. *"That!* Good luck," he sang smugly before trailing back to his own lane.

"What the–" Danforth laughed. "Good one Trey! I owe you!"

Brad looked stunned, but Lyndi was the most bewildered of the bunch. "How is that supposed to help *me* bowl?" Brad muttered. "Hey Trey! Next time you want to kiss something, you can kiss *this*," he said, swatting his own backside. He threw the ball haphazardly down the lane only skimming three pins, much to Danforth's great delight.

Chantry grinned at the look of defiant ferocity on Brad's face as he levied his second bowl. "He doesn't like to lose, but then again, who does?"

Brad only knocked four more down. Danforth celebrated Brad's performance with a little dance, mimicking a pivoting sprinkler head.

"Fine! I'm kissing Tahnee before you bowl next time, Dan. We'll see how you like it," Brad grumbled.

"Nobody's kissing me," Tahnee assured. "I don't mix kissing with business."

Chantry smiled at the athletic girl. "Good thinking, Tahnee! I might like to draft you onto my baseball team. These boys better all shape up by springtime and learn how to focus. I want all of their minds on baseball, not on who's kissing whom."

"I've noticed you've been doing a little kissing of your own," Brad sneered saucily in Chantry's direction, not caring a hoot about baseball.

"But it's not effecting my game," Chantry said, slamming the pins to bits. "Looks like my game's spot on."

In the end Tahnee and Danforth took the money. The overall high score belonged to Chantry, but of course Sabrina's bowling had weakened his average. Everyone seemed to have a fun time and each of Sabrina's friends wished the couple well. Chantry and Sabrina helped Dorian and Amanda bus tables and tidy up the bowling alley before leaving.

Chantry's arm pulled Sabrina against him. "Do you have homework?"

"No, luckily."

"Good. I'm not done with you yet."

They drove back to the apartment. Chantry turned on the television set then patted a spot for Sabrina to join him on the couch. Sabrina didn't have a clue what was dancing across the screen. She was too busy enjoying the closeness with Chantry. "Do you know why I call you Little Bird?"

Sabrina shook her head. "No."

"Because your heart trills so rapidly when we are alone like this... and I'm always about half afraid that you'll spook and fly away."

"I'm not flying anywhere--accept for possibly away with you."

"Remember that time we spotted the little robin in your yard?"

"Yes!" Sabrina smiled at the faint memory. "You grabbed a piece of bread and baited it with a trail of crumbs. It would gobble and hop, gobble and hop, until it hopped right into the palm of your hand for the last bite. I remember lying on my stomach in the grass, not even daring to breath, for fear it would flutter away."

"It was exhilarating when it finally landed in my hand. I had to hold very still to keep from frightening it. Crushing it would have been easy but what would the conquest have been in that?"

"I would have hated you!"

"It's kind of the same with you. I had to bait a trail *so* carefully. Sliding that ring on your finger was the most exhilarating feeling of my life! I feel like I'm holding you now in the palm of my hand. I don't want to scare you away and I definitely don't want to crush you."

"You won't."

Chantry was combing his fingers through Sabrina's let-down hair as he spoke. "Sabrina, I really want to get married before school gets out. Does that make you want to flutter away?"

"No."

"I also want us to stay temple-worthy but that's getting trickier. Maybe we need to see each other less, but that only seems to make it harder on me when I am with you as my feelings get too pent up. Just don't let me crush you, okay?"

"Let's get married during Spring Break then."

"I was hoping you'd say that. Then I can begin baseball with a clear head. You can even come with me on some of the ball trips, if you'd like."

"That sounds fun. Mom's baby is due the week after my birthday anyway. She really won't feel up to anything and I don't want to postpone it further into summer."

"So, the first day of Spring Break, okay? Let's not have our reception until we're back from our honeymoon."

Sabrina punched the calendar on her phone. "Thursday, March twelve? How does that sound?"

"It sounds like my favorite day. Will that be okay with Amanda?"

"Dorian's kind of on my side. He'll help persuade her. What colors do you want?"

"Breezy, I'll just leave all of that to you. You're the professional, and I'm sure you know what you want. You just do whatever you want to, and I'll go along with it."

"Seriously? What if I like pink?"

"I don't have a problem with it, whatever you want."

"No argument? I always have so much fun arguing with you. Where are we going for our honeymoon?"

"We'll have to talk about that, I guess. Where do you want to go?"

"In there," Sabrina said, pointing down the hall toward the bedroom.

A smile curled Chantry's lips. "Besides that."

"Someplace where we can dance with the moon like we did in Corvallis. The mountains, or the beach, the country, or the city, I don't even care. Just as long as I'm with you. Hey, Chantry? You didn't have to bait a trail for me to hop into your hand. All you had to do was whistle and I would have flown right to you."

"I don't think so. There were too many other bird hunters all out laying their bait." Chantry kicked his feet up on the couch, reclining. He pulled Sabrina down with him. Her head rested on his arm.

"You're funny," Sabrina said, nestling against him. Chantry's arms folded around her. His eyes were black and beautiful, smoldering and searching, in their usual way.

Sabrina leaned her head forward, pressing her lips against his. "I love you, Chantry."

"Even if I'm dragging you away from your new house and enormous bathroom? There's no sunken tub here, you know."

"That's okay. I can always run home to soak, if I get the urge."

"Dorian told me you finished your herbal medicine course."

"I did. I'm just waiting for the certificate. I've just started another one in nutrition."

"I'm proud of you. You're an interesting little person aren't you? Marriage really won't spoil any of your dreams will it?"

"No, it will just fulfill them."

"How do you feel about children?"

"In what way, exactly?"

"Our own?"

"Well, of course I want to have a family. Frankly speaking, I want to have *your* children."

"I'm sort of feeling envious of Dorian. You won't lace our kids to a cradle-board will you?"

Sabrina giggled against Chantry's shoulder. "No. I'll try to refrain."

Chantry kissed Sabrina again. It was dangerously good. Sabrina's heart pounded with adrenaline slamming into her bloodstream. "Your heart is racing Little Bird," Chantry murmured between kisses.

"Don't fly away."

"I won't, but perhaps you'd better drive me home before I beg you to crush me."

CHAPTER THIRTY-NINE

Sabrina finished work with a heavy sense of foreboding. She didn't know what was wrong. She felt creepy as she turned the closed sign in the window and locked the front door. She quickly stole upstairs just to make sure everything was okay in the work room. It seemed normal with objects strewn in typical organized chaos, but she couldn't deny the fiery chilled feeling that unseen eyes were trailing her. Her stomach knotted nervously beneath the specter of haunting melancholy. "Here Mia, here kitty," Sabrina called; making sure the cat was safely in the house. She fed and watered her then locked the back door and climbed into her jeep.

School had been okay. Chantry had taken a couple of personal days off to help his father work cattle. Randy Cantrell worked as a mine foreman, ranching on the side. He owned four hundred acres and ran seventy head of cows. Chantry had worked for Grandpa Ashley since there was more to do. Joseph's spread was sizeable; with two thousand acres and more than four hundred and fifty cows. Grandpa and Randy Cantrell always shipped their cattle together in the fall. Chantry had gone to Idaho to help in his father's stead.

Is that why I feel so weird–because I haven't seen Chantry for a couple of days? Sabrina hoped she hadn't gotten that soft and sappy. Her thoughts tumbled haphazardly as she drove through Morgan. The closer she got to home the faster she drove. *Perhaps it's Mom?* The yellow jeep screeched in the driveway and Sabrina dashed into the house.

The comforts of home embraced her just as soon as she hit the door. She could smell dinner cooking. The lights were on and she could hear her mother and Dorian singing and laughing in the kitchen. She felt better just being there. "I'm home!"

"Hello, Sabrina. How was school and work?"

"Good...actually, I don't know. I've had a weird feeling this afternoon. Is everybody okay?"

Amanda looked quizzically at Dorian. "I think everything's fine—look, I'm cooking! Hooray for me!"

"It smells good," Sabrina said lifting lids off pots to see what was for dinner. "How's Brad?"

"He's upstairs if you want to talk to him."

"Do you need any help with anything down here?"

Dorian eyed Sabrina. "Bree, you've been at school and work all day. How about you go relax for a few minutes before we eat okay? You're too responsible all of the time."

Sabrina forced a smile, trying to forget the knife twisting in her gut. "I guess I will then." She climbed the stairs feeling heavy and tired. She knocked on Brad's door. "Can I come in?"

"Entre," Brad called.

Sabrina stepped into his bedroom. As an ode to all things Disney, Brad's room was uncommonly cheery. His hat collection lined one wall and Disney posters were plastered everywhere. Instead of an enormous bathroom suite like Sabrina had in her room, Brad had a home gym, complete with uneven parallel bars, rings, a pommel horse, and a floor trampoline. He also had an elliptical and weight station. His buddies were crazy about Brad's lair and it was becoming a popular after-school hangout. Of course Brad didn't mind showing off his skills. He could run through his whole Tarzan routine anytime he felt like it.

"Thanks for the bowling party the other day. I really appreciated it."

Brad nodded, hefting himself onto the pommel horse. "Sure," he said, between clenched teeth as he maneuvered his body with strength and finesse. "No problem." He finished his routine then walked over to his desk and sat facing Sabrina. "What's wrong? You look sick."

"I just feel upset about something. I don't know why."

"That's too bad, for I happen to have some very good news."

"What?"

Brad spun around in his chair, clicking his mouse a couple of times. "Come read this E-mail from Grandpa Haskel".

Sabrina's eyes scanned the text. She had to smile, as Haskel's eloquent words seemed to twinkle and waltz behind the screen. He asked how they were enjoying their autos and wondered if Sabrina was working on any smashing artwork. He reported progress on the *Delphinia Movie*, thanking them for landing him such a marvelous opportunity. "And now," he wrote, "I'd like to share my innermost feelings concerning the present which you two delightful grandchildren have given me. I have examined *The Book of Mormon* thoroughly. It seems that I have feasted on its words, partaking of their delectable bounty, and digesting the beautiful truths. My heart feels merry and my heels are clicking together with enthusiasm for that which I'm learning. I've quite decided to settle myself with the believers of this marvelous book. I want to be baptized. What say you Brad? Shall we take the big plunge together? Consider being baptized while I'm in Utah for Thanksgiving. We could share this auspicious occasion together. Perhaps Sabrina's tall, dark and handsome fiancé would do us the honors? If he is good enough for Sabrina then he's surely qualified to dunk us under..."

"I love Haskel! Thanks for sharing."

"He's awesome. So don't worry about stuff–it's all good."

"So...do you really want to be baptized?"

"I think so."

Amanda's voice called from downstairs, "Dinner!" Brad peeled from the bedroom exuberantly. Sabrina marveled at his ability to celebrate the simple things. After supper the family gathered comfortably in front of the fireplace. Brad and Sabrina were stretched out on the floor playing a game of Battleship. Dorian and Amanda hovered over a baby name book, tossing suggestions back and forth. "How about Doriana? We could call her Dori for short," Amanda suggested.

"I kind of like that one. She'd be named after me! We could give her your middle name of Jean, maybe call her Dori Jean."

"I like it." Amanda wrote the suggestion in a notebook. "Maybe since we have Brad, Bree, and Brian, we should name this baby something that starts with BR, like Brooke, Bridget, Brandy, or Brielle..."

"Why do you keep talking about girl names?" Brad complained. "Hasn't Sabrina been enough?"

Dorian scowled at the boy. "I would take another ten daughters just like her."

Amanda smiled, flipping the book to the boy names. "Brayson, Brighton, Brock, Bridger, Brandon..."

"Technically," Brad offered smartly, "Sabrina is an S name. If you have a girl you could name her an S name, too. How do you like Sabotage for instance? That sounds just like Sabrina!" Brad grinned at his clever comment.

The hair on the back of Sabrina's neck stood up and a sickening chill crept down her spine, like the touch of a cold, dead, mummy's finger. Her heart began to race violently. She bolted upright, grabbing her stomach, trying to hush the cramping, twisting, knots inside of her.

"What's wrong?" Brad asked. "Did I hit your sub?" Sabrina shook her head. "Oh, I got your little tug?" Brad smiled.

"Something's wrong!" *Whoosh, whoosh, whoosh!*

"You're having an attack," Amanda quickly diagnosed. "I'm sorry, Honey. It's been awhile since you had a bad one. I'll go get your stuff." She quickly slipped into the kitchen.

"Dorian, something's seriously wrong! I can *feel* it."

394

His face was etched with concern. "Nonsense, Sabrina. It's okay," he soothed, putting his arms around her. "Do you need to call Chantry?" He hit Chantry's number on his phone. It rang and rang until a recorded message said his cell phone was out of the service area. That didn't help.

"Dorian! Something is wrong!"

"Come on Honey. Let's get you into the kitchen. I'll make you some cocoa or something."

Sabrina stood but the hammering in her heart made her chest feel like it would explode and fly into a million pieces. "I can't." Dorian caught her arm and helped her lay back on the couch. He propped her up with pillows.

Amanda quickly returned, bringing a cool cloth and Sabrina's anxiety medicine. "Here you go, you'll soon feel better."

Brad watched helplessly. He forced a big smile and said, "What about Frank? I've always admired that name. Good old-fashioned Frank! It kind of has a neat ring to it: *Frank, Frank, Frank.*"

The doorbell rang. Dorian stepped to the entry way and swung it open. His body stood rigid and stiff before letting out a shocked hissing sound. "Cate?" His right hand braced against the door frame. It tightened into a hard fist. His left hand gripped the doorknob. He mumbled something soft and low.

Amanda peered around the entry wall, trying to see what was causing Dorian so much duress, but couldn't get a clear view. The fact that something was wrong was obvious.

He pivoted away from the door then, spitting out a sentence which must have choked him to utter. "Brad, your mother is here... if you can call her that."

Cate? Evil, *pure evil,* was silhouetted in the door way. Sabrina felt a wicked fire light inside her veins. It spread throughout her body like burning venom. A sickening cold sweat crept against her skin, trying to extinguish the tortured flames. She stared into the cold cruel eyes of Larielle Pritchett. There was no *Cate* to it.

Every nerve in Sabrina's body began to flinch and tremble. Her feelings were harrowed up at the sight of her father's murderess. She wanted to spit, scratch, and claw the woman out of the house and back into the haunted dregs of darkness where she belonged! But Sabrina lay paralyzed with utter, dark, suffocating fear and loathing. Brad's so-called mother was the epitome of every nightmare.

Sabrina cast a sideways glance at Brad. His expression was peculiar and strange. His eyes seemed glassy and dazed. He too was trembling. *Dear, wonderful, beautiful Brad, who thinks all women are princesses. Couldn't he see the villain in her?* He was gasping for a breath. "Mom?" Like the world's greatest oxymoron, the word was tinged with hopeful doubt. *How often has he prayed that she would come back? How dearly has he yearned for her love?* Brad smiled and stepped toward the spidery woman.

"No, Brad! Don't go with her!"

Brad scowled at his sister. "But it's my Mom."

"That's right," Larielle whispered. "It's time we got to know each other." Larielle's sentence was drenched with honeyed tones, thick and dripping. "Come with me and we'll talk."

"Dorian! Don't let him go!" The front door closed. Sobs and shakes racked Sabrina's body as she battled the torturing demons of yesterday. "Dorian! Dorian!"

Amanda squeezed her hand. "Stop it Sabrina! Stop it right now! Dorian's facing his own grief. Let him be. It will be okay."

"I hate her! I hate her!"

"I do too. I have always hated Larielle Pritchett."

"Dorian!" Sabrina called again, but Dorian wasn't there. Sabrina heard the garage door slam. "Don't go!"

Amanda's hand cracked against Sabrina's cheek. "Stop it! Sabrina, pull yourself out of this spiral! You're scaring the living daylights out of me right now."

Sabrina's hand flew to her burning cheek. Her mother had never struck her before. She stared at the lovely blond face. It was frightened and pale. Sabrina turned inwardly, calling on every ounce of sheer grit that she had in her, to draw together and reconstruct the iron shell which she hid behind. She drew several breaths then quieted like a zombie. Her trembling turned inside of her, rattling her innards with a ravaging hell but she looked calmly at her mother. "I'm sorry. Are you okay?"

Amanda shook her head. "No I'm not. I'm upset. I feel sick! I *hate* that Pritchett woman. I can't even conceive that she's Brad's mother. Brad--the boy whom I love *so* dearly! How can he possibly be that woman's son?"

"Let me help you Mom. You don't look good," Sabrina guided her to a kitchen stool then quickly mixed minerals with the raspberry leaf tincture. "Don't be upset Mom. It won't be good for the baby." Sabrina felt as if her life had been sucked backward through time in a vacuum. She was seven again, traumatized, hurting, battered; yet the adult, the guardian, the caretaker of one who was much more fragile. "You're looking better now. Come on, let's get you to bed. I'll help you undress. Brad will be okay," she soothed, hardly believing the sound of her own words; unable to convince herself. "He's intelligent enough to realize how terrible she's treated him. He'll be okay."

"Brad's guileless. He's too forgiving. He's going to get hurt."

"Let's say a prayer for him then." She helped her Mother pull a nightgown over her head then folded down the bedding. "Climb in. You snuggle under the covers and I'll kneel." Sabrina prayed with all of the power she could muster. She kissed her mother's forehead. "Sleep well. I love you. I'm sorry I lost it for a minute. Just a spell, I guess." She turned off the lamp and slipped from the room.

Sabrina leaned against the door, listening to Amanda's sobs muffling against her pillow until she could stand it no longer. She dialed Dorian's number.

"Hello?"

"Where are you?"

"I just had to get out for a minute."

"Your wife needs you. I'm sure that you're ignorant of this fact, but your *ex*-wife happens to be an *ex*-acquaintance of ours. She's been Mom's arch-enemy."

"You're kidding?"

"No, I am not. Haven't you learned that truth is stranger than fiction? Your mind would be boggled if you realized just how sickly twisted the fates have truly been with our two families. *Cowboy up*, Dorian Manning! Your wife needs you." Sabrina slammed the phone down and tromped upstairs.

Sabrina walked past Brad's room, remembering Haskel's E-mail and baptismal challenge to his great grandson. "Satan blew the most evil thing he could find right onto our doorstep to frustrate things," she said out loud. "Larielle Pritchett is certainly a devout minion of the dark side."

She closed the door to her bedroom, managing to hold her steel reserve in place until she reached her bed. Soon the violent shaking overtook her once again. She could feel a fever spread across her brow. Her attacks had always been this severe when she was young, complete with spiking temperature. The pain was dying to get out while Sabrina was dying to hold it in. Throughout the sadistic hours of the night the battle raged.

Sabrina shook with shock and fever, occasionally feeling delirious. She saw Dorian stumbling up the walk, drunk and swaggering. She was so angry she kicked him but her leg just flew into the emptiness above her bed for none of it was real. She saw Sundance standing on both hind legs pawing into the sky. Tessie galloped past dragging her hackamore and whinnying. A dust devil whirled in the corner of Sabrina's bedroom, madly swirling cats and envelopes. Jennifer flew from the spinning wind and landed on Sabrina's bed. Sabrina tried to comfort the frightened kitty but she couldn't find her, and then she realized the cat was long since dead.

She wandered in the pasture and beyond, stumbling through a ground mist, looking for her Daddy. She stumbled again and again, not able to see where she was stepping. She tripped over something very solid and scraped her knee. She bent low to see what had done it. A headstone said *Benjamin Joseph Ashley.* "He's dead, he's dead," Sabrina mourned in the mist.

Coherent thoughts tried to saw through the muddle. *Chantry! I love Chantry!* She felt one ray of hope streaking through the blackness and haze of the battle, but the murky, inky, fiends of darkness closed around it and Sabrina was alone.

"Come play dominoes with me," Grandma called through the void.

"I don't have the time for it," Sabrina said.

"I'm making fudge. Come help me stir it. Chantry will lick the pan."

"Chantry? I love Chantry! I'll be right there." She ran, tumbling through the darkness, but she tripped again, sprawling over a stack of laundry and dirty dishes. "I have to be a grown up," she said, sorting through the heaps. Princess Pussy Willow wailed from her cradle board. Sabrina threw the doll into the field. "You be quiet! I can't play with you anymore. I'm no longer a child and you were never real."

Sabrina cried out with anguish wishing the madness would stop. "Heavenly Father," she mumbled, "please make it go away..."

A hand wiped against her brow. The hand was cool and wonderful. It was soothing and kind. Sabrina didn't know whose hand to bless, nor thank, nor praise, but she settled against her pillow and the jarring twitches subsided to some degree. "That's it, Honey. You're carrying this thing around like an infected sliver. It's abscessed and festering. Let's draw it out of there."

The voice was familiar. "Daddy?"

"You have a sliver. We need to get it out."

"Will it hurt?"

"Yes Sabrina, because it hurt going in, remember? I'm sorry it hurt so badly."

"Daddy? Are you there?"

"I'm here."

"Are you in my fever or are you real?"

"I'm here, Sabrina."

"Give me a blessing."

The hands. *Those hands!* Sabrina felt them close against her head and she tumbled backwards into her pillow and slept.

CHAPTER FORTY

Sabrina pushed against the mosquito. It was huge and sucking the blood from her hand. She swiped again then a voice said, "Sabrina? Leave it in okay? It's just an I.V."

One eye cracked open. Splintering fluorescence exploded against her vision. Gradually a few items came into focus. Sabrina was staring at an I.V. pump and the mosquito was a needle taped to her hand. A nurse was fidgeting and fluttering with a monitor then taking a temperature. Sabrina tried to swallow but her lips were thick and cracked, and her tongue felt scummy and coated. "I'm thirsty," she moaned.

The nurse removed the thermometer. "I'll get you a swab."

"I don't think I like a swab," Sabrina mumbled, but the nurse was gone.

She awoke a few moments later to a wet sensation rolling against her tongue, moistening it. The nurse slid it against the parched dry lips. It felt good. Sabrina's head turned on her pillow. Her mom was looking at her. "Where's Brad?"

"He's here."

"Where?"

"In the hall."

"I need to talk to him alone."

Amanda's cool hand wiped against Sabrina's brow. "I'll get him."

It seemed like a long time before Sabrina's consciousness fought again through the haze, yet perhaps it had only been a minute. Brad was looking at her. "You scared the crap out of me last night."

"Turnabout is fair play."

"I came in the house after midnight and you were shrieking from your bed. I went into your room. Your sheets were soaked through and you were completely out of it. I ran and got Mom and Dad. They put you in a bath several times through the night, but by five this morning they gave up and called the ambulance."

"Am I drugged?"

"Yes."

"I hate that feeling. Why would anybody purposefully feel this way? I don't get it."

"Search me, but the shot was a blessing for the rest of us. It was a relief to see you settle down."

"I don't remember bathing in the night."

"We changed your bed three different times."

"That's gross."

"I know, right?"

"Brad...your birth mom is no good. She's poisonous like a viper. I would think that you would have immersed yourself hard enough in Storybook Land to recognize a villain when you see one. Larielle Pritchett makes Maleficent look like Snow White."

"She invited me to stay with her in Geneva this summer. Do you know where that is?"

"Geneva is just the next spot up the road from Raymond. That's where I went to elementary school and church, duh! I knew your mother and I'm telling you to stay away."

"She said that I should be staying away from *your* mother. She told me not to get baptized. She's known Mormons for a long time and all they preach are lies."

"If you choose to believe that then you're no brother of mine. Does *my* mother seem like a liar to you, Brad? Do I? Remember last summer, when you told me how welcome you felt in our tiny little house? Would you have felt like that in a liars' den?"

Brad stared at Sabrina. "Well, I'm probably not going to go there this summer. I have my work…"

"Good!"

"But I might not get baptized…"

The words were punishing to hear. Sabrina rolled her eyes and they grated against her sockets. "I wish Regina Raduccio really was your mother! She would want you to be happy and follow your heart. I can tell you one thing; Larielle Pritchett would never have worn your homemade macaroni necklaces! And come to think about it, she never did, did she? Where was she do you think?"

"She said she was confused."

"Ha! That's the understatement of the century. Brad, stay away from her. She's lethal."

"Don't be a drama queen."

"Get out then. You are forcing me to do something which could get me killed! You are forcing me to do something which may cause everyone around us to suffer."

"Stop over reacting!"

"I want my mother."

"She's talking to the doctor. They can't figure out why your fever spiked so high. It was over a hundred and five when the ambulance picked you up, but your white count looks okay."

"I'm suffering from an unseen infection. My Dad says it's abscessed and festering."

"There you go again, rambling and mumbling about someone who isn't even here anymore." Brad walked away.

A moment later a white coat stood next to the bed. "Hello Sabrina. I'm Dr. Roberts. How are you?"

"Groovy."

"You've been one sick girl. We've run a couple of I.V. bags through you, so that will help to hydrate your tissues. Your fever is down for the moment but we're sending you with some medication, okay? We also have a prescription to help you with anxiety. We've dripped some antibiotics in with your I.V. fluids, which should help just in case there's something we've missed. We're still waiting on some of the cultures."

"My adrenal glands are whacked out. It doesn't matter what emotion I have, I'm slammed with too much adrenaline. It makes my heart race then leaves me shaky and trembling. Anger, joy, fear, excitement, love, hate...it's all the same. Can you check my adrenals?"

Dr. Roberts tilted his head. "Just anxiety." He scratched something on Sabrina's chart. "You should be okay to go home," he said, ignoring her request. "Make sure and get lots of rest and fluids, okay? I want to see you in my office on Wednesday."

"So you're blowing me off? Figures," Sabrina said solemnly. "How much arrogance does it take to help a person feel better? I just wanted to make sure you used enough."

Dr. Roberts' eyes narrowed at the girl's stinging words. "I'll be glad to recommend a counselor if you'd like to see one."

"So I'm crazy? Okay, thank you. I'll just fix myself. Don't worry about it. I've heard it all before! Nobody ever listens to me."

Amanda stepped back into the room during the exchange. "Dr. Roberts! We appreciate all you have done," she smoothed. "We really do. I'm sure Sabrina's just a little bit groggy—not quite herself yet. Please don't mind her."

"Sure, don't mind me. I appreciate your arrogance and prejudgments. I feel much better now. I'd love that counselor's number. I've been collecting them since I was seven." Sabrina rolled away from the white coat.

"Sabrina!" Amanda scolded.

"Thank you for the I.V., Doctor. I know I needed it and I do appreciate it."

"You're going to be okay," Dr. Roberts said sternly. "I'll have a nurse come and take that needle out of your vein and then you can shower up and be on your way."

"Here's my coat, there's the door, what's my hurry?" Sabrina couldn't keep herself from smarting off. *Is it the drugs? Or am I really awful?* "If I'm really good can I try another swab for lunch before I go? They are the most addicting little buggers."

"Don't worry Mrs. Manning, it's the medication talking." Dr. Roberts heaved an exasperated sigh before strutting from the room. He bumped into Dorian as he was leaving.

"Hi honey," Dorian said. "Chantry's called a dozen times checking on you. Would you like to talk to him?"

Sabrina considered the possibility. "No. Tell him to focus."

"Sabrina?"

"They have a lot of cows to ship. I'm fine. I don't want to talk to anybody."

"Are you sure?"

"I want Grandpa Haskel."

"He's not here. Who else will do?"

"Nobody. Get me out of here! I have a lot of work to do."

Dorian, Amanda, and Brad looked ill at ease, casting peculiar glances back and forth. A nurse came in to help Sabrina shower then forced a little medicine cup of liquid down her throat. "There, now you can go home and rest well," she said kindly.

Dang it! Drugged again.

Chapter Forty-one

Sabrina slept for fourteen hours, blissfully dreaming of nothing. She planned and schemed for the next four, waiting for her parents to go to church. She was interested to see Brad don his Sunday clothes as well. "Church?"

"The ward choir is singing today. I actually have a small part. I don't want to miss that. Too bad you can't come and applaud."

"Mormons don't clap in church."

"Darn it."

"But I'm sure the congregation would if they could. Good luck."

Amanda carried a breakfast tray to Sabrina's room. "Here honey. Don't forget to take the medicine."

"I won't," Sabrina lied. "Thanks for everything." The girl was fully dressed, snuggling convincingly beneath the covers.

Just as soon as Dorian's Escalade left the premises, Sabrina was up, grabbing her coat, self-prescribed supplements, car keys, and sealed white envelope. She dumped them into her bag. She snatched a note paper and scrawled, *"Don't worry, I'll be fine and home later."* She left the note on her pillow.

It was a clear day and traffic was light on the freeway. Sabrina stopped in Evanston for gas and a sandwich for later, although she still didn't have much of an appetite. It was only noon when the yellow jeep turned at the Idaho border. Three miles from the turn she cruised past the Raymond turn-off. Another eight miles and

Sabrina hit her blinker at the Geneva Junction. She was now beyond the point of no return.

The Pritchett Ranch was located on the northern most tip of the Thomas Fork Valley. A sprawling log house graced the property. The Pritchett's were all about showing off. Sabrina passed Ely Pritchett. He was driving toward the one local bar. *Good! It helps not having him to deal with.*

The jeep obeyed Sabrina as she hit her breaks in the driveway. She locked her doors then leaned against the side of the vehicle for a long minute. She took a big breath and began walking toward the front door of the big house, but the sound of merry whinnies called on the late autumn breeze. Larielle Pritchett was riding up behind her.

*How ironic! She's riding a horse...*Sabrina's eyes cast about for a stray cat. She was disappointed not to see one. She watched her nemesis ride closer. She could not see any trace of Brad in her features.

"What can I do for you?" Her violet eyes locked on Sabrina's. "You are so beautiful Sabrina. No wonder Brad fell in love with you."

Strange! Sabrina wasn't prepared for kindness. She had steeled herself to face cold calloused cruelty and wicked black sorcery, but not normalcy--not kindness. "You know who I am, then?"

"Yes." Larielle reached a hand through her jet-black mane. "I hear you are engaged. Don't do it, Sabrina, you are much too young. I think you should run around with dozens of boys—give them all a try."

"As if I need to take advice from the likes of you! I need to talk to you. It's urgent."

"Come to tell me off? Don't want me interfering in Brad's world?"

"Basically."

"It's done then so you can leave." She dismounted the Palomino, leading it into the barn.

"It isn't done! It hasn't even started."

Larielle slid the saddle from the honey-colored mount. She began currying the pretty hide. "I'm listening,"

"I like your horse. I've always been fond of horses."

"You sound like a girl after my own heart."

"Hardly." Sabrina drew in a labored breath. "Ten years ago I was sitting in the loft of our horse barn. My father was working with a couple of colts and I was sketching them. You showed up. My father never saw the light of another day."

Larielle's hand froze against the horse. "I don't know what you're talking about."

"Yes you do!"

"Ben's death was ruled as accidental."

"Because they didn't know the truth! I saw what happened! I am a witness. You threw my cat through the air and then you turned and walked away. Directly or indirectly you killed my father!" Sabrina's voice was shrill. The horse's ears skittered back.

Larielle swept herself from the stall, closing the gap between herself and the girl. "Shut up!"

"You rained chaos all around. Since you didn't stay for the grand finale let me catch you up on what you missed. The cat sailed through the air and landed on one of the colts. There was an explosion of bucking, rearing, and kicking. My father dove for safety but a hard hoof clipped him on the back of the head. That was it; he was dead before he hit the ground. I saw it! Damn you Larielle Pritchett, I saw my father fall!"

Larielle slapped Sabrina across the jawbone. "Shut up, before I shut you up! Get off my property."

"Yeah, how does that feel to have somebody barge in here and refuse to leave?"

Taut lines twisted Larielle's mouth into an ugly grimace. Her eyes were narrow and mean like an artist's rendering of a wicked witch. "You're a little Mormon liar. You come from a long line of them."

"Religion has nothing to do with this!" Sabrina was sick of that line of argument before it even started. She snagged the envelope from her bag, whipping it visibly yet keeping a tight grip on it. "You left this behind."

The woman paled significantly. "Give me that!"

"No, hell no, I won't. Look! I've never even opened it. You walk away from Brad. Walk and never return, *ever*! Don't you so much as wink in his direction or this letter will be published in every paper I can find, and mailed to the police as well. I'll request a manslaughter investigation."

"Give me the letter!" The witch's eyes were blazing and wild. Her cheeks were flaming crimson, and she was shaking out of control. "I went back to get it after the emergency vehicles left, but I couldn't find it. I hoped it had blown away with the wind."

"Hardly! I'm giving *you* one minute to blow away on the wind and then I'm calling the police. What's it going to be?" A full minute of silence ticked away while Sabrina stared unflinching.

"I'll walk away." Larielle's hands shot up in a mock surrendering motion. A slight smile twisted her mouth.

Everything about the sentence seemed wrong. Sabrina didn't trust her, didn't even dare turn her back on the woman. *How can a person really sign a contract with a snake?* "You are purely evil! You think you're so smart and invincible. You think you've fooled the world, well you haven't fooled me. One little girl in this entire universe knows who you are and what you've done. Stay away from my family! Stay away from all of us."

Larielle was gazing sickly at Sabrina. Shivers of danger tingled on Sabrina's scalp. Her flesh crawled beneath the witch's transfixed gaze. "You are so beautiful Sabrina."

"Stop saying that!" Sabrina wondered why that sentence sounded normal and nice a few minutes ago. It was disturbing and disjointed to their particular argument. It didn't fit!

"You were only a year and a half old when Ely moved me here from California. We drove to Raymond to buy a load of hay from Randy Cantrell. Ely saw your father in the yard and pulled the truck in to visit. Your father was holding you. I was smitten! I couldn't get enough of you! I watched you grow month by month, and I wanted you."

Sabrina shuddered with disgust. "Maybe you should have stayed with your own baby. He was beautiful too! Maybe you should have tried being *his* mother!"

"But I didn't and my arms ached desperately for a child. You had the most enchanting eyes I'd ever seen. And your eyelashes! You were like a taunting little pixie child. I wanted you; your curly hair, your freckles, your dimples."

"You walked away from your own son and never looked back! How can any mother do that?"

Larielle didn't answer the question, instead she kept rambling about the infant Sabrina. "Your little mouth was so red and pretty, like a little cherry."

Mummy fingers returned, tracing eerie shivers up and down Sabrina's spine again and again. This conversation was more than Sabrina had bargained for. The moment felt deranged and surreal, like a broken fragment of reality. Sabrina tried to reconstruct the shattered shards into sense, but nothing fit.

"I followed your mother to town sometimes, tailing her through the grocery store just to see you. When you were a little bit older I stood in the cattails and watched you play in the meadow."

"Stop it!" Sabrina shouted. "Stop it right now! You're twisted. You're the most screwed-up person I've ever seen."

Larielle's eyes were glassy and her words were growing thick, as if she herself were the victim of too much anesthetic. Her features looked savage and unsettling. "I wanted a child just like you. I begged Ben to give me one. I begged and begged. You looked just like him! I came into your house several times and watched you sleep. I watched you *both* sleep. Amanda didn't deserve either one of you! I would have indulged you Sabrina. I would have indulged any child *like* you. Your father had no right to deny me." Larielle touched a strand of Sabrina's hair before the girl shied away.

"Shut up!"

"I was hiding in the work room of the flower shop when you snuck up the stairs two nights ago. You were so becoming, looking all around as if something was wrong. You left in a panic and I watched from the window as you backed out of the driveway. I followed you home. That's how I knew where to find Brad. You actually led me right to him."

"What do you mean you were in the floral shop?" Sabrina was horrified by this tale of recent stalker activity.

"It wasn't the first time. I've been there a few times over the past decade. I would have to drive to Morgan for my "Sabrina fix" every now and then. I watched you play in the school yard. Once I hid in the willows while you fiddled around by the river, thinking it was a pity your own mother was letting you get so close to the water. It would have been easy to take you. Surely the authorities would have suspected a drowning."

Sabrina backed up several steps. "That's enough!"

"After I followed you to your new house the other night, I stood outside the dining room window and watched you all eat dinner. At one point I was just a couple of feet away from you, separated only by the window glass. I wished I might have reached out and touched your curls just as I did when you were small. I cursed the window for stopping me."

The confessions grew worse and worse. Sabrina's flesh was jumping and crawling. "Please stop, Larielle! I've said what I've come to say. Stay away from Brad and I'll never divulge this letter." Sabrina backed away from the woman. "You're so possessed! I think you could frighten the devil himself."

Larielle's head lolled back and she laughed madly. Sabrina ran toward the jeep, hitting the keyless entry button. She couldn't drive quickly enough, nor put enough of a distance behind her. Her tires spun gravel, spraying tiny rocks onto the yard.

"I'll get that letter!" a wild voice screamed in the distance. All of the hellish, haunted howls of Halloween couldn't replicate the spooky sound which shattered the Sabbath Day.

Sabrina's foot hit the accelerator even harder. Her heart was thumping audibly, and Sabrina had to grip the steering wheel to keep a handle on the tremors. "It's over," she said to herself. "It's over, it's over. Just drive."

She was thankful to make it to the highway without someone following her! She studied her rearview mirror and rejoiced. Ely's truck was still parked at the bar across the road. Sabrina drove dangerously fast. She didn't feel the overwhelming relief she was hoping for as residual creeps continued to gnaw against her guts and haunt her spirit. She knew she would now have to notify the authorities regardless, for Larielle was unhinged and dangerous. Sabrina again checked her rearview mirror, relieved to find an empty road behind her. She hoped Larielle had only meant to scare her into a hasty retreat. She pacified herself with that hope, wanting to believe that Larielle was playing mind games.

Familiar landscape blurred by Sabrina's windows. Her eyes swept the mountainside as she motored along, allowing the jeep to chew up at least ten miles of distance. No snow had yet fallen in the valley and the dirt road leading to the Ashley cabin was still barren and dry. Sabrina suddenly hit her blinker. She felt compelled to walk on the land that had meant so much to her father.

The jeep rumbled steadily toward the private mountain paradise. Childhood memories tumbled from rocks and rills while the laughter of yesterday echoed from the trees. Sabrina parked near some chokecherry bushes near the reservoir and hiked toward the cabin and clearing. It was a drab season to visit. The network of naked branches was skeletal, appearing old and bent against the grey sky. Fallen leaves carpeted the forest floor and they crunched beneath Sabrina's boots as she walked. Had she but once scanned the vista down the hillside, she may have seen the green truck, slowly tracing her movements from the highway.

CHAPTER FORTY-TWO

Sabrina sat on the crude bench her father had built near the fire pit, remembering the last night of his life. Memories flickered instead of flames. *We were here celebrating my birthday. Chantry sat right over there.* Sabrina's eyes trailed across the empty fire pit, resting upon the exact spot. *I was angry with him that night.* Sabrina's eyes swept further around the fire circle. *Dad stood behind Mom, right there, and Grandpa and Grandma were on the other side.* Sabrina studied the memory in her mind, hearing the laughter and feeling the moment. *Daddy loved it up here. He worked so hard to make it nice for us.* Sabrina walked toward the little cabin.

It was dark inside, and there was no electricity to hit a switch. Sabrina leaned against the cook stove, letting her eyes adjust to the shadows. The bed still sat in the right corner. A table and four chairs were clustered in the left corner. There was a counter with low cupboards near the door. Sabrina tossed her bag onto the counter top. Everything was just as she had remembered it. *Hasn't anyone stayed here in the last ten years?* Sabrina's thoughts answered their own question. *No--Grandpa Ashley says it's too painful to come and enjoy it anymore.*

Sabrina pulled the drawers open, one by one, smiling at the contents. She had filled some of the drawers herself. There were Daddy's red speckled camp dishes and utensils. Another drawer revealed an old first-aid kit, matches, lantern mantels, flashlights, and batteries. Another drawer held Yahtzee, Uno, Rook, Hearts and Old Maid. Sabrina smiled, spying a couple of coloring books and her cabin crayons. She pulled the coloring books up for closer inspection, flipping the pages open. She had proudly signed and dated each picture. There were several pages colored by her parents also. One picture was signed, *Ben Ashley, June 1st, 2000.* Sabrina urged him to color the picture with her before they went to bed after her birthday party. He colored the picture on the eve of his death.

Sabrina put the books into her bag. She wanted to add them to her treasure box at home. She then climbed the ladder into the small loft. Princess Pussy Willow stared from her cradle board in the corner, where Sabrina tucked her in for the night more than ten years earlier. Sabrina remembered leaving the doll just as the family had returned home the next morning, but Ben was in a hurry to get outside and move sprinkler pipe. "But I need my baby," Sabrina wailed.

"I'll drive up and get her after lunch," her daddy told her.

"Take me with you when you go."

"It's a promise." Sabrina bit her lip, wiping tears as she realized it was the only promise he never kept. Her mind kept churning. "I left my jacket anyway and I need to go get it." Sabrina's head jerked toward the nail near the door. Sure enough, the jacket still hung, faded and dusty.

Sabrina climbed down the rungs, stepping quickly to retrieve it. She shook it hard, stirring dust around the room. She put it on and looked into the mirror above the counter. It was more of a shirt than a jacket, as it was merely lined denim, but it had been her father's favorite. Sabrina buried her face in the collar, hoping to still catch the scent of him, but the fabric smelled only of the musty cabin.

Her hands slipped into the pockets. She pulled out a pocketknife. *Another treasure!* Something felt heavy in a chest pocket. Sabrina investigated the bulky item, finding a brown wallet.

Another round of tears stung against her eyes. Amanda had searched for the missing wallet for weeks after Ben's death, but never found it. *It was hanging here all along.*

Sabrina sat down on the bed and began pulling sentimental articles from the leather compartments. She studied the face on his driver's license. "Benjamin Joseph Ashley," she read.

"Brown hair, hazel eyes. Height: six feet, two inches. Weight: Two hundred and five pounds."

His social security card tumbled into her hands, followed by a visa. The credit card still had the sticker in place with an activation number to call. *He never even used it.* Next was his temple recommend, two photographs of her mother, and four of her. A folded yellow paper was stuffed between the pictures. Sabrina wondered if it might be a receipt but it was a note, scrawled in the penmanship of a child. *"I love you Daddy. You are my friend. Love, Sabrina."* The bill fold held twenty-two dollars and a small white card containing the Bear Lake Bears' baseball schedule. Her father had written, *Chantry's Games* across the top. "I should become an archaeologist, digging up so many bones." Sabrina gathered the items back into the wallet and added it to the contents of her bag.

Sabrina wondered what time it was. The dusty clock on the wall ticked still at some point in the past decade, at six minutes past six. Sabrina flipped her phone open. No service of course, but the time was just past two. "Chantry's probably just sitting down to dinner with his parents. If I had any sense at all I'd be with him."

Sabrina shut the cabin door. She remembered a glen further up the mountain where she used to play as a child. She started hiking through the trees toward it. She wanted to pray and pray until the heaviness left her chest, until the festering sliver was removed from her cankered pain center. "All I want is to feel better," she mumbled as she crunched through the trees. "I need some stinking peace!"

The sound of breaking branches snapped behind her. She whipped around, scanning the woods, seeing nothing. "Don't get spooked," she coaxed to herself, weaving through the trees again. She remembered Dorian's words and tried to comfort herself by thinking about them. *"...Others may be masters of their own destinies, but they have no jurisdiction over mine."*

She stepped from the stand of aspen and pine onto the seldom-traveled road which led higher up a steep canyon. Eerie strands of uneasiness clasped around her. Sabrina cast her eyes again down the road. From her vantage point she could see the cabin and the clearing. The reservoir was obstructed by brambles of chokecherry bushes as well as her view to the south. She was penned in on the north by a steep rocky ridge. Fear was bottling in her throat like a fizzing soda pop, ready to explode. Her heart hammered sideways. Sabrina didn't know if the danger was real or imagined. "I'm certain I wasn't followed," she whispered to herself. She had two choices; she could run further up the hill or flee back toward the cabin. Her ears strained for noise. *Nothing.* She took a quick step backward, concealing herself again in a thick thatch of trees. Every sense in her body was on high alert.

An icy wind gusted against her then. She noticed angry clouds roiling and boiling over the top of the mountain, covering the sun and casting the air with troubled, shadowy shades. *Maybe that's it– the danger. A storm is building.* Thunder began belching over the ridge, rumbling and reverberating down the mouth of the canyon. Lightening was zigzagging from the turbulent rolling clouds. It was an alarmingly violent sky.

Snap, crunch, pop! Sabrina sucked in her ragged breathing as she strained against the wind to separate the sounds of the coming storm from something possibly more threatening. *Dear God in Heaven! Please help me! Everything is wrong. I only came here to pray and find some peace, but there is no peace. Help me, help me, help me...*

A micro burst of wind suddenly ignited against the ridge line, forcing dirt, leaves and debris to swirl like raging banshees. Sabrina ducked her face toward an aspen tree to protect her eyes. *Kaboom!* Lightening hissed and thunder cracked simultaneously overhead. The ground quaked from the shock. Sabrina stumbled from her hiding place against the trees. *What was I thinking? You don't hug a tree in lightening storm!* She lunged back onto the road, running for the cabin. Dirt blew in her eyes and branches were falling and cracking around her. Sabrina ducked low, shielding her face with one arm as she lumbered toward the snug comforts of the cabin. *Schrrwipp!* A blazing hot trail suddenly tore through Sabrina's upper arm. A millisecond later she heard the bang of a gun. *Of course the bullet would travel faster than the sound.* She noticed the steely glint of a rifle barrel through a tangled network of chokecherry branches. Sabrina dove behind the outhouse. "God, help me!"

Hail began pelting fiercely, bruising Sabrina's flesh like pebbles where they hit. The atmosphere was charged with the thunderous sound of them, hammering against the tin roofs of the outhouse and cabin. The icy stones drowned out any sounds of footsteps, or movements. Sabrina didn't know which way to crawl, lunge, or run. Her jeep was straight behind her, parked against the tangled mass of bushes, but her keys were in her bag inside the cabin. *Kaboom!* Another jolt of lightning pounded the ground. It ripped the thundercloud to pieces and drenching torrents of rain rushed toward the earth, liquefying the hailstones. Sabrina couldn't feel her arm, shoulder, wrist, or hand; just a burning blaze of numb heat.

She leaned carefully behind the outhouse chancing a quick view. She could no longer see the gun or any signs of life. Whatever was after her was also being crushed by nature's fury. She leaned toward the cabin then, craning her neck to study the other route. Larielle Pritchett suddenly materialized in the windy drizzle. She was standing between the outhouse and cabin, about fifteen yards from Sabrina.

Sabrina struggled to her feet. She wasn't going to face her executioner sitting down. Larielle stood unflinching in the rain and howling wind. Her lips were curled like a growling dog. "Who do you think you are?" The words were shrill and howled against the wind.

"Put that gun down!"

"No. You have something I want. Give me that letter and then we'll see what happens. Maybe I won't kill you and maybe I will."

"It's down in my jeep," Sabrina lied. If only the insane eyes would look away for one second Sabrina would run.

"I'm not stupid!"

"Neither am I! You've already shot me. Do you think I want to stand here, bleeding to death in the rain?"

"That's a good idea! The rain is washing all the evidence away. I should have just smothered you with a pillow when you were small. It would have saved me a lot of trouble. I was tempted you know. If I couldn't have you, I didn't want Amanda to hold you either."

Sabrina was content to let the gun-toting woman ramble. Her mind spun with possibilities for an escape. "Put that gun down!"

"Don't marry Chantry Cantrell! Your beautiful blood will be diluted."

"What does that mean? I'm going to marry Chantry and your opinion certainly doesn't matter. You are insane! Put that gun down and I'll go get the letter."

"You're too young to know your own mind. I should have drowned you before now. I didn't want to kill you this way but you are causing me a lot of trouble."

Fury rose in Sabrina's bosom like the flood waters rushing down the hill. Larielle's ugly words were tainted, twisted, and poisonous, and Sabrina refused to listen any longer. "Burn in hell!" Sabrina had never exploded with so much anger before. Raw passion burbled from her throat and she heard herself scream, "In the name of Jesus Christ, I tell you, Larielle Pritchett, you cannot hurt me anymore!" She lowered her shoulder and began running toward the woman. She would not beg, plead, or hide any longer. The sensation was empowering and she felt as if the hosts of Heaven were flanking her rear as she charged.

The gun was leveled against Larielle's shoulder and her finger was squeezing off the shot when Sabrina saw it. A blue finger of twisted, popping, electricity flashed. The force knocked Sabrina backward several yards, throwing her onto her back. Larielle's black hair stood on end, flaming with a circular fire. The scene was terrible as the woman burned beneath the scorching, sizzling hiss of lightning. The air was putrid with the stench of charring flesh. Sabrina pulled her shirt over her nose to block the offensive odor. It was over!

The sounds of the storm suddenly quieted and the pelting needles softened into soothing drops.

A tall raven-haired figure was running across the clearing toward Sabrina. "Chantry?" She wanted to leap to her feet and run into his arms, but she was too dizzy from the jolt.

Chantry's arms closed around her, lifting her from the ground. "Sabrina! Oh, my precious Little Bird!" He kissed her wet hair as he ran with her to the comfort of the cabin's shelter. "You're hurt! I heard the shot and I ran faster than I ever have in my life, praying with every step! Why on earth did that woman want to kill you? Sabrina, *why* are you here?" Chantry's questions were spilling out rapid fire. "We've got to get you warmed up," he said, before hearing any explanations from the girl. He quickly loaded the cook stove with wood and lit the tinder with a match. Striking another match he lit a lantern. A soft glow illuminated shadows in the cabin, making it feel warmer almost instantly. He then knelt in front of the girl, pulling her boots from her feet and peeling the socks from her chilled skin. "The road's all washed out. No emergency vehicles can get up here and it will be awhile before we can head down the mountain. We need to get you dried up and warm. Unfasten your pants, Breezy." Sabrina's left hand was out of commission and her other hand was icy and stiff. She struggled with the button, feeling frustrated and embarrassed. "Let me help you," Chantry whispered. "It will be okay. I've seen your underwear before anyway."

"In a box! It's not the same."

Chantry quickly flipped the button open. "Be quiet Sabrina, you are disrupting the hymn in my head."

Sabrina started laughing as Chantry fiddled with her zipper and pulled her pants from her legs. "You are thinking of a hymn?"

"*Choose the Right.*" Chantry winked at the giggling crimson cheeked girl. Her heavily drenched sweatshirt and bloody t-shirt came next. Instead of trying to pull them over Sabrina's head, he cut the wet, bloody, muddy clothes from her body with Ben's pocketknife. "I don't want to hurt your arm," he whispered. His hands felt hot against her skin where he touched her. Chantry flipped the bedspread around her to protect her modesty and warm her up.

"Let's look at your arm." He wiped blood away with her wet T-shirt, studying the wound. "It's bled a lot which is probably good, but don't go into shock on me, okay Sabrina?"

Sabrina pointed out the first aid kit and Chantry grabbed it. "Oh there are all kinds of good stuff in here." He poured peroxide into the bloody hole. Sabrina could hear it fizzing but she didn't feel any pain yet, just a strange, searing numbness. "Does that hurt?"

"No, I can't feel anything, luckily."

"Don't worry, you will." Chantry scowled over his patient as he carefully dressed the arm. "I remember what those cleat spikes felt like after my nerves woke up and it was not pleasant."

"Well, maybe I'll be lucky. This isn't as bad as that was."

Chantry arched a brow. "It's not?"

"Hand me Dad's jacket over there. I'll put it on while my clothes get dry."

"Okay but slip out of your underwear too. They might as well dry on the oven door with the rest of your things." He turned around to give her privacy, peering out of the small window in the door at the dead body outside. Steam rose beneath the chilly drizzle.

"Um, Chantry? Can you help me with this? I can't get my bra undone." Sabrina backed up to him with the bedspread secured tightly under her arms, covering the front of her.

Strong hands unfastened the clasps. "I must confess I've never done that before."

"Thanks for taking care of me."

"My pleasure." He helped her into the denim shirt. Sabrina held it shut with her good hand while Chantry fastened the buttons. It hung to mid thigh like a mini dress. It was warm and dry, and felt wonderful against her cold skin. "Congratulations Breezy, you are now an official member of the Redneck Lingerie Society. I *love* a girl in denim. Are you hungry Sabrina?"

"There's a sandwich in my bag. I bought it in Evanston this morning but I didn't feel like eating it."

Chantry pulled the bed down and Sabrina scrambled in. He propped the pillows behind her back, tucking her in nice and cozy. "Enjoy the fresh sheets," he teased. "The bed was just made up ten years ago."

"I don't care." Sabrina snuggled under the covers, shivering.

Chantry handed her the sandwich. "Please eat."

"I will if you'll come snuggle up with me and get me warm."

"I'm a little damp myself so I'm not sure that I can warm you up too much."

"Take your clothes off then," Sabrina teased, closely studying his brooding expression.

Chantry's head cocked off to one side and he looked sternly at the girl. "No way Breezy, haven't you enjoyed enough excitement for one day? You want to invite more danger into your life?" He smiled and it was beautiful to behold. Sabrina's eyes drank in his features like a tonic. "But I *will* do this," he said, sitting on the bed on top of the covers. One arm scooped around Sabrina, pulling the burrowing cocoon close to his side. He held her while she ate, careful not to bump against her arm.

"How did you find me?"

"I was sitting in priesthood meeting and the ward clerk came and told me I was wanted on the phone. Your mother was frantic on the other end."

"What?"

"Apparently Delphinia Blue approached Brad after church. She was very upset and said, 'Sabrina's other brother just told me that she is in trouble on the mountain.' Well, Amanda, Dorian, and Brad went peeling out of church, driving a million miles an hour back to your house, hoping that Delphinia was delusional, but she wasn't, was she? They found your note and your jeep was gone. Amanda called me immediately.

I raced out of church, hauling butt up the road, and scanning the hills for any sign of your jeep. I drove up here first, but couldn't see anything, so I tried Raymond Canyon next, and nothing. Of course Amanda was calling me, every ten seconds, wondering if I'd found you yet. Phillip and Vidalia were scouting in the hills above Porterville, just in case that was the mountain that Delphinia was referring to.

I decided to drive west then, up Wood Canyon Road. I followed it until it spat me out at the highway. I drove down Montpelier Canyon and followed the road back into Geneva. Driving again from Geneva to Raymond, I saw a green pickup parked alongside the highway and your bright yellow jeep up on the hill against the trees. Apparently you showed up after I was here looking for you the first time. I phoned your mother and told her I found your jeep while I still had cell service. Half way up here, a thunder burst hit and a flood of water came barreling down the hill, washing the road away. I skidded along until I was almost to the reservoir. I was looking around your car when I heard gunfire. My heart nearly gave out on me! I came around the trees just in time to see you charging Larielle Pritchett, with a gun aimed right in your face." Chantry's expression was smoldering and intense. "Little Bird, why did you fly away?"

"I had to Chantry."

"Why?"

"Oh Chantry!" Sabrina realized the moment was finally right to remove the infected sliver. Who else in the entire world could she tell but him? "Well, it all started when my Dad was killed..."

Chantry listened patiently while Sabrina labored, telling her tale for the first time. The unedited version had never before been uttered. After the secrets were finally out and the heavy burden exposed,

Sabrina was infused with the sweetest and most overwhelming sense of peace. It was what she had for so long been looking for. It broke over the top of her head like a bucket of warm water, trickling downward until she was saturated with it. The inner calm was delicious to her soul.

"Where's the envelope?"

"In my bag."

Chantry climbed off of the bed and retrieved it, ripping it open.

"Hey! It's taken me ten years to even deal with that letter and you ripped it open in less than two seconds? No fair."

"There's no sense dragging this out any longer." He read through the letter, grimacing a time or two. The more he read the angrier he became. His brows furrowed and his eyes glowered at the words. "She was mad, completely off her rocker. It gives me the willies just reading the words! How did you ever handle talking to her face to face?"

Sabrina shuddered. "It was the creepiest, most disturbing and twisted conversation, *ever*. What does the letter say?"

Chantry lifted the page and began reading. *"Ben, after several years of pleading with you, I am growing impatient. Ely cannot give me children and I want a child like Sabrina! She is my greatest obsession; she is my drug. I have watched her in the past, from secret places, and I gaze upon her now, when and where you least expect it. Does that unsettle you? Because it should. Give me what I want, Ben, and I'll leave your daughter alone. If you don't, I'm warning you...the girl will die! It will be your own fault that Amanda will cry from the agony of empty arms. Could loving me really be so bad? I have pleasured many men in the past and I can also please you. Pleasure is my particular art form... you really should try it. If you tell me no again, the cost will be great. Sabrina will die. What's it going to be?"*

Chantry swallowed. "I had no idea what kind of danger you have always been in! It makes me physically sick! You know Breezy;

your dad would gladly have faced death himself before letting anything happen to you."

"He did." Her arm felt wet and she asked Chantry to check the bandage. The wound was bleeding again and the gauze pad was saturated. Chantry applied a dry bandage, holding pressure against the arm to quiet the flow. He glanced out of the windows. The rain had stopped.

"Well, Little Bird, what do you think? Should we take our chances slipping and sliding down the hill?"

"I'd rather just stay here with you. I don't want to leave."

"I know but we've got to get some help." Chantry checked the clothes on the oven door. The panties were dry. He tossed them to Sabrina. "Everything else is still wet. Wrap up in your blankets and I'll carry you down to my truck."

"What about my jeep?"

"We'll get it later. Let's not worry about that right now."

"Chantry, I've missed you. I'm not leaving until you kiss me; a full-on serious kiss."

"I think I can take care of that." His eyes were deep and black, brimming with every kind of emotion from the day. Concern etched against his brow and set in lines around his mouth.

"Chantry, you are smoldering, smoking hot, and I will never get tired of looking at you."

His mouth softened into a tiny smile. Chantry's eyes searched her face intently. One hand rested against her throat, the other supported her neck as he laid her back on the bed. The perfect tenderness of his touch made Sabrina ache with longing. "I won't break," she whispered.

"I'm not taking any chances." His mouth closed around hers then, kissing her softly and gently, yet the intimacy felt insane. Sabrina had never known the pleasure of such a kiss. It was almost as if Chantry's lips were the conduit to his whole spirit and soul. The kiss felt nourishing and life-sustaining. It was warm and wet and Sabrina savored the exquisite aching passion of it. "There now... consider yourself kissed. The next time I undress you and put you to bed it had better be our wedding night."

He pulled himself upright and gathered a few of Sabrina's things together. Chantry stuffed Larielle's ranting letter inside of his shirt pocket. "The police and your folks will want to see this. No more secrets, Breezy." He dug in the drawers until he found a dish towel and fashioned a sling for Sabrina's arm. He secured her arm against her body with a second towel. "This will protect it from bouncing around so much in the truck. It's apt to be a wild ride off the mountain."

CHAPTER FORTY-THREE

Dorian, Brad, Amanda, all of the Ashley's, the Cantrell's, police cars and an ambulance were all bottling up at the highway as Chantry's Dodge fish-tailed toward the bottom of the hill. Sabrina's arm was starting to ache and every bump sent a jarring jolt coursing from her fingertips to her neck. "It's hurting now. Every time my heart beats it throbs." She fished her minerals from her bag and took a shot of the bitter liquid. Her body was now beginning to react to the shock of the day.

"I'm sorry, Breeze. I'm going to have to change your name to Old Wounded Wing. Look at that stir you're causing down there." Chantry pointed to the traffic jam at the bottom of the dirt road.

"I wonder why the police and ambulance are already here. Who called them?"

"Probably your mother. Too much time has elapsed since I told her I found your jeep."

"I didn't mean to worry everybody. Look, even Uncle Brant and Aunt Jessie are milling around down there."

Chantry's truck was surrounded with a swarm as soon as it stopped. He motioned to the EMT's to bring the stretcher. Amanda looked frightfully pale. "I'm okay Mom," Sabrina assured.

"What's happened to you?" Everyone was craning and milling about, trying to learn the details.

Chantry took over and Sabrina was glad. "She was shot." Gasps were heard all around. Sabrina pulled her blanket down, showing off her slings and bloody jacket sleeve.

"Is that your Dad's shirt?" Amanda asked, even more confused.

The EMT's were loading Sabrina into the ambulance. "I'll talk to you guys in a while," she called to the concerned onlookers and loved ones.

She heard Chantry explain to the officers that a dead woman was still lying on the hill near the Ashley's cabin. Sabrina saw Chantry put an arm around Brad. "I've got to talk to you," he said. "Ride with me to town."

"But who shot Sabrina?" A look of pensive fear shadowed his good looking face, as if he somehow already knew the answer.

"Your mother, I guess. I'm sorry Brad. She's dead. Lightning hit her."

Tears began spilling from the piercing blue, guileless eyes. Brad sprang toward the ambulance. "Sabrina! I'm sorry, Sabrina! You told me she was dangerous. You said I was forcing you to do something which could get you killed, but I–I–"

"I'm sorry too. She was never any good and you are lucky she left when you were little. You have no idea how lucky you were to grow up without a mother!"

Brad digested the words. "I didn't mean to sound like a jerk at the hospital yesterday! It's just that I was angry and confused. My mother finally came to claim me but all she wanted to talk about was *you*! She didn't really care about me at all...just you. It was so freaky." A sob strangled oddly in his throat.

Chantry's arm reached around the boy's shoulders again. "Come on Brad, let's talk. We'll follow the ambulance."

Amanda climbed into the back of the ambulance to ride with Sabrina and the others followed with Chantry's red Dodge leading the procession. All of the way to Montpelier Sabrina offered up heart-felt prayers of thanks to the Lord. Her newfound peace was stronger and more powerful than the throbbing pain in her arm.

The next several hours were a blur. X-rays showed bullet fragments were still lodged in her upper arm, near the bone. An emergency surgery remedied that situation. Sabrina found herself once again with a heavy head and sucking on a swab to moisten her mouth. Again a giant mosquito poked against her hand.

"Sabrina?"

Her eyes worked the room, trying to focus. Chantry was bent over her. "I love you. I want to marry you right now. I am your Little Bird and I want to live in your nest." Chuckles sounded around the room. Sabrina would have flushed with embarrassment but she was too hazy, fading in and out of consciousness for a few minutes.

The next time she surfaced, Chantry spoke first. "I love you too, Breezy. You are crazy amazing!" His lips caressed her fingertips.

"I am?"

"Sure. I don't know anyone else who would charge their would-be assassin, proclaiming in the name of Jesus Christ, that they could not hurt them anymore. Every time I replay the scene in my mind, I get goose bumps. Your innocent faith is so profound. Heaven was bound to deliver you. Sabrina, ever since you were only seven years old, your courage and spunk have been remarkable. You are definitely the woman I want in my life." Chantry kissed her hand again and then rested her palm against his cheek.

Tears trickled against Sabrina's temples. Chantry wiped them away. "Is Brad okay?"

Brad stepped to the other side of the bed, taking Sabrina's other hand. "I'm okay, Sabrina."

"I couldn't bear to see her destroy you. I had to stop her."

"I know. Chantry let me read the letter and she was sick. I picked up on that when we were talking the other night. It was a pretty big disappointment. I never considered for one minute that I should believe anything she said. For the record I know you and Mom aren't liars."

"You'd better after all of this! It's a good thing I love you so much, Brad! It's a good thing I love you like a brother." Sabrina smiled as she felt both Chantry and Brad squeeze her hands at the same time.

"Chantry?" Brad asked, "Will you baptize me and my Grandpa Haskel when he comes for Thanksgiving?" The words sent a thrill through Sabrina. She smiled exuberantly through the hazy after-effects of anesthetic.

"What about Dorian?"

"I'm thinking about it," a voice said near the window.

"I'll do it on one condition."

"What's that?"

"You stand up for me as Best Man at our reception."

"If I'm the Best Man how come you got the girl?" Laughter echoed around the bed. A nurse glanced into the crowded hospital room, scowling.

Dorian scooted Brad out of the way. He knelt down. "Do you remember a few days ago, when I said you were low maintenance?"

"Yeah?"

"Well I take it all back!" Laughter rolled again. Sabrina noticed her Grandpa was smiling at her.

"Dorian, why did you marry that woman?"

"Bree, twenty years ago I married a girl named Cate Steele. She loved horses and dreamt of someday owning a big horse ranch. She was a good mother and claimed Brad made her happier than anything else in the world. We were young and broke, but I thought everything was going fine in our lives until she split. I've now learned she ran away with a cowboy named Ely Pritchett, who just happened to have inherited a large horse ranch. I guess he had money at the time and I didn't. When she ditched her old life she must have dumped it all; including her old name and identity. After talking to Chantry and reading her unhinged letter, I've concluded that her guilty conscience drove her over the brink. She couldn't forgive herself for walking out on Brad. She eventually became a monster, Sabrina, but she didn't start out that way."

Sabrina considered the words. Things seemed to take a long while to process in her groggy mind. Her mother was rubbing her feet and the end of the bed. "Mom? What time is it?"

"Nine thirty."

"It's night?"

"Yes Honey."

"Don't wear yourself out. I'm okay. You should get some rest."

"Dr. Bainbridge thinks he'll let you come home tomorrow. He's been on the phone with Dr. Robert's to transfer your care closer to home. I think Dorian and I will head home so Brad won't miss school tomorrow. Brad's going to drive your jeep."

"It's down from the mountain?"

"Uncle Brant, Joe and B.J. got it down. I guess it was quite a process. Joe says your yellow Jeep is now mud brown."

"I'll bet...well, how am I supposed to get home if you all leave me?"

"Duh!"

Sabrina looked at Chantry. "But you've already missed a couple of days of school, shipping cows."

"I'm not leaving you, Sabrina! I've already phoned Mr. Hodges. He sends his best wishes to you and told me not to worry about it."

Amanda stooped to kiss her daughter. "I really don't want to leave you, Honey."

"Mom, I'm probably better than I've been for ten years. Please don't worry about me anymore. I feel a hundred times better than I did with that high fever! That was the tortured night. That was the worst."

"I'm sorry for all of it! I'm sorry you've had to pack it all around for so long! But, and maybe this is selfish of me, I'm glad I didn't know the truth any sooner. I would have been paranoid to ever let you leave my side! I would have been utterly crippled by the dark danger looming around you, and smothered you with over-protection."

"Strangled by the apron strings," Grandpa offered.

"I'm so grateful that your tender, innocent, seven year old eyes never read that letter! It would have shattered your spirit with fear. What you had already seen and heard was enough of a burden. No wonder you've struggled with such violent anxiety."

"Brian told me not to open the envelope so I never did. When I left home this morning I didn't have a clue what it said, but I had to make that woman leave us alone."

"I love you, Honey. Sleep well. Chantry's staying through the night. He loves you so much! Call me if you need me." Again she bent an exhausted face to kiss her daughter's forehead. "No fever– I'm so happy. Dr. Roberts is amazed at that."

"Those episodes are all in the past, I hope." Sabrina said goodbye to her family. "Don't wreck my jeep Brad! Drive it more carefully than you do your own!"

"Ha ha! Good one Sabrina," he mumbled, leaving the room.

Grandpa and Grandma Ashley also bid Sabrina a pleasant night's rest. Grandpa extended a hand toward Chantry before leaving the room. The gesture turned into an emotional embrace. Joseph thumped Chantry on the back several times thanking him for bringing Sabrina safely from the mountain. Both men wiped tears from their cheeks. "You're a good man, Chantry! I've always regarded you as a son. Take good care of her. She's our only granddaughter and we love her so much."

Chantry nodded. "I will Joseph. I love her too."

"I know. You always have. You were so kind and patient with her when she was little. You've watched her grow up right along with the rest of us."

Joe and B.J. slipped into the room just as their grandparents were leaving. Joe was carrying a bundle of items. "This was left on the oven door," Joe said, casually tossing a blood-stained bra toward Chantry. "Boy, I'd like to have been a fly on the wall during triage." Joe paused, wrinkling his freckled nose at his cousin. "Here's your boots and stuff," Sabrina. "I brought you your cut-to-pieces t-shirt and hoodie just in case you wanted them as a souvenir." Joe sent a taunting look in Chantry's direction.

"Maybe Chantry would like to sew them back on you once your arm heals," B.J. quipped.

Joe grinned, "Yes sir, I surely would have liked to pass off my first-aid merit badge under your tutelage."

Chantry endured their teasing with a faint smile. "Keep it up boys," he said pleasantly. "I can still whip both of you at the same time."

Joe and B.J. laughed at the comment. "Well, uh...get better Sabrina," Joe mentioned, patting her foot.

B.J. nodded, "Try to stay out of trouble for five minutes if you can. I know that's difficult for you. One thing about it you sure know how to liven up a Sunday afternoon."

"Thanks for bringing my jeep down."

"It's a sweet ride and we just pretended we were diggin' in it."

"I hope there's a gear left," Chantry muttered.

"There is, but Grandpa's road is trashed. It will take four bulldozers, three road-graders, two loads of gravel, and one big miracle to fix it," B.J. offered. "Well, see you guys around...keep better track of your underwear from now on Sabrina." They sauntered out, chuckling at their sport.

Sabrina closed her eyes. When she opened them the room was quiet. Chantry was settled into a chair next to Sabrina. "You can watch television if you want to. It won't bother me."

"I don't want any noise," he whispered.

"I'm thirsty."

Chantry dipped the swab into a cup of icy water and slid it across Sabrina's lips, teeth, and tongue. "Here," he said playfully, "pretend this is a vicarious kiss."

Sabrina smiled. She felt too exhausted to laugh. "What time is it?"

"It's now eleven thirty."

"Have I been sleeping?"

"Yes."

"Did I just wake you up then?"

"No Sabrina. I've been content just to watch you. I love you!"

Sabrina gazed at him in the dim hospital light. He looked like he'd been crying. The sight wrenched Sabrina's heart. "Chantry, I'm okay!"

"I know. Isn't it wonderful?" The words rolled off his tongue like a beautiful melody. "I'm so thankful to have you! I just keep thinking about how messed up my night could have been if that bullet hadn't veered three or four inches off course, or if the lightning hadn't cracked with such fine precision...I *need* you, Sabrina!"

Her right arm reached out to him and he laced his fingers between hers and knelt by the side of her bed. He laid his head against her neck and wept with gratitude. Sabrina's hand stroked his hair, his cheek, and neck. "It's okay Chantry. I'm yours. I'm not going anywhere. I need you too! It's okay." His tears fell wet against her throat and it was good. Sabrina sealed the moment into her heart and mind as one of the sweetest keepsakes her memory could ever possess.

CHAPTER FORTY-FOUR

Sabrina adjusted her cap as Mr. Hodges' voice presented her name into the microphone, "Sabrina Lyn Ashley Cantrell, daughter the late Benjamin Ashley, and Dorian and Amanda Manning, *and* wife of Coach Chantry Cantrell." Sabrina reached for her diploma, shaking the hands of the principal, Superintendent Casey, and members of the school board. She glided back to her seat, smiling triumphantly at the handsome class advisor. Chantry telegraphed a small kiss and a wink.

Sabrina noticed a sea of flashes snapping from her families' section in the audience. Phillip and Vidalia, Vandaline, Grandpa and Grandma Ashley, Randy and Tashina Cantrell, Dorian, a miserably pregnant Amanda, and Grandpa Haskel all craned from their seats. The same people would stir when Mr. Hodges hit the M's, and it was Brad's turn to receive his diploma.

Sabrina's mind stretched over the past year. One year ago she had shivered against the biting wind and stinging rain near the Weber River. How her life had changed! In twelve precious months she had acquired a first love, a step-father, a brother, a beloved great-grandfather, lasting love in the form of a husband, and a whole new family of in-laws. She would soon meet a new little brother and she looked forward to cradling the little stranger.

The tiniest of all tiny flutters then stirred within her womb; the most delicious secret she had ever kept! She intended to tell Chantry that evening. He had been crowing with excitement over the future opportunity of coaching his forth-coming brother-in-law in baseball. Would he also coach a son on the same team? Sabrina relished the thought of an uncle and nephew playing ball together.

She knew she would again hear the snide comments of other people; that she was too young, that she didn't know what she was doing, but Sabrina didn't care. Her own heart was soaring with the knowledge and her mind was in agreement. There had been plenty of naysayers, brooking argument over her early marriage as well, and yet Sabrina knew marrying Chantry was the right path for her to follow. Sometime over the past few months Sabrina had stopped saying, *"This will ruin everyday life for me from now on,"* whenever good things happened. She realized her life was a beautiful, dancing stage of opportunity and promise. Tears seared against her lashes as she contemplated her own state of happiness. She gazed again in Chantry's direction. His eyes were on her, ever searching and deep.

Those eyes! Sabrina loved to reminisce again and again the way they had gazed at her over the holy altar of the temple when he covenanted to love her for an eternity. Chills splashed down Sabrina's arms as she contemplated the sacred ordinance which sealed her to Chantry forever.

"You are mine!" he whispered against her ear as they left the temple together, posing for pictures on that sunny spring day. "You are mine!" he whispered during the wedding breakfast. Sabrina rejoiced at the sound of the words, again and again as the day progressed.

Grandpa Haskel had given them a week's stay at a private chalet in Tahoe. They flew to Reno, then rented a car and enjoyed the scenery over the Sierra Nevada Mountains. Snow still blanketed the slopes and peaks but green grass was edging the roads and coloring yards and brilliant shoreline with the renewed promise of spring. The vista was a blessed merging of two seasons and Sabrina's artistic sensibilities soaked it up. No matter how she mentally dabbed colors together she knew she would never be able of capture the magic of the occasion.

The sun was setting over the western mountains when Chantry carried his bride over the thresh hold. They explored the beautiful

chalet together. Double French doors led out to a balcony overlooking the water. The moon was beginning to weave a shimmering silvery path. Chantry's arms enfolded Sabrina in her requested dance.
"You wanted to dance with the moon?" he asked against her hair.

"Yes." She leaned against him. Around and around they spun,
basking in the celestial glow. Waves lapped rhythmically. "I love you
Chantry. Guess what? I'm *yours!*"

"Yes you are," he mused, smiling down at her. "So why are we
out here dancing, may I ask?"

Sabrina giggled softly. "I don't know--because I don't really *need*
the moon, remember?"

Chantry's mouth covered hers with a hunger that could finally
be satisfied. He waltzed her into the privacy of their new life, kicking the doors shut behind them as they went. Every night began
and ended the same way. The magical, loving, deliciously satiating
moments had definitely been worth the wait.

Sabrina's mind jerked back to the present. "Bradley Haskel
Manning," Mr. Hodges announced, "the son of Dorian and Amanda
Manning," There was no mention of Cate Steele, nor Larielle
Pritchett. Amanda received the rightful honor as the boy's mother.
The tiniest, minutest flutter stirred again. Sabrina slid a protective
hand across her stomach, smiling again at Chantry.

There was a family dinner following the commencement exercises at the Manning's. Amanda waddled around the kitchen, happy
to feed her guests but apologizing for her slow speed. Sabrina tried
to help but Dorian and Vidalia chased her from the kitchen. Brad
spent most of his time talking to Whitlee on the phone. Whitlee
was now legal dating age and Brad apparently had big plans for the
summer.

"Do I need to send Vidalia to live with you?" Sabrina asked him
between phone calls.

"Are you kidding? Her dad's huge! He'd throttle me if I tried anything. Plus he's a stake president. I'll be too scared to get out of line! I want to go on a mission you know."

Phillip, Randy Cantrell, and Grandpa Ashley seemed completely enthralled with Haskel. They listened attentively to his statements, amused by his spirit and captivating mannerisms. The party was nice but Sabrina was happy when Chantry's arm slid around her, leading her from the noisy house. "I have a present for you," he murmured against her hair.

"You do?"

"Yes," he said, driving with one arm around her. She was surprised when the truck headed up the Richville road toward Porterville. He stopped in front of a newly-built house and turned off the truck.

Sabrina didn't know who lived there. "Doesn't look like any-body's home."

"Not until we walk in."

"What?" Sabrina stared incredulously at Chantry in the darkness.

"I wanted you to have a walk-in shower and sunken tub." He pressed a key into her hand. "Happy Graduation, Mrs. Cantrell."

Sabrina began crying. "What? You can't be serious!"

"Oh, but I am," he laughed, pulling her from the truck. He packed her to the door. He held her while she stuck the key into the lock and opened it. Chantry set her down inside their new home and flipped a switch.

Sabrina walked through the spacious rooms in a daze. It was a perfect house; roomy, yet cozy too. "When did you buy this?"

"I started looking the week after I brought you home from the hospital. This house is only three years old. There are some unbeliev-ably great deals on homes right now. I closed on it a month ago."

"Surely all of this furniture isn't ours?" Sabrina asked, looking around.

"The furniture is your graduation gift from Grandpa Haskel. I tried to refuse such an offering but he wouldn't hear of it. You know how he is! 'I desire to be just a little bit like the Lord,' he said, 'showering blessings, every once in a while.' I couldn't do anything but go along with him."

"No, that's all a person *can* do with Haskel. Isn't he wonderful?"

"He's planning on coming to see us in the morning, to see how you liked everything. In fact, we're cooking breakfast for the crew. My folks' are spending the night at our apartment, and your Grandma and Grandpa Ashley are crashing at the flower shop. Are you up to feeding them all in the morning? Grandpa Ashley has requested pancakes."

"Absolutely! It will be my birthday party. I finally get to say I'm old enough to be grown up."

"Believe me; you're grown up alright." Chantry's smile caused a pleasant acceleration in Sabrina's heart rate.

Sabrina wandered through the rooms, examining everything closely. She sucked her breath in when she saw the master bedroom. An identical mural of the Raymond Mountains covered one wall. The bathroom revealed another depiction of Sabrina's Thinking Place, surrounding a large sunken tub. "The artwork is a gift from your mother."

She was startled to see all of her things already hanging in her closet. Chantry had certainly been busy! Sabrina looked towards a sturdy king-size bed. Strewn rose petals graced the pillows and a note card said, "Welcome to your nest Little Bird."

Sabrina sat on the bed, wiping tears away, trying to take it all in. "Thank you Chantry! I love it...but I was happy at the apartment, too."

"I know. You're so easily satisfied that it's terrific fun to spoil you. I'm glad you like it."

"Four bedrooms--*wow!* This is a lot of house for the two of us."

"We'll have to work on filling it up then," Chantry said, kissing Sabrina and tipping her back against the pillow.

"I have a gift for you too."

He was leaning over her, his perfect features just inches from her face. "What?"

Sabrina took his hand, guiding it along her body until it reached her lower abdomen. "A baby."

The dark, smoldering, searching eyes turned to liquid in a heartbeat. Chantry's brows furrowed intently. "Not really?"

Sabrina nodded. "It's true and even though it's *so* early, I actually felt the tiniest flutter tonight. I felt it twice actually."

"Twins?"

The question startled Sabrina and she began laughing. "Well... either I felt the fluttering of one baby twice or two babies once, but I didn't consider twins as a possibility—until just now. You crack me up, Chantry!"

Chantry kissed Sabrina's belly. "Your present to me is even better than a new house. I love you Sabrina! I can't wait for every second of the rest of our lives. Let's celebrate." A sultry smile tugged against his mouth as he turned off the lights. Moonlight tumbled through the window, providing proper mood lighting. "Oh Sabrina, the moon and I are happy to dance with you for the rest of eternity."